THE HERMANN HESSE MEGAPACK®

THE HERMANN HESSE MEGAPACK®

HERMANN HESSE

WILDSIDE PRESS

CONTENTS

INTRODUCTION, by John Betancourt 7

DEMIAN 9

SIDDHARTHA 109

STEPPENWOLF 185

INTRODUCTION

JOHN BETANCOURT

Hermann Hesse was born on July 2, 1877, in Calw, Germany, and died on August 9, 1962, in Montagnola, Switzerland. Raised in a deeply religious family, Hesse struggled with traditional values and authority from an early age, experiences that would strongly shape his later work. As a young man, he traveled widely, searching for deeper meaning and a sense of purpose. These personal journeys and his emotional struggles became powerful influences in his novels and poetry. His writings gained wide attention, eventually leading him to win the Nobel Prize in Literature in 1946, cementing his legacy as one of the most important writers of his time. Today, Hesse is best remembered for exploring spiritual themes, human self-discovery, and the tension between individuality and society.

This MEGAPACK® assembles three of Hesse's most important works: *Demian* (1919), *Siddhartha* (1922), and *Steppenwolf* (1927). Each novel reflects Hesse's fascination with the inner struggles of individuals searching for meaning in a confusing and changing world. *Demian*, published shortly after World War I, explores youthful rebellion, self-realization, and the mysterious nature of human consciousness. It captured the uncertainty and restlessness of post-war Europe. *Siddhartha* delves into spiritual enlightenment, following the journey of a young man in ancient India seeking personal fulfillment beyond religious dogma. Its simple yet profound message resonated strongly with readers, becoming especially popular among young people in the 1960s. *Steppenwolf* explores existential themes of isolation, the duality of human nature, and the quest for personal identity, becoming a defining text for many readers in the mid-20th century, particularly those grappling with similar personal and cultural anxieties.

In his time, Hermann Hesse occupied a unique literary position, admired by intellectuals for addressing universal concerns of spirituality, psychology, and identity in the turbulent decades between the World Wars. His works drew on philosophies from East and West, combining literary artistry with psychological depth. Hesse's impact extends far beyond his lifetime; he significantly influenced authors and thinkers such as Jack Kerouac, Paulo Coelho, and Thomas Mann. Today, Hesse is still widely read for his honest, thought-provoking portrayal of the human condition. His writings continue to resonate, attracting new generations who seek deeper meaning and personal freedom in an increasingly complex world.

RECOMMENDED READING

Hesse's Greatest Books:

> *Demian* (1919)
> *Siddhartha* (1922)
> *Steppenwolf* (1927)
> *Narcissus and Goldmund* (1930)

Recommended Short Story Collections:

> *Strange News from Another Star* (1919)
> *Stories of Five Decades* (1972)

DEMIAN

PREFATORY

THE STORY OF EMIL SINCLAIR'S YOUTH

I wanted only to try to live in obedience to the promptings which came from my true self. Why was that so very difficult?

In order to tell my story, I must begin far back. If it were possible, I should have to go back much further still, to the earliest years of my childhood, and even beyond, to my distant ancestry.

Authors, in writing novels, usually act as if they were God, and could, by a broadness of perception, comprehend and present any human story as if God were telling it to Himself without veiling anything, and with all the essential details. That I cannot do, any more than can the authors themselves. But I attach more importance to my story than can any other writer to his: because it is my own, and it is the story of a human being—not that of an invented, possible, ideal or otherwise, non-existent creature, but that of a real, unique, living man. What that is, a real living man, one certainly knows less today than ever. For men are shot down in heaps—men, of whom each one is a precious, unique experiment of nature. If we were nothing more than individuals, we could actually be put out of the world entirely with a musket-ball, and in that case there would be no more sense in relating stories. But each man is not only himself, he is also the unique, quite special, and in every case the important and remarkable point where the world's phenomena converge, in a certain manner, never again to be repeated. For that reason the history of everyone is important, eternal, divine. For that reason every man, so long as he lives at all and carries out the will of nature, is wonderful and worthy of every attention. In everyone has the spirit taken shape, in everyone creation suffers, in everyone is a redeemer crucified.

Few today know what man is. Many feel it, and for that reason die the easier, as I shall die the easier, when I have finished my story.

I must not call myself one who knows. I was a seeker and am still, but I seek no more in the stars or in books; I am beginning to listen to the promptings of those instincts which are coursing in my very blood. My story is not pleasant, it is not sweet and harmonious like the fictitious stories. It smacks of nonsense and perplexity, of madness and dreams, like the lives of all men who do not wish to delude themselves any longer.

The life of everyone is a way to himself, the search for a road, the indication of a path. No man has ever yet attained to self-realization; yet he strives thereafter, one ploddingly, another with less effort, each as best he can. Each one carries the remains of his birth, slime and eggshells of a primeval world, with him to the end. Many a one will remain a frog, a lizard, an ant. Many a one is top-part man and bottom-part fish. But everyone is a projection of nature into manhood. To us all the same origin is common, our mothers—we all come out of the womb. But each of us—an experiment, one of nature's litter, strives after his own ends. We can understand one another; but each one is able to explain only himself.

CHAPTER 1

TWO WORLDS

I will begin my story with an event of the time when I was ten or eleven years old and went to the Latin school of our little town. Much of the old-time fragrance is wafted back to me, but my sensations are not unmixed, as I pass in review my memories—dark streets and bright houses and towers, the striking of clocks and the features of men, comfortable and homely rooms, rooms full of secrecy and dread of ghosts. I sense again the atmosphere of cosy warmth, of rabbits and servant-girls, of household remedies and dried fruit. Two worlds passed there one through the other. From two poles came forth day and night.

The one world was my home, but it was even narrower than that, for it really comprised only my parents. This world was for the most part very well known to me; it meant mother and father, love and severity, good example and school. It was a world of subdued lustre, of clarity and cleanliness; here were tender friendly words, washed hands, clean clothes and good manners. Here the morning hymn was sung, and Christmas was kept.

In this world were straight lines and paths which led into the future; here were duty and guilt, evil conscience and confession, pardon and good resolutions, love and adoration, Bible texts and wisdom. To this world our future had to belong, it had to be crystal-pure, beautiful and well ordered.

The other world, however, began right in the midst of our own household, and was entirely different, had another odor, another manner of speech and made different promises and demands. In this second world were servant-girls and workmen, ghost stories and breath of scandal. There was a gaily colored flood of monstrous, tempting, terrible, enigmatical goings-on, things such as the slaughter house and prison, drunken men and scolding women, cows in birth-throes, plunging horses, tales of burglaries, murders, suicides. All these beautiful and dreadful, wild and cruel things were round about, in the next street, in the next house. Policemen and tramps passed to and fro, drunken men beat their wives, crowds of young girls flowed out of factories in the evening, old women were able to bewitch you and make you ill, robbers dwelt in the wood, incendiaries were rounded up by mounted policemen—everywhere seethed and reeked this second, passionate world, everywhere, except in our rooms, where mother and father were. And that was a good thing. It was wonderful that here in our house there were peace, order and repose, duty and a good conscience, pardon and love—and wonderful that there were also all the other things, all that was loud and shrill, sinister and violent, yet from which one could escape with one bound to mother.

And the oddest thing was, how closely the two worlds bordered each other, how near they both were! For instance, our servant Lina, as she sat by the sitting-room door at evening prayers, and sang the hymn with her bright voice, her freshly washed hands laid on her smoothed-out apron, belonged absolutely to father and mother, to us, to what was bright and proper. Immediately after, in the kitchen or in the woodshed, when she was telling me the tale of the headless dwarf, or when she quarreled with the women of the neighborhood in the little butcher's shop, then she was another person, belonged to the other world, and was enveloped in mystery. It was the same with everything and everyone, especially with myself. To be sure, I belonged to the bright, respectable world, I was my parents' child, but the other world was present in everything I saw and heard, and I also lived in it, although it was often strange and foreign to me, although one had there regularly a bad conscience and anxiety. Sometimes I even liked to live in the forbidden world best, and often the homecoming into the brightness—however necessary and good it might be—seemed almost like a return to something less beautiful, to something more uninteresting and desolate. At times I realized this: my aim in life was to grow up like my father and mother, as bright and pure, as systematic and superior. But the road to attainment was long, you had to go to school and study and pass tests and examinations. The road led past the other dark world and through it, and it was not improbable that you would remain there and be buried in it. There were stories of prodigal sons to whom that had happened—I was passionately fond of reading them. There the return home to father and to the respectable world was always so liberating and so sublime, I quite felt that this alone was right and good and desirable. But still that part of the stories which dealt with the wicked and profligate was by far the most alluring, and if one had been allowed to acknowledge it openly, it was really often a great pity that the prodigal repented and was redeemed.

But one did not say that, nor did one actually think it. It was only present somehow or other as a presentiment or a possibility, deep down in one's feelings. When I pictured the devil to myself, I could quite well imagine him down below in the street, openly or in disguise, or at the annual fair or in the public house, but I could never imagine him with us at home.

My sisters also belonged to the bright world. It often seemed to me that they approached more nearly to father and mother; that they were better and nicer mannered than myself, without so many faults. They had their failings, they were naughty, but that did not seem to me to be deep-rooted. It was not the same as for me, for whom the contact with evil was strong and painful, and the dark world so much nearer. My sisters, like my parents, were to be treated with regard and respect. If you had had a quarrel with them, your own conscience accused you afterwards as the wrongdoer and the cause of the squabble, as the one who had to beg pardon. For in opposing my sisters I offended my parents, the representatives of goodness and law. There were secrets which I would much sooner have shared with the most depraved street urchins than with my sisters. On good, bright days when I had a good conscience, it was often delightful to play with my sisters, to be gentle and nice to them, and to see myself under a halo of goodness. That was how it must be if you were an angel! That was the most sublime thing we knew, to be an angel, surrounded by sweet sounds and fragrance like Christmas and happiness. But, oh, how seldom were such days and hours perfect! Often when we were playing one of the nice, harmless, proper games I was so vehement and impetuous, and I so annoyed my sisters that we quarreled and were unhappy. Then when I was carried away by anger I did and said things, the wickedness of which I felt deep and burning within me, even while I was doing and saying them. Then came sad, dark hours of remorse and contrition, the painful moment when I begged pardon, then again a beam of light, a peaceful, grateful happiness without discord, for minutes or hours.

I used to go to the Latin school. The sons of the mayor and of the head forester were in my class and sometimes used to come to our house. They were wild boys, but still they belonged to the world of goodness and of propriety. In spite of that I had close relations with neighbors' boys, children of the public school, whom in general we despised. With one of these I must begin my story.

One half-holiday—I was little more than ten at the time—I went out with two boys of the neighborhood. A public-school boy of about thirteen years joined our party; he was bigger than we were, a coarse and robust fellow, the son of a tailor. His father was a drunkard, and the whole family had a bad reputation. I knew Frank Kromer well, I was afraid of him, and was very much displeased when he joined us. He had already acquired manly ways, and imitated the gait and manner of speech of the young factory hands. Under his leadership we stepped down to the bank of the stream and hid ourselves from the world under the first arch of the bridge. The little bank between the vaulted bridge wall and the sluggishly flowing water was composed of nothing but trash, of broken china and garbage, of twisted bundles of rusty iron wire and other rubbish. You sometimes found there useful things. We had to search the stretch under Frank Kromer's direction and show him what we found. He then either kept it himself or threw it away into the water. He bid us note whether the things were of lead, brass or tin. Everything we found of this description he kept for himself, as well as an old horn comb. I felt very uneasy in his company, not because I knew that father would have forbidden our playing together had he known of it, but through fear of Frank himself. I was glad that he treated me like the others. He commanded and we obeyed; it seemed habitual to me, although that was the first time I was with him.

At last we sat down. Frank spat into the water and looked like a full grown man; he spat through a gap in his teeth, directing the sputum in any direction he wished. He began a conversation, and the boys vied with one another in bragging of schoolboy exploits and pranks. I was silent, and yet, if I said nothing, I was afraid of calling attention to myself and inciting Kromer's anger against me. My two comrades had from the beginning turned their backs on me, and had sided with him; I was a stranger among them, and I felt my clothes and manner to be a provocation. It was impossible that Frank should like me, a Latin schoolboy and the son of a gentleman, and the other two, I felt, as soon as it came to the point, would disown me and leave me in the lurch.

At last, through mere fright, I also began to relate a story. I invented a long narration of theft, of which I made myself the hero. In a garden by the mill on the corner, I recounted, I had one night with the help of a friend stolen a whole sack of apples, and those none of the ordinary sorts, but russets and golden pippins, the very best. In the danger of the moment I had recourse to the telling of this story, which I invented easily and recounted readily. In order not to have to finish off immediately, and so perhaps be led from bad to worse, I gave full scope to my inventive powers. One of us, I continued, always had to stand sentinel, while the other was throwing down apples from the tree, and the sack had become so heavy that at last we had to open it again and leave half the apples behind; but we returned at the end of half an hour and took the rest away with us.

I hoped at the end to gain some little applause, I had warmed to my work and had let myself go in my narration. The two small boys waited quiet and expectant, but Frank Kromer looked at me penetratingly through half-closed eyes and asked me in a threatening tone:

"Is that true?"

"Yes," I said.

"Really and truly?"

"Yes, really and truly," I asserted defiantly, though inwardly I was stifling through fear.

"Can you swear to it?"

I was terribly frightened, but I answered without hesitation: "Yes."

"Then say: 'I swear by God and all that's holy'!"

I said: "I swear by God and all that's holy!"

"Aw, gwan!" said he and turned away.

I thought that everything was now all right, and was glad when he got up and made for the town. When we were on the bridge I said timidly that I must now go home. "Don't be in such a hurry," laughed Frank, "we both go the same way." He dawdled on, and I dared not tear myself away, especially as he was actually taking the road to our house. As we arrived, I looked at the heavy brass-knocker, the sun on the window and the curtains in my mother's room, and I breathed a sigh of relief. Home at last! What a blessing it was to be at home again, to return to the brightness and peace of the family circle!

As I quickly opened the door and slipped inside, ready to shut it behind me, Frank Kromer forced his way in as well. He stood beside me in the cool, dark stone corridor which was only lighted from the courtyard, held me by the arm and said softly: "Not so fast, you!"

Terrified, I looked at him. His grip on my arm was one of iron. I tried to think what he had in his mind, whether he was going to maltreat me. I wondered, if I should scream, whether anyone would come down quickly enough to save me. But I gave up the idea.

"What's the matter?" I asked. "What d'you want?"

"Nothing much. I only want to ask you something—something the others needn't hear."

"Well, what do you want me to tell you? I must go upstairs, you know."

"You know, don't you, whose orchard that is by the mill on the corner?" said Frank softly.

"No, I don't know; I think it's the miller's."

Frank had wound his arm round me, and he drew me quite close to him, so that I had to look up directly into his face. His look boded ill, he smiled maliciously, and his face was full of cruelty and power.

"Now, kid, I can tell you whose the garden is. I have known for a long time that the apples had been stolen, and I also know that the man said he would give two marks to anyone who would tell him who stole the fruit."

"Good heavens!" I exclaimed. "But you won't tell him anything?" I felt it was useless to appeal to his sense of honor. He came from the other world; for him betrayal was no crime. I felt that for a certainty. In these matters people from the "other" world were not like us.

"Say nothing?" laughed Kromer. "Look here, my friend, d'you think I am minting money and can make two shilling pieces myself? I'm a poor chap, and I haven't got a rich father like yours, and when I get the chance of earning two shillings I must take it. He might even give me more."

Suddenly he let me go free. Our house no longer gave me an impression of peace and safety, the world fell to pieces around me. He would report me as a criminal, my father would be told, perhaps even the police might come for me. The terror of utter chaos menaced me, all that was ugly and dangerous was aligned against me. The fact that I had not stolen at all did not count in the least. I had sworn to it besides. O dear, O dear!

I burst into tears. I felt I must buy myself off. Despairingly I searched all my pockets. Not an apple, not a penknife, absolutely nothing. All at once I thought of my watch. It was an old silver one which wouldn't go. I wore it for no special reason. It came down to me from my grandmother. I drew it out quickly.

"Kromer," I said, "listen, you mustn't give me away, that wouldn't be nice of you. Look here, I will give you my watch; I haven't anything else, worse luck! You can have it, it's a silver one; the mechanism is good, there is one little thing wrong, that's all, it needs repairing."

He smiled and took the watch in his big hand. I looked at his hand and felt how coarse and hostile it was, how it grasped at my life and peace.

"It's silver," I said, timidly.

"I wouldn't give a straw for your silver and your old watch!" he said with deep scorn. "Get it repaired yourself!"

"But, Frank," I exclaimed, quivering with fear lest he should go away. "Wait a minute. Do take the watch! It's really silver, really and truly. And I haven't got anything else." He gave me a cold and scornful look.

"Very well, then, you know who I am going to; or I can tell the police. I know the sergeant very well."

He turned to go. I held him back by the sleeve. I could not let that happen. I would much rather have died than bear all that would take place if he went away like that.

"Frank," I implored, hoarse with emotion, "please don't do anything silly! Tell me it's only a joke, isn't it?"

"Oh, yes, a joke, but it might cost you dear."

"Do tell me, Frank, what to do. I'll do anything!" He examined me critically through his screwed-up eyes and laughed again.

"Don't be silly," he said with affected affability. "You know as well as I do. I've got the chance of earning a couple of marks, and I'm not such a rich fellow that I can afford to throw it away, you know that well enough. But you're rich, why, you've even got a watch. You need only give me just two marks and everything will be all right."

I understood his logic. But two marks! For me that was as much, and just as unobtainable, as ten, as a hundred, as a thousand marks. I had no money. There was a money box that my mother kept for me, with a couple of ten and five pfennig pieces inside which I received from my uncle when he paid us a visit, or from similar sources. I had nothing else. At that age I received no pocket-money at all.

"I have nothing," I said sadly. "I have no money at all. But I'll give you everything I have. I've got a book about red Indians, and also soldiers, and a compass. I'll get that for you."

But Kromer only screwed up his evil mouth, and spat on the ground.

"Quit your jawing," he said commandingly. "You can keep your old trash yourself. A compass! Don't make me angry, d'you hear? And hand over the money!"

"But I haven't any. I never get money. I can't help it."

"Very well, then, you'll bring me the two marks in the morning. I shall wait for you in the market after school. That's all. If you don't bring any money, look out!"

"Yes; but where shall I get it, then? Good Lord! If I haven't any—"

"There's enough money in your house. That's your business. Tomorrow after school, then. And I tell you: If you don't bring it—"

His eyes darted a terrible look at me, he spat again and vanished like a shadow.

I could not go upstairs. My life was ruined. I wondered if I should run away and never come back, or go and drown myself. But these thoughts were not clearly formulated. I sat crouched in the dark on the bottom step and I surrendered myself to my misfortune. There Lina found me in tears as she came down with a basket to get wood.

I begged her to say nothing on her return and I went up. My father's hat and my mother's sunshade hung on the rack near the glass door. All these things reminded me of home and tenderness, my heart went out to them imploringly and, grateful for their existence, I felt like the prodigal son when he looked into his old homely room and sensed its familiar atmosphere. All this, the bright father-and-mother world, was mine no longer, and I was buried deeply and guiltily in the strange flood, ensnared in sinful adventures, beset by enemies and dangers, menaced by shame and terror. The hat and sunshade, the good old sandstone floor, the big picture over the hall cupboard, and the voice of my elder sister in the living-room, all this was dearer and more precious to me than ever, but it was no longer consolation and secure possession. All of it was now a reproach. All this belonged to me no more, I could share no more in its cheerfulness and peace. I carried mud on my shoes that I could not wipe off on the mat, I brought shadows in with me, of which the home-world had no knowledge. How many secrets had I already had, how many cares—but that was play, a mere nothing compared with what I was bringing in with me that day.

Fate was overtaking me, hands were stretched out after me, from which even my mother could not protect me, of which she was to be allowed no knowledge. It was all the same, whether my offense was thieving, or a lie (had I not taken a false oath by God?). My sin was not this or that, I had tendered my hand to the devil. Why did I follow him? Why had I obeyed Kromer, more than ever I did my father? Why had I falsely invented the story of the theft? Why had I plumed myself on having committed a crime, as if it had been a deed of heroism? Now the devil had me by the hand, now the evil one was pursuing me.

For a moment I felt no further dread of the morrow, but I had the terrible certainty that my way was leading me further and further downhill and into the darkness. I realized clearly that from my wrongdoing other wrongdoings must result, that the greetings and kisses I gave to my parents would be a lie, that a secret destiny I should have to conceal hung over me.

For an instant confidence and hope came to me like a lightning flash as I gazed at my father's hat. I would tell him everything, would accept his judgment and the punishment he might mete out; he would be my confidant and would save me. Confession was all that would be necessary, as I had made so many confessions before—a difficult bitter hour, a serious, remorseful plea for forgiveness.

How sweetly that sounded! How tempting that was! But nothing came of it. I knew that I should not do it. I knew that I had now a secret, that I was burdened with guilt for which I myself would have to bear the responsibility alone. Perhaps I was at this very moment at the cross-roads, perhaps from this hour henceforth I should have to belong to the wicked, forever share secrets with the bad, depend on them, obey them, and become as one of themselves. I had pretended to be a man and a hero, now I had to take the consequences.

I was glad that my father, as he entered, found fault with my wet boots. It diverted his attention from something worse, and I allowed myself to suffer his reproach, secretly thinking of the other. That gave birth to a peculiar new feeling in me, an evil cutting feeling like a barbed hook. I felt superior to my father! I felt, for an instant's duration, a certain scorn of his ignorance; his scolding over the wet boots seemed to me petty. "If you only knew!" I thought, and looked upon myself as a criminal who is being tried for having stolen a loaf of bread, while he ought to confess to having committed murder. It was an ugly and repugnant feeling, yet strong and not without a certain charm, and it chained me to my secret and my guilt more securely than anything else. Perhaps Kromer has already gone to the police and given me away, I thought, and a storm is threatening to break over my head, while here I am looked upon as a mere child!

This was the important and permanent element of the whole event up to this point of my narration. It was the first cleft in the sacredness of parent-hood, it was the first split in the pillar on which my childhood had reposed, and which everyone must overthrow, before he can attain to self-realization. The inward, fundamental basis of our destiny is built up from these events, which no outsider observes. Such a split or cleft grows together again, heals up and is forgotten, but in the most secret chamber of the soul it continues to live and bleed.

I myself felt immediate terror in the presence of this new feeling, I would have liked to embrace my father's feet there and then, to beg his forgiveness. But one cannot beg pardon for something fundamental, and a child knows and feels that as well and as deeply as any adult.

I felt the need to think over the affair and to consider ways and means for the morrow; but I did not get around to it. My whole evening was taken up solely in accustoming myself to the changed atmosphere of our living-room. Clock and table, Bible and looking-glass, bookcase and pictures seemed all to be saying good-bye to me. With freezing heart I had to stand by and watch my world, the good happy time of my life, sever itself from me, to be rel-egated to the past. I was forced to realize that I was being held fast to new sucking roots in the darkness of the unfamiliar world outside. For the first time I tasted death, and death tasted bitter, for it is birth, with the terror and fear of a formidable renewal.

I was glad to be lying at last in bed. But first I had passed through pur-gatory in the form of evening prayers, and we had sung a hymn, one of my favorite ones. Alas! I did not join in, and each note was gall and poison for me. I did not join in the common prayer, either, when my father gave the blessing, and when he finished: "Be with us all!" I tore myself convulsively from the circle. The grace of God was with them all, but with me no longer. Cold and very tired, I went away.

After I had lain awhile in bed, wrapped around in warmth and safety, my troubled heart strayed back once again, and fluttered uneasily in the past. Mother had wished me good-night, as she always did, her step sounded yet in the room, the light of her candle gleamed through the crack in the door. Now, I thought, now she will come back again—she has felt my need, she will give me a kiss and will ask, in tones kind and full of promise, what is the matter. Then I can weep, the lump in my throat will melt away, I will throw my arms about her and will tell her, and everything will be right—I shall be saved! And when the crack in the door had become dark again I still listened for a while and thought—she must come, she must.

Then I came back to reality, and looked my enemy in the face. I saw him clearly, he had one eye closed, his mouth laughed uncouthly. While I gazed at him and the inevitable gnawed at my heart, he became bigger and more ugly, and his wicked eye lit up devilishly. He was close beside me, until I dropped off to sleep. But I did not dream of him, nor of the day's events. I dreamed instead that we were in a boat, my parents, my sisters and I, lapped in peace and the brightness of a holiday. I woke up in the middle of the night, with the aftertaste of bliss. I still saw the white summer dresses of my sisters glistening in the sun, and then fell from my paradise back to reality, and the enemy with the wicked eye stood opposite me.

I looked ill when mother came in quickly in the morning and told me how late it was and wanted to know why I was still in bed, and when she asked what was the matter with me, I vomited.

But I seemed to have gained a point. I rather liked to be somewhat ill and to be allowed to spend the morning in bed drinking chamomile tea, to listen to mother clearing-up in the next room, and to hear Lina outside in the corridor opening the door to the butcher. To stay away from morning school was rather like a fairy-story, and the sun which played in the room was not the same you saw through the green curtains at school. But today all this had lost its charm for me. It had a false ring about it.

If I had died! But I was only slightly ill, as I had often been before, and nothing was gained by that. It prevented me from going to school, but it did not protect me in any way from Kromer, who would be waiting for me in the market at eleven o'clock. And mother's friendliness was this time without comfort; it was burdensome and painful. I soon pretended to be asleep again, and thought the matter over, but all to no purpose—I had to be in the market at eleven o'clock. For that reason I got up at ten, and said that I was better. As usual in such cases I was told that either I must go back to bed or go to school in the afternoon. I said I would rather go to school. I had formed a plan.

I dared not go to Kromer without money. I had to get possession of the little savings box which belonged to me. There was not enough money in it, far from enough, I knew; but it was still a little, and something told me that a little was better than nothing; for at least Kromer had to be appeased.

I felt horrible as I crept in my socks into my mother's room and took my box from her writing table; but it was not so horrible as the previous day's experience. My heart beat so fast I nearly died, and it was no better when I found, at the first look, down below on the stairs, that the box was locked. It was easy to break it open, it was only necessary to cut through a thin plate of tin; but the action caused me pain, for only in doing this was I committing theft. Up to then I had only taken lumps of sugar and fruit on the sly. Now I had stolen something, although it was my own money. I realized I had taken a step nearer Kromer and his world, that I was slipping gradually downwards—and I adopted an attitude of defiance. The devil could run away with me if he liked, there was no way out. I anxiously counted the money, it had sounded so much in the box, now in my hand it was miserably little. There were sixty-five pfennigs. I hid the box in the basement, held the money in my closed fist and went out of the house, with a feeling different from any with which I had ever left the portal before. Someone called to me from above, I thought, but I went quickly on my way.

There was still plenty of time. I sneaked by a roundabout way through the streets of a changed town, beneath clouds I had never seen before, by houses which seemed to spy on me, and people who suspected me. On the way I recollected that one of my school friends had once found a thaler in the cattle market. I would have liked to pray to God to work a miracle and allow me to make such a treasure-trove. But I had no longer the right to pray. And even then the box would not be made whole again.

Frank Kromer saw me in the distance. However, he came along very slowly and seemed not to be looking out for me. As he approached me he beckoned me commandingly to follow. He passed on tranquilly, without once looking round, went down Straw Street and over the bridge, and stopped on the outskirts of the town in front of a new building. No one was working there, the walls stood bare, without doors or windows. Kromer looked round and then went through the doorway. I followed him. He stepped behind the wall, beckoned to me and stretched out his hand.

"That makes sixty-five pfennigs," he said and looked at me.

"Yes," I said timidly. "That's all I have—it's too little, I know, but it's all. I haven't any more."

"I thought you were cleverer than that," he exclaimed, blaming me in what were almost mild terms. "Between men of honor there must be honest dealing. I will not take anything from you, except what is right. You know that. Take your pfennigs back, there! The other—you know who—doesn't try to beat me down. He pays."

"But I have absolutely nothing else. That was my money box."

"That's your affair. But I don't want to make you unhappy. You still owe me one mark thirty-five pfennig. When can I have it?"

"Oh, you will soon have it, certainly, Kromer. I don't know yet—perhaps tomorrow, or the day after, I shall have some more. You understand that I can't tell my father, don't you?"

"That's no concern of mine. I don't want to harm you. If I liked, I could get the money before noon, you see, and I'm poor. You wear nice clothes, and you get something better to eat for dinner than I do. But I won't say anything. I am willing to wait a few days. The day after tomorrow, in the afternoon, I will whistle for you, then you will bring it along. You can recognize my whistle?"

He gave me a whistle that I had often heard before.

"Yes," I said, "I know it."

He went away, as if I didn't belong to him. It had been only a transaction between us, nothing further.

Even today, I believe, Kromer's whistle would terrify me if I heard it again suddenly. From then on I heard it often. It seemed I heard it continually and always. No place, no game, no work, no idea in which this whistle would not sound. I was dependent on it, it was now the messenger of my fate. On mild, glowing autumn afternoons I was often in our little flower garden, which I loved dearly. A peculiar impulse made me take up again boyish games which I had played formerly. I played, as it were, that I was a boy who was younger than I, who was still good and free, innocent and secure. But in the middle of the game, always expected and yet always terribly disturbing and surprising sounded Kromer's whistle, destroying the picture my imagination had painted.

Then I had to go, I had to follow my tormentor to evil and ugly places, had to render an account and let myself be dunned. The whole business may have lasted a few weeks, but it seemed to me like a year, or an eternity. I seldom had money—a five or ten pfennig piece stolen from the kitchen table when Lina left the market basket standing there. Each time I was blamed by Kromer, and heaped with abuse; it was I who deceived him and kept back what was his due, it was I who robbed him and made him unhappy! Seldom in life has need so oppressed me, seldom have I felt a greater helplessness, a greater dependence.

I had filled up the savings box with toy money—no one made any enquiries. But that as well could be discovered any day. I was even more afraid of mother than of Kromer's harsh whistle, especially when she stepped up to me softly—was she not going to ask me about the money box?

As I presented myself to my evil genius several times without money he began to torment and to make use of me after a different fashion. I had to work for him. He had to see to various things for his father. I did that for him or he made me do something more difficult, hop on one leg for ten minutes, or fasten a scrap of paper on to the coat of a passer-by. Many nights these torments realized themselves in my dreams, and I wept and broke out in a cold sweat in my nightmare.

For a time I was ill. I often vomited and felt cold, but at night I lay in a fever, bathed in perspiration. Mother felt that something was wrong and displayed much sympathy on my behalf, but this tortured me because I could not respond by confiding in her.

One evening, after I had already gone to bed, she brought me a piece of chocolate. This action was a souvenir of former years when, if I had been good, I was often rewarded in this way before going off to sleep. Now she stood there and held the piece of chocolate out to me. This so pained me that I could do nothing but shake my head. She asked what was the matter with me and stroked my hair. I could only sob out: "Nothing! Nothing! I won't have anything." She put the chocolate on my bed table and went away. When she wished subsequently to question me on the matter I made as if I knew nothing about it. Once she brought the doctor to me, who examined me and prescribed cold ablutions in the morning.

My state at that time was a sort of insanity. I was shy and lived in torment like a ghost in the midst of the well-ordered peace of our house. I had no part in the others' lives, and could seldom, even for as much as an hour, forget my miserable existence. In the presence of my father, who often took me to task in an irritated fashion, I was reserved and wrapped up in myself.

CHAPTER 2

CAIN

Deliverance from my troubles came from quite an unexpected quarter, and with it something new entered into my life, which has up to the present day exercised a strong influence.

A short time before we had had a new boy at our Latin school. He was the son of a well-to-do widow who had moved to our town. He was in mourning and wore a crape band round his sleeve. His form was above mine, and he was several years older, but I soon began to take notice of him, as did all of us. This remarkable boy impressed one as being much older than he looked. He made on no one the impression of being a mere schoolboy. With us childish youngsters he was as distant and as mature as a man, or rather, as a gentleman. He was by no means popular, he took no part in the games, much less in the fooling. It was only the self-conscious and decided tone which he adopted towards the masters that pleased the others. His name was Max Demian.

One day it happened, as it occasionally did in our school, that for some cause or other, another class was sent into our large schoolroom. It was Demian's form. We little ones were having Biblical history, the big ones had to write an essay. While we were having the story of Cain and Abel knocked into us, I kept looking across at Demian, whose face fascinated me strangely, and saw his wise, bright, more than ordinarily strong features bent attentively and thoughtfully over his task. He did not look at all like a schoolboy doing an exercise, but like a research worker solving a problem. I did not find him really agreeable. On the contrary, I had one or two little things against him. With me he was too distant and superior, he was much too provokingly sure of himself, and the expression of his eyes was that of an adult—which children never like—rather sad with occasional flashes of scorn. Yet I could not resist looking at him, whether I liked him or not. But the minute he looked in my direction I looked away, somewhat frightened. If today I consider what he looked like as a schoolboy, I can say that he was in every respect different from the others, and bore the stamp of a striking personality and therefore attracted attention. But at the same time he did everything to prevent himself from being remarked—he bore and conducted himself like a disguised prince who finds himself among peasant boys and makes every effort to appear like them.

He was behind me on the way home from school. When the others had run on, he overtook me and said: "Hello!" Even his manner of greeting, although he imitated our schoolboy tone of voice, was polite and like that of a grownup person.

"Shall we go a little way together?" he questioned in a friendly way. I was flattered and nodded. Then I described to him where I lived.

"Oh, there?" he said laughingly. "I know the house already. There is a remarkable work of art over your door, which interested me at once."

I did not guess immediately to what he was referring, and was astonished that he seemed to know our house better than I did. There was indeed a sort of crest which served as a keystone over the arch of the door, but in course of time it had become faint and had often been painted over. As far as I knew, it had nothing to do with us, or with our family.

"I don't know anything about it," I said timidly. "It's a bird, or something like it; it must be very old. They say that the house at one time belonged to the abbey."

"Very likely," he nodded. "We'll have another good look at it. Such things are often interesting. It is a hawk, I think."

We continued our way. I was considerably embarrassed. Suddenly Demian laughed, as if something funny had struck him.

"Oh, I was present at your lesson," he said with animation. "The story of Cain, who carried the mark on his forehead, was it not? Do you like it?"

Generally I used not to like anything of all the things we had to learn. But I did not dare to say so—it was as though a grownup person were talking to me. I said I liked the story very much.

Demian tapped me on the shoulder. "No need to impose on me, old fellow. But the story is really rather remarkable. I think it is much more remarkable than most of the others we get at school. The master didn't say very much about it, only the usual things about God and sin, et cetera. But I believe—" he broke off, smiled, and questioned: "But does it interest you?"

"Well," he continued, "I think one can conceive this story of Cain quite differently. Most things we are taught are certainly quite true and right, but one can consider them all from a different standpoint from the master's, and most of them have a much better meaning then. For instance, we can't be quite content with the explanation given us with regard to this fellow Cain and the mark on his forehead. Don't you find it so, too? It certainly might happen that he should kill one of his brothers in a quarrel, it is also possible that he should afterwards be afraid, and have to come down a peg. But that he should be singled out into the bargain with a decoration for his cowardice, which protects him and strikes terror into everyone else, that is really rather odd."

"Certainly," I said, interested. The case began to interest me. "But how else should one explain the story?" He clapped me on the shoulder.

"Quite simply! The essential fact, and the point of departure of the story, was the sign. Here was a man who had something in his face which terrified other people. They did not dare to molest him, he made a big impression on them, he and his children. Perhaps, or rather certainly, it was not really a sign on his forehead like an office stamp—things are not as simple as that in real life. I would sooner think it was something scarcely perceptible, of a peculiar nature—a little more intelligence and boldness in his look than people were accustomed to. This man had power, other people shrank from him. He had a 'sign.' One could explain that as one wished. And one always wishes what is convenient and agrees with one's opinions. People were afraid of Cain's children, they had a 'sign.' And so they explained the sign not as it really was, a distinction, but as the contrary. The fellows with this sign were said to be peculiar, and they were courageous as well. People with courage and character are always called peculiar by other people. That a race of fearless and peculiar men should rove about was very embarrassing. And so people attached a surname and a story to this race, in order to revenge themselves on it, in order to compensate themselves more or less for all the terror with which it had inspired them. Do you understand?"

"Yes—that means to say, then—that Cain was not at all wicked? And the whole story in the Bible isn't really true?"

"Yes and no. Such ancient, primitive stories are always true, but they have not always been recorded and explained in the proper manner. In short, I mean that Cain was a thundering good fellow, and this story got attached to his name simply because people were afraid of him. The story was merely a report, something people might have set going in a gossiping way, and it was true in so far as Cain and his children did actually wear a sort of 'sign' and were different from most people."

I was much astonished.

"And do you believe then, that the affair of the murder is absolutely un-true?" I asked, much impressed.

"Not at all! It is certainly true. The strong man killed a weak one. One may doubt of course whether it was really his brother or not. It is not important, for, in the end, all men are brothers. A strong man, then, has killed a weak one. Perhaps it was a deed of heroism, perhaps it was not. But in any case the other weak people were terrified, they lamented and complained, and when they were asked: 'Why don't you simply kill him as well?' they did not answer, 'Because we are cowards,' but they said instead: 'You can't. He has a sign. God has singled him out!' The humbug must have arisen something after this style— Oh, I am keeping you from going in. Good-bye, then!"

He turned into Old Street and left me alone, more astonished than I had ever been before. Scarcely had he gone when everything that he had said seemed to me quite unbelievable! Cain a noble fellow, Abel a coward! Cain's sign a distinction! It was absurd, it was blasphemous and infamous. What was God's part in the matter? Had he not accepted Abel's sacrifice, did he not love Abel? Demian's story was nonsense! I suspected him of making fun of me and of wishing to mislead me. The devil of a clever fellow, and he could talk, but—well—

Still, I had never thought so much about any of the Biblical or other stories before. And for some time past I had never so completely forgotten Frank Kromer, for hours, for a whole evening. At home I read through the story once again, as it stands in the Bible, short and clear. It was quite foolish to try to find a special, secret meaning. If it had one, every murderer could look upon himself as a favorite of God! No, it was nonsense. But Demian had a nice way of saying such things, so easily and pleasantly, as if everything were self-evident—and then his eyes!

My ideas were certainly a little upset, or rather they were very much confused. I had lived in a bright, clean world, I myself had been a sort of Abel, and now I was so firmly fixed in the other and had sunk so deeply, but really what could I do to help it? What was my position now? A reminiscence glowed in me which for the moment almost took away my breath. I remembered that wretched evening, from which my present misery dated, when I looked for an instant into the heart of my father's bright world and despised his wisdom! Then I was Cain and bore the sign; I imagined that it was in no way shameful, but a distinction, and in my wickedness and unhappiness I stood on a higher level than my father, higher than good and pious people.

It was not in such a clear-thinking way that my experience then presented itself to me, but all this was contained therein. It was only a flaming up of feeling, of strange emotions which caused me pain and yet filled me with pride.

When I considered the matter, I saw how strangely Demian had spoken of the fearless and the cowards! How curiously he had explained the mark on

Cain's forehead. How singularly his eyes had lit up, those peculiar eyes of a grown person! And indistinctly it shot through my brain: Is not he himself, this Demian, a sort of Cain? Why did he defend him, if he did not feel like him? Why had he this force in his gaze? Why did he speak so scornfully of the "others," of the fearsome, who are really the pious and the well-considered of God?

This thought led me to no definite conclusion. A stone had fallen into the well, and the well was my young soul. And this business with Cain, the murder and the sign, was for a long, a very long, time the point from which my seekings after knowledge, my doubts and my criticisms took their departure.

I noticed that the other boys also occupied themselves a good deal with Demian. I had not told anyone of his version of the story of Cain, but he appeared to interest the others as well. At least, many rumors concerning the "new boy" became current. If only I still knew all of them, each would help to throw fresh light on him, each would serve to interpret him. I only remember the first rumor was that Demian's mother was very rich. It was also said that she never went to church, nor the son either. Another rumor had it that they were Jews, but they could just as easily have been, in secret, Mohammedans. Furthermore, tales were told of Max Demian's strength. So much was certain, that the strongest boy in his form, who challenged him to a fight, and who at his refusal branded him coward, suffered a terrible humiliation at his hands. Those who were there said that Demian had simply taken him by the nape of the neck with one hand and had brought such a pressure to bear that the boy went white and afterwards crawled away, and that for several days he was unable to use his arm. For a whole evening a rumor even ran that he was dead. For a time everything was asserted and believed, everything that was exciting and wonderful. Then there was a satiety of rumors for a while. A little later new ones circulated, which asserted that Demian had intimate relations with girls and "knew everything."

Meanwhile my affair with Frank Kromer took its inevitable course. I could not get away from him, for although he left me in peace for days together, I was still bound to him. In my dreams he lived as my shadow, and thus my fantasy credited him with actions which he did not, in reality, do; so that in dreams I was absolutely his slave. I lived in these dreams—I was always a deep dreamer—more than in reality. These shadowy conceptions wasted my strength and my life force. I often dreamed, among other things, that Kromer ill-treated me, that he spat on me and knelt on me and, what was worse, that he led me to commit grave crimes—or rather I was not led, but simply forced, through his powerful influence. The most terrible of these dreams, from which I woke up half mad, presented itself as a murderous attack on my father. Kromer whetted a knife and put it in my hand, as we were standing behind the trees of a lane, and lying in wait for someone—whom I knew not; but when someone came along and Kromer through a pressure of the arm informed me that this was the man, whom I was to stab, it turned out to be my father! Then I woke up.

With all these troubles, I still thought a great deal about Cain and Abel, but much less about Demian. It was, strangely enough, in a dream that he first came in contact with me again. I dreamed once more, of assault and ill-treatment which I suffered, but instead of Kromer, this time it was Demian who knelt upon me. And, what was quite new and profoundly impressive, everything that I suffered resistingly and in torment at the hands of Kromer, I suffered willingly from Demian, with a feeling which was composed as much of joy as of fear. I had this dream twice, then Kromer occupied his old position in my thoughts.

For a long time I have not been able to separate what I experienced in these dreams from what I underwent in reality. But in any case my evil relation with Kromer took its course, and was by no means at an end, when I had at last, by petty thefts, paid the boy the sum owed. No, for now he knew of these thefts, as he always asked me where the money came from, and I was more in his hands than ever. He frequently threatened to tell my father everything, and my terror then was scarcely as great as the profound regret that I had not myself done that in the beginning. However, miserable as I was, I did not repent of everything, at least not always, and sometimes felt, I thought, that things could not have helped being as they were. The hand of fate was upon me, and it was useless to want to break away.

I conjecture that my parents suffered not a little in these circumstances. A strange spirit had come over me, I no longer fitted into our community which had been so intimate, and for which I often felt a maddening homesickness, as for a lost paradise. I was treated, particularly by mother, more like a sick person than like a miserable wretch. But the actual state of affairs I was able to observe best in the conduct of my two sisters. It was quite evident from their behavior, which was very considerate and which yet caused me endless pain, that I was a sort of person possessed, who was more to be pitied than blamed for his condition, but yet in whom evil had taken up residence. I felt that I was being prayed for in a different way from formerly, and realized the fruitlessness of these prayers. I often felt burning within me an intense longing for relief, an ardent desire for a full confession, and yet I realized in advance that I should not be able to tell everything to father and mother properly, in explanation of my conduct. I knew that I should be received in a friendly way, that much consideration and compassion would be shown me, but that I should not be completely understood. The whole affair would have been looked upon as a sort of backsliding, whereas it was really the work of destiny.

I know that many people will not believe that a child scarcely eleven years old could feel thus. But I am not relating my affairs for their benefit. My narration is for those who know mankind better. The grownup person who has learned to convert part of his feelings into thoughts, feels the absence of these ideas in a child, and comes to believe that the experiences are likewise lacking. But they have seldom been so vivid and not often in my life have I suffered as keenly as then.

One rainy day I was ordered by my tormentor to Castle Place, and there I stood, waiting and digging my feet in the wet chestnut leaves, which were still falling regularly from the black, dripping branches. Money I had none, but I had brought with me two pieces of cake that I had stolen in order at least to be able to give Kromer something. I had long since been accustomed to stand about in any odd corner waiting for him often for a very long time, and I put up with the unalterable.

Kromer came at last. That day he did not stay long. He poked me several times in the ribs, laughed, took the cake, and even offered me a mouldy cigarette, which however I did not accept. He was more friendly than usual.

"Oh," he said, as he went away, "before I forget—next time you can bring your sister along, the elder one. What's her name? Now tell the truth."

I did not understand, and gave no answer. I only looked at him wonderingly.

"Don't you get me? You must bring your sister along."

"But Kromer, that won't do. I mustn't do that, and besides she wouldn't come."

I thought this was only another pretext for vexing me. He often did that, requiring me to do something impossible, and so terrifying me. And often, after humiliating me, he would by degrees become more tractable. I then had to buy myself off with money or with some other gift.

This time he was quite different. He was really not at all angry at my refusal.

"Well," he said airily, "you'll think about it, won't you? I should like to make your sister's acquaintance. It will not be so difficult. You simply take her out for a walk, and then I come along. Tomorrow I'll whistle for you, and then we can talk more about it."

When he had gone, a glimpse of the meaning of his request dawned on me. I was still quite a child, but I knew by hearsay that boys and girls, when they were somewhat older, did things which were forbidden, things of a secret and scandalous nature. And now I should also have to—it was suddenly quite clear to me how monstrous it was! I immediately resolved never to do that. But I scarcely dared think of what would happen in that case and how Kromer would revenge himself on me. A new torment began, I had not yet been tortured enough.

I walked disconsolately across the empty square, my hands in my pockets. Fresh torments, a new servitude!

Suddenly a fresh, deep voice called to me. I was terrified and began to run on. Someone ran after me, a hand gripped me from behind. It was Max Demian.

I let myself be taken prisoner. I surrendered.

"It's you?" I said uncertainly. "You frightened me so!"

He looked at me, and never had his glance been more like that of an adult, of a superior and penetrating person. For a long time past we had not spoken with one another.

"I am sorry," he said in his courteous and at the same time very determined manner. "But listen, you mustn't let yourself be frightened like that."

"Oh, that can happen sometimes."

"So it appears. But look here: If you shrink like that from someone who hasn't hurt you, then this someone begins to think. It makes him curious, he wonders what can be the matter. This somebody thinks to himself, how awfully frightened you are, and he thinks further: one is only like that when one is terrified. Cowards are always frightened; but I believe you aren't really a coward. Ain't I right? Of course, you aren't a hero either. There are things of which you are afraid. There are also people of whom you are afraid. And that should never be. No one should ever be afraid of other people. You aren't afraid of me? Or are you, perhaps?"

"Oh no, of course not."

"There, you see. But there are people you are afraid of?"

"I don't know…let me go, what do you want of me?"

He kept pace with me—I was going quicker with the idea of escaping—I felt his look directed on me from the side.

"Just assume," he began again, "that I mean well with you. In any case you needn't be afraid of me. I would very much like to try an experiment with you—it's funny, and you can learn something that's very useful. Listen: I often practise an art which is called mind-reading. There's no witchcraft in it, but it seems very peculiar if one doesn't know how to do it. You can surprise people very much with it. Well, let us try it. I like you, or I interest myself in you, and I would like to find out what your real feelings are. I have already made the first step towards doing that. I have frightened you—you are, then, easily frightened. There are things and people of which and of whom you are afraid. Why is it? One need be afraid of no one. If you fear somebody then it is due to the fact that he has power over you. For example, you have done something wrong, and the other person knows it—then he has power over you. D'you get me? It's clear, isn't it?"

I looked helplessly into his face, which was serious and prudent as always, and kind as well, but without any tenderness—his features were rather severe. Righteousness or something akin lay therein. I was not conscious of what was happening; he stood like a magician before me.

"Have you understood?" he questioned again.

I nodded. I could not speak.

"I told you mind-reading looked rather strange, but the process is quite natural. I could for example tell you more or less exactly what you thought about me when I once told you the story of Cain and Abel. But that has nothing to do with the matter in hand. I also think it possible that you have dreamed of me. But let's leave that out! You're a clever kid, most of 'em are so stupid. I like talking now and then with a clever fellow whom I can trust. You have no objections, have you?"

"Oh, no! Only I don't understand."

"Let's keep to our old experiment! We have found that: the boy S. is easily frightened—he is afraid of somebody—he apparently shares a secret with this other person, which causes him much disquietude. Is that about right?"

As in a dream I lay under the influence of his voice, of his personality. I only nodded. Was not a voice talking there, which could only come from myself? Which knew all? Which knew all in a better, clearer way than I myself?

Demian gave me a powerful slap on the shoulder.

"That's right then. I thought so. Now just one question more: Do you know the name of the boy who has just gone away?"

I sank back, he had the key to my secret, this secret which twisted back inside me as if it did not want to see the light.

"What sort of a fellow? There was no one there, except myself."

He laughed.

"Don't be afraid to tell me," said he laughingly. "What's his name?"

I whispered: "Do you mean Frank Kromer?"

He nodded contentedly.

"Bravo! You're a smart chap, we shall be good friends yet. But now I must tell you something else: this Kromer, or whatever his name is, is a nasty fellow. His face tells me he's a rascal! What do you think?"

"Oh yes," I sobbed out, "he is nasty, he's a devil! But he mustn't know anything! For God's sake, he mustn't know anything. D'you know him? Does he know you?"

"Don't worry! He's gone, and he doesn't know me—not yet. But I should like to make his acquaintance. He goes to the public school?"

"Yes."

"In which standard?"

"In the fifth. But don't say anything to him! Please, don't say anything to him!"

"Don't worry, nothing will happen to you. I suppose you wouldn't like to tell me a little more about this fellow Kromer?"

"I can't! No, let me go!"

He was silent for a while.

"It's a pity," he said, "we might have been able to carry the experiment still further. But I don't want to bother you. You know, don't you, that it is not right of you to be afraid of him? Such fear quite undermines us, you must get rid of it. You must get rid of it, if you want to become a real man. D'you understand?"

"Certainly, you are quite right…but it won't do. You don't know…."

"You have seen that I know a lot, more than you thought. Do you owe him any money?"

"Yes, I do, but that isn't the essential point. I can't tell, I can't!"

"It won't help matters, then, if I give you the amount you owe him? I could very well let you have it."

"No, no, that is not the point. And please: don't say anything to anybody! Not a word! You are making me miserable!"

"Rely on me, Sinclair. Later you can share your secrets with me."

"Never, never!" I exclaimed vehemently.

"Just as you please. I only mean, perhaps you will tell me something more later on. Only of your own free will, you understand. Surely you don't think I shall act like Kromer?"

"Oh no—but you don't even know anything about it!"

"Absolutely nothing. But I think about it. And I shall never act like Kromer, believe me. Besides, you don't owe me anything."

We remained a long time silent, and I became more tranquil. But Demian's knowledge became more and more of a puzzle to me.

"I'm going home now," he said, and in the rain he drew his coat more closely about him. "I should only like to repeat one thing to you, since we have gone so far in the matter—you ought to get rid of this fellow! If there is nothing else to be done, then kill him! It would impress me and please me, if you were to do that. Besides, I would help you."

I was again terrified. I suddenly remembered the story of Cain. I had an uncanny feeling and I began to cry softly. So much that was weird seemed to surround me.

"All right," Max Demian said, smilingly. "Go home now! We will put things square, although murder would have been the simplest. In such matters the simplest way is always the best. You aren't in good hands, with your friend Kromer."

I came home, and it seemed to me as if I had been away a year. Everything looked different. Between myself and Kromer there now stood something like future freedom, something like hope. I was lonely no longer! And then I realized for the first time how terribly lonely I had been for weeks and weeks. And I immediately recollected what I had on several occasions turned over in my mind: that a confession to my parents would afford me relief and yet would not quite liberate me. Now I had almost confessed, to another, to a stranger, and as if a strong perfume had been wafted to me, sensed the presentiment of salvation!

Still my fear was far from being overcome, and I was still prepared for long and terrible mental wrestlings with my evil genius. So it was all the more remarkable to me that everything passed off so very secretly and quietly.

Kromer's whistle remained absent from our house for a day, two days, three days, a whole week. I dared not believe my senses, and lay inwardly on the watch, to see whether he would not suddenly stand before me, just at that moment when I should expect him no longer. But he was, and remained, away! Distrustful of my new freedom, I still could not bring myself to believe in it whole-heartedly. Until at last I met Frank Kromer. He was coming down the street, straight in my direction. When he saw me, he drew himself together, twisted his features in a brutal grimace, and turned away without more ado, in order to avoid meeting me.

That was a wonderful moment for me! My enemy ran away from me! My devil was afraid of me! Surprise and joy shook me through and through!

In a few days Demian showed himself once again. He waited for me outside school.

"Hullo," I said.

"Good morning, Sinclair. I only wanted to hear how you're getting on. Kromer leaves you in peace, doesn't he?"

"Did you manage that? But how did you do it? How? I don't understand it. He hasn't come near me."

"Splendid. If he should come again—I don't think he will, but he's a cheeky fellow—then simply tell him to remember Demian."

"But what does it all mean? Have you had a fight with him and thrashed him?"

"No, I'm not so keen on that. I simply talked to him, as I did to you, and I made it clear to him that it is to his own advantage to leave you in peace."

"Oh, but you haven't given him any money?"

"No, kid. You have already tried that way yourself."

I attempted to pump him on the matter, but he disengaged himself. The old, embarrassed feeling concerning him came over me—an odd mixture of gratitude and shyness, of admiration and fear, of affection and inward resistance.

I had the intention of seeing him again soon, and then I wanted to talk more about everything, about the Cain affair as well. But I did not see him. Gratitude is not one of the virtues in which I believe, and to require it of a child would seem to me wrong. So I do not wonder very much at the complete ingratitude which I evinced towards Max Demian. Today I believe positively that I should have been ruined for life if he had not freed me from Kromer's clutches. At that time also I already felt this release as the greatest event of my young life—but I left the deliverer on one side as soon as he had accomplished the miracle.

As I have said, ingratitude seems to me nothing strange. Solely, the lack of curiosity I evinced is odd. How was it possible that I could continue for a single day my quiet mode of life without coming nearer to the secrets with which Demian had brought me in contact? How could I restrain the desire to hear more about Cain, more about Kromer, more about the thought-reading?

It is scarcely comprehensible, and yet it is so. I suddenly saw myself extricated from the demoniacal toils, saw again the world lying bright and cheerful before me. I was no longer subject to paroxysms of fear. The curse was broken, I was no longer a tormented and condemned creature, I was a schoolboy again. My temperament sought to regain its equilibrium and tranquillity as quickly as possible, and so I took pains above all things to put behind me all that had been ugly and menacing, and to forget it. The whole, long story of my guilt, of my terrifying anxiety, slipped from my memory wonderfully quick, apparently without having left behind any scars or impressions whatsoever.

The fact that I likewise tried as quickly to forget my helper and deliverer, I understand today as well. Instinctively my mind turned from the damning recollection of my awful servitude under Kromer, and I sought to recover my former happy, contented mental outlook, to regain that lost paradise which opened once more to me, the bright father-and-mother world, where my sisters dwelt in the fragrant atmosphere of purity, in loving kindness such as God had extended to Abel.

On the very next day after my short conversation with Demian, when I was at last fully convinced of my newly-born freedom and feared no longer a relapse to my condition of slavery, I did what I had so often and so ardently desired to do—I confessed. I went to mother and showed her the little savings box with the broken lock, filled with toy mark pieces instead of with real money, and I told her how long I had been in the thrall of an evil tormentor, through my own guilt. She did not understand everything, but she saw the money box, she saw my altered look and heard my changed voice—she felt that I was healed, that I had been restored to her.

And then with lofty feelings I celebrated my readmission into the family, the prodigal son's return home. Mother took me to father, the story was repeated, questions and exclamations of wonder followed in quick succession, both parents stroked my hair and breathed deeply, as in relief from a long oppression. It was all lovely, like the stories I had read, all discords were resolved in a happy ending.

I surrendered myself passionately to this harmonious state of affairs. I could not have enough of the idea that I was again free and trusted by my parents. I was a model boy at home and played more frequently than ever with my sisters. At prayers I sang the dear, old hymns with the blissful feeling of one converted and redeemed. It came straight from my heart, it was no lie this time.

And yet it was not at all as it should have been. And this is the point which alone can truly explain my forgetfulness of Demian. I ought to have made a confession *to him*! The confession would have been less touching and less specious, but for me it would have borne more fruit. I was now clinging fast to my former paradisaical world, I had returned home and had been received in grace. But Demian belonged in no wise to this world, he did not fit into it. He also—in a different way from Kromer—but nevertheless he also was a seducer, he too bound me to the second, evil, bad world, and of this world I never wanted to hear anything more. I could not now, and I did not wish to give up Abel and help to glorify Cain, now when I myself had again become an Abel.

So much for the outward correlation of events. But inwardly it was like this: I had been freed from the hands of Kromer and the devil, but not through my own strength and effort. I had ventured a footing on the paths of the world, and they had been too slippery for me. Now that the grasp of a friendly hand had saved me, I ran back, without another glance round, to mother's lap, to the protecting, godly and tender security of childhood. I made myself younger, more dependent on others, more childlike than I really was. I had to replace my dependence on Kromer by a new one, since I was powerless to strike out for myself. So I chose, in the blindness of my heart, the dependence on father and mother, on the old, beloved, "bright world," on this world which I knew already was not the sole one. Had I not done this, I should have had to hold to Demian, to entrust myself to him. The fact that I did not, appeared to me then to be due to justifiable distrust of his strange ideas; in reality it was due to nothing else than fear. For Demian would have required more of me than did my parents, much more. By stimulation and exhortation, by scorn and irony he would have tried to make me more independent. Alas, I know that today: nothing in the world is so distasteful to man as to go the way which leads him to himself!

And yet, about half a year later, I could not resist the temptation to ask my father while we were out for a walk, what was to be made of the fact that many people declared Cain to be better than Abel.

He was much surprised, and explained to me that this was a conception by no means novel. It had even emerged in the early Christian era, and had been professed by sects, one of which was called the "Cainites." But naturally this foolish doctrine was nothing else than an attempt of the devil to undermine our belief. For, if one believes that Cain was right and Abel was wrong, then it follows that God has erred, and that the God of the Bible is not the true and only God, but a false one. The Cainites really used to profess and preach something approximating this doctrine; but this heresy vanished from among mankind a long time ago and he wondered the more that a school friend had been able to learn something on the subject. Nevertheless, he earnestly exhorted me not to let these ideas occupy my attention.

CHAPTER 3

THE THIEF ON THE CROSS

I could describe scenes of my childhood, spent in peaceful security at the side of father and mother, relate how I passed this period of my life, playing contentedly in the midst of surroundings brightened by love and tenderness. But others have done that. I am only interested in the steps I took in life, in order to attain self-realization. All the pretty resting-places, happy isles and children's paradises, whose charm is not unknown to me, I leave lying behind me in the shimmer of a distant horizon, and I have no desire to set foot there again.

For that reason I will speak, so far as I intend to dwell on the period of my childhood, only of new events which overtook me, of what impelled me forward enabling me to throw off my shackles.

These impulses always came from the "other" world, they always brought fear, coercion and a bad conscience in their train, they were always of a revolutionary tendency and a danger to the peace in which I would willingly have been allowed to remain.

There came the years in which I had to discover anew that there was within me an instinct which had to lie close and concealed in the bright world of moral sanction. As to every man, the slowly awakening sense of sex came to me as an enemy and a destroyer, as something forbidden, as seduction and sin. What my curiosity sought to know, what caused me dreams, desire and fear, the great secret of puberty, that was not at all in keeping with the guarded happiness of my peaceful childhood. I did as everyone else. I led the double life of a child, who is yet a child no longer. My conscious self lived under the conditions sanctioned at home; it denied the existence of the new world whose dawn glimmered before me. But I lived as well in dreams, impelled by desires of a secret nature, upon which my conscious self anxiously attempted to build a new fabric, as the world of my childhood fell in ruins about me. Like almost all parents, my own did nothing to help the awakening life-instincts, about which not a syllable was uttered. They only aided, with untiring care, my hopeless attempts to deny the reality, and to continue my existence in a child-like world which was ever becoming more unreal and more mendacious. I do not know whether parents can do much in such a case, and I make mine no reproach. It was my own affair, to settle my difficulties and to find my way, and I carried through the business badly, like most of those who are well brought up.

Every man passes through this difficulty. For the average person, this is the point in his life where the demands of his own life come most in conflict with his surroundings, where the road forward has to be attained through the bitterest fighting. For many people this is the only time in their lives that they experience the sequence of death and rebirth that is our fate, when they become conscious of the slow process of the decay and breaking up of the world of their childhood, when everything beloved of us leaves us, and we suddenly feel the loneliness and deathly cold of the universe around us. And for very many this pitfall is fatal. They cling their whole life long painfully to the irrevocable past, to the dream of a lost paradise, the worst and most deadly of all dreams.

But to return to the story. The sensation and dream pictures in which the close of childhood presented itself to me are not important enough to be described. The important point was that I was once again conscious of the existence of the "dark" world, the "other" world. What Frank Kromer had once been to me, was now present within myself. And so, from the outside as well, the other world once more gained power over me.

Several years had passed since my affair with Kromer. That dramatic and guilty time of my life lay far behind me at that time and seemed to have passed like a quick nightmare into nothingness. Frank Kromer had long since disappeared from my life; I scarcely gave it a moment's thought if I chanced to meet him. But the other important figure in my tragedy, Max Demian, never entirely disappeared from my life. However, for a long time he stood on the far horizon, visible, but not affecting me. Only by degrees he approached me again, and I came once more under the ray of his power and influence.

I will try to recollect what I know of Demian in that period. Perhaps for a year, or longer, I did not have a single conversation with him. I avoided him, and he in no wise forced himself on me. Once or twice, when we met, he nodded to me in friendly greeting. Then it seemed to me at times that there was a note of scorn or ironical reproach in his friendliness, but that might only have been imagination on my part. My relation with him, and the strange influence he had exercised over me, were as if forgotten, by him as well as by me.

I try to recall his face—as I recollect him, I see that I was conscious of his existence after all, and took notice of him. I can see him going to school, alone or with some of the other big boys. I see him walking among them like a stranger, lonely and still like a celestial body, enveloped in a different atmosphere and subject to his own laws. No one liked him, he was intimate with no one, except his mother, and his relations with her did not seem like those of a child, but those of a grownup person. The masters left him as much as possible in peace. He was a good pupil, but he did not go out of his way to please them. From time to time we heard, in gossip, of a word, a comment or a retort he had made to a master, and which left nothing to be desired in the way of blunt challenge or irony.

I call him to mind, as I close my eyes, and I see his picture emerge. Where was it? Ah, now I have it again. It was in the street, in front of our house. There one day I saw him standing, a note book in his hand. I saw that he was drawing. He was drawing the old crest with the bird over the door of our house. And I stood at a window, concealed behind a curtain, and gazed at him. I saw with astonishment his attentive, cool, bright features turned to the crest, the features of a man, of a research worker, or an artist, superior and full of will-power, oddly bright and cool, with knowing eyes.

And again I can see him. It was a little later, in the street; we had come out of school and were all standing round a horse that had fallen down. It lay, still harnessed to the shaft, in front of a peasant's cart, and sniffed the air pitifully with open nostrils, while blood flowed from an invisible wound, so that the white dust in the street darkened as it became slowly saturated. As I, with a feeling of nausea, turned my gaze away, I saw Demian's face. He had not pressed forward, he stood furthest back of all, rather elegant, quite at his ease, as was proper to him. His gaze seemed to be directed at the horse's head, and expressed again that deep, quiet, almost fanatical and yet calm attentiveness. I could not resist watching him some considerable time, and I remember feeling, though quite unconsciously, that there was something very peculiar about him. I saw Demian's face, I saw not only that he had not the face of a boy, but that of a man; I saw still more, I thought I saw, or felt, that it was not the face of a man either but something else besides. There seemed to be also something of the woman in his features, and particularly it seemed to me for a moment, not manly or boyish, nor old or young, but somehow or other a thousand years old, not to be measured by time, bearing the stamp of other epochs. Animals could look like that, or trees, or stones—I did not realize that precisely, I did not experience the exact sensation which I, a grownup person, am now describing, but what I felt then approximated in some way to what I have just related. Perhaps he was beautiful, perhaps he pleased me, perhaps even he was repugnant—I could not then determine. I saw only that he was different from us, he was like an animal, or a spirit, or a picture, I know not what he was like, but he was different, inconceivably different from us all.

My reminiscence tells me nothing more, and perhaps even what has been described has arisen, in part, from later impressions.

Until I was several years older, I did not come into close contact with him again. Contrary to custom, Demian had not been confirmed with the boys of his year, and in consequence fresh rumors concerning him were set afloat. In school they were again saying that he was really a Jew, or no, a heathen, and others pretended to know that he and his mother professed no religion, or that they belonged to a bad sect in mythology. In connection with this I seem to remember that he was suspected of living with his mother as with a mistress. Presumably the facts were that he had been, up to that time, brought up without any denominational creed, and that it was now thought that this might be disadvantageous for his future career. In any case, his mother now decided after all to allow him to be prepared for confirmation, two years later than the boys of his own age. Hence it came about that for months he was my classmate in the confirmation class.

For a time I kept out of his way, I did not want to have anything to do with him; too many mysterious rumors had become attached to his name. But above all things I was worried by a sense of obligation, implanted in me since my affair with Kromer. And just at that time I had enough to do with my own secrets. For the confirmation class coincided with the period when I was definitively enlightened on matters of sex, and in spite of my good will, my interest in the pious instruction was on that account greatly diminished. The things of which the clergyman spoke lay far from me in a still, sacred unreality; they may have been quite beautiful and valuable, but in no way real and stirring, as were in the highest degree, these other things.

The more indifferent I became, under these conditions, to our spiritual instruction, the more was my interest drawn towards Max Demian again. Something or other seemed to unite us. As nearly as I remember it began in class early one morning, while the light was still burning in the schoolroom. The clergyman taking the confirmation class happened to be talking about Cain and Abel. I hardly paid any attention, I was sleepy and scarcely listened. Then with raised voice the clergyman began to speak fervently of Cain's sign. At this moment I felt a sort of contact or exhortation and looking up I saw Demian's face turned toward me from a row of desks in front, with a bright speaking look, which could have expressed scorn as much as seriousness. He looked at me for a moment only, and suddenly I was listening intently to the clergyman's words. I heard him speak of Cain and the mark on his forehead, and suddenly I felt deep within me the knowledge that the story could have a different signification, that it could be looked at from another view, that it was possible to be critical.

From that instant the bond of communication between Demian and myself was again established. And oddly enough, scarcely had this sense of a certain solidarity between us presented itself to my mind, than I saw it transferred as if by magic from the ideal world to the world of space. I did not know whether he had been able to arrange it himself, or whether it was pure chance—at that time I believed firmly in chance—but a few days after I noticed Demian had suddenly changed his place and was now sitting directly in front of me. (I recollect still how pleasant it was, in the midst of the miserable workhouse atmosphere of the overcrowded schoolroom, to sense the delicate, fresh aroma of soap from his neck in the morning.) A few days later he had changed again, and now sat next to me. And there he stayed, occupying the same place through the whole of that winter and spring.

Morning lessons had quite changed. They were no longer sleepy and boring. I looked forward to them. Sometimes we both listened to the clergyman with the greatest attention. A glance from my neighbor would suffice, calling my attention to a strange story or a peculiar text. And another glance from him, a very decided one, acted on me as an admonition, arousing criticism and doubt.

But very often we were bad pupils and heard nothing of the lesson. Demian was always courteous towards masters and schoolfellows. I never saw him commit a schoolboy prank, never heard him laugh out loud or talk in class; he never drew on himself the master's blame. But noiselessly, rather by signs and glances than by whispered words, he knew how to let me share in his own occupations. These were, in part, of a peculiar nature.

For instance, he told me which of the fellows interested him; and in what manner he studied them. He judged many of them with accuracy. He used to say to me before the lesson: "When I signal to you with my thumb, so and so will look round at us, or will scratch his neck, etc." Then during the lesson, when I scarcely gave a thought to what he had told me, Max would attract my attention by suddenly bending his thumb. I would look up quickly at the boy already designated, and every time, as if attached to a wire, the fellow would make the gesture required of him. I bothered Max to try this on the master, but he did not want to do it. But once, when I came into class and told him I had not done my preparation, and that I hoped the clergyman would not question me that day, he helped me. The master looked round for a boy to recite a portion of the catechism, and his roving eye rested on me. He approached me slowly, stretched out his finger in my direction, and already had my name on his lips—when suddenly he became absent-minded or uneasy, put his hand to his collar, stepped up to Demian who looked fixedly into his face. He seemed to want to ask him something but he turned away, to our surprise, coughed a little, and put his question to another boy.

These jokes amused me very much, but only gradually did I notice that my friend frequently played the same game with me. It would happen that on my way home from school I had suddenly the feeling Demian was a little way behind me, and when I turned round, there he was, sure enough.

"Can you really make another person think what you want him to?" I asked him.

He gave me information on the subject readily enough, quietly and pertinently, in his grownup manner.

"No," he said, "that can't be done. That is to say, one hasn't a free will, even if the person acts that way. Neither can the other person think as he will, nor can I make him think what I want him to. But you can observe someone well, and then you can say fairly exactly what he thinks or feels; in this way you can generally predict what he will do the moment after. It's quite simple, but people merely do not know it. Naturally it requires practice. To take an example from the butterfly world, there is a certain species of moth, of which the female is much rarer than the male. The moths reproduce like other animals, the male impregnates the female, who then lays the egg. Suppose you have in your possession a female of this type of moth—naturalists have often made the experiment—then the male moths fly in the night to this female, they even make a flight of several hours' duration! Think of it! For many miles around all the males are conscious of the whereabouts of the only female moth in the district. People have tried to explain that, but it is not easy. Moths must have a sense of smell, or something like it, which allows them to pick up and follow an almost imperceptible scent, like a good hound. You understand? There are such things, nature is full of them, and no one can explain them. Now I draw the conclusion that if among this class of moths the females were as abundant as the males, then these latter would not have such a refined sense of smell! They have it simply because they have been trained like that. If an animal or a man concentrates his whole attention and his whole will-power on a certain thing then he attains it. That's all. And it is just the same with what you have asked me. Observe a man sufficiently well, and you will know more about him than he does himself."

It lay on the tip of my tongue to mention the word "mind-reading," and so to remind him of the scene with Kromer, now relegated to such a distant past. But the odd thing between us both was that neither he nor I ever made the slightest reference to the fact that several years ago he had intervened so decisively in my life. It was as if formerly there had been nothing between us, or as if each of us reckoned that the other had forgotten the affair. It even happened once or twice when we were together that we met Frank Kromer in the street, but we exchanged no look, neither did we speak of him.

"But what has that got to do with will-power?" I asked. "You said there was no such thing as free will. And then you said one only had to concentrate one's will on something to be able to attain one's ends. That doesn't agree! If I am not master of my will, then I can't direct it here or there as I wish."

"A good question!" he said, laughing. "You should always ask questions, you must always doubt. But the explanation is very simple. If a moth for instance wants to concentrate his will-power on a star or something like that, he can't do it. Only—he doesn't try. He seeks only what has sense and value for him, satisfies his needs, he gets what he absolutely must have. And it is just there that the unbelievable succeeds—he develops a marvelous sixth sense, that no other animal besides him has! People in our position have more elbow-room, certainly, and more interests than an animal. But even we are confined to a comparatively small space, beyond which we cannot go. To be sure, I can imagine this or that, or make myself believe that I absolutely want to get to the North Pole or somewhere, but I can only carry that out and wish it strongly enough when the desire lies right in myself, when my whole being is really filled with it. As soon as that is the case, as soon as you try to carry out an inward command, then you succeed, then you can harness your will as you would a good nag. If for instance I resolved that our good Mr. Parson shall not wear his spectacles for the future, then that wouldn't work. That is merely play. But when last autumn I had the fixed intention of getting myself moved to another desk, I succeeded. Someone suddenly arrived who came before me in the alphabet and who up to then had been ill. Because someone had to make room for him, it was naturally I who did it, because my willing it had made me ready to seize the opportunity."

"Yes," I said, "that seemed to me very strange at the time. From the moment we began to get interested in one another, you managed to get nearer and nearer to me. But how was that? You did not immediately take a place next to me; for a few lessons at first you were sitting in the row of desks in front of me, weren't you? How did that come about?"

"It was like this. I wasn't quite certain where I wanted to go when I wished to move from my first place. I only knew that I wanted to sit further back. It was my wish to move towards you, but I was not conscious of this at the time. Simultaneously your own will was working with mine and helped me. It was only when I sat in front of you that I realized my wish was only half fulfilled—I noticed that really I had desired nothing else than to sit next to you."

"But on that occasion no newcomer arrived."

"No, but then I simply did what I wished, and sat next to you without hesitation. The boy with whom I changed places was simply surprised, and let me do it without further say. And the parson indeed noticed once that a change had taken place—in fact, whenever he looks at me something worries him secretly. That is to say, he knows my name is Demian, and that something must be wrong that I, whose initial is D, am sitting back there among the S's! But that does not penetrate his consciousness because my will is against it, because I prevent him again and again from becoming conscious of it. He notices now and then that something is wrong. He looks at me and begins to study the question, the good fellow. But I have a simple means at my disposal. I look at him very, very fixedly in the eyes. Hardly anyone can bear that. They always get restive. If you want to get something out of a person, and you fix him unexpectedly with your eyes, and if he doesn't get restive, then give it up! You won't get anything out of him, ever! But that happens seldom. I know only one single person with whom this trick won't help me."

"Who is that?" I asked quickly.

He looked at me, with eyes somewhat closed; as his fashion was when he meditated. Then he looked away and gave no answer, and in spite of my lively curiosity I could not bring myself to repeat the question.

But I believe he was referring to his mother. He seemed to live on very intimate terms with her, but he never spoke about her, never invited me to his house. I scarcely knew what his mother looked like.

* * * *

Several times I attempted to imitate his example by concentrating my will-power on something so firmly that I would have to attain it. I had desires which seemed to me sufficiently pressing. But nothing came of it. I could not bring myself to talk matters over with Demian. I should not have been able to make him understand what I wanted. He did not ask, either.

My faith in matters of religion had meanwhile suffered many a breach. Yet in my manner of thinking, which was entirely under the influence of Demian, I was to be distinguished from those of my schoolfellows who professed an entire disbelief. There were a few such who let occasional phrases be overheard, to the effect that it was laughable and unworthy of man's dignity to believe in a God, and that stories such as those of the Trinity and the immaculate conception of the Virgin Mary were simply a joke. It was disgraceful, they said, that such rubbish was peddled about today. This was by no means my way of thinking. Even where I had doubts, the whole experience of my childhood taught me to believe in the efficacy of a godly life such as that led by my parents, which I knew to be neither contemptible nor hypocritical. On the contrary, now as before, I had the greatest reverence for the spirit of religion. Only Demian had accustomed me to consider and explain the stories and articles of belief from a more liberal and more personal point of view, a point of view in which fantasy and imagination had their share. At least, I always took great pleasure and enjoyment in the interpretations he suggested to me. To be sure much seemed to me too crude; such as the affair of Cain. And once, during the preparation for confirmation, I was terrified by a conception, which, if that were possible, seemed to me even still more daring. The master had been speaking of Golgotha. The Biblical account of the Passion and Death of Christ had, from my earliest years, made a deep impression on me. As a little boy, on such days as Good Friday, after my Father had read out to us the story of the Passion, I had lived in imagination and with much emotion in Gethsemane and on Golgotha, in that world so poignantly beautiful, pale and ghostlike, and yet so terribly alive. And when I listened to the Passion according to St. Matthew by Bach, I felt the mystical thrills of this dark, powerful, mysterious world of passion and suffering. I find in this music, even today and in the "actus tragicus," the essence of all poetry and of all artistic expression.

At the conclusion of the lesson Demian said to me contemplatively:

"There's something in this, Sinclair, which I don't like. Read through the story, consider it, there's something there which sounds insipid. I mean this business of the two thieves. It's sublime, the three crosses standing side by side on the hill! But what about this sentimental story of the honest thief, which reads more like a tract? First he was a criminal who had perpetrated crimes, and God knows what, and now he breaks out in tears and is consumed by feelings of contrition and repentance. I ask you what's the sense of such a repentance two steps from the grave? It's nothing but a real parson's story, mawkish and mendacious, larded with emotion, and having a most edifying background. If today you had to choose one of the two thieves as your friend, or if you consider which of the two you would the sooner have trusted, it would most certainly not be this weeping convert. No, it's the other, who's a real fellow with plenty of character. He doesn't care a straw about conversion, which in his case can mean simply nothing more than pretty speeches. He goes his way bravely to the end, without being such a coward as to renounce the devil in the last moment who up to that point has had to help him. He is a character, and in Biblical history people of character always come off second best. Perhaps he's a descendant of Cain. Don't you think so?"

I was dismayed. I had believed myself to be quite familiar with the story of the crucifixion, and now I saw for the first time what little personal judgment I had brought to bear on it, with what little force of imagination and of fantasy I had listened to it and read it. Demian's new ideas, therefore, were quite annoying, threatening to overthrow conceptions, the stability of which I had believed it necessary to maintain. No, one could not deal with anything and everything like that, certainly not with the All Holiest.

As always, he noticed my opposition immediately, even before I had spoken a word.

"I know," said he, in a tone of resignation, "it's the old story. Everything is all right until you're serious about it! But I'll tell you something: this is one of the points where one can clearly see the shortcomings of this religion. The fact is that this God, of the old and of the new dispensation, may be an excellent conception, but He is not what He really ought to be. He is everything that is good, noble, fatherly, beautiful, sublime and sentimental certainly! But the world consists of other things which are simply ascribed to the devil. All this part of the world, a good half, is suppressed and hushed up. Just the same as they praise God as the Father of all life, but pass over the whole sex-life, on which all life depends, and declare it to be sinful and the work of the devil! I have nothing to say against honoring this God Jehovah, nothing at all. But I think we should reverence everything and look upon the whole world as sacred, not merely this artificially separated, official half of it! We ought then to worship the devil as well as God. I should find that quite right. Or we ought to create a God, who would embody the devil as well, and before whom we should not have to close our eyes, when the most natural things in the world take place."

Contrary to his custom, he had become almost vehement, but he smiled again immediately and pressed me no further.

But in me these words encountered the riddle of my whole boyhood, which I had hourly carried with me, but of which I had never spoken to anyone. What Demian had said about God and the devil, about the official godly world and the suppressed devil's world, that was exactly my own idea, my own myth, the idea of the two worlds or two halves of the world—the light and the dark. The realization that my problem was a problem of humanity as a whole, of life and thought in general, suddenly dawned on me, and this recognition inspired me with fear and awe as I suddenly felt to what an extent my own innermost personal life and thought were part of the eternal stream of great ideas. The realization was not joyful, although it confirmed my mode of thought and made me happy to a certain extent. It was hard and tasted raw, because a hint of responsibility lay therein, telling me to put away childish things and to stand alone.

I told my friend—the first time in my life I had revealed so deep a secret—of my conception of the "two worlds," a conception which had been formed since the earliest years of my childhood. He at once saw that I was in thorough agreement with him. But he was not the kind to make the most of this. He listened with greater attention than he had ever given me, and looked me in the eyes until I had to turn away. I again noticed in his look this odd, animal-like timelessness, this inconceivably old age.

"We will talk more about that another time," he said considerately: "I see that you think more than you can express. But if that is so, then you also know that you have never lived in experience all that you have thought, and that is not good. Only the thought that we live through in experience has any value. You knew that your 'world of sanction' was simply one-half of the world, and yet you tried to suppress the other half in you, as do the parsons and teachers. You will not succeed. No one succeeds who has once began to think."

This impressed me deeply.

"But," I almost shouted, "there *are* horrible things which are really and actually forbidden—you can't deny that fact. And they are forbidden once for all, and so we must renounce them. I know of course that there are such things as murder, and all possible kinds of vice, but shall I then, simply because such things exist, go and become a criminal?"

"We shan't be able to finish our discussion today," said Max, in a milder tone. "You must certainly not commit murder or rape, no. But you haven't yet reached that point where one can see what is 'permitted' and what is really 'taboo.' You have realized only a part of the truth. The remainder will come after, rely on it. For instance, for the past year or so you have had in you an instinct which is stronger than all the others, and which is held to be 'taboo.' The Greeks and many other people, on the contrary, made a sort of divinity out of this instinct, and honored it by great celebrations. What is now 'taboo' is therefore not eternally so, it can change. Today everyone is permitted to sleep with a woman as soon as he has been with her to a parson and has gone through the ceremony of marriage. With other races it is different, even today. For that reason each one of us must find out for himself what is permitted and what is forbidden—forbidden, that is, to himself. You need never do anything that is forbidden and yet be a thorough rascal. And vice versa. It is really merely a question of convenience. Whoever is too lazy to think for himself and to constitute himself his own judge simply conforms to the taboos, whatever they happen to be. He has an easy time of it. Others realize they carry laws in themselves. For them things are forbidden which every man of honor does daily. On the other hand things are permitted them which are otherwise taboo. Everyone must stand up for himself."

Suddenly he seemed to regret having said so much, and broke off. I felt I could understand to a certain extent what his sentiment was. That is to say, however agreeably he used to present his ideas (apparently in a cursory manner) he could on no account tolerate a conversation made simply "for the sake of talking," as he once said. He realized in my case that, although my interest was genuine enough, I was too much inclined to look upon discussion as a game, too fond of clever talking—in short I was lacking in perfect seriousness.

* * * *

As I read again the words I have just written—"perfect seriousness"—another scene suddenly comes into my mind, the most impressive experience I lived through with Max Demian in those still half-childlike times.

Our confirmation classes were drawing to an end, and the closing lessons were devoted to the Last Supper. The clergyman thought this very important, and he took pains to make us feel something of the inspiration and sacred character of his teaching. However, precisely in those last few lessons, thoughts were diverted to another object, to the person of my friend. Looking forward to my confirmation, which was explained to us as being our solemn admission into the community of the Church, the thought presented itself imperatively to me that the value of this half-year's religious instruction did not lie for me in what I had learned in class, but rather in Demian's presence and influence. It was not into the Church that I was ready to be received, but into something else, into an order of ideas and of personalities which surely existed somewhere or other on earth, and of which I felt my friend was the representative or messenger.

I tried to repress this thought. In spite of everything, I earnestly intended to go through the ceremony of confirmation with a certain dignity, and the new notions I was forming seemed scarcely compatible with this. Yet do what I would, the idea was there, and gradually identified itself with the approaching religious ceremony. I was ready to celebrate it in a different fashion from the other confirmation candidates. For me it would mean admission into a world of ideas, with which I had become acquainted through Demian.

In those days it happened that I had another discussion with him; it was just before a lesson. My friend was wrapped up in himself and took little pleasure in my talk, which was perhaps rather precocious and bombastic.

"We talk too much," he said with unwonted gravity. "Wise speeches have no value at all, absolutely none. You only escape from yourself. To escape from yourself is a sin. You should be able to creep right into yourself, like a tortoise."

We entered the schoolroom immediately after. The lesson began. I took pains to listen, and Demian did not disturb me in my effort. After a while I began to feel something peculiar at my side where his place was, a sort of emptiness or coolness or something like that, as if his seat had suddenly become vacant. The feeling became oppressive and I turned round.

There I saw my friend sitting, upright and in his customary attitude. But he looked quite different from usual. Something I did not know went out from him, enveloped him. I thought his eyes were closed, until I saw he held them open. But they were stiff as if gazing within or directed to an object a great way off. He sat there perfectly motionless; he seemed not to be breathing and his mouth was as if carved out of wood or stone. His face was white, uniformly white, as stone. His brown hair showed more signs of life than did any other feature. His hands lay before him on the desk, without life, as still as inanimate objects, like stones or fruit, white and motionless, yet not relaxed, but as if controlling the secret springs of a powerful life force.

The sight made me tremble. He is dead, I thought. I almost said it out loud. But I knew he was not dead. Mesmerized, I hung on his look; my eyes were riveted to this white, stone mask. I felt it was the real Demian.

The Demian who was in the habit of walking and talking with me, that was only one side of him, a half. Demian, who from time to time played a part, who accommodated himself to circumstances out of mere complacence. But the real Demian looked like this, with just this look of stone, prehistorically old, like an animal, beautiful and cold, dead yet secretly full of fabulous life force. And around him this still emptiness, this infinite ethereal space, this lonely death!

"Now he has quite retired into himself," I felt with a shudder. Never had I been so isolated. I had no part in him, he was unattainable, he was further from me than if he had been on the most distant isle in the world.

I scarcely understood why no one besides myself noticed it. I thought that everyone would have to remark him, that everyone would shudder. But no one gave him any attention. He sat like a picture and, as I could not prevent myself from thinking, as stiff as a strange idol. A fly settled on his forehead, moved slowly down over his nose and lips—not a muscle, not a nerve in his face twitched.

Where, where was he now? What was he thinking, what was he feeling? Was he in heaven or in hell?

It was impossible for me to question him. When I saw him at the end of the lesson living and breathing again, when his glance met mine, was he as he formerly had been? Where did he come from? Where had he been? He seemed tired. His face had its normal color, his hands moved again, but his brown hair was lustreless and fatigued, as it were.

In the days following I practised a new exercise in my bedroom several times. I sat stiffly on a chair, kept my eyes fixed, and held myself perfectly motionless. I waited to see how long I could maintain this attitude, and what the sensation would be like. However, I merely got very tired, and suffered from a violent twitching of the eyelids.

The confirmation took place soon after, of which no important recollections remain with me.

Everything was now quite changed. Childhood fell about me in ruins. My parents used to look at me with a certain embarrassment. My sisters had become quite strange in their conduct towards me. A disillusionment falsified and weakened the old sentiments and pleasures, the garden was without fragrance, the wood was no longer inviting, the world around me seemed like a clearance-sale of old articles, insipid and without charm, books were merely paper, music a noise. The leaves fall thus from a tree in autumn, the tree feels it not, rain drips on it, sun comes and frost, and the life in it recedes slowly into the narrowest and most inward recess. The tree is not dying. It is waiting.

It was decided that after the holidays I should go to another school, leaving home for the first time. My mother meanwhile approached me with especial tenderness, a sort of preliminary good-bye, endeavoring to charm me with a love from which I should go with homesickness and unforgetfulness in my heart. Demian had gone away. I was alone.

CHAPTER 4

BEATRICE

Without having seen my friend again, I traveled at the end of the holidays to St. ——. Both my parents came with me, and handed me over with all possible care to the protection of a master of the school, in whose house I was to board. They would have been numb with horror, had they only known to what sort of fate they were leaving me.

It still hung in the balance whether I should become with time a good son and a useful citizen, or whether my nature would break out in other directions. My last attempt to be happy under the roof of my father's house and the spirit prevailing there had lasted for a considerable period, and at times had almost succeeded, only in the end to fail completely.

The curious emptiness and isolation which I had begun to feel for the first time in the holidays after my confirmation (how I learned to know it later, this emptiness, this thin atmosphere) did not pass immediately. The parting from home was for me peculiarly easy. I was really rather ashamed of not being sadder—my sisters wept without reason, I could not. I was astonished at myself. I had always been an emotional child, and at bottom, tolerably good. Now I was quite changed. I was completely indifferent towards the outside world. For days together my sole occupation was hearkening to my inner self, listening to the flood of dark, forbidden instincts which roared subterraneously within me. I had grown very quickly in that last half-year, and appeared lanky, thin and immature. The amiability of boyhood had completely disappeared from my character; I realized myself that it was impossible to like me thus, and I by no means loved myself. I had often a great longing for Max Demian; on the other hand, I hated him not seldom, and looked upon him as responsible for the moral impoverishment of my life, to which I resigned myself as to a sort of nasty disease.

In the beginning I was neither liked nor respected in our school boarding house. First they ragged me, then kept out of my way, looking upon me as a rotter and an eccentric character; I was pleased with myself and I even overplayed my part, withdrawing into my solitary self, growling occasional cynicisms. Superficially I appeared to despise the world in most manly fashion, whereas in reality I was secretly consumed by melancholy and despair. In school I could fall back on a knowledge amassed at home. The form I was in was not so advanced as the same form in the school I had just left, and so

I acquired the habit of despising my school contemporaries, regarding them as mere children.

This attitude lasted a year and longer. My first holiday visits at home brought no change, I went gladly away again.

It was in the beginning of November. I had formed the habit of taking short, meditative walks in all kinds of weather, during which I often experienced a sort of joy, a joy full of melancholy, contempt of the world and contempt of self. I was sauntering thus one evening through the damp, foggy twilight in a suburb of the town. The broad drive of a public park stood completely deserted, inviting me to enter. The road lay thick with fallen leaves, into which I dug voluptuously with my feet. It smelt damp and bitter; in the distance the trees stood up tall and shadowy, ghostlike in the fog.

At the end of the drive I stood still and undecided, staring into the black foliage, scenting eagerly the damp odor of decomposition and death, which seemed to be in harmony with my own mood. Oh, how insipid life tasted!

A man, with the collar of his raincoat blowing about him, came out of a side path. I was just going on when he called to me.

"Hello, Sinclair!"

It happened to be Alphonse Beck, the senior boy of the house. I was always glad to see him and had nothing against him, except that he always treated me as he did all the younger boys, in an ironical and grandfatherly manner. He passed for being as strong as a bear, was said to have great influence on the house master, and was the hero of many school stories.

"What are you doing here?" he asked affably, in the tone the seniors always used when they condescended on occasion to talk to us. "Composing verse, I bet?"

"Shouldn't dream of it," I disclaimed gruffly.

He laughed, came up to me, and we chatted together in a manner to which I had not been accustomed for some time past.

"You needn't be afraid, Sinclair, that I shouldn't understand. I know the feeling, when one goes for a walk on a foggy evening—the thoughts autumn inspires in one. And one writes poetry about dying nature, of course, and spent youth; which is very much like it. Read Heinrich Heine?"

"I am not so sentimental," I said in self-defense.

"Oh, all right. But in this weather, I think, it does a man good to find a quiet place where one can take a glass of wine or something. Are you coming with me for a bit? I happen to be quite alone. Or wouldn't you care to? I wouldn't like to lead you astray, old man, if you are one of those model boys."

A little while after we sat clinking our thick glasses in a little tavern in the suburbs, drinking wine of a doubtful quality. At first I wasn't much pleased, still it was rather a novelty for me. But unaccustomed to wine, I soon became talkative. It was as if a window had been flung open within me, and the world shining in—for how long, how terribly long, had I not eased my heart by talking. I gave full play to my imagination, and once started, I related the story of Cain and Abel.

Beck listened to me with pleasure—someone at last, to whom I was giving something! He clapped me on the shoulder, told me I was the devil of a good fellow and a clever rascal. How I reveled in communicating my opinions, as I relieved myself of all the pent-up thought of the past months! My heart swelled with pride at finding my talents recognized by someone older than I was. When he called me a clever rascal the effect was like a sweet, strong wine running through me. The world lit up in new colors, thoughts came to me as from a hundred sources, wit and fire blazed up in me. We spoke of masters and schoolfellows, and I thought we understood one another wonderfully well. We talked of Greeks and of pagans, and Beck wished absolutely to draw me out on the subject of women. But on this point I could not converse. I had no experience, nothing to relate. True, all that I had felt and imagined was burning within me, but I could not impart my thoughts, not even under the influence of wine. Beck knew much more about girls, and I listened to his tales with glowing eyes. The things I heard were unbelievable. What I should never have conceived to be possible entered the sphere of commonplace reality and seemed self-evident. Alphonse Beck, who was perhaps eighteen years old, was already a man of experiences. Among other things, he told me that girls liked boys to play the gallant with them, but in general were too frightened to go any further. You could hope for more success with women. Women were much cleverer. For instance, there was Mrs. Jaggelt, who sold pencils and copybooks, who was much easier to deal with. All that had happened behind the counter in her shop was unprintable in any book.

I sat on captivated; my head was swimming. To be sure, I could not exactly have loved Mrs. Jaggelt, but still, it was unheard of. It seemed as if things happened, at least to older people, of which I had never dreamed. There was a false ring about it, to be sure, everything seemed more trivial and commonplace, and did not coincide with my own ideas about love, but still, it was reality, it was love and adventure, someone sat next to me who had lived it in experience, to whom it seemed a matter of course.

Our conversation had reached a lower level, had deteriorated. I was no longer a clever little fellow, I was just a mere boy listening to a man. But even then—in comparison with what my life had been for months and months, this was delicious, this was heaven. Besides, as I gradually began to realize, all this was forbidden, absolutely forbidden, everything from sitting in a public house, down to the subject of our conversation. In any case, I thought I was showing spirit; I was in revolt.

I can recollect that night with the greatest clearness. We both of us wended our way home at a late hour under the dimly burning gas lamps through the cool, damp night, and for the first time in my life I was drunk. It was not agreeable, it was in the highest degree unpleasant, but there was a sort of charm about it, a sweetness—it smacked of orgy and revolt, of spirit and life. Beck bravely took me in hand, and although he grumbled at me as being a bloody novice, he half carried, half dragged me home, where, by good fortune, he was able to smuggle us both through a window which stood open on the ground floor.

But a maddening pang accompanied the sobering up as I painfully awoke after a short heavy sleep. I sat up in bed and saw that I was still wearing my shirt. My clothes and shoes lay round about on the floor, smelling of tobacco and vomit. And between headache, nausea and a maddening thirst, a picture came before my mind on which I had not set eyes for many a long day. I saw my home, the house where dwelt my parents. I saw father and mother, my sisters and the garden. I saw my peaceful, homely bedroom, the school and the marketplace. Demian and the confirmation class—and all this was bright, lustrous, all was wonderful, godly and pure, all that, I realized now, had until yesterday belonged to me, had waited for me. But now, in this hour, it was mine no longer, it spurned me and looked upon me with disgust. All that was loving and intimate, all that I had received from my parents since the first golden days of my childhood, each kiss mother had given me, each Christmas, each godly bright Sunday morning there at home, each flower in the garden, all that was laid waste, I had trampled on it all with my foot! If the police had come for me then and had bound me and led me away to the gallows as a desecrator and as the scum of humanity, I should have acquiesced; should have gone gladly. I would have found it right and fitting.

That was the state of my feelings. I, who had gone about despising the world! I, who had been so proud in spirit and who had shared Demian's thoughts! So I appeared a filthy pig, to be classed with the scum of the earth, drunk and befouled, disgusting and common, a dissolute beast, carried away by abominable instincts. So I appeared, I who came from those gardens whose bright flowers had been purity and sweet gentleness, I who had loved Bach's music and beautiful poetry! I could still hear, with aversion and disgust, my own laugh, the drunken, uncontrolled, convulsive and silly laugh which escaped me. That was I!

But in spite of everything there was a certain enjoyment in suffering these torments. I had lived for so long a blind, dull existence, for so long had my heart been silent, impoverished and shut up, that even this self-accusation, this self-aversion, this entirely dreadful feeling was welcome. At least it was feeling; flowers were flaring up, emotion was quivering therein.

I experienced in the midst of my misery a confused sensation of liberation, of the approach of spring.

However, as far as outward appearances went, I was going fast down the hill. The first debauch was soon followed by others. There was much drinking at school, and other things not in accord with study. I was among the youngest who carried on in this way, but from being just tolerated and looked upon as a mere youngster, I soon rose to be considered as a leader and a star. I was renowned as a daredevil and could drink with the best. Once again I belonged entirely to the dark world, to the devil, and I passed in this world for being a splendid fellow.

But at the same time I was in a pitiful state of mind. I lived in a whirl of self-destroying debauchery, and while I was looked up to by my friends as a leader and the devil of a good fellow, as a cursed witty and spirited drinking companion, my anxious soul was full of apprehension. I remember on one occasion tears started to my eyes when, on coming out of a tavern one Sunday morning, I saw children playing in the street, bright and contented, with freshly combed hair, and in their Sunday clothes. And while I amused and often terrified my friends with monstrous cynicisms, as we sat at dirty tables stained with puddles of beer, in low public houses, I had in my heart a secret, deep reverence for everything at which I scoffed—inwardly I was weeping bitterly at the thought of my past life, of my mother, of God.

There is a good reason for the fact that I was never one with my companions, that I remained lonely even in their midst, that I suffered in the manner above described. I was a hero of drinking bouts, with the roughest of them, I was a scoffer after their own heart. I showed courage and wit in my ideas and in my talks about masters, school, parents, the church—I listened to their smutty stories unflinchingly and even ventured one or two myself—but I was never about when my boon companions went off with girls. I remained behind alone, filled with an ardent desire for love, a hopeless longing, whereas to judge from my conversation I must have been a hardened rake. No one was more vulnerable, no one more chaste than I. And when from time to time I saw young girls pass by in the town, pretty and clean, bright and charming, they seemed to me like wonderful, pure dream women, a thousand times too good and too pure for me. For a long time I could not bring myself to enter Mrs. Jaggelt's stationery shop, because I blushed when I saw her and thought of what Alphonse Beck had told me about her.

The more I realized how different I was from the members of my new set, how isolated I was in their midst, the less easy was it for that very reason to break with them. I do not really know whether the toping and bragging ever caused me much pleasure, and I could never so accustom myself to hard drinking that I did not feel the painful consequences after each bout. I was as if coerced into doing this. I did it because I had to, because I was otherwise absolutely ignorant of a course to follow, I knew not where to begin. I was afraid of being long alone. I was frightened of the many tender, chaste, intimate moods to which I constantly felt myself inclined, I was afraid of the tender notions of love which so often came to me.

One thing I lacked most of all—a friend. There were two or three school-fellows whom I liked very much. But they belonged to the good set and my vices had for a long time been a secret to no one. They avoided me. With all I passed for a hopeless gamester under whose feet the very earth quaked. The masters knew much about me, severe punishments were several times inflicted on me, my final expulsion from the school was waited for with more or less certainty. I knew that myself; for a long time I had ceased to be a good pupil; I got through my work by hook or by crook, with the feeling that the state of affairs could not last much longer.

There are many ways by which God can make us feel lonely and lead us to a consciousness of ourselves. With me it was in this way: it was like a bad dream, in which I saw myself ostracized, foul and clammy, creeping rest-lessly and painfully over broken beer glasses, down an abominably unclean road. There are such dreams, when you imagine you have set out to find a beautiful princess, but you stick in stinking back streets full of rubbish and dirty puddles. So it was with me. In this scarcely refined way I was destined to become lonely and to put between myself and my childhood a locked door of Eden over against which stood merciless sentinels on guard in beaming rays of light. It was a beginning, an awakening of that homesickness, that longing to return to my true self.

I was terribly frightened when my father, alarmed by a letter from my house master, appeared for the first time in St. —— and faced me unexpect-edly. When he came for the second time, towards the end of that winter, I was hard and indifferent, I let him heap blame on me, I let him beg me to think of my mother, I was unmoved. Finally he grew very angry and said that if I did not turn over a new leaf he would have me disgraced and chased out of the school, and would have me placed in a reformatory. Little I cared! When he went away I felt sorry for him, but he had accomplished nothing; he had found no approach to me, and for a few moments I felt that it served him right.

I was indifferent as to what might become of me. In my peculiar and unlovely manner, with my carrying on and my frequenting of public houses, I was at odds with the world—this was my way of protesting. I was ruining myself thereby, but what of it? Sometimes the case presented itself to me in this wise: If the world had no use for such as me, if there was no better place for us, if there were no higher duties, then people like myself simply went to the devil. So much the worse for the world.

The Christmas holidays of that year were exceedingly unpleasant. My mother was terrified when she saw me again. I had grown taller, and my thin face looked gray and ravaged by dissipation, with flabby features and inflamed rings round the eyes. The first indications of a moustache, and the spectacles which I had but lately taken to wearing, made me look stranger still. My sisters started back and giggled when they saw me. It was all very pleasant. Unpleasant was the conversation with my father in his study, unpleasant the greeting of a couple of relations, unpleasant above all things was Christmas night. That has been since my birth the great day of our house, the evening of festivity and love, of gratitude, of the renewal of the bond between my parents and myself. This time everything was depressing and embarrassing. As usual my father read the portion of the gospel about the shepherds in the field "keeping watch over their flock by night"; as usual my sisters stood radiantly before the table on which the presents were laid out. But my father's voice was sad, and he looked old and constrained. Mother was unhappy; for me everything was equally painful and unwished for, presents and good wishes, Gospel and Christmas tree. The ginger-bread smelt delicious and exhaled thick clouds as of sweet remembrances. The Christmas tree was fragrant and told of things which existed no longer. I longed for the end of the evening and of the holidays.

So passed the whole winter. It was not long before I was severely reprimanded by the faculty and threatened with expulsion. It could not last much longer. Well it made no difference to me.

I had a special grudge against Max Demian, whom I had not seen for the whole of this period. In my first term at St. —— I had written to him twice, but had received no reply; for that reason I had not paid him a visit in the holidays.

* * * *

In the same park, where I had met Alphonse Beck in the autumn, it chanced that in the first days of spring, just as the thorn hedges were beginning to turn green, a girl attracted my attention. I was out for a walk by myself, full of gnawing cares and thoughts, for my health was bad. Besides that I was in continual financial embarrassment. I owed various sums to my friends and had to invent excuses to procure some money from home. In several shops I had run up accounts for cigars and such things. Not that these cares were very pressing—if the end of my school career was approaching, and if I drowned myself or was sent to a reform school, these trifles would not make much difference either. But I was nevertheless constantly facing these unpleasant things and I suffered from it.

On that spring day in the park I met a girl who had a strong attraction for me. She was tall and slender, elegantly dressed, and had a wise, boyish face.

She pleased me at once, she belonged to the type that I loved, and she began to work upon my imagination. She was scarcely older than I, but she was more mature; she was elegant and possessed a good figure, already almost a woman, but with a touch of youthful exuberance in her features, which pleased me exceedingly.

It was never my good fortune to approach a girl with whom I could have fallen in love, neither was it my luck in this case. But the impression was deeper than all the former ones, and the influence of this infatuation on my life was powerful.

Suddenly I had again a picture standing before me, a revered picture—ah, and no need, no impulse was so deep or so strong in me as the desire to revere, to adore. I gave her the name of Beatrice, of whom, without having read Dante, I knew something from an English painting, a reproduction of which I had in my possession. The picture was of an English pre-Raphaelite girlish figure, very long-limbed and slender, with a small, long head and spiritualized hands and features. My beautiful young girl did not completely resemble this, although she had the same slenderness and boyish suppleness of figure, which I loved, and something of the spiritualization of the face, as if her soul lay therein.

I never spoke a single word to Beatrice. Yet at that time she exercised the deepest influence over me. Her picture fastened itself on my mind; in my imagination she opened a sanctuary for me, she caused me to pray in a temple. From one day to another I remained absent from the drinking bouts and the nightly excursions. Once more I could bear being alone, I read gladly, I liked to go for walks again.

I was much scoffed at for my sudden conversion. But I had now something to love and to worship, I had again an ideal, life was once more full of suggestion, of gaily colored secret nuances, that made me insensible to the jeers of my companions. I again felt at home with myself, although I was now the servant and slave of a picture which I revered.

I cannot think of that time without a certain emotion. With earnest striving, I again endeavored to build a "bright world" out of the ruins of that period of my life which had broken up around me, I again lived entirely and single-mindedly in the desire to put away the dark and the bad, and to dwell completely in the light, on my knees before my gods. Still, this "bright world" I built up was to a certain extent my own creation. It was not the action of flying back or of crawling back to mother, to a security without responsibilities. It was a new service upon which I entered, invented by myself for my own requirements, with responsibilities and discipline of self. The sex consciousness from which I suffered and before which I was in constant flight was now transmuted in this sacred fire to spirit and devotion. The grim and horrible would disappear, I should groan through no more agonizing nights, there would be no more heart-beatings in front of lewd pictures, no more listening at forbidden doors, no more lasciviousness. Instead of all this, I set up my altar, with the picture of Beatrice, and in dedicating myself to her I dedicated myself to the spirit and to the gods. That part of myself which I withdrew from the powers of darkness I brought as a sacrifice to the powers of light. Not lust was my aim, but purity; not happiness, but beauty and spirituality.

This cult for Beatrice completely changed my life. A precocious cynic but a short while before, I had now become a servant in the temple, whose aim it was to be a saint. I not only renounced the evil life to which I had accustomed myself, but I endeavored to change everything, to set myself a standard of purity, nobility and dignity, which I even applied to eating and drinking, to my manner of speech and dress. I began each morning to wash with cold water, to the use of which I had, in the beginning, to force myself. I behaved with gravity and dignity, carried myself erect and acquired a slower and more dignified gait. To an observer it might have seemed rather ludicrous, but to me it was the performance of a divine worship.

Of all the ways in which I sought to find expression for my new faith, one bore fruit. I began to paint. To start with, the English picture of Beatrice I had in my possession did not bear a sufficient resemblance of Beatrice. I wanted to try to paint her for myself. Full of new pleasure and hope I carried into my room—I had recently been given a room to myself—beautiful paper, colors, and a paint-brush. I made ready my palette, porcelain bowls, glass and pencils. The fine water colors in little tubes which I had bought captivated me. There was a bright chromic green which I think I can see yet as it flashed out for the first time from the little white tube.

I began with caution. To paint a face was difficult; I wished first of all to try something else. I painted ornaments, flowers, and small landscapes from imagination, a tree near a chapel, a Roman bridge with cypresses. I often lost myself completely in this pastime, I was as happy as a child with a box of paints. At last I began to paint Beatrice.

The first few attempts were abortive, and I threw them away. The more I tried to conjure up in my mind the face of the girl, whom I met from time to time in the street, the less I seemed able to transfer my impressions to paper. Finally I gave up the idea, and began simply to paint a face according to the guidance of my imagination, a face which gradually grew out of the one already begun, as if by itself, at the mercy of color and brush. The result was a face I had dreamed of, and I was not ill pleased with it. Yet I made another essay immediately, and each new picture was clearer, and approached more nearly to the type, but was by no means like the reality.

More and more I accustomed myself, in a dreamy sort of way, to draw lines with my brush, to fill in surfaces. My sketches grew out of a few strokes of the brush, out of the unconscious. At last one day I finished a face, almost unconsciously, which made a stronger appeal to me than the former ones. It was not the face of the girl, for I had long since given up the idea of trying to paint my Beatrice to the life. It was something else, something unreal, and yet not of less value for me on that account. It looked more like the head of a youth than of a girl. The hair was not blond like that of my pretty girl, but brown with a tinge of red; the chin was strong and firm, but the mouth was red as a blossom. The features were rigid, like a mask, but impressive and full of secret life.

As I sat before the finished sketch, it made a peculiar impression on me. It seemed to me a sort of picture of a god or of a sacred mask, half man, half woman, ageless, the expression being at once dreamy and strong-willed, stiff and yet secretly alive. This face seemed to have something to say to me, it belonged to me; its look was rather imperative, as if requiring something of me. And there was a certain resemblance to someone or other, to whom I knew not.

The picture played an important rôle for a while, sharing my thoughts and my life. I kept it concealed in a drawer, in order that one should not get possession of it and so be able to sneer at me. But as soon as I found myself alone in my little room I took out the picture and communed with it. Each evening I pinned it on to the wall over against my bed, and gazed at it until I dropped off to sleep. In the morning it was the first object which met my gaze.

Just at that time I began again to dream a great deal, as I had constantly done when a child. It seemed to me that for years I had had no more dreams. Now they came again, quite a new kind of pictures, and often and often the painted image appeared therein, living and speaking, friendly or inimical, with the features sometimes twisted into a grimace, sometimes infinitely beautiful, harmonious and noble.

And one morning, as I awoke out of such a dream, I suddenly realized who was the original of the picture, I recognized it. It gazed at me in such a fabulously well-known way, and seemed to be calling my name. It seemed to know me, like a mother, seemed to love me as if since the beginning of time. With beating heart I stared at the paper, at the thick brown hair, at the half-womanly mouth, the strong forehead with the wonderful brightness (it had dried that way of itself) and more and more I felt in me the knowledge, the certainty of having somewhere met the original of the picture.

I sprang out of bed, placed myself in front of the face, and gazed at it from the closest proximity, straight into the wide open, greenish, staring eyes, the right eye somewhat higher than the other. And all at once this right eye twitched perceptibly, but still decidedly, and from this twitching I recognized the picture....

How was it that I had found it out so late? It was Demian's face. Later I often and often compared the picture with Demian's real features, as they had remained in my memory. They were not quite the same, although there was a resemblance. But it was Demian, nevertheless.

Once, on an evening in early summer the red sun shone obliquely through my window, which looked towards the west. In the room the dusk was gathering. I suddenly had the idea of pinning the picture of Beatrice, or of Demian, to the cross-bar of the window and of gazing at it, while the evening sun was shining through. The whole outline of the face disappeared, but the reddish ringed eyes, the brightness of the forehead and the strong red mouth glowed deeply and wildly from the surface of the paper. I sat opposite it for a long time, even after the light had died away. And by degrees the feeling came to me that this was not Beatrice or Demian but—myself. The picture did not resemble me—it was not meant to, I felt—but there was that in it which seemed to be made up of my life, something of my inner self, of my fate or of my dæmon. My friend would look like that, if I ever found another. My mistress would look like that, if ever I had one. My life and death would be like that. It had the ring and rhythm of my fate.

In those weeks I had begun to read a book which made a deeper impression on me than anything I had read before. Even in later years I have seldom chanced upon books which have made such a strong appeal to me, except perhaps those of Nietzsche. It was a volume of Novalis, containing letters and apothegms. There was much that I did not understand. But the book captivated me and occupied my thoughts to an extraordinary degree. One of the aphorisms now occurred to me. I wrote it with a pen under the picture: "Fate and soul are the terms of one conception." That I now understood.

I frequently used to meet the girl I called Beatrice. I felt no emotion on seeing her, but I was often sensible of a harmony of sentiment, which seemed to say: we are connected, or rather, not you and I, but your picture and I; you are a part of my destiny.

* * * *

My longing for Max Demian was again eager. I had had no news of him for several years. On one occasion only I had met him in the holidays. I see now that I have failed to mention this short meeting in my narrative, and I see that this was owing to shame and self-conceit on my part. I must make up for it now.

So then, once in the holidays, I was parading my somewhat tired, blasé self through the town. As I was sauntering along, swinging my stick and examining the old, unchanged features of the bourgeois Philistines whom I despised, I met my one-time friend. Scarcely had I caught sight of him when I started involuntarily. With lightning rapidity my thoughts were carried back to Frank Kromer. I hoped and prayed Demian had really forgotten the story! It was so disagreeable to be under this obligation to him—simply owing to a silly, childish affair—still, I was under an obligation....

He seemed to be waiting to see whether I would greet him. I did, as calmly as possible under the circumstances, and he gave me his hand. That was indeed his old handshake! So strong, warm and yet cool, so manly!

He looked me attentively in the face and said: "You've grown a lot, Sinclair." He himself seemed quite unchanged, just as old, just as young as ever.

He proposed we should go for a walk, and we talked of secondary matters, not of the past. I remembered that I had written to him several times, without having received an answer. I hoped he had forgotten this as well, those silly, silly letters. He made no mention of them.

At that time there was no Beatrice and no picture, I was still in the period of my dissipation. Outside the town I invited him to come with me into an inn. He came. With much ostentation I ordered a bottle of wine and filled a couple of glasses. I clinked glasses with him, showing him how conversant I was with student drinking customs, and I emptied my first glass at a gulp.

"Do you frequent public houses often?" he asked me.

"Oh yes," I said with a drawl, "what else is there to do? It's certainly more amusing than anything else; after all."

"You think so? Perhaps. It may be so. There's certainly something very pleasing about it—intoxication, bacchanalian orgies! But I find, with most people who frequent public houses, this sense of *abandon* is lost. It seems to me there is something typically Philistine, bourgeois, in the public house habit. Of course, for just one night, with burning torches, to have a proper orgy and drunken revel. But to do the same thing over and over again, drinking one glass after another—that's hardly the real thing. Can you imagine Faust sitting evening after evening drinking at the same table?"

I drank, and looked at him with some enmity.

"Yes, but everyone isn't a Faust," I said curtly.

He looked at me with a somewhat surprised air.

Then he laughed, in his old superior way. "What's the good of quarreling about it? In any case the life of a toper, of a libertine, is, I imagine, more exciting than that of a blameless citizen. And then—I have read it somewhere—the life of a profligate is one of the best preparations for a mystic. There are always such people as Saint Augustine, who become seers. Before, he was a sort of rake and profligate."

I was distrustful and wished by no means to let him take a superior attitude towards me. So I said, with a blasé air: "Well, everyone according to his taste! I haven't the slightest intention of doing that, becoming a seer or anything."

Demian flashed a glance at me from half-closed eyes.

"My dear Sinclair," he said slowly, "it wasn't my intention to hurt your feelings. Besides—neither of us knows to what end you drink. There is that in you, which orders your life for you, and which knows why you are doing it. It is good to realize this; there is someone in us who knows everything, wills everything, does everything better than we do ourselves. But excuse me, I must go home."

We did not linger over our leave-taking. I remained seated, very dejected, and emptied the bottle. I found, when I got up to go, that Demian had already paid for it. That made me more angry still.

* * * *

This little event recurred to my thoughts, which were full of Demian. And the words he had spoken in the inn came back to my mind, retaining all their old freshness and significance: "It is good to know there is one in us who knows everything!"

I looked at the picture hanging in the window, now quite dark. The eyes glowed still. It was Demian's look. On it was the look of the one inside me, who knows all.

Oh, how I longed for Demian! I knew nothing of his whereabouts, for me he was unattainable. I knew only that he was supposed to be studying somewhere or other, and that after the conclusion of his school career his mother had left the town.

I called up in my mind all my reminiscences of Max Demian, from the Kromer affair onwards. A great deal he had formerly said came back to me. Today everything still had a meaning, all was of real concern to me! And what he had said at our last, not very agreeable, meeting, about the libertine and the saint, suddenly crossed my mind. Was it not just so with me? Had I not lived in filth and drunkenness, my senses blunted by dissipation, until a new life impulse, the direct contrary of the old, awoke in me, namely the desire for purity, the longing to be saintly?

So I went on, from reminiscence to reminiscence. Night had long since fallen, and outside it was raining. In recollection, as well, I heard it rain; it was the hour under the chestnut trees when he first questioned me concerning Frank Kromer, so guessing my first secrets. One after another these souvenirs came to mind, conversations on the way to school, the confirmation class. And then I recollected my very first meeting with Max Demian. What had we been talking about? I could not for the moment recollect, but I took my time, I thought deeply. At last I remembered. We were standing in front of our house; after he had imparted to me his opinion about Cain. Then he spoke to me about the old, almost obliterated crest which stood over the door, in the keystone which widened as it got higher. He said it interested him and that one ought not to let such things escape one's notice.

That night I dreamt of Demian and of the crest. It changed perpetually, now Demian held it in his hands, now it was small and grey, now very large and multicolored, but he explained to me that it was always one and the same. But at last he forced me to eat the crest. As I swallowed it, I felt with terror that the bird on the crest was alive inside me, my stomach was swollen and the bird was beginning to consume me. With the fear of death upon me, I commenced to struggle. Then I woke up.

I felt relieved. It was the middle of the night, and I heard the rain blowing into the room. I got up to close the window; and in doing so trod on a bright object which lay on the floor. In the morning I found it was my painting. It was lying there in the wet and had rolled itself up. In order to dry it I stretched it out between two sheets of blotting paper and placed it under a heavy book. When I looked at it the next day it was dry. But it had changed. The red mouth had paled and had become smaller. Now it was exactly Demian's mouth.

I now began to paint a new picture, namely, that of the bird on the crest. I could not recollect any more what it really looked like, neither could I form a clear image of the whole, as even if one stood directly in front of our door, the crest was scarcely recognizable, it was so old and had several times been painted over. The bird stood or sat on something, perhaps on a flower, or on a basket or nest, or on a tree-top. I did not bother about that, and began with the part I could picture clearly. In answer to a confused prompting, I began straight away with strong colors; on my paper the head of the bird was golden yellow. I continued my work at intervals, when I was in the mood for it, and after a few days the thing was completed.

Now it was a bird of prey, with a sharp, bold hawk's head. The lower half of the body was fixed in a dark terrestrial globe, out of which it was working to escape, as if out of a giant egg. The background was sky-blue. The longer I gazed at the sheet, the more it seemed to me this was the colored crest which I had visualized in my dream.

It would not have been possible for me to have written a letter to Demian, even if I had known where to send it. But I decided, acting under a suggestion which came to me in a dreamy sort of way, as under all my promptings of that period, to send him the picture with the hawk—whether it would reach him or not. I wrote nothing thereon, not even my name. I carefully cut the border, bought a large paper cover and wrote on it my friend's former address. Then I sent it off.

The approach of an examination caused me to work harder than usual in school. The masters had again received me into grace, since I had suddenly changed my vile conduct. I was not, even now, by any means a good pupil, but neither I nor anyone else seemed to remember that, half a year before, my expulsion from the school had been imminent.

My father now wrote to me as formerly, adopting his old cheerful tone, without reproaches or threats. Yet I had no impulse to explain to him or to anyone how the change was brought about. It was merely chance that this change coincided with the wishes of my parents and the masters. It did not bring me into closer contact with the others but isolated me still more. I myself was ignorant of the tendency of the change in me, it might be leading me to Demian, to a distant fate. It had begun with Beatrice, but for some time past I had been living in quite an unreal world with my paintings and my thoughts of Demian, so that she quite disappeared from my mind, as she did from my view. I should not have been able to say a word to anyone of my dreams, of my expectations, of the inner change realized in me, not even if I had wished to do so.

But I had not the faintest desire ever to broach the subject.

CHAPTER 5

THE BIRD FIGHTS ITS WAY OUT OF THE EGG

My painted dream-bird was on its way, searching out my friend. An answer came to me in the most curious manner.

In my classroom in school I found at my desk, in the interval between two lessons, a piece of paper slipped between the pages of my book. It was folded in the manner we used for passing notes to one another in class. I wondered who could have sent me such a note, as I was not so intimate with any of the boys that one of them should wish to write to me. I thought it was a summons to participate in some school rag or other, in which however I should not have taken part, and I replaced the note unopened in my book. During the lesson it fell by chance into my hands again.

I toyed with the paper, unfolded it without thinking, and discovered a few words written thereon. I threw a glance at the writing, one word riveted my attention. Terrified, I read on, while my heart seemed to become numb with a sense of destiny.

"The bird fights its way out of the egg. The egg is the world. Whoever will be born must destroy a world. The bird flies to God. The name of the god is Abraxas."

I sank into deep meditation after I had read the words through several times. It admitted of no doubt: this was Demian's answer. None could know of the bird, except our two selves. He had received my picture. He had understood and helped me to explain its significance. But where was the connection in all this? And—what worried me above all—what did Abraxas mean? I had never read or heard of the word. "The name of the god is Abraxas!"

The hour passed without my hearing anything of the lesson. The next lesson began, the last of the morning. It was taken by quite a young assistant master, fresh from the University, to whom we had already taken a liking, because he was young and pretended to no false dignity with us.

We were reading Herodotus under Doctor Follen's guidance. This was one of the few school subjects which interested me. But this time my attention wandered. I had mechanically flung open my book, but I did not follow the translation, and remained lost in thought. For the rest, I had already several times had the experience that what Demian had said to me in the confirmation class was right. If you willed a thing strongly enough, it happened. If during the lesson I was deeply immersed in thought, I need not fear that the master would disturb my peace. Certainly, if you were absent-minded or sleepy, then he stood suddenly there; that had already happened to me several times. But if you were really thinking, if you were genuinely sunk in thought, then you were safe. And I had already put to the test what he had said to me about fixing a person with one's eyes. When at school with Demian I had never been successful in this attempt, but now I often realized that you could accomplish much simply by a fixed look and deep thinking.

So I was sitting now, my thoughts far from Herodotus and school. But the master's voice unexpectedly fell on my consciousness like a thunder-crash, so that I started with fright. I listened to his voice, he was standing quite close to me, I thought he had already called me by name. But he did not look at me. I breathed a sigh of relief.

Then I heard his voice again. Loudly the word "Abraxas" fell from his lips.

Continuing his explanation, the beginning of which had escaped me, Doctor Follen said: "We must not imagine the ideas of those sects and mystical corporations of antiquity to be as naïve as they appear from the standpoint of a rationalistic outlook. Antiquity knew absolutely nothing of science, in our sense of the word. On the other hand more attention was paid to truths of a philosophical, mystical nature, which often attained to a very high stage of development. Magic in part arose therefrom, and often led to fraud and crime. But none the less, magic had a noble origin and was inspired by deep thought. So it was with the teaching of Abraxas, which I have just cited as an example. This name is used in connection with Greek charm formulas. Many opinions coincide in thinking it is the name of some demon of magic, such as some savage people worship today. But it appears that Abraxas had a much wider significance. We can imagine the name to be that of a divinity on whom the symbolical task was imposed of uniting the divine and the diabolical."

The learned little man continued his discourse with much seriousness, no one was very attentive, and as the name did not recur, I was soon immersed in my own thoughts again.

"To unite the divine and the diabolical," rang in my ears. Here was a starting-point. I was familiar with that idea from my conversations with Demian in the very last period of our friendship. Demian told me then, we had indeed a God whom we revered, but this God represented part of the world only, the half which was arbitrarily separated from the rest (it was the official, permitted, "bright" world). But one should be able to hold the whole world in honor. One should either have a god who was at the same time a devil, or one should institute devil worship together with worship of God. And now Abraxas was the god, who was at the same time god and devil.

For a long time I zealously sought to follow up the trail of ideas farther, without success. In addition, I rummaged through a whole library to find out more about Abraxas, but in vain. However, it was not my nature to concentrate my energies on a methodical search after knowledge, a search which would reveal truths of a dead, useless, documentary kind.

The figure of Beatrice, which had for a certain time occupied so much of my attention, vanished by degrees from my mind, or rather receded slowly, drawing nearer and nearer to the horizon, becoming paler, more like a shadow, as it retreated. She satisfied my soul no longer. A new spiritual development now began to take place in the dreamy existence I led, this existence in which I was strangely wrapped up in myself. The longing for a full life glowed in me, or rather the longing for love. The sex instinct, which for a time had been merged into my worship of Beatrice, required new pictures and aims. Fulfillment was denied me, and it was more impossible than ever for me to delude myself by expecting anything of the girls who seemed to have the happiness of my comrades in their keeping. I again dreamed vividly, even more by day than by night. Images presented themselves to me, desires in the shape of pictures rose up in my imagination, withdrawing me from the outside world, so that my relations with these pictures, with these dreams and shadows, were more real and more intimate than with my actual surroundings.

A certain dream, or play of fantasy, which recurred to me, was full of significance. This dream, the most important and the most enduring of my life, was as follows: I returned home—over the front door shone the crest with the yellow bird on the blue ground—my mother came to meet me—but as I entered and wished to embrace her, it was not she, but a shape I had never before seen, tall and powerful, resembling Max Demian and my painting, yet different, and quite womanly in spite of its size. This figure drew me towards it, and held me in a quivering, passionate embrace. Rapture and horror were mixed, the embrace was a sort of divine worship, and yet a crime as well. Too much of the memory of my mother, too much of the memory of Max Demian was contained in the form which embraced me. The embrace seemed repulsive to my sentiment of reverence, yet I felt happy. I often awoke out of this dream with a deep feeling of contentment, often with the fear of death and a tormenting conscience as if I were guilty of a terrible sin.

It was only gradually and unconsciously that I realized the connection between this mental picture and the hint which had come to me from outside concerning the god of whom I was in search. However, this connection became closer and more intimate, and I began to feel that precisely in this dream, this presentiment, I was invoking Abraxas. Rapture and horror, man and woman, the most sacred things and the most abominable interwoven, the darkest guilt with the most tender innocence—such was the dream picture of my love, such also was Abraxas. Love was no longer a dark, animal impulse, as I had felt with considerable anxiety in the beginning. Neither was it a pious spiritualized form of worship any longer, such as I had bestowed upon the picture of Beatrice. It was both—both and yet much more, it was the image of an angel and of Satan, man and woman in one, human being and animal, the highest good and lowest evil. It was my destiny, it seemed that I should experience this in my own life. I longed for it and was afraid of it, I followed it in my dreams and took to flight before it; but it was always there, was always standing over me.

The next spring I was to leave school and go to some university to study, where and what I knew not. A small moustache grew on my lip, I was a grown man, and yet completely hopeless and aimless. Only one thing was firm: the voice in me, the dream picture. I felt it my duty to follow this guidance blindly. But it was difficult, and daily I was on the point of revolting. Perhaps I was mad, I often used to think; perhaps I was not as other men? But I could do everything the others did; with a little pains and industry I could read Plato, I could solve a trigonometrical problem or work out a chemical analysis. Only one thing I could not do: Discover the dark, concealed aim within me and make up my mind, as others did—others, who knew well enough whether they wanted to be professors or judges, doctors or artists. They knew what career to follow and what advantages they would gain by it. But I was not like that. Perhaps I would be like them some day, but how was I to know? Perhaps I should have to seek and seek for years, and would make nothing of myself, would attain no end. Perhaps I should attain an end, but it might be wicked, dangerous, terrible.

I wanted only to try to live in obedience to the promptings which came from my true self. Why was that so very difficult?

I often made the attempt to paint the powerful love-figure of my dream. But I never succeeded. If I had been successful I would have sent the picture to Demian. Where was he? I knew not. I only knew there was a bond of union between us. When should I see him again?

The pleasant tranquillity of those weeks and months of the Beatrice period was long since gone. I thought at that time I had reached a haven and had found peace. But it was ever so—scarcely did I begin to adapt myself to circumstances, scarcely had a dream done me good, when it faded again. In vain to complain! I now lived in a fire of unstilled desires, of tense expectation, which often rendered me completely wild and mad. I frequently saw before me the picture of my dream-mistress with extraordinary clearness, much more clearly than I saw my own hand. I spoke to it, wept over it, cursed it. I called it mother and knelt before it in tears. I called it my beloved and felt its ripe kiss of fulfilled desire. I called it devil and whore, vampire and murderer. It invited me to the tenderest dreams of love and to the most horrible abominations—nothing was too good and precious for it, nothing too bad and vile.

I passed the whole of that winter in a state of inward tumult difficult to describe. I had long been accustomed to loneliness—that did not depress me. I lived with Demian, with the hawk, with my picture of the big dream-figure, which was my fate and my mistress. It sufficed to live in close communion with those things, since they opened up a large and broad perspective, leading to Abraxas. But I was not able to summon up these dreams, these thoughts, at will. I could not invest them in colors, as I pleased. They came of themselves, taking possession of me, governing me and shaping my life.

I was secure in so far as the outside world was concerned. I was afraid of no one. My schoolfellows had learned to recognize that, and observed a secret respect towards me, which often caused me to smile. When I wished, I could penetrate most of them with a look, thereby surprising them occasionally. Only, I seldom or never wanted to do this. It was my own self which occupied my attention, always myself. And yet I longed ardently to live a bit of real life, to give something of myself to the world, to enter into contact and battle with it. Sometimes as I wandered through the streets in the evening and could not, through restlessness, return home before midnight, I thought to myself: Now I cannot fail to meet my beloved, I shall overtake her at the next corner, she will call to me from the next window. Sometimes all this seemed to torture me unbearably, and I was quite prepared to take my own life some day.

At that time I found a peculiar refuge—by "chance," as one says. But really such happenings cannot be attributed to chance. When a person is in need of something, and the necessary happens, this is not due to chance but to himself; his own desire leads him compellingly to the object of which he stands in need.

Two or three times during my wanderings through the streets I had heard the strains of an organ coming from a little church in the suburbs, without, however, stopping to listen. The next time I passed by the church I heard it again, and recognized that Bach was being played. I went to the door, which I found to be locked. As the street was practically empty I sat down on a curb-stone close to the church, turned up the collar of my coat and listened. It was not a large organ, but a good one nevertheless. Whoever was playing played wonderfully well, almost like a virtuoso, but with a peculiar, highly personal expression of will and perseverance, which seemed to make the music ring out like a prayer. I had the feeling that the man who was playing knew a treasure was shut up in the music and he struggled and tapped and knocked to get at the treasure, as if his life depended on his finding it. In the technical sense I do not understand very much about music, but this form of the soul's expression I have from my childhood intuitively understood; I feel music is something which I can comprehend without initiation.

The organist next played something modern, it might have been Reger. The church was almost completely dark, only a very narrow beam of light shone through the window nearest to me. I waited until the end, and then walked up and down till the organist came out. He was still a young man, though older than myself, robust and thick-set. He walked quickly, taking powerful strides, but as if forcing the pace against his will.

Many an evening thereafter I sat before the church, or walked up and down. Once I found the door open, and for half an hour I sat shivering and happy inside, while the organist played in the organ loft by the dim gas light. Of the music he played I heard not only what he himself put into it. There seemed also to be a secret coherence in his repertory, each piece seemed to be the continuation of the one preceding. Everything he played was pious, ex-pressing faith and devotion. But not pious like church-goers and clergymen, but like pilgrims and beggars of the Middle Ages, pious with a reckless sur-render to a world-feeling, which was superior to all confessions of faith. He frequently played music by the pre-Bach composers, and old Italian music. And all the pieces said the same thing, all expressed what the musician had in his soul: longing, a longing to identify oneself with the world and to tear oneself free again, listening to the workings of one's own dark soul, an orgy of devotion and lively curiosity of the wonderful.

I once secretly followed the organist as he left the church. He continued his way to the outskirts of the town and entered a little tavern. I could not resist the temptation to go in after him. For the first time I had a clear view of him. He sat at the table in the corner of the little room, a black felt hat on his head, a measure of wine before him, and his face was just as I had expected it to be. It was ugly and somewhat uncouth, with the look of a seeker and of an eccentric, obstinate and strong-willed, with a soft and childish mouth. The expression of what was strong and manly lay in the eyes and forehead; on the lower half of the face sat a look of gentleness and immaturity, rather effeminate and showing a lack of self-mastery. The chin indicated a boyish indecision, as if in contradiction with the eyes and forehead. I liked the dark brown eyes, full of pride and hostility.

Silently I took my place opposite him. There was no one else in the tavern. He glared at me, as if he wished to chase me away. Nevertheless I maintained my position, looking at him unflinchingly, until at last he growled testily: "What the deuce are you staring at me for? Do you want anything of me?"

"I don't want anything," I said. "You have already given me much."

He wrinkled his forehead.

"Ah, you're a music enthusiast, are you? I think it's disgusting to go mad over music."

I did not let myself be intimidated.

"I have so often listened to your playing, there in the church," I said. "But I don't want to bother you. I thought perhaps I should discover something in you, something special, I don't know exactly what. But please don't mind me. I can listen to you in the church."

"Why, I always lock the door!"

"Just lately you forgot, and I sat inside. Otherwise I stand outside or sit on the curb-stone."

"Is that so? Another time you can come inside, it's warmer. You've simply got to knock on the door. But loudly, and not while I'm playing. Now— what did you want to say? But you're quite young, apparently a schoolboy or student. Are you a musician?"

"No. I like music, but only the kind you play, absolute music, where one feels that someone is trying to fathom heaven and hell. I like music so much, I think, because it is not concerned with morals. Everything else is a question of morals, and I am looking for something different. Whatever has been concerned with morals has caused me only suffering. I don't express myself properly. Do you know that there must be a god who is at the same time god and devil? There must have been one, I have heard so."

The organist pushed back his broad hat and shook the dark hair from his forehead. He looked at me penetratingly and bent forward his face towards me over the table.

Softly and tensely he questioned:

"What's the name of the god of whom you are talking?"

"Unfortunately I know practically nothing about him really, only his name. His name's Abraxas."

The musician looked distrustfully around, as if someone might be eavesdropping. Then he bent towards me and said in a whisper: "I thought so. Who are you?"

"I'm a student from the school."

"How do you know about Abraxas?"

"By chance."

He thumped on the table, so that his wine spilled over.

"Chance! Don't talk nonsense, young man! One doesn't know of Abraxas by chance, mark you. I will tell you something more of him. I know a little about him!"

He ceased talking and pushed back his chair. I looked at him expectantly, and he made a grimace.

"Not here! Another time. There, take these!"

He dug his hand into the pocket of his overcoat, which he had not taken off, and pulled out a couple of roasted chestnuts, which he threw to me.

I said nothing. I took and ate them, and was very contented.

"Well," he whispered after a while. "How do you know about—him?"

I did not hesitate to tell him.

"I was lonely and perplexed," I related. "I called to mind a friend of former years who, I think, knows a great deal. I had painted something, a bird coming out of a terrestrial globe. I sent this to him. After a time, when I had begun to lose hope of a reply, a piece of paper fell into my hands. On it was written: 'The bird fights its way out of the egg. The egg is the world. Whoever will be born must destroy a world. The bird flies to God. The name of the god is Abraxas.'"

He answered nothing. We peeled our chestnuts and ate them, and drank our wine.

"Shall we have another drink?" he asked.

"Thanks, no. I don't care much for drinking."

He laughed, somewhat disappointedly.

"As you wish! I am different. I am staying here. You can go now!"

The next time I saw him after the organ recital, he was not very communicative. He conducted me through an old street to an old, stately house and upstairs into a large, somewhat gloomy and untidy room where, besides a piano, there was nothing to indicate that its occupant was a musician. Instead, a huge bookcase and writing table gave the room a somewhat scholarly air.

"What a lot of books you have!" I said appreciatively.

"A part of them belongs to the library of my father, with whom I live. Yes, young man, I live with my father and mother, but I cannot introduce you to them, as I and my acquaintances meet with but scant respect at home. I am a prodigal son, you see. My father is very much looked up to, he is a well-known clergyman and preacher in this town. And I, to let you know at once, am his talented and promising son, who, however, is guilty of many backslidings, and, to a certain extent, mad. I was studying theology, and deserted this worthy faculty shortly before my final examination, although really I am still in the same line, as far as concerns my private studies. For me it is still of the highest importance and interest what sort of gods people have invented for themselves at various times. I am a musician into the bargain, and shall soon get a post as organist, I think. Then I shall be in the church again."

I glanced over the backs of the books and found Greek, Latin, Hebrew titles, as far as I could see by the feeble light of the lamp on the table. My acquaintance, meanwhile, had taken up a position on the floor in the dark by the wall.

"Come here," he called after a while, "we will practice a little philosophy. That means keeping one's mouth shut, lying on one's stomach and thinking."

He struck a match and applied it to the paper and wood in the fireplace, in front of which he was lying. The flame leapt up; he poked and blew the fire with great skill. I lay down near him on the ragged carpet. He stared into the flames, which drew my attention as well, and we lay silent for perhaps a whole hour stretched out in front of the flaring wood fire. We watched it flame and roar, die down and flicker up again, until finally it settled down into a subdued glow.

"Fire worship was not by any means the silliest form of worship invented," he murmured without looking up. Those were the only words spoken. With staring eyes I gazed into the fire. Lulled by the tranquillity of the room, I sank in dreams, seeing shapes in the smoke and pictures in the ashes. Once I started up. My companion had thrown a little bit of resin into the glow. A little slender flame shot up, I saw in it the bird with the gold hawk's head. In the glow which died away in the fireplace, golden glittering threads wove themselves together into a net, letters and pictures, memories of faces, of animals, of plants, of worms and serpents. When I woke from my reveries and looked across at my companion, he was absorbed, staring at the ashes with the fixed gaze of a fanatic, his chin in his hands.

"I must go now," I said softly.

"Well, go then, good-bye!"

He did not get up, and as the lamp had gone out, I had to feel my way across the dark room, through dark corridors and down the stairs, and so out of the enchanted old dwelling. Once in the street I stopped and looked up at the house. In not one of the windows was a light burning. A little brass-plate shone in the gleam of the gas-lamp before the door.

"Pistorius, vicar," I read thereon. As I sat in my little room after supper I remembered that I had learnt nothing about Abraxas, or anything else from Pistorius. We had scarcely exchanged ten words. But I was quite contented with the visit I had paid him. And he had promised to play next time an exquisite piece of organ music, a Passacaglia by Buxtehude.

Without my having realized it, the organist Pistorius had given me a first lesson, as we lay on the floor in front of the fireplace of his melancholy hermit's room. Staring into the fire had done me good, it had confirmed and set in activity tendencies which I had always had, but had never really followed. Gradually and in part I saw light on the subject.

When quite a child I had from time to time the propensity to watch bizarre forms of nature, not observing them closely, but simply surrendering myself to their peculiar magic, absorbed by the contemplation of their curling shapes. Long dignified tree-roots, colored veins in stone, flecks of oil floating on water, flaws in glass—all things of a similar nature had had great charm for me at that time, above all, water and fire, smoke, clouds, dust, and especially the little circulating colored specks which I saw when I closed my eyes. In the days following my first visit to Pistorius this began to come back to me. I noticed that I was indebted solely to staring into the open fire for a certain strength and pleasure, for the increase in my depth of feeling which I had felt since. It was curiously beneficial and enriching—dreaming and staring into the fire!

To the few experiences I had gained on the road to the attainment of my proper ends in life was added this new one: The contemplation of such shapes, the surrendering of oneself to these irrational, twisting, odd forms of nature, engenders in us a feeling of the harmony of our inner being with the will which brought forth these shapes; we soon feel the temptation to look upon them as our own creations, as if made by our own moods; we see the boundary between ourselves and nature waver and vanish; we learn to know the state of mind by outside impressions, or by inward. In no way so simply and so easily as by this practice do we discover to what a great extent we are creators, to what a great extent our souls have part in the continual creation of the world. Or rather, it is the same indivisible godhead, which is active in us and in nature. If the outside world fell in ruins, one of us would be capable of building it up again, for mountain and stream, tree and leaf, root and blossom, all that is shaped by nature lies modeled in us, comes from the soul, whose essence is eternity, of whose essence we are ignorant, but which is revealed to us for the most part as love-force and creative power.

Many years later I found this observation confirmed in a book, one of Leonardo da Vinci's, who in one passage remarks how good and deeply moving it is to look at a wall on which many people have spat. He felt the same sensation before those spots on the wet wall as Pistorius and I before the fire.

At our next meeting the organist enlightened me still further on the subject.

"We confine our personality within much too narrow bounds. We count as composing our person only that which distinguishes us as individuals, only that which we recognize as irregular. But we are made up from the entire world stock, each one of us, and just as in our body is displayed the genealogical table of development back to the fish stage and still further, so we have accumulated in our souls all the experiences through which a human soul has ever lived. All the gods and devils which have ever been, whether those of the Greeks or Chinese or Zulus, all are in us, are there as potentialities, as desires, as starting points. If all mankind died out, with the exception of a single moderately gifted child, who had not enjoyed the slightest instruction, so would this child rediscover the whole process of things; it would be able to produce gods, demons, paradises, the commandments and prohibitions, old and new testaments—everything."

"Well and good," I objected; "but then what does the worth of the individual consist of? Why do we continue to strive if everything has already been achieved in us?"

"Stop!" exclaimed Pistorius vehemently. "There is a great difference between whether one merely carries the world in oneself, or whether one is conscious of that as well. A madman can have ideas which remind one of Plato, and a pious little boy in a Moravian boarding school will recreate in his thought profound mythological ideas which occur in the gnostics or in Zoroaster. But he does not realize it! He is a tree or a stone, at best an animal, as long as he does not know it. But, when the first spark of this knowledge glimmers in him he becomes a man. You will not consider all the two-legged creatures who walk out there in the street as human beings, simply because they walk erect and carry their young nine months in the womb? Look how many of them are fish or sheep, worms or leeches, how many are ants or bees. Well, in reach of them are the possibilities of becoming human creatures, but only when they feel this, it is only when, if even in part, they learn to make them conscious, that these potentialities become theirs."

Our conversations were somewhat after this style. They seldom taught me anything completely new, anything absolutely surprising. But all, even the most banal, hit like a light persistent hammer-stroke on the same point in me, all helped in my development, all helped to peel off skins, to break up eggshells, and after each talk I held my head somewhat higher, I was more sure of myself until my yellow bird pushed his beautiful bird-of-prey crest through the ruins of the world-shell.

We frequently related our dreams to one another. Pistorius knew how to interpret them. A curious example comes to my mind. I dreamed I was able to fly. I was flung through the air, so to speak—impelled by a great force over which I had not the mastery. The sensation of this flight was exhilarating, but soon changed to fear as I saw myself snatched up involuntarily to risky heights. There I made the saving discovery that I could control my rise and fall by arresting my breath and by breathing again.

Pistorius interpreted it as follows: "The swing, which sent you up into the air, is the great property of mankind, which everyone possesses. It is the feeling of close relationship with the springs of every force, but it soon causes anxiety. It is cursedly dangerous! For that reason most people willingly renounce flying, preferring to walk according to prescribed laws along the footpath. But not you. You fly higher, as befits an intelligent fellow. And behold, you make a wonderful discovery there, namely, you gradually get the mastery over the impelling force. In other words, you acquire a fine little force of your own, an instrument, a rudder. That is splendid. Without that one goes floating into the air without any will of one's own; madmen, for instance, do that. They have deeper presentiments than the people on the footpath. But they have no key and no rudder, they fall whistling through the air, down into the fathomless depths. But you, Sinclair, you manage all right! And how, pray? You probably don't even know. You manage with a new instrument, with a breath regulator. And now you can see, that your soul isn't really 'personal' at bottom. I mean that you didn't invent this regulator. It isn't new. It is a loan, it has existed for thousands of years. It is the balancing organ fish have—the air-bladder. Even today we actually still have a few very rare kinds of fish whose air-bladder is at the same time a sort of lung; and on occasion can use it to breathe with. In your dream you made use of your lungs in exactly the same way as these fish do their air-bladder."

He even brought me a volume on zoölogy, and showed me the original drawings of these ancient fish. And with a peculiar thrill I felt an organ of early evolutionary epochs functioning in me.

CHAPTER 6

JACOB WRESTLES WITH GOD

I cannot relate in brief all that I learned from the singular musician Pistorius about Abraxas. The most important result of his teaching was that I made a further step forward on the road to self-realization. I was then about eighteen years old. I was a young man rather out of the ordinary, precocious in a hundred things, in a hundred other things backward and helpless. When from time to time I used to compare myself with others, I was often proud and conceited, but just as frequently I felt depressed and humiliated. I had often looked upon myself as a genius, often as half mad. I could not share the pleasures and life of the fellows of my age, and often I heaped reproaches on myself and was consumed with cares, thinking I was hopelessly cut off from them, and that life was closed to me.

Pistorius, himself full-grown and an eccentric, taught me to preserve my courage and my self-esteem. In constantly finding some value in my words, in my dreams, in the play of my imagination and in my ideas, in taking them seriously and discussing them, he set me an example.

"You have told me," he said, "that you like music because it is not moral. Well, all right. But you should be no moralist yourself! You should not compare yourself with others. If nature had created you to be a bat, you ought not to want to make yourself into an ostrich. You often consider yourself as singular, you reproach yourself with going ways different from most people. You must get out of that habit. Look in the fire, look at the clouds, and as soon as you have presentiments, and the voices of your soul begin to speak, yield to them and don't first ask what the opinion of your master or your father would be, or whether they would be pleasing to some god or other. One spoils oneself that way. In doing that one treads the common road, becomes a fossil. Sinclair, my dear fellow, the name of our god is Abraxas. He is God and he is Satan; he has the light and the dark world in him. Abraxas has no objection to urge against any of your ideas or against any of your dreams. Never forget that. But he deserts you if you ever become blameless and normal. He deserts you and seeks out another pot in order to cook his ideas therein."

Of all my dreams, that dark love-dream recurred most frequently. Often, often have I dreamed of it; often I stepped under the crest with the bird on it into our house, and wished to draw my mother to me, but instead of her I found I was embracing the tall, manly, half-motherly woman, of whom I was afraid, and yet to whom I was drawn by a most ardent desire. And I could never relate this dream to my friend. I kept it back, although I had opened my heart to him on everything else. It was my secret, my retreat, my refuge.

When I was depressed, I used to beg Pistorius to play me the Passacaglia of old Buxtehude. I sat in the dark church in the evening, engrossed in this singularly intimate music, which seemed to be hearkening to itself, as if entirely self-absorbed. Each time it did me good and made me more ready to follow the promptings of my inward self.

Sometimes we stayed awhile in the church after the strains of the organ had died away. We sat and watched the feeble light shine through the high lancet window; the light seemed to lose itself in the body of the church.

"It sounds funny," said Pistorius, "that I once did theology and almost became a parson. But it was only an error in form that I committed. To be a priest, that is my vocation and my aim. Only I was too easily satisfied, and gave myself to the service of Jehovah before ever I knew Abraxas. Ah, every religion is beautiful! Religion is soul. It is all one whether you take communion as a Christian or whether you make a pilgrimage to Mecca."

"Then really you might have been a clergyman," I suggested.

"No, Sinclair, no. I should have had to have lied in that case. Our religion is so practised, as if it were none. It is carried on as if it were a work of the understanding. A Catholic I could well be, if need were, but a Protestant clergyman—no! There are two kinds of genuine believers—I know such—

who hold gladly to the literal interpretation. I could not say to them that for me Christ was not a mere person, but a hero, a myth, a wonderful shadow-picture, in which mankind sees itself painted on the wall of eternity. And what should I find to say to the other sort, those who go to church to hear wise words, to fulfill a duty, in order to leave nothing undone, etc.? Convert them, you think, perhaps? But that is not at all my idea. The priest does not wish to convert. He only wants to live among the believers, among those of his own kind, so that through him they may find expression for that feeling out of which we make our gods."

He broke off. Then he continued: "Our new faith, for which we have now chosen the name of Abraxas, is beautiful, my friend. It is the best we have. But it is still a nestling. Its wings have not yet grown. Alas, a lonely religion, that is not yet the true one. It must become an affair of many, it must have cult and orgy, feasts and mysteries...."

He was sunk in reflection.

"Can one not celebrate mysteries alone, or in a very small circle?" I asked hesitatingly.

"Yes, one can," he nodded. "I have been celebrating them for a long time past. I have celebrated cults for which I should have been imprisoned for years in a convict station, if they had been found out. But I know it is not the right thing."

He suddenly clapped me on the shoulder, making me jump. "Young friend," he said impressively, "you also have mysteries. I know that you must have dreams of which you make no mention to me. I don't wish to know them. But I tell you: Live them, these dreams, play your destined part, build altars to them! It is not yet the perfect religion, but it is a way. Whether you and I and a few other people will one day renew the world remains to be seen. But we must renew it daily within us, otherwise we are of no account. Think over it! You are eighteen, Sinclair, you don't go with loose women, you must have love-dreams, desires. Perhaps they are such that you are frightened by them! They are the best you have! Believe me! I have lost a great deal by doing violence to these love-dreams when I was your age. One should not do that. When one knows of Abraxas, one should do that no more. We should fear nothing. We should hold nothing forbidden which the soul in us desires."

Frightened, I objected: "But you can't do everything which comes into your mind! You can't murder a man because you can't tolerate him."

He pressed closer to me.

"There are cases where you can. Only, generally it's a mistake. I don't mean that you can simply do everything which comes into your mind. No, but you shouldn't do injury to those ideas in which there is sense, you shouldn't banish them from your mind or moralize about them. Instead of getting one-self crucified or crucifying others, one can solemnly drink wine out of a cup, thinking the while on the mystery of sacrifice. One can, without such actions, treat one's impulses and one's so-called temptations with esteem and love. Then you discover their meaning, and they all have meaning. Next time the idea takes you to do something really mad and sinful, Sinclair, if you would like to murder someone or to do something dreadfully obscene, then think a moment, that it is Abraxas who is indulging in a play of fancy. The man you would like to kill is never really Mr. So and So, that is really only a disguise. When we hate a man, we hate in him something which resides in us ourselves. What is not in us does not move us."

Never had Pistorius said anything to me which went home so deeply as this. I could not reply. But what moved me most singularly and most powerfully was that Pistorius in this conversation had struck the same note as Demian, whose words I had carried in my mind for years and years past. They knew nothing of one another, and both said to me the same thing.

"The things we see," said Pistorius softly, "are the same things which are in us. There is no reality except that which we have in ourselves. For that reason most people live so unreally, because they hold the impressions of the outside world for real, and their own world in themselves never enters into their consideration. You can be happy like that. But if once you know of the other, then you no longer have the choice to go the way most people go. Sinclair, the road for most people is easy, ours is hard. Let us go."

A few days later, after I had on two occasions waited for him in vain, I met him late one evening in the street. He came stumbling round a corner, blown along by the cold night wind. He was very drunk. I did not like to call him. He passed by without noticing me, staring in front of him with strange, glowing eyes, as though he were moving in obedience to a dark call from the unknown. I followed him down one street. He drifted along as if drawn by an invisible wire, with the swaying gait of a fanatic, or like a ghost. Sadly I went home, to the unsolved problems of my dreams.

"Thus he renews the world in himself!" I thought, and felt instantly that my thought was base and moral. What did I know of his dreams? Perhaps in his intoxication he was going a surer way than in my anxiety.

* * * *

In the intervals between lessons it struck me once or twice that a boy who had never before attracted my notice was hovering about in my proximity. It was a little, weak-looking, slim youngster with reddish-blond thin hair, who had something peculiar in his look and behavior. One evening as I came home he was on the watch for me in the street. He let me pass by, then walked behind me; and remained standing in front of the door of the house.

"Can I do anything for you?" I asked.

"I only want to speak to you," he said timidly. "Be good enough to come a few steps with me."

I followed him, observing that he was deeply excited and full of expectation. His hands trembled.

"Are you a Spiritualist?" he asked quite suddenly.

"No, Knauer," I said, laughing. "Not a bit. How did you get hold of that idea?"

"But you are a Theosophist?"

"No again."

"Oh, please don't be so reserved. I feel with absolute certitude there is something singular about you. It is in your eyes. I thought it certain you communed with spirits. I am not asking out of curiosity, Sinclair, no! I am myself a seeker, you know, and I am so lonely."

"Tell me, then!" I encouraged him. "I know absolutely nothing of ghosts. I live in my dreams: that is what you have felt about me. Other people live in dreams as well, but not in their own, that is the difference."

"Yes, perhaps so," he whispered. "Only it depends on the sort of dreams you live in. Have you ever heard of white magic?"

I had to admit my ignorance.

"It's when you learn to get the mastery over yourself. You can be immortal, and have magical powers as well. Have you never practised such experiments?"

On my evincing curiosity with regard to those practices, he was mysteriously silent, but when I turned to go he burst out in explanation.

"For example, when I go to sleep or when I wish to concentrate my thoughts I do such exercises. I think of something or other, a word for instance, or a name, or a geometrical figure. Then I think it into myself, as strongly as I can. I try to get it into my head, until I feel it is there. Then I think it in my neck, and so on, until I am quite full of it. Then my thoughts are concentrated and nothing more can disturb my repose."

I understood to a certain degree what he meant. Yet I felt he had something else in his mind, he was oddly excited and hasty. I tried to make the questions easy for him, and he soon gave me an indication of what immediately concerned him.

"You are also continent?" he asked me anxiously.

"What do you mean by that? Do you mean it from the sex point of view?"

"Yes, yes. I have been continent for two years, since I knew of what I have told you. Before that I practised a vice, you know what. You have never been with a woman, then?"

"No," I said. "I haven't found the right one."

"But if you should find her, the one you consider the right one, then would you sleep with her?"

"Yes, naturally. If she had nothing against it," I said with some scorn.

"Oh, then you are on a false track! One can only perfect one's inner forces if one remains entirely continent. I have done it, for two whole years. Two years and a little more than a month! It's so hard. Often I can scarcely hold out any longer."

"Listen, Knauer, I don't believe that continency is so terribly important."

"I know," he parried, "they all say that. But I did not expect to hear it from you. Whoever will go the higher spiritual way must remain pure, unconditionally!"

"Well, then, do so! But I don't understand why one man should be purer than another, because he represses his sex instincts. Or can you switch off all sexual matters from your thoughts and dreams?"

He looked despairingly at me.

"No, that's just it. God! And yet it must be. At night I have dreams which I couldn't relate even to myself. Terrible dreams, terrible!"

I recollected what Pistorius had said to me. But however much I felt his words to be right I could not pass them on. I could not give advice which did not result from my own experience, advice the observance of which I did not yet feel myself equal to. I was silent and felt humiliated that someone should come to me for counsel when I had none to give.

"I have tried everything!" wailed Knauer beside me. "I have done all that a man can do, with cold water, with snow, with gymnastic exercises and running, but all that doesn't help a bit. Each night I wake up out of dreams on which I dare not think. And most dreadful of all, I am by degrees losing everything that I had gained spiritually. It is almost impossible for me any longer to concentrate my thoughts or to lull myself to sleep. Often I lie awake the whole night through. I shall not be able to bear that much longer. Finally, when I can carry on the struggle no further, when I give in and make myself impure again, then I shall be worse than all the others who have never struggled against it. You understand that, don't you?"

I nodded, but could say nothing to the point. He began to bore me, and I was horrified at myself, because his obvious need and despair made no deep impression on me. My only sentiment was: I can't help you.

"Then you know nothing that would help me?" he asked at last, exhausted and sad. "Nothing at all? There must be some way! How do you manage?"

"I cannot tell you anything, Knauer. People can't help one another in this case. No one has helped me, either. You must think of something yourself, and you must obey the prompting which really comes from your own nature. There is nothing else. If you cannot find yourself, you won't find any spirits, either."

Disappointed, and suddenly become dumb, the little fellow looked at me. Then his look suddenly glowed with hate, he made a grimace at me and cried with rage: "Ah, you're a nice sort of saint! You have your vice as well, I know! You pretend to wisdom, and secretly you stick in the same filth as I and all of us! You're swine, swine, like myself. We are all swine!"

I went away and left him standing there. He made two, three steps in my direction, then he stopped, turned round and ran away. I felt sick from a feeling of pity and horror. I could not get rid of the feeling until I got home to my little room, and placing my few pictures before me, I surrendered myself up with passionate fervor to my dreams. My dreams came back at once, the dream of front door and crest, of mother and the strange woman, and I saw the features of the woman so very clearly that I began to draw her picture the same evening.

In a few days this drawing was finished, painted in as if unconsciously in dreamy quarter-of-an-hour periods. In the evening I hung it on the wall, put the reading lamp in front of it, and stood before it as before a spirit with whom I had to fight until victory should be decided one way or the other. It was a face similar to the former, resembling my friend Demian, in certain traits even resembling myself. One eye stood perceptibly higher than the other, the look passed over me, sunk in a staring gaze, full of destiny.

I stood before it. Such was my inward exertion that I became cold to the marrow. I questioned the picture, I abused it, I caressed it, I prayed to it. I called it mother, I called it beloved, called it strumpet and whore, called it Abraxas. Meanwhile words of Pistorius crossed my mind, or of Demian? I could not recollect on what occasion they had been spoken, but I thought I heard them again. They were the words of Jacob wrestling with the angel of God. "I will not let thee go, except thou bless me."

The painted face in the lamplight changed at each appeal. It was bright and shining, was black and gloomy; it closed pale lids over dead eyes, opened them again and flashed a burning look. It was woman, man, girl, was a little child, an animal, vanished to a speck, was again tall and clear. At last, in response to a strong inward prompting, I closed my eyes, and saw the picture inwardly in me, stronger and more powerful. I wished to kneel down before it, but it was so much within me, that I could separate it from myself no more; it seemed as if it had entirely identified itself with me.

Then I heard a loud confused roar as of a spring storm. I trembled in an indescribably new feeling of fear and excitement. Stars darted before me and died out, recollections even of the first forgotten years of my childhood, of a time further back still, of a pre-existence and the early stages of existence, pressed through me. But the recollections which seemed to piece together my life's whole history even to its most secret details did not cease with yesterday and today, they went farther, mirrored the future, tearing me away from today, changing me into new forms of life, of which the pictures were very bright and blinding. But of none of them could I call up a just image later.

In the night I woke up out of a deep sleep. I was dressed and lying transversely across the bed. I struck a light, feeling that I must try to remember something important that had happened. I knew nothing of the hours just passed. I turned on the light, and recollection came back gradually. I looked for the picture. It was not hanging on the wall, neither was it lying on the table. I thought confusedly that I must have burned it. Or was it a dream, that I had burned it in my hands and had eaten the ashes?

A great inquietude convulsed me and drove me forth. I put on my hat, went out of the house and down the street, as if under coercion. I walked and walked through streets and squares as if blown along by a storm, I listened in front of the gloomy church of my friend, searched in obedience to a blind impulse, without knowing what I was looking for. I went through a suburb, where brothels stood. Here and there a light was still shining. Further on stood new buildings and brick heaps, covered in part with grey snow. I went on through this wilderness, driven forward by a strange impulse, like a man walking in a dream. The thought of the new building in my native town crossed my mind, that building to which my tormentor Kromer had drawn me to settle accounts with him. In the grey night a similar building stood there in front of me, its black doorway yawning wide. I was drawn towards it, but wanted to shun it and stumbled over sand and rubbish. The impulse was stronger than I, I had to go in.

I staggered over planks and broken bricks into the deserted room. There was a mouldy smell of damp, cold stones. A heap of sand lay there, a grey bright speck, otherwise all else was dark.

Suddenly a terrified voice called to me: "In God's name, Sinclair, where have you come from?"

And a human figure rose out of the darkness close to me, a little thin shape like a ghost. I recognized, while yet my hair was standing on end, my school companion Knauer.

"How did you get here?" he asked, as if mad with excitement. "How have you been able to find me?"

I did not understand.

"I wasn't looking for you," I said, dazed. I spoke with difficulty, the words came from me painfully, as if from dead, heavy, frozen lips.

"You weren't looking for me?"

"No. I was drawn here. Did you call me? You must have called. But what are you doing here? It's still night."

He put his thin arms convulsively round me.

"Yes, night. But it must soon be morning. Oh, Sinclair, to think that you didn't forget me! Can you ever forgive me?"

"What then?"

"Ah, I was so hateful!"

Then I recollected our conversation. Had that taken place four, five days ago? It seemed to me like a lifetime. But suddenly I knew all. Not only what had occurred between us, but also why I had come and what Knauer wanted to do there.

"You wanted, then, to take your life, Knauer?"

He shuddered through cold and fear.

"Yes, I wanted to. I don't know whether I could have. I wished to wait until the morning came."

I drew him into the open. The first oblique rays of day glimmered indescribably cold through the grey atmosphere.

I led the boy on my arm a little way. I heard my own voice saying: "Now go home, and don't say anything to anybody. You were on a false track, a false track! And we are not swine, as you think. We are men. We make gods, and we wrestle with them, and they bless us."

Silently we went on, and separated. When I came home it was day.

The best that mystery in St. —— had yet to give me was the hours with Pistorius at the organ or by the chimney fire. We read a Greek text about Abraxas together. He read to me portions of a translation of the Veda and taught me to say the sacred "Om." However, it was not this learned instruction which was of service to my inner self, but rather the contrary. What did me good was the self-progression I made, the increasing confidence in my own dreams, thoughts and presentiments, and the consciousness of the power that I carried in me.

I had an excellent understanding with Pistorius in every way. I needed only to think intently of him, and I could be sure that he, or a greeting from him, would come to me. I could ask him, just as I could Demian, something or other, without his being there in person. I needed only to imagine his presence and to put my questions to him as intensive thoughts. Then all the soul-force I had put into the question came back to me as answer. Only it was not the person of Pistorius which I called up in my imagination; nor that of Max Demian, but it was the picture I had painted and of which I had dreamed. It was the half-man, half-woman, dream picture of my dæmon, to which I called. It lived now not only in my dreams, it was no longer painted on paper, but it was in me, as a desire-picture and an enhancement of my spiritual self.

The relation into which the unsuccessful suicide Knauer entered with me was peculiar and sometimes amusing. Since the night I had been sent to him, he dogged my steps like a faithful servant or hound, sought to attach himself to me and followed me blindly. He came to me with curious questions and wishes. He wanted to see spirits, to learn the Cabbala, and he did not believe me when I assured him I understood nothing of all these things. He credited me with being able to do anything. But it was singular that he often came to me with his strange and silly questions just at the moment when I myself had a mental knot to be disentangled. His moody ideas and concerns often gave me the cue, the impulse which helped me in the solution of my own problems. He was often tiresome and I imperiously drove him away. I felt, however, that he had been sent to me, and what I gave to him, I received twofold in return. He also was a guide, or rather a way. The mad books and publications he brought me, and in which he sought the key to happiness, taught me more than I realized at the time.

This Knauer vanished later from my path, neither did I miss him. No arrangement, no understanding was necessary with him. But it was with Pistorius. Towards the close of my school career in St. —— I lived through another peculiar experience with my friend.

Even innocuous, innocent people are not altogether spared the shock of a conflict. Even they come once in their lives in conflict with the beautiful virtues of piety and gratitude. Each must make the step which parts him from his father, from his teachers. Each must once feel something of the bitterness of loneliness, though most people cannot support it for long and soon creep back to their homes again. It was not a great struggle for me to part from my parents and their world, the "bright" world of my beautiful childhood. But slowly and almost imperceptibly I had got further from them and become more of a stranger to them. I regretted it; it often caused me bitter hours during my visits home; but it was not deep. I could bear it.

But when we have offered love and reverence of our own accord, and not out of habit, when we have been disciples and friends with our innermost feelings—then it is a bitter and terrible moment when the realization is suddenly brought home to us that the guiding current of our life is bearing us away from those we love. Then every thought of ours which rejects our friend and teacher enters our own heart like a poisoned sting, every blow of self-defense strikes back into our own face. Then he who felt that the dictates of his own conscience were an authentic guide reproaches himself with the terms "faithlessness" and "ingratitude." Then the terrified heart flees anxiously back to the valleys of childhood virtues, and cannot believe that the rupture must take place, that another bond must be severed.

In the course of time a feeling had slowly developed in me which refused to recognize my friend Pistorius unconditionally as my guide. What I experienced in the most important moments of my youth was my friendship with him, his counsel, his consolation, his proximity. God had spoken to me through him. Through him my dreams returned to me, from his mouth came their explanation, from him I learned their significance. He had given me the courage to realize myself. And now, alas, I felt a growing opposition against him. In his conversation he evinced too clearly a desire to instruct me. I felt it was only one side of my nature that he thoroughly understood.

There was no quarrel, no scene between us, no rupture. I said to him only a single, really harmless word, but nevertheless it was the moment when an illusion between us fell in colored pieces.

The presentiment had for some time already oppressed me, but one Sunday in his scholarly old room this presentiment changed to a definite feeling. We were lying on the floor before the fire. He was speaking of mysteries and religious forms which he was studying, and on which he was meditating. He occupied himself with trying to picture their possible future. To me all this seemed curious and interesting, but scarcely of vital importance. It smacked of erudition. It was like a fatiguing search among the ruins of former worlds. And all at once I felt an aversion from the whole business, from this cult of mythology, from this sort of piecing together, this mosaic work of religious forms which had been handed down to posterity.

"Pistorius," I said suddenly, in a malicious outburst which surprised and frightened even myself, "relate a dream, a real dream, one that you have had in the night. What you have just been talking about is so—so cursedly antiquarian!"

He had never heard me speak thus. With shame and terror I realized the very same moment that the arrow I had shot at him, and which had entered his heart, was taken from his own quiver—I realized that I had heard him reproach himself in an ironical tone on this very account, and that now I had maliciously turned one of his own reproaches against him like a resharpened arrow.

He felt it instantly, and was silent. I looked at him with terror in my heart and saw that he had become very pale.

After a long, heavy pause he put some wood on the fire and said quietly: "You are quite right, Sinclair. You're a wise fellow. I will spare you all this antiquarian business."

He spoke very quietly, but his tone told me how deeply he had been wounded. What had I done!

I was on the point of tears. I wanted to beg his pardon with all my heart, to assure him of my affection and gratitude. Moving words came into my mind—but I could not utter them. He was silent as well, and so we lay there, while the flames leaped up and then sank, and with each flame that paled fell something beautiful and fervid that ceased to glow and had vanished—never again to come back.

"I fear you have misunderstood me," I said at last, much crushed, and with a dry, hoarse voice. The silly, senseless words came as if mechanically from my lips, as if I had been reading them out of a news sheet.

"I understood you perfectly," said Pistorius softly. "You are quite right." We waited. Then he continued slowly: "So far as one man can be right in his judgment of another."

No, no, a voice inside me said, I am wrong; but I could not say anything. I knew that I had aimed my single little word at his one essential weakness. I had touched the point of which he himself was distrustful. His idea was "antiquarian." He was a seeker, but retrogressive, he was a romantic. And suddenly I realized that it was just what he had been to me and had given me that he could not be and give to himself. He had guided me to a point on the road, beyond which he, the guide, could not go.

God knows how I could have uttered such a word! I had not meant it badly. I had had no idea it would lead to a catastrophe. I had uttered something, the import of which I did not myself realize at the moment of utterance. I had surrendered myself to a somewhat witty, somewhat malicious inspiration, and fate used it as her instrument. I had been guilty of a little thoughtlessness, crudeness, and he had accepted it as a judgment.

Oh, how much I wished then that he would have got angry, have defended himself, have shouted at me! But he did nothing. I had all that to do within myself. He would have smiled, had he been able. The fact that he could not, showed me more than anything else how hard I had hit him.

And because Pistorius took the blow from me, his presumptuous and ungrateful pupil, so quietly, because he silently agreed with me, because he recognized my word as a judgment of fate, he caused me to hate myself, he made my thoughtlessness seem a thousand times greater than it was. As I struck, I had thought to hit a strong man, capable of defending himself—now he was a meek, suffering creature, defenseless, who surrendered in silence.

We remained a long time lying before the dying fire, in which each glowing figure, each crumbling ash heap called to my memory happy, beautiful, rich hours, making my guilt and my obligation to Pistorius greater and greater. Finally I could bear it no longer. I got up and went. A long time I stood before his door, a long time I listened on the dark staircase, a long time I stood outside in front of the house, waiting to see whether perhaps he would come out to me. Then I went on, walking for hours and hours through town and suburbs, park and wood, until evening fell. At that moment I felt for the first time the mark of Cain on my forehead.

I fell to pondering and rumination. I had every intention, in thinking matters over, to accuse myself and to defend Pistorius. But all ended to the contrary. A thousand times I was ready to repent of my rash word and to withdraw it—but it had been true, nevertheless. Now I succeeded in understanding Pistorius, in building up his whole dream. This dream had been to be a priest, to proclaim a new religion, to invent new forms of exultation, of love, of worship, to set up new symbols. But this was not within his province.

He lingered too long in the past, he knew too much of what had been, he knew too much of Egypt, of India, of Mithras, of Abraxas. His love was attached to ideas with which the world was already familiar. And in his inmost self he probably recognized that the new religion had to be different, that it had to spring from fresh sources and not be drawn out of collections and libraries. His office was, perhaps, to help men to find themselves, as he had done with me. But to found a new doctrine, to give new gods to the world, was not his function in life.

And at this point the realization came upon me that everyone has an "office," a charge. But to no one is it permitted to choose his office for himself, and to discharge it as he likes. It was wrong to want new gods, it was entirely wrong to wish to give the world anything. A man has absolutely no other duty than this: to seek himself, to grope his own way forward, no matter whither it leads. That thought impressed itself deeply on me; that was the fruit of this new event for me. Often had I pictured the future. I had dreamed of filling rôles which might be destined for me, as poet perhaps or as prophet, as painter, or some such rôle. All that was of no account. I was not here to write, to preach, to paint, neither I nor anyone else was here for that purpose. All that was secondary. The true vocation for everyone was only to attain to self-realization. He might end as poet or as madman, as prophet or as criminal—that was not his affair, that was of no consequence in the long run. His business was to work out his own destiny, not any destiny, but his own, to live for that, entirely and uninterruptedly. Everything else was merely an attempt to shun his fate, to fly back to the ideals of the masses, to adapt himself to circumstances. It was fear of his own inner being. There rose before me this new picture, terrible and sacred, suggested to me a hundred times ere this, perhaps often already expressed, but now for the first time lived. I was a throw from nature's dice box, a projection into the unknown, perhaps into something new, perhaps into the void, and my sole vocation was to let this throw-up from primeval depths work itself out in me, to feel its will in me and to make it mine. That solely!

I had already known what it was to be very lonely. Now I felt I could be lonelier still, and that I could not escape from it.

I made no attempt to reconcile myself with Pistorius. We remained friends, but our relation towards one another had changed. Only one single time did we mention it, or rather, it was only he who spoke of the matter. He said: "I want to be a priest, you know that. I would best of all like to be the priest of the religion of which we have so many presentiments. I can never be that, I know. I have known it already for some time, without fully admitting it. I will do some other priestly service, perhaps at the organ, perhaps in another way. But I must always be surrounded by something which I find beautiful and sacred, organ music and mysteries, symbol and myth, I need that and cannot persuade myself to leave it—that is my weakness. I often realize, Sinclair, that I should not have such desires, that they are a luxury and a weakness. It would be greater, it would be more right, if I placed myself quite simply at the disposition of fate, without pretensions. That is the sole thing I cannot do. Perhaps you will some time be able to do it. It is hard, it is the only thing really hard there is, my friend. I have often dreamed of it, but I cannot do it, I tremble at the thought of it. I cannot stand so completely naked and alone. I am a poor, weak hound, who needs a little warmth and food, who occasionally likes to feel the proximity of his own kind. He whose only desire it is to work out his own destiny has no kith or kin, but stands alone and has only the cold world space around him. Do you know, that is Jesus in the garden of Gethsemane? There have been martyrs who willingly let themselves be nailed to the cross, but even they were not heroes, they were not free, they also wished for something to which they had been accustomed, which they had loved; with which they had felt at home. They had examples or ideals. He who will fulfill his destiny has neither examples nor ideals, he has nothing dear to him, nothing to comfort him. And one really ought to go this way. People like you and I are certainly very lonely, but we still have each other, we have the secret satisfaction of being different, of revolting, of wanting the unusual. But we must drop that, too, if we would go the whole way. We must not wish to be revolutionaries, or examples, or martyrs. To think the thought to its logical end—"

No, one could not think beyond that. But one could dream of it, could sense it, could anticipate it. A few times I realized something of this, in a very quiet hour. Then I looked straight into the open, staring eyes of my fate. They could have been full of wisdom, or full of madness, they could be full of love or full of wickedness, it was all one. One was to choose nothing of all that; one was to want nothing, one was only to want oneself, one's destiny. In that way had Pistorius served me, for a time, as guide.

In those days I walked about as if I were blind, storms roared within me, every step meant danger. I was conscious of nothing but the precipitous darkness in front of me, down to which all the roads I had trodden hitherto seemed to lead. And in my inward self I saw the picture of the guide, who resembled Demian, and in whose eyes stood my fate.

I wrote on a sheet of paper: "A guide has left me. I stand in complete darkness. I cannot take a step alone. Help me!"

I wished to send that to Demian. Yet I omitted to do this, for each time I wished to do it, it seemed foolish and meaningless. But I knew that little prayer by heart, and often said it to myself. It accompanied me hourly. I began to realize what prayer is.

* * * *

My school career was over. My father had arranged that during the holidays I was to travel and then I was to go to the University. In which faculty, I knew not. I was to be allowed to take philosophy for one semester. I should have been equally content with anything else.

CHAPTER 7

MOTHER EVE

In the holidays I went once to the house in which, years before, Max Demian and his mother had lived. An old lady was walking in the garden. I entered into conversation and learned that the house belonged to her. I enquired after the Demians. She remembered them very well. But she did not know where they were living at that moment. As she felt my interest, she took me into the house, searched through a leather album and showed me a photograph of Demian's mother. I scarcely had any recollections of what she was like. But when I saw the little picture my heart stood still. It was my dream picture! There it was, the tall, almost masculine woman's figure, resembling her son, with traits of motherliness, traits which denoted severity, and deep passion, beautiful and alluring, beautiful and unapproachable, demon and mother, destiny and mistress. That was she!

I was filled with a wild wonder, when I learned that my dream picture lived on earth! There was a woman, then, who looked like that, who bore my fate in her features! Where was she? Where? And she was Demian's mother!

I started on my travels soon after. A strange journey! I went restlessly from place to place as impulse directed, always in search of this woman. There were days when I met shapes which reminded me of her, and which resembled her. These shapes led me on through the streets of strange towns, into railway stations, into trains, as in a tangled dream. There were other days when I saw how useless my search was. Then I sat inactive, anywhere, in a park or the garden of a hotel, in a waiting room; I looked into myself and tried to make the picture live in me. But it was now shy and elusive. I could not sleep, I only nodded for a quarter of an hour or so on railway journeys through country unknown to me. Once in Zürich, a woman followed me, a pretty, rather forward woman. I scarcely noticed her and went on, as if she were air. I would rather have died at once, than have shown sympathy for another woman, even if only for an hour.

I felt that my destiny was leading me on. I felt that fulfillment was nigh. I was mad with impatience, to think that I could do nothing to help myself. Once at a station, I think it was at Innsbruck, I saw, at the window of a train which was just moving out, a form which reminded me of her, and I was miserable for days. And suddenly the form appeared again to me at night in a dream. I woke up with a feeling as of shame, realizing the fruitlessness and senselessness of my chase, and I went home by the most direct route.

A couple of weeks later I matriculated in the University of H——. Everything disappointed me. The course of lectures I followed, on the history of philosophy, was just as vain and mechanical as the common ground of student life. Everything was so much according to pattern, one person did as the other, and the boyish faces, although inflamed with a forced gaiety, looked so distressingly vacant. It was like the gloss of a ready-made article! But I was free, I had the whole day to myself, and lived quietly in a beautiful old building outside the town. I had a couple of volumes of Nietzsche on my table. I lived with him, feeling the loneliness of his soul, sensing his destiny, which impelled him onwards unceasingly. I suffered with him, and was happy that there had been one who had gone his way so inflexibly.

Late one evening I wandered through the town; an autumn wind was blowing and I heard the student societies singing in their taverns. Tobacco smoke rose in clouds through the open windows; songs were being roared out, loudly and tensely; but the noise did not soar up, it fell dully on the ear, and was lifelessly uniform.

I stood at a street corner and listened. From two cafés the flood of song rolled forth into the night. Everywhere community, everywhere this huddling together, everywhere this unloading of the burden of destiny, this flight into the warm proximity of the herd!

Two men passed me by slowly. I caught a phrase of their conversation.

"Isn't it just like an assembly of youths in a negro village?" said one. "They all do the same things. Even tattooing is in fashion. Look, that's the young Europe."

The voice rang suggestively in my ear. I followed behind the two in the dark street. One of them was a Japanese, small and elegant. I saw his yellow smiling face shine under the lamp.

The other spoke again.

"Well, I don't suppose it's any better with you in Japan. People who do not follow the herd are everywhere rare. There are a few here, too."

Every word went through me. I felt pleasure and dread. I recognized the speaker. It was Demian.

In the windy night I followed him and the Japanese through the dark streets, listening to their conversation and enjoying the ring of Demian's voice. It had the old tone, the old, beautiful sureness and tranquillity, and it had the same power over me. Now everything was right. I had found him.

At the end of a street in the suburbs the Japanese took leave and closed a house door behind him. Demian took the way back. I had remained standing, and awaited him in the middle of the street. With beating heart I saw him approaching erect and walking with an elastic step. He wore a brown raincoat and carried a thin stick, hanging from his arm. He advanced without altering his regular stride until he got right up to me. He took off his hat, displaying his old, bright face with the determined mouth and the peculiar brightness on the broad forehead.

"Demian!" I called.

He stretched out his hand to me.

"So it's you, then, Sinclair? I expected you."

"Did you know I was here?"

"I did not know for certain, but I hoped it might be true. I saw you first this evening. You have been behind us the whole time."

"You recognized me then at once?"

"Of course. You're very much changed to be sure; but you have the sign. We used to call it the mark of Cain, if you recollect. It is our sign. You have always had it; for that reason I became your friend. But now it is clearer."

"I did not know. Or rather I did. I once painted a picture of you, Demian, and was astonished that it was also like me. Was that the sign?"

"That was it. It's fine that you are here now! My mother will be glad as well."

I started.

"Your mother? Is she here? She doesn't know me a bit."

"Oh, she knows of you. She will know, without even my asking her, who you are. You haven't let me hear from you for a long time."

"Oh, I often wanted to write, but nothing came of it. For some time past I have felt I should find you. I was waiting for it every day."

He pushed his arm through mine and we went on. Tranquillity seemed to emanate from him and pass on to me. We were soon chatting together as formerly. We mentioned our schooldays, the confirmation class and that unlucky meeting of ours in the holidays—only no mention was made of the earliest and closest bond between us, of the affair with Frank Kromer.

Unexpectedly we found ourselves in the middle of a singular and ominous conversation. Having recalled Demian's discourse with the Japanese, we spoke of student life in general and from that we had branched off to something else, which seemed to be rather out of the way of the former trend of our talk. Nevertheless, from Demian's manner of introducing the subject, there seemed to be no lack of coherence in our conversation.

He spoke of the spirit of Europe, and of modern tendencies. Everywhere, he said, reigned a desire to come together, to form herds, but nowhere was freedom or love. All this life in common, from the student clubs and choral societies to the state, was an unnatural, forced phenomenon. The community owed its origin to a sense of fear, of embarrassment, to a desire for flight; inwardly it was rotten and old, and approaching a general break-up.

"Community," Demian said, "is a beautiful thing. But what we see blossoming everywhere is by no means that. It will arise anew from the mutual understanding of individuals, and after a time the world will be remodeled. What is now called community is merely a formation of herds. Mankind seeks refuge together because men have fear of one another—the masters combine for their own ends, the workmen for theirs, and the intellectuals for theirs! And why are they afraid? One is only afraid when one is not at one with oneself. They are afraid because they have never had the courage to be themselves. A community of men who are afraid of the unknown in themselves! They all feel that the laws of their life no longer hold good, that they are living according to outworn commandments. Neither their religion nor their morals conform to our needs. For a hundred years and more Europe has simply studied and built factories. They know exactly how many grams of powder it takes to kill a man, but they do not know how to pray to God. They have no idea how to amuse themselves, even for an hour. Look at these students drinking in their tavern! Or take any place of amusement where rich people go! Hopeless! My dear Sinclair, no cheerfulness, no serenity can come of all that. These creatures, who move about so uneasily in crowds, are full of fear and full of wickedness, no one trusts the other. They adhere to ideals which have ceased to exist, and they stone everyone who proposes a new one. I feel that there are troubles ahead of us. They will come, believe me, they will come soon! Of course the world won't be bettered! Whether the workmen kill the manufacturers, or whether the Russians and Germans shoot at one another, it will only be a change of proprietors. But it will not be in vain. It will free the world from the chains of present-day ideals, there will be a clearing away of Stone-Age gods. The world, as it is now, wants to die, it wants to perish, and it will."

"And what will happen to us then?" I asked.

"To us? Oh, perhaps we shall perish as well. They can also murder people in our position. Only we shall not be entirely wiped out. The will of the future will realize itself from what remains of our influence, or with the aid of those of us who survive. The will of humanity will make itself felt, which our Europe has for a long time past tried to drown in its sale yard of scientifically manufactured articles. And then it will be seen that there is nothing in common between the will of humanity and that of our present-day communities, of the states and peoples, of the societies and churches. But what nature wills with man, is written in the individual few, in you and in me. It is found in Jesus, in Nietzsche. For these (the only important currents of thought which naturally can alter their course each day) there will be place when the present-day communities break up together."

It was late when we made a halt before a garden by the river.

"We live here," said Demian. "Come and see us soon! We shall expect you."

I cheerfully wended my long way home through the night, which had become cold. Here and there brawling students were lurching through the town. I had often felt, sometimes with a feeling of privation, sometimes with scorn, the contrast between their curious sort of gaiety and my lonely life. But now, tranquil and strong in a sense of secret power I felt as never before how little that affected me, how far removed was their world from mine. I reminded myself of officials of my native town, worthy old gentlemen, who clung to memories of the semesters they had passed in drinking, as they would to memories of a blissful paradise, and who practised a cult, calling up reminiscences of the vanished "freedom" of their University life with all the seriousness which some poet or other romantic would devote to an account of his childhood. Everywhere the same! Everywhere they sought "liberty" and "happiness" behind them, in the past, for fear of being reminded of their own responsibility, of being warned they were not striking out for themselves, but merely going the way of all the world. Two or three years passed in drinking and jollification, and then they crept under the common shelter and became serious gentlemen in the service of the state. Yes, it was rotten, our whole system was rotten and these student sillinesses were less stupid and not so bad as a hundred others.

However, when I reached my distant dwelling and went to bed, all these thoughts had flown. Everything else was in suspense as I looked forward to the fulfillment of the promise made to me that day. As soon as I wished, in the morning if I liked, I could see Demian's mother. Let the students hold their drinking bouts and tattoo their faces, let the world be rotten and on the brink of ruin—what had that to do with me? I was waiting for one single thing, that my fate might meet me in a new picture.

I woke up late in the morning from a deep sleep. The day broke for me as a solemn festal day, such as I had not experienced since the Christmas celebrations of my boyhood. I was full of a deep unrest, yet entirely without fear. I felt that an important day had broken for me. I saw and felt the world around me changed: it was full of secret portent, expectant and solemn. Even the gently falling autumn rain was beautiful, full of the quiet, glad, serious music of a festal day. For the first time the outer world was in tune with my inner world—then it is a feast-day for the soul, then living is worth while! No house, no shop window, no face in the street disturbed me. Everything was as it had to be, but did not wear the empty features of every day and of the habitual. It was like expectant nature, standing full of awe to meet its fate. Thus, as a little boy, I used to see the world on the morning of a great feast-day, at Christmas or at Easter. I had not known that this world could still be so beautiful. I had been accustomed to living shut up in myself, and to content myself with the idea that my understanding for the outside world had been lost, that the loss of glistening colors was inevitably connected with the loss of childish vision.

So the hour came when I found again that garden in the suburbs, at the gate of which I had taken leave of Max Demian the night before. Concealed behind trees in a grey mist of rain stood a little house, bright and homely, tall flowers stood behind a big glass partition, and behind shining windows were dark room walls with pictures and bookcases. The front door led immediately into a little hall, and a silent old servant, black, with white apron, showed me in and took my raincoat from me.

She left me alone in the hall. I looked about me. I looked round; and immediately I was in the middle of my dream. On the dark wood wall above a door, under glass and in a black frame, hung a picture I knew well, my bird with the golden yellow hawk's crest, forcing its way out of the sphere. Much moved, I remained standing. My heart felt glad and sorry, as if in that moment everything I had done and had experienced came back to me as answer and fulfillment. Like a lightning flash a crowd of pictures passed through my soul: my home, the house of my father, with the old stone crest over the arch of the door, the boy Demian drawing the crest, myself as a boy, fearsome under the evil spell of my enemy Kromer, myself, as a youth, at the table in my little room at school painting the bird of my dream, the soul caught in a web of its own weaving, and everything, everything up to this moment found echo in me again, and was confined, answered, approved.

With misty eyes I stared at my picture and read in the book of my soul. My glance dropped. In the open door under the picture of the bird stood a tall lady in a dark dress. It was she.

I could not utter a word. The beautiful woman smiled at me in a friendly way beneath features like her son's, timeless and without age, full of an animated will. Her look was fulfillment, her greeting meant home-coming. In silence I stretched out my hands to her. She seized both mine with her strong, warm ones.

"You are Sinclair. I knew you at once. I am very glad to see you!"

Her voice was deep and warm, I drank it in like sweet wine. And now I looked up in her tranquil face, into the black eyes of unfathomable depth. I looked at her fresh, ripe mouth, queenly forehead, which bore the sign.

"How glad I am!" I said to her and kissed her hands. "I believe I have been on my way all my life long—but now I have come home."

She smiled in a motherly way.

"One never comes home," she said gently. "But where friendly roads converge, the whole world looks for an hour like home."

She gave expression to what I myself had felt on my way to her. Her voice and her words were like those of her son, and yet quite different. Everything was more mature, warmer, more assured. But just as Max in years past had made on no one the impression of being a mere boy, so his mother did not look like the mother of a grownup son, so young and sweet was the breath of her face and hair, so smooth her golden skin, so blossoming her mouth. More queenly still than in my dream she stood before me. Her presence was love's happiness, her look was fulfillment.

This, then, was the new picture, in which my fate displayed itself, no longer severe, no longer isolating, but mature and full of promise. I took no resolutions, I made no vows. I had attained an end, I had reached a point of vantage on the way, from which the further road displayed itself, broad and lovely, leading on to lands of promise, shaded by treetops of happiness near at hand, cooled by gardens of delight. Come what might, I was happy to know of this woman's existence in the world, to drink in her voice, to sense her presence. Whether she would be to me mother, mistress, goddess—what mattered it as long as she was present! As long as my way lay near to hers!

She indicated my picture of the hawk.

"You have never given Max more pleasure than by sending this bird," she said musingly. "And I was pleased as well. We expected you, and when the picture arrived we knew that you were on the way to us. When you were a little boy, Sinclair, my son came one day from school and said: 'There's a boy who has the sign on his forehead, he must be my friend.' That was you. You have not had an easy time of it, but we had confidence in you. Once in the holidays when you were at home, Max met you again. You were at that time about sixteen years old. Max told me—"

I interrupted: "Oh, that he should have told you that. It was the most miserable time I have had!"

"Yes, Max said to me: 'Now Sinclair has the hardest time before him. He is making an attempt to escape to the community, he has even taken to drinking with the others; but he won't succeed in that. His sign has become dulled, but it shines secretly.' Was not that the case?"

"Oh yes, it was, exactly. Then I found Beatrice, and finally a guide came to me. His name was Pistorius. For the first time it was clear to me why my boyhood was so bound up with Max's, why I could not break away from him. Dear lady—dear mother, at that time I often thought I should have to take my life. Is the way so hard for everyone?"

She let her fingers stray through my hair, as gently as if a light breeze were blowing.

"It is always hard, to be born. You know, it is not without effort that the bird comes out of the egg. Look back and ask yourself: was the way then so hard?—only hard? Was it not beautiful as well? Could you have had one more beautiful, more easy?"

I shook my head.

"It was hard," I said, as if in sleep, "it was hard, until the dream came."

She nodded and looked at me penetratingly.

"Yes, one must find one's dream, then the way is easy. But there is no dream which endures for always. Each sets a new one free, to none should one wish to cleave."

I started. Was that already a warning? Was that already a warding-off? But no matter, I was ready to let myself be led by her, and not enquire after the end.

"I do not know," I said, "how long my dream is to last. I wish it would be forever. My fate received me under the picture of the bird, like a mother, and like a mistress. To it I belong and to no one else."

"As long as the dream is your fate, so long must you remain true to it," she said, in earnest confirmation of my remark.

I was very sad, and I wished ardently to die in this hour of enchantment; I felt the tears—for what an interminably long time had I not wept—rise irresistibly and overmaster me. I turned violently away from her. I stepped to the window, and looked out, my eyes blinded with tears, away over the flower-pots.

I heard her voice behind me; it rang out calmly and yet was so full of tenderness, like a cup filled to the brim with wine.

"Sinclair, what a child you are! Of course your fate loves you. One day it will belong to you entirely, just as you dreamt it, if you remain true to it."

I had composed myself and turned my face to her again. She gave me her hand.

"I have a few friends," she said, smiling, "very few, very close friends, who call me Mother Eve. You may call me so as well, if you like."

She led me to the door, opened it and indicated the garden. "You will find Max out there, I think."

I stood under the tall trees, stunned and stupefied. I knew not whether I was more awake or more dreaming than ever. Softly the rain dripped from the branches. I went slowly through the garden, which stretched far along the river bank. At last I found Demian. He stood in an open summer house. Naked to the waist, he was doing boxing exercises with a little sack of sand hung from a beam.

Astonished, I remained standing there. Demian looked magnificent; his broad chest, the firm manly head, the uplifted arms were strong and sturdy. The movements came from the hips, the shoulders, the joints of the arm, as easily as if they bubbled out of a spring of strength.

"Demian!" I called. "What are you doing there?"

He laughed gaily.

"I am exercising. I have promised to box with the little Jap; the fellow is as agile as a cat, and naturally just as sly. But he won't be able to manage me. I owe him just one little beating."

He drew on shirt and coat.

"You have already seen mother?" he asked.

"Yes, Demian, what a marvellous mother you have! Mother Eve! The name suits her perfectly; she is like the mother of all being."

He gazed for an instant musingly in my face.

"You know her name already? You ought to be proud, young friend. You are the only one to whom she has said it in the first hour's acquaintance."

From this day on I went in and out of the house like a son and a brother, but also like a lover. When I closed the gate behind me, even when I saw the tall trees of the garden emerge in the distance, I was happy. Outside was "reality," outside were streets and houses, human beings and institutions, libraries and lecture rooms—here inside were love and the life of the soul, here was the kingdom of fairy stories and dreams. And yet we lived by no means shut off from the world. In thought and word we often lived in its midst, only on another plane. We were not separated from the majority of creatures by boundaries, but rather by a different sort of vision. Our task was to be, as it were, an island in the world, perhaps an example, in any case to proclaim that it was possible to live a different sort of life. I, who had been isolated for so long, learned to what extent community of feeling is possible between people who have experienced complete loneliness. I no longer desired to be back at the tables of the happy, at the feasts of the merry. I no longer felt envious or homesick when I saw others living in community. And slowly I was initiated into the mystery of those who bore "the sign."

We, who bore the sign, were probably justly considered by the world as peculiar—yes, mad even, and dangerous. For we were awake, or were waking, and our endeavor was to be more and more completely awake, whereas the others strove to be happy, attaching themselves to the herd, the opinions and ideals of which they made their own, taking up the same duties, making their life and happiness depend on common interests. True, there was a certain greatness, a vigorousness, in their endeavor. But whereas, from our point of view, we who bore the sign carried out the will of nature as individuals and as men of the future, the others persisted in a stubbornness which hindered all progress. For them mankind, which they loved just as we did—was something already complete, which must be maintained and protected. For us mankind was a distant future, to which we were all on the way. No one could image this future, neither did its laws stand written in any book.

Besides Mother Eve, Max and myself, there belonged to our circle in a greater or lesser degree of intimacy many seekers of very various sorts. Many of them were going along their own special paths, had set up special aims and adhered to special opinions and duties. Amongst these were astrologers and cabbalists, also an adherent of Count Tolstoy, and all kinds of tender, timid, sensitive people, followers of new sects, men who practised Indian cults, vegetarians and others. With all these we had really nothing of a spiritual nature in common, except the esteem which each accorded the secret life-dream of the other. Some were in closer contact with us, such as those who traced the searchings of mankind after gods and new ideals in the past, and whose studies often reminded me of my friend Pistorius. They brought books with them, translated for us texts from ancient tongues and showed us illustrations of ancient symbols and rites. They taught us to see how all the ideals of mankind up to the present have their origin in dreams of the subconscious soul, dreams in which humanity is, as it were, feeling its way forward into the future, guided by premonitions of the future's potentialities. So we went through the religious history of the ancient world with its thousand gods, to the dawn of Christianity. The confessions of the isolated saints were known to us, and the changes of religion from race to race. And from all the knowledge we thus acquired resulted a criticism of our era and of present-day Europe, of this continent which through enormous exertions had created powerful new weapons for humanity, only to fall finally into a deep spiritual devastation, the effects of which were at last being felt. For it had gained the whole world, only to lose its own soul.

There were with us believers as well, advocates of doctrines of salvation, in the efficacy of which they were very hopeful. There were Buddhists who wished to convert Europe, and disciples of Tolstoy, and of other confessions. We in our narrow circle listened, but accepted none of these doctrines except as symbols. We who bore the sign had no cares as regarded the formation of the future. To us every confession, every doctrine of salvation appeared in advance dead and useless. Our whole duty, our destiny, was, we felt, to attain to self-realization, in order that in us nature might find scope for its full activities, and that the unknown future might find us ready to fill any rôle which should be allotted us.

Whether we expressed our opinion in so many words or not, it was clear to all of us that a break-up of the present-day world was approaching, to be followed by a new birth. Demian said to me on more than one occasion: "What will come is beyond conception. The soul of Europe is an animal which has been chained up for an immeasurably long period. When it is set free, its first movements will not display much amiability. But the way it will take, whether direct or indirect, is not of importance, provided that the soul's true need is realized, this soul which has been deluded and dulled for so long. Then our day will come, then we shall be needed, not as guides or new law-givers—we shall not live to see the new laws—but rather as volunteers, as those who are ready to follow and to stand wherever fate shall call us. Look, all men are ready to perform the incredible, when their ideals are threatened. But no one comes forward when a new ideal, a new, perhaps dangerous and uncanny impulse of spiritual growth declares itself. We shall be of those few who are there, ready to go forward. For that purpose have we been singled out just as Cain was marked with the sign to inspire fear and hate, to drive the men of his time out of a narrow idyllic existence into the broad pastures of a greater destiny. All men whose influence has affected the march of humanity, all such, without differentiation, owe their capabilities and their efficacy to the fact that they were ready to do the bidding of destiny. That applies to Napoleon and Bismarck. The immediate purpose to which they direct their energies does not lie within their choice. If Bismarck had understood the social democrats and had thrown in his lot with them, he would have been a prudent fellow, but he would never have been the instrument of fate. The same applies to Napoleon, to Caesar, to Loyola, to all of them! One must always look at such things from the point of view of biology and evolution! When the changes which took place in the earth's surface transferred to the land animals which lived in water, and vice versa, then those specimens which were ready to fulfill their functions as instruments of fate, brought new and unheard-of things to pass and were able, through new adaptations, to save their kind. Whether these specimens were the same that had previously been conservatives and preservers of the status quo or the eccentrics and revolutionaries, is not known. They were ready to be used by fate, and for that reason were able to help their race through a new stage of evolution. That we do know. For that reason we want to be ready."

Mother Eve was often present when such conversations took place, but she did not join in. For each of us who chose to express his thoughts she was as it were a listener and an echo, full of confidence, full of understanding. It appeared as if our ideas all emanated from her and returned to her again. My happiness consisted in sitting near her, in hearing her voice from time to time, and in participating in that atmosphere of maturity and of the soul, which surrounded her.

She felt immediately when a change was taking place in me, when my soul was troubled, or when a renewal was in progress. It seemed to me as if the dreams I had in my sleep were inspired by her. I often related them to her. She found them quite comprehensible and natural, there were no peculiarities which she could not follow clearly. For a time I had dreams which were like reproductions of the day's conversation. I dreamed that the whole world was in revolt, and that I, alone or with Demian, tensely waited the signal of fate. Fate remained half concealed, but bore somehow or other the traits of Mother Eve—to be chosen or rejected by her, that was fate.

Sometimes she said with a smile: "Your dream is not complete, Sinclair, you have forgotten the best part"—and it sometimes happened that I recalled it then, and I could not understand how I had come to forget any of it.

At times I was discontented and was tormented by desire, I thought I could not bear to see her near me any longer without taking her in my arms. She noticed that immediately. Once, when I had stayed away for several days and had returned distraught, she took me aside and said: "You should not give yourself up to wishes in which you do not believe, I know what you wish. You must give up these desires, or else surrender yourself to them completely. If one day you are able to ask, convinced that your wishes will be fulfilled, then you will find satisfaction. But you wish, and repent again, and are afraid. You must overcome all that. I will tell you a fairy-tale."

And she told me of a youth who was in love with a star. He stood on the sea-shore, stretched out his hands, and prayed to the star. He dreamed of it and all his thoughts were of it. But he knew, or thought he knew, that a star could not be embraced by a man. He held it to be his fate to love a star without hope of fulfillment, and he created from this thought a whole life-poem about renunciation, and mute, faithful suffering which should better him and purify him. But his dreams all went up to the star. Once again he stood at night by the sea-shore, on a high cliff. He gazed at the star, and his love for it flamed up within him. And in a moment of great longing he made a spring, throwing himself into space to meet the star. But at the moment of leaping, the thought flashed through his mind: it is impossible! And so he was dashed to pieces on the rocks below. He did not know how to love. Had he had the strength of soul, at the moment of leaping, to believe in the fulfillment of his wish, he would have flown up and have been united with the star.

"Love must not beg," she said, "nor demand either. Love must have the force to be absolutely certain of itself. Then it is attracted no longer, but attracts. Sinclair, I am attracting your love. As soon as you attract my love, I shall come. I do not want to make a present of myself. I want to be won."

On a later occasion she told me another fairy-story. There was a lover, who loved without hope of success. He withdrew entirely into himself and thought his love would consume him. The world was lost to him, he saw the blue sky and the green wood no longer, he did not hear the murmuring of the stream, or the notes of the harp; all that meant nothing to him, and he became poor and miserable. But his love grew, and he would much rather have died and have made an end of it all than renounce the chance of possessing the beautiful woman whom he loved. Then he suddenly felt that his love had consumed everything else in him, it became powerful and exercised an irresistible attraction, the beautiful woman had to follow, she came and he stood with outstretched arms to draw her to him. But as she stood before him, she was completely transformed, and with a thrill he felt and saw that he had drawn into his embrace the whole world, which he had lost. She stood before him and surrendered herself to him, sky and wood and brook, all was decked out in lovely new colors, all belonged to him, and spoke his tongue. And instead of merely winning a woman, he had taken the whole world to his heart, and each star in the heaven glowed in him, and twinkling, communicated desire to his soul. He had loved, and thereby had found himself. But most people love only to lose themselves thereby.

My whole life seemed to be contained in my love for Mother Eve. But every day she looked different. Many times I felt decidedly that it was not her person for which my whole being was striving, but that she was a symbol of my inward self, and that she wished only to lead me to see more deeply into myself. I often heard words fall from her lips, which sounded like answers to the burning questions asked by my subconscious self. Then again there were moments when in her presence I burnt with desire, and afterwards kissed objects she had touched. And by degrees sensual and unsensual love, reality and symbol merged into one another. Then it happened that I could think of her at home in my room with quiet fervor. I thought I felt her hand in mine and my lips pressed to hers. Or I was at her house, gazing up into her face, talking with her and listening to her voice; and I did not know whether it was really she, or whether it was a dream. I began to foresee how one can have a lasting and immortal love. In reading a book I had acquired new knowledge, and it was the same feeling as a kiss from Mother Eve. She stroked my hair and smiled at me, I sensed the perfume of her warm ripe mouth, and I had the same feeling as if I had been making progress within myself. All that was important and fateful for me seemed to be contained in her. She could transform herself into each of my thoughts, and every one of my thoughts was transformed into her.

I feared that it would be torture to spend the two weeks of the Christmas holidays, separated from Mother Eve, with my parents at home. But it was no torture, it was lovely to be at home and to think of her. When I returned to H—— I remained away from her house another two days, in order to enjoy the security and independence of her actual presence. I also had dreams in which my union with her was accomplished by way of allegory. She was a sea, into which I, a river, flowed. She was a star, and I myself was a star on my way to her. We felt drawn to one another. We met, and remained together always, turning blissfully round one another in close-lying orbits, to the music of the spheres.

I related this dream to her, when I visited her again after the holidays.

"It is a beautiful dream," she said softly. "See that it comes true!"

There came a day in early spring that I shall never forget. I entered the hall. A window stood open and the heavy scent of hyacinths, wafted by a warm breath of air, permeated the room. As no one was to be seen, I went upstairs to Max Demian's study. I knocked softly on the door and entered without waiting for permission, as I was in the habit of doing with him.

The room was dark. The curtains were all drawn. The door to a little room adjoining stood open, where Max had set up a chemical laboratory. From there came the bright, white light of the spring sun, shining through rain clouds. I thought no one was there and pulled back one of the curtains.

There I saw Max Demian, sitting on a stool by a curtained window. His attitude was cramped and he was oddly changed. The thought flashed through me: You have seen him like this once before! His arms were motionless at his side, his hands in his lap; his face inclined slightly forward, with open eyes, was without sight, as if dead. In the eyes there glimmered dully a little reflex of light, as in a piece of glass. The pale face was self-absorbed and without any expression, save that of great rigidity. He looked like a very ancient mask of an animal at the door of a temple. He appeared not to be breathing.

The recollection came to me—thus, exactly thus, had I once seen him, many years ago, when I was still quite a boy. Thus had his eyes stared inwards, thus his hands had been lying motionless, close to one another, a fly had been crawling over his face. And he had then, six years ago perhaps, looked just as old and as ageless, not a wrinkle in his face had changed.

I was frightened, and went softly out of the room and down the stairs. In the hall I met Mother Eve. She was pale and seemed tired: I had not seen her like that before. A shadow came through the window, the bright white sun had suddenly disappeared.

"I went into Max's room," I whispered hastily. "Has anything happened? He is asleep, or absorbed, I don't know what; I once saw him like that before."

"But you didn't wake him?" she asked quickly.

"No. He did not hear me. I came out immediately. Mother Eve, tell me, what is the matter with him?"

She passed her hand over her forehead.

"Don't worry, Sinclair, nothing has happened to him. He has retired into himself. It will not last long."

She got up and went out into the garden, although it had begun to rain. I felt that I must not follow her. So I walked up and down in the hall, inhaling the scent of the hyacinths which dulled my senses, and gazing at my picture of the bird over the door. I felt oppressively the odd shadow which seemed to fill the house that morning. What was it? What had happened?

Mother Eve came back soon. Rain drops hung in her dark hair. She sat down in her easy chair. She was very tired. I went to her, bent down and kissed the raindrops in her hair. Her eyes were bright and soft, but the raindrops tasted like tears.

"Shall I go and see how he is?" I asked in a whisper.

She smiled weakly.

"Don't be a child, Sinclair!" she admonished loudly, as if to relieve her own feelings. "Go now and come back later, I cannot talk to you now."

I went. I walked out of the house and out of the town, towards the mountains. The thin rain was falling obliquely, and clouds were driving at a low altitude under heavy pressure, as if in fear. Down below there was hardly any breeze, but on the heights above a storm seemed to be raging. Several times the sun, pale and bright, broke for an instant through the steely grey of the clouds.

There came a fleecy, yellow cloud driving across the sky. It collided with the grey cloud wall, and in a few seconds the wind formed a picture of the yellow and blue, of a bird of giant size, which tore itself free from the blue mêlée and with wide fluttering wings disappeared in the sky. Then the storm became audible and rain mixed with hail rattled down. A short burst of thunder with an unnatural and terrific sound cracked over the whipped landscape. Immediately after the sun broke through and on the mountains close at hand above brown woods glistened, pale and unreal, the fresh snow.

When I returned after several hours, wet from the rain and wind, Demian himself opened the front door to me.

He took me with him up to his room. A gas flame burned in the laboratory, paper lay about, he appeared to have been working.

"Sit down," he invited, "you must be tired, it was a terrible storm; it's evident, you were overtaken by it. Tea is coming at once."

"Something is the matter today," I began hesitatingly, "it can't only be that bit of a storm."

He looked at me penetratingly.

"Have you seen anything?"

"Yes. I saw a picture clearly in the clouds, for an instant."

"What sort of a picture?"

"It was a bird."

"The hawk? Was it that? The bird of your dream?"

"Yes, it was my hawk. It was yellow and of giant size, it flew up into the blue-black heaven."

Demian took a deep breath. Someone knocked at the door. The aged servant brought in tea.

"Take a cup, Sinclair, do. I don't think it was by chance you saw the bird."

"Chance? Does one see such things by chance?"

"Well, no. It means something. Do you know what?"

"No. I only feel, it means a violent shock, the approach of fate. I think it will affect all of us."

He walked violently up and down.

"The approach of fate!" he exclaimed loudly. "I dreamed the same thing myself last night, and my mother yesterday had a premonition, portending the same thing. I dreamed I was going up a ladder, placed against a tree trunk or a tower. When I reached the top I saw the whole country. It was a wide plain, with towns and villages burning. I cannot yet relate everything, because it isn't all quite clear to me."

"Do you interpret the dream as affecting you?" I asked.

"Me? Naturally. No one dreams of what does not concern him. But it does not concern me alone, you are right. I distinguish tolerably well between the dreams which indicate agitation of my own soul, and the others, the rare ones, which bear on the fate of all humanity. I have seldom had such dreams, and never one of which I can say that it was a prophecy, and that it has been fulfilled. The interpretations are too uncertain. But this I know for a certainty, I have dreamed of something which does not concern me alone. For the dream belongs to others, former ones I have had; this is the continuation. These are the dreams, Sinclair, in which I had the premonitions which I have already mentioned to you. We know that the world is absolutely rotten, but that is no reason to prophesy its ruin, or to make a prophecy of a like nature. But for several years past I have had dreams, from which I conclude, or feel, or what you will, which, then, give me the feeling that the break-up of an old world is drawing near. At first they were simply faint presentiments, but since they have become more and more significant. Even now I know nothing more than that something big and terrible is approaching, which will concern me. Sinclair, we shall go through the experiences of which we have so often talked. The world is about to renew itself. It smacks of death. Nothing new comes without death. It is more terrible than I had thought."

Frightened, I looked at him fixedly.

"Can't you tell me the rest of your dream?" I begged timidly.

He shook his head.

"No."

The door opened and Mother Eve entered.

"There you are, sitting together! Children, I hope you aren't sad?"

She looked fresh, her fatigue had quite vanished. Demian smiled at her, she came to us as a mother comes to frightened children.

"We aren't sad, mother. We were simply trying to solve the riddle of these new signs. But that is of no importance; what is to come, will be here all of a sudden, and then we shall learn what we need to know."

But I did not feel happy. When I said good-bye and went down alone through the hall, I felt that the hyacinths were faded and withered, reminding me of corpses. A shadow had fallen over us.

CHAPTER 8

BEGINNING OF THE END

It had been decided that I should remain in H—— for the summer semester. Instead of staying in the house, we were almost always in the garden by the river. The Japanese, who by the way had been thoroughly beaten in the boxing match, was away, and the disciple of Tolstoy was also missing. Demian had procured a horse, and went for long rides every day. I was often alone with his mother.

Sometimes I wondered greatly at the peaceableness of my life. I had been so long accustomed to being alone, to practise renunciation, to fight toilfully my own battles, that these months in H—— seemed to me like a time passed on a dream island, where I might live tranquilly in beautiful, enchanted surroundings. I felt that this was a foretaste of that new, higher community, on which we meditated. And now and then I was seized by a deep feeling of sadness, for I knew that this happiness could not last. I was not destined to breathe in the fulness of peace and comfort, I needed torment to spur me on. I felt that one day I should wake up from these dreams of beautiful love-pictures to find myself standing once more alone, in the cold world of others, where for me there would be only loneliness and fighting, no peace, no community of spirit.

Then I yielded myself to the charms of Mother Eve's presence. My feeling for her was now doubly tender. I was glad that my fate bore still these beautiful, tranquil features.

The summer weeks passed quickly and easily. Already the semester was drawing to a close. Leave-taking was near, I dared not think of it, and did not, but clung to the beautiful days like a butterfly to a honeyed flower. That was my period of happiness, the first fulfillment of my life's wishes, and my reception into the league—what was to come next? I would again have to fight my battles, be consumed by longing, have dreams, be alone.

At this time the feeling, the foretaste of separation, came over me so strongly that my love for Mother Eve blazed up suddenly, causing me pain. My God! How soon would the time come to say good-bye, and I should see her no more, no more hear her firm step in the house, should find no more her flowers on my table! And what had I attained? I had dreamed and had lulled myself in comfort, instead of winning her, instead of fighting for her and drawing her to me for always! All that she had said to me about genuine love crossed my mind, hundreds of fine, suggestive words, a hundred tender invitations, promises perhaps—and what had I made of them? Nothing! Nothing!

I took up a position in the middle of my room, collected my whole conscious self together and thought of Eve. I wished to concentrate the forces of my soul, in order to let her feel my love, in order to draw her to me. She was to come, longing for my embrace. My kisses were to suck insatiably the ripe fruit of her lips.

I stood tense, until fingers and feet became stiff with cold. I felt force was going out of me. For a few seconds something seemed to take shape with me, something bright and cool; I had for a moment the sensation as if I carried a crystal in my heart, and I knew that was myself. A cold chill pierced to my heart.

As I woke out of my fearful state of tension I felt something was approaching. I was exhausted to the point of death, but I was prepared to see Eve step into the room, burning with passion, ravished.

The sound of horse's hoofs clattering down the long street rang nearer and nearer, then suddenly ceased. I sprang to the window. Below Demian was dismounting.

"What is the matter, Demian? Nothing can have happened to your mother?"

He did not listen to my words. He was very pale, and perspiration ran down both sides of his forehead over his cheeks. His horse was flecked with foam. He tied the reins to the garden fence, then he took my arm and walked with me down the street.

"Have you already heard the news?" I had heard nothing.

Demian pressed my arm and turned his face to me, with a dark, compassionate, singular look.

"Yes, old man, now we're in for it. You know of the strained relations with Russia—"

"What? Is it war? I had never believed it."

He spoke in an undertone, although no one was near.

"It is not yet declared. But it's war. Rely on it. I haven't worried you lately, but I have seen three new omens since. It will be no foundering of the world, no earthquake, no revolution. It's war. You will see how that strikes everybody. It will be a joy to people; everyone already rejoices that hostilities are about to commence. So insipid has life become for them. But you will see now, Sinclair, that is only the beginning. This will perhaps be a great war, a very great war. The new dispensation commences and for those who adhere to the old, the new will be terrible. What will you do?"

I was perplexed, everything sounded so strange and improbable.

"I don't know—and you?"

He shrugged his shoulders.

"As soon as mobilization orders are out, I join up. I am a lieutenant."

"You? I had no idea of that."

"Yes. It was one of my adaptations. You know, I have never wanted to appear out of the ordinary, and have rather done too much, in order to be correct, to do the right thing. In eight days, I think, I shall be already in the field."

"For God's sake!"

"Look here, old fellow, you mustn't take things so sentimentally. At bottom it certainly won't give me pleasure to order machine gunfire to be turned on living creatures, but that is a secondary matter. Now each one of us will be seized by the great wheel of fate. You as well. You will certainly be called up."

"And your mother, Demian?"

Then for the first time I recollected what I was doing a quarter of an hour before. How the world had changed! I had summoned together all my force in order to conjure up the sweetest picture, and now fate had suddenly put on a new, horrible mask.

"My mother? We need have no cares for her safety. She is safe, safer than anyone else in the world today. You love her so very much?"

"You knew it, Demian?" He laughed brightly and without any embarrassment.

"You child! Naturally I knew it. No one has yet called my mother Mother Eve without loving her. By the way, how was that? You have called to either her or myself today, haven't you?"

"Yes, I called—I called to Mother Eve."

"She felt it. She suddenly sent me away, I was to come to you. I had just told her the news about Russia."

We turned back, scarcely speaking, he untied his horse and mounted.

I first realized in my room how exhausted I was by Demian's message, and even more so by my previous spiritual exertions. But Mother Eve had heard me! My thoughts had reached her. She would have come herself, if—how wonderful all this was, and how beautiful! Now it was to be war. Now what we had so often spoken of was about to happen. And Demian had known so much in advance. How strange that the world's stream would no longer flow somewhere or other by us—that now it was suddenly flowing through us, that fate and adventure called us, and that now, or soon, the moment would come when the world would need us, when it would be transformed. Demian was right, one should not be sentimental over it. Only it was strange that I was now to experience that lonely thing, "fate," with so many, with the whole world. Good then!

I was ready. In the evening, when I went through the town, every corner was alive with bustle and excitement. Everywhere the word "war"!

I went to Mother Eve's house. We had supper in the summer house. I was the only guest. No one spoke a word about the war. But later, shortly before

I left, Mother Eve said: "Dear Sinclair, you called me today. You know why I did not come myself. But don't forget, you know the call now and if ever you need someone who bears the sign, call me again."

She rose and went out through the gloaming into the garden. Tall and queenly, invested with mystery, she stepped between the trees, the foliage ceased its whispering at her approach, and over her head glimmered tenderly the many stars.

* * * *

I am coming to the end. Events marched quickly. War was declared. Demian, who looked strange in uniform, with a silver-grey cloak, went away. I brought his mother home. Soon after I also said good-bye to her. She kissed me on the lips and held me a moment on her breast, and her large eyes burned steadily close to mine.

And all men were like brothers. They had in mind their country and their honor. But it was fate, they peeped for a moment into the unveiled face. Young men came out of barracks, stepped into trains, and on many a face I saw a sign—not ours—a beautiful and dignified sign, signifying love and death. I as well was embraced by people I had never seen before. I understood and responded gladly. It was an atmosphere of intoxication in which they moved, not that of a fated will. But the intoxication was sacred, it was due to the fact that they had all looked into the rousing eyes of destiny.

It was already nearly winter when I went to the front.

At first, in spite of the sensation of the bombardment, I was disappointed with everything. Formerly I had often wondered why people so seldom were able to live for an ideal. Now I saw that many, yes, all men, are capable of dying for an ideal, provided that such an ideal is not personal, not chosen of their own free will. For them it had to be an ideal accepted by and common to a great number.

But with time I saw that I had underestimated men. Although service and a common danger renders them uniform, I saw many, living and dying, approach fate magnificently. Not only in an attack, but the whole time, many, very many of them had a fixed, far-away look, rather like that of a person possessed, a look which indicates entire ignorance of the end pursued, and a complete surrender of self to the unknown. No matter what they might believe and think they were ready, they were there in case of need, out of them would the future be formed. And, however strongly the world's attention appeared to be focused on war and heroic deeds, on honor and other old ideals, however distantly and unnaturally sang the voices of humanity—all this was merely the surface, just as the question with regard to the foreign and political aims of the war was superficial. Deep down, below the surface of human affairs, something was in process of forming. Something which might be a new order of humanity. For I could see many—many such died at my side—to whom the understanding was brought home that hate and rage, murder and destruction had no connection with the real object of the war. No, the object, just as the aims in view, was purely a matter of chance. Their deepest and most primitive feelings, even their wildest instincts were not actually directed against the enemy, their murderous and bloody work was an expression of their own inner being, of their cleft soul, which wished to rave and kill, to destroy and die, in order to be able to be born anew. A giant bird was fighting its way out of the egg, and the egg was the world, and the world had to go to ruin.

One night in early spring I was doing sentry duty in front of a farm we had occupied. The wind was blowing in fitful gusts, shrieking and moaning according to the vagaries of its mood; over the high Flanders sky rode an army of clouds, somewhere or other behind was a suspicion of moon. I had been restless throughout the whole of that day, troubled by cares which I could not precisely define. Now, at my dark post, I thought with fervor of the picture of my life up to that time, of Mother Eve, of Demian. I stood leaning against a poplar, staring into the agitated sky, the mysterious quivering brightness of which soon resolved itself into a series of pictures. I felt by the odd slowness of my pulse, by the insensibility of my skin to wind and rain, by the lively wakefulness of my inner being, that a guide was near me.

In the clouds a large city could be seen, out of which millions of men were streaming, spreading in swarms over the broad countryside. In their very midst there appeared the mighty figure of a god, as big as a mountain, with glittering stars in its hair, and with the features of Mother Eve. Into it disappeared the processions of men, as into a gigantic cave, and were lost to view. The goddess shrank down on the ground, the sign on her forehead glittered brightly. She seemed to be under the influence of a dream. She closed her eyes and her large features were twisted in pain. Suddenly she cried out, and out of her forehead sprang stars, which hurried in lovely arcs and half-circles over the black sky.

One of the stars rushed noisily through the air to meet me, as if seeking me out. With a crash it burst into a thousand sparks, lifting me off my feet and hurling me on to the ground. The world broke up thunderously about me.

They found me close to the poplar, covered with earth and wounded in several places.

I lay in a cellar, guns growled and rumbled overhead, I lay in a cart, and was jolted over empty fields. For the most part I was either asleep or unconscious. But the more deeply I slept, the more strongly I felt that I was being drawn, that I followed at the will of a force over which I was not master.

I lay on straw in a stable, it was dark, someone trod on my hand. But my inner self willed to go further, the mysterious force drew me on. Again I lay in a cart, and later on a stretcher. Even more strongly I felt in me the command to go forward, I was conscious only of the pressure, the force which seemed to be controlling my journeying thus from place to place.

At last I was there. It was night. I was fully conscious and I felt strongly the secret attraction and power which had brought me to that place. Now I was lying in a room, on a bed made up on the floor. I felt I had arrived at the place to which I had been called. I glanced around, close to my mattress was another, on which someone was lying, someone who bent over and looked at me. It was Max Demian.

I could not speak, and he either could not or would not. He only looked at me. A lamp which hung over him on the wall cast a light on his face. He smiled at me.

For what seemed an immeasurably long time he gazed unwaveringly into my eyes. Slowly he inclined his face towards me, until we almost touched.

"Sinclair!" he said in a whisper.

I signaled to him with my eyes that I understood him.

He smiled again, almost as if in compassion.

"Little one!" he said, smiling.

His mouth lay now quite close to mine. Softly he continued to speak.

"Can you still remember Frank Kromer?" he asked.

I winked at him, and could even manage to smile.

"Sinclair, old man, listen: I shall have to go away. Perhaps you will need me once again, on account of Kromer, or something. When you call me, I shall not come riding on a horse, or in a train. You must hearken to the voice inside you, then you will notice it is I, that I am in you. Do you understand? And one other thing: Mother Eve said that if ever you were ill I was to give you a kiss from her, which she gave me.... Close your eyes, Sinclair!"

I obediently closed my eyes. I felt a light kiss on my lips, on which there was a trace of blood, which never seemed to stop flowing. And then I fell asleep.

In the morning I was awakened to have my wounds dressed. When at last I was properly awake, I turned quickly to the mattress by my side. A stranger lay upon it, a man on whom I had never before set eyes.

The bandaging hurt me. All that has happened to me since hurt me. But my soul is like a mysterious, locked house. And when I find the key and step right down into myself, to where the pictures painted by my destiny seem reflected on the dark mirror of my soul, then I need only stoop towards the black mirror and see my own picture, which now completely resembles Him, my guide and friend.

SIDDHARTHA

An Indian Tale

FIRST PART

To Romain Rolland, my dear friend.

THE SON OF THE BRAHMAN

In the shade of the house, in the sunshine of the riverbank near the boats, in the shade of the Sal-wood forest, in the shade of the fig tree is where Siddhartha grew up, the handsome son of the Brahman, the young falcon, together with his friend Govinda, son of a Brahman. The sun tanned his light shoulders by the banks of the river when bathing, performing the sacred ablutions, the sacred offerings. In the mango grove, shade poured into his black eyes, when playing as a boy, when his mother sang, when the sacred offerings were made, when his father, the scholar, taught him, when the wise men talked. For a long time, Siddhartha had been partaking in the discussions of the wise men, practising debate with Govinda, practising with Govinda the art of reflection, the service of meditation. He already knew how to speak the Om silently, the word of words, to speak it silently into himself while inhaling, to speak it silently out of himself while exhaling, with all the concentration of his soul, the forehead surrounded by the glow of the clear-thinking spirit. He already knew to feel Atman in the depths of his being, indestructible, one with the universe.

Joy leapt in his father's heart for his son who was quick to learn, thirsty for knowledge; he saw him growing up to become great wise man and priest, a prince among the Brahmans.

Bliss leapt in his mother's breast when she saw him, when she saw him walking, when she saw him sit down and get up, Siddhartha, strong, handsome, he who was walking on slender legs, greeting her with perfect respect.

Love touched the hearts of the Brahmans' young daughters when Siddhartha walked through the lanes of the town with the luminous forehead, with the eye of a king, with his slim hips.

But more than all the others he was loved by Govinda, his friend, the son of a Brahman. He loved Siddhartha's eye and sweet voice, he loved his walk and the perfect decency of his movements, he loved everything Siddhartha did and said and what he loved most was his spirit, his transcendent, fiery thoughts, his ardent will, his high calling. Govinda knew: he would not become a common Brahman, not a lazy official in charge of offerings; not a greedy merchant with magic spells; not a vain, vacuous speaker; not a mean, deceitful priest; and also not a decent, stupid sheep in the herd of the many. No, and he, Govinda, as well did not want to become one of those, not one of those tens of thousands of Brahmans. He wanted to follow Siddhartha, the beloved, the splendid. And in days to come, when Siddhartha would become a god, when he would join the glorious, then Govinda wanted to follow him as his friend, his companion, his servant, his spear-carrier, his shadow.

Siddhartha was thus loved by everyone. He was a source of joy for everybody, he was a delight for them all.

But he, Siddhartha, was not a source of joy for himself, he found no delight in himself. Walking the rosy paths of the fig tree garden, sitting in the bluish shade of the grove of contemplation, washing his limbs daily in the bath of repentance, sacrificing in the dim shade of the mango forest, his gestures of perfect decency, everyone's love and joy, he still lacked all joy in his heart. Dreams and restless thoughts came into his mind, flowing from the water of the river, sparkling from the stars of the night, melting from the beams of the sun, dreams came to him and a restlessness of the soul, fuming from the sacrifices, breathing forth from the verses of the Rig-Veda, being infused into him, drop by drop, from the teachings of the old Brahmans.

Siddhartha had started to nurse discontent in himself, he had started to feel that the love of his father and the love of his mother, and also the love of his friend, Govinda, would not bring him joy forever and ever, would not nurse him, feed him, satisfy him. He had started to suspect that his venerable father and his other teachers, that the wise Brahmans had already revealed to him the most and best of their wisdom, that they had already filled his expecting vessel with their richness, and the vessel was not full, the spirit was not content, the soul was not calm, the heart was not satisfied. The ablutions were good, but they were water, they did not wash off the sin, they did not heal the spirit's thirst, they did not relieve the fear in his heart. The sacrifices and the invocation of the gods were excellent—but was that all? Did the sacrifices give a happy fortune? And what about the gods? Was it really Prajapati who had created the world? Was it not the Atman, He, the only one, the singular one? Were the gods not creations, created like me and you, subject to time, mortal? Was it therefore good, was it right, was it meaning-ful and the highest occupation to make offerings to the gods? For whom else were offerings to be made, who else was to be worshipped but Him, the only one, the Atman? And where was Atman to be found, where did He reside, where did his eternal heart beat, where else but in one's own self, in its in-nermost part, in its indestructible part, which everyone had in himself? But where, where was this self, this innermost part, this ultimate part? It was not flesh and bone, it was neither thought nor consciousness, thus the wisest ones taught. So, where, where was it? To reach this place, the self, myself, the At-man, there was another way, which was worthwhile looking for? Alas, and nobody showed this way, nobody knew it, not the father, and not the teach-ers and wise men, not the holy sacrificial songs! They knew everything, the Brahmans and their holy books, they knew everything, they had taken care of everything and of more than everything, the creation of the world, the origin of speech, of food, of inhaling, of exhaling, the arrangement of the senses, the acts of the gods, they knew infinitely much—but was it valuable to know all of this, not knowing that one and only thing, the most important thing, the solely important thing?

Surely, many verses of the holy books, particularly in the Upanishades of Samaveda, spoke of this innermost and ultimate thing, wonderful verses. "Your soul is the whole world" was written there, and it was written that man in his sleep, in his deep sleep, would meet with his innermost part and would reside in the Atman. Marvellous wisdom was in these verses, all knowledge of the wisest ones had been collected here in magic words, pure as hon-ey collected by bees. No, not to be looked down upon was the tremendous amount of enlightenment which lay here collected and preserved by innu-merable generations of wise Brahmans. —But where were the Brahmans, where the priests, where the wise men or penitents, who had succeeded in not just knowing this deepest of all knowledge but also to live it? Where was the knowledgeable one who wove his spell to bring his familiarity with the Atman out of the sleep into the state of being awake, into the life, into every step of the way, into word and deed? Siddhartha knew many venerable Brah-mans, chiefly his father, the pure one, the scholar, the most venerable one. His father was to be admired, quiet and noble were his manners, pure his life, wise his words, delicate and noble thoughts lived behind its brow—but even he, who knew so much, did he live in blissfulness, did he have peace, was he not also just a searching man, a thirsty man? Did he not, again and again, have to drink from holy sources, as a thirsty man, from the offerings, from the books, from the disputes of the Brahmans? Why did he, the irreproach-able one, have to wash off sins every day, strive for a cleansing every day, over and over every day? Was not Atman in him, did not the pristine source spring from his heart? It had to be found, the pristine source in one's own self, it had to be possessed! Everything else was searching, was a detour, was getting lost.

Thus were Siddhartha's thoughts, this was his thirst, this was his suffering.

Often he spoke to himself from a Chandogya-Upanishad the words: "Truly, the name of the Brahman is satyam—verily, he who knows such a thing, will enter the heavenly world every day." Often, it seemed near, the heavenly world, but never he had reached it completely, never he had quenched the ultimate thirst. And among all the wise and wisest men, he knew and whose instructions he had received, among all of them there was no one, who had reached it completely, the heavenly world, who had quenched it completely, the eternal thirst.

"Govinda," Siddhartha spoke to his friend, "Govinda, my dear, come with me under the Banyan tree, let's practise meditation."

They went to the Banyan tree, they sat down, Siddhartha right here, Govinda twenty paces away. While putting himself down, ready to speak the Om, Siddhartha repeated murmuring the verse:

Om is the bow, the arrow is soul, The Brahman is the arrow's target, That one should incessantly hit.

After the usual time of the exercise in meditation had passed, Govinda rose. The evening had come, it was time to perform the evening's ablution. He called Siddhartha's name. Siddhartha did not answer. Siddhartha sat there lost in thought, his eyes were rigidly focused towards a very distant target, the tip of his tongue was protruding a little between the teeth, he seemed not to breathe. Thus sat he, wrapped up in contemplation, thinking Om, his soul sent after the Brahman as an arrow.

Once, Samanas had travelled through Siddhartha's town, ascetics on a pilgrimage, three skinny, withered men, neither old nor young, with dusty and bloody shoulders, almost naked, scorched by the sun, surrounded by loneliness, strangers and enemies to the world, strangers and lank jackals in the realm of humans. Behind them blew a hot scent of quiet passion, of destructive service, of merciless self-denial.

In the evening, after the hour of contemplation, Siddhartha spoke to Govinda: "Early tomorrow morning, my friend, Siddhartha will go to the Samanas. He will become a Samana."

Govinda turned pale, when he heard these words and read the decision in the motionless face of his friend, unstoppable like the arrow shot from the bow. Soon and with the first glance, Govinda realized: Now it is beginning, now Siddhartha is taking his own way, now his fate is beginning to sprout, and with his, my own. And he turned pale like a dry banana-skin.

"O Siddhartha," he exclaimed, "will your father permit you to do that?"

Siddhartha looked over as if he was just waking up. Arrow-fast he read in Govinda's soul, read the fear, read the submission.

"O Govinda," he spoke quietly, "let's not waste words. Tomorrow, at daybreak I will begin the life of the Samanas. Speak no more of it."

Siddhartha entered the chamber, where his father was sitting on a mat of bast, and stepped behind his father and remained standing there, until his father felt that someone was standing behind him. Quoth the Brahman: "Is that you, Siddhartha? Then say what you came to say."

Quoth Siddhartha: "With your permission, my father. I came to tell you that it is my longing to leave your house tomorrow and go to the ascetics. My desire is to become a Samana. May my father not oppose this."

The Brahman fell silent, and remained silent for so long that the stars in the small window wandered and changed their relative positions, 'ere the silence was broken. Silent and motionless stood the son with his arms folded, silent and motionless sat the father on the mat, and the stars traced their paths in the sky. Then spoke the father: "Not proper it is for a Brahman to speak harsh and angry words. But indignation is in my heart. I wish not to hear this request for a second time from your mouth."

Slowly, the Brahman rose; Siddhartha stood silently, his arms folded.

"What are you waiting for?" asked the father.

Quoth Siddhartha: "You know what."

Indignant, the father left the chamber; indignant, he went to his bed and lay down.

After an hour, since no sleep had come over his eyes, the Brahman stood up, paced to and fro, and left the house. Through the small window of the chamber he looked back inside, and there he saw Siddhartha standing, his arms folded, not moving from his spot. Pale shimmered his bright robe. With anxiety in his heart, the father returned to his bed.

After another hour, since no sleep had come over his eyes, the Brahman stood up again, paced to and fro, walked out of the house and saw that the moon had risen. Through the window of the chamber he looked back inside; there stood Siddhartha, not moving from his spot, his arms folded, moonlight reflecting from his bare shins. With worry in his heart, the father went back to bed.

And he came back after an hour, he came back after two hours, looked through the small window, saw Siddhartha standing, in the moon light, by the light of the stars, in the darkness. And he came back hour after hour, silently, he looked into the chamber, saw him standing in the same place, filled his heart with anger, filled his heart with unrest, filled his heart with anguish, filled it with sadness.

And in the night's last hour, before the day began, he returned, stepped into the room, saw the young man standing there, who seemed tall and like a stranger to him.

"Siddhartha," he spoke, "what are you waiting for?"

"You know what."

"Will you always stand that way and wait, until it'll becomes morning, noon, and evening?"

"I will stand and wait."

"You will become tired, Siddhartha."

"I will become tired."

"You will fall asleep, Siddhartha."

"I will not fall asleep."

"You will die, Siddhartha."

"I will die."

"And would you rather die, than obey your father?"

"Siddhartha has always obeyed his father."

"So will you abandon your plan?"

"Siddhartha will do what his father will tell him to do."

The first light of day shone into the room. The Brahman saw that Siddhartha was trembling softly in his knees. In Siddhartha's face he saw no trembling, his eyes were fixed on a distant spot. Then his father realized that even now Siddhartha no longer dwelt with him in his home, that he had already left him.

The Father touched Siddhartha's shoulder.

"You will," he spoke, "go into the forest and be a Samana. When you'll have found blissfulness in the forest, then come back and teach me to be blissful. If you'll find disappointment, then return and let us once again make offerings to the gods together. Go now and kiss your mother, tell her where you are going to. But for me it is time to go to the river and to perform the first ablution."

He took his hand from the shoulder of his son and went outside. Siddhartha wavered to the side, as he tried to walk. He put his limbs back under control, bowed to his father, and went to his mother to do as his father had said.

As he slowly left on stiff legs in the first light of day the still quiet town, a shadow rose near the last hut, who had crouched there, and joined the pilgrim—Govinda.

"You have come," said Siddhartha and smiled.

"I have come," said Govinda.

WITH THE SAMANAS

In the evening of this day they caught up with the ascetics, the skinny Samanas, and offered them their companionship and—obedience. They were accepted.

Siddhartha gave his garments to a poor Brahman in the street. He wore nothing more than the loincloth and the earth-coloured, unsown cloak. He ate only once a day, and never something cooked. He fasted for fifteen days. He fasted for twenty-eight days. The flesh waned from his thighs and cheeks. Feverish dreams flickered from his enlarged eyes, long nails grew slowly on his parched fingers and a dry, shaggy beard grew on his chin. His glance turned to ice when he encountered women; his mouth twitched with contempt, when he walked through a city of nicely dressed people. He saw merchants trading, princes hunting, mourners wailing for their dead, whores offering themselves, physicians trying to help the sick, priests determining the most suitable day for seeding, lovers loving, mothers nursing their children—and all of this was not worthy of one look from his eye, it all lied, it all stank, it all stank of lies, it all pretended to be meaningful and joyful and beautiful, and it all was just concealed putrefaction. The world tasted bitter. Life was torture.

A goal stood before Siddhartha, a single goal: to become empty, empty of thirst, empty of wishing, empty of dreams, empty of joy and sorrow. Dead to himself, not to be a self any more, to find tranquility with an emptied heart, to be open to miracles in unselfish thoughts, that was his goal. Once all of my self was overcome and had died, once every desire and every urge was silent in the heart, then the ultimate part of me had to awake, the innermost of my being, which is no longer my self, the great secret.

Silently, Siddhartha exposed himself to burning rays of the sun directly above, glowing with pain, glowing with thirst, and stood there, until he neither felt any pain nor thirst any more. Silently, he stood there in the rainy season, from his hair the water was dripping over freezing shoulders, over freezing hips and legs, and the penitent stood there, until he could not feel the cold in his shoulders and legs any more, until they were silent, until they were quiet. Silently, he cowered in the thorny bushes, blood dripped from the burning skin, from festering wounds dripped pus, and Siddhartha stayed rigidly, stayed motionless, until no blood flowed any more, until nothing stung any more, until nothing burned any more.

Siddhartha sat upright and learned to breathe sparingly, learned to get along with only few breathes, learned to stop breathing. He learned, beginning with the breath, to calm the beat of his heart, learned to reduce the beats of his heart, until they were only a few and almost none.

Instructed by the oldest of the Samanas, Siddhartha practised self-denial, practised meditation, according to a new Samana rules. A heron flew over the bamboo forest—and Siddhartha accepted the heron into his soul, flew over forest and mountains, was a heron, ate fish, felt the pangs of a heron's hunger, spoke the heron's croak, died a heron's death. A dead jackal was lying on the sandy bank, and Siddhartha's soul slipped inside the body, was the dead jackal, lay on the banks, got bloated, stank, decayed, was dismembered by hyaenas, was skinned by vultures, turned into a skeleton, turned to dust, was blown across the fields. And Siddhartha's soul returned, had died, had decayed, was scattered as dust, had tasted the gloomy intoxication of the cycle, awaited in new thirst like a hunter in the gap, where he could escape from the cycle, where the end of the causes, where an eternity without suffering began. He killed his senses, he killed his memory, he slipped out of his self into thousands of other forms, was an animal, was carrion, was stone, was wood, was water, and awoke every time to find his old self again, sun shone or moon, was his self again, turned round in the cycle, felt thirst, overcame the thirst, felt new thirst.

Siddhartha learned a lot when he was with the Samanas, many ways leading away from the self he learned to go. He went the way of self-denial by means of pain, through voluntarily suffering and overcoming pain, hunger, thirst, tiredness. He went the way of self-denial by means of meditation, through imagining the mind to be void of all conceptions. These and other ways he learned to go, a thousand times he left his self, for hours and days he remained in the non-self. But though the ways led away from the self, their end nevertheless always led back to the self. Though Siddhartha fled from the self a thousand times, stayed in nothingness, stayed in the animal, in the stone, the return was inevitable, inescapable was the hour, when he found himself back in the sunshine or in the moonlight, in the shade or in the rain, and was once again his self and Siddhartha, and again felt the agony of the cycle which had been forced upon him.

By his side lived Govinda, his shadow, walked the same paths, undertook the same efforts. They rarely spoke to one another, than the service and the exercises required. Occasionally the two of them went through the villages, to beg for food for themselves and their teachers.

"How do you think, Govinda," Siddhartha spoke one day while begging this way, "how do you think did we progress? Did we reach any goals?"

Govinda answered: "We have learned, and we'll continue learning. You'll be a great Samana, Siddhartha. Quickly, you've learned every exercise, often the old Samanas have admired you. One day, you'll be a holy man, oh Siddhartha."

Quoth Siddhartha: "I can't help but feel that it is not like this, my friend. What I've learned, being among the Samanas, up to this day, this, oh Govinda, I could have learned more quickly and by simpler means. In every tavern of that part of a town where the whorehouses are, my friend, among carters and gamblers I could have learned it."

Quoth Govinda: "Siddhartha is putting me on. How could you have learned meditation, holding your breath, insensitivity against hunger and pain there among these wretched people?"

And Siddhartha said quietly, as if he was talking to himself: "What is meditation? What is leaving one's body? What is fasting? What is holding one's breath? It is fleeing from the self, it is a short escape of the agony of being a self, it is a short numbing of the senses against the pain and the point-lessness of life. The same escape, the same short numbing is what the driver of an ox-cart finds in the inn, drinking a few bowls of rice-wine or fermented coconut-milk. Then he won't feel his self any more, then he won't feel the pains of life any more, then he finds a short numbing of the senses. When he falls asleep over his bowl of rice-wine, he'll find the same what Siddhartha and Govinda find when they escape their bodies through long exercises, stay-ing in the non-self. This is how it is, oh Govinda."

Quoth Govinda: "You say so, oh friend, and yet you know that Siddhar-tha is no driver of an ox-cart and a Samana is no drunkard. It's true that a drinker numbs his senses, it's true that he briefly escapes and rests, but he'll return from the delusion, finds everything to be unchanged, has not become wiser, has gathered no enlightenment—has not risen several steps."

And Siddhartha spoke with a smile: "I do not know, I've never been a drunkard. But that I, Siddhartha, find only a short numbing of the senses in my exercises and meditations and that I am just as far removed from wisdom, from salvation, as a child in the mother's womb, this I know, oh Govinda, this I know."

And once again, another time, when Siddhartha left the forest together with Govinda, to beg for some food in the village for their brothers and teachers, Siddhartha began to speak and said: "What now, oh Govinda, might we be on the right path? Might we get closer to enlightenment? Might we get closer to salvation? Or do we perhaps live in a circle—we, who have thought we were escaping the cycle?"

Quoth Govinda: "We have learned a lot, Siddhartha, there is still much to learn. We are not going around in circles, we are moving up, the circle is a spiral, we have already ascended many a level."

Siddhartha answered: "How old, would you think, is our oldest Samana, our venerable teacher?"

Quoth Govinda: "Our oldest one might be about sixty years of age."

And Siddhartha: "He has lived for sixty years and has not reached the nirvana. He'll turn seventy and eighty, and you and me, we will grow just as old and will do our exercises, and will fast, and will meditate. But we will not reach the nirvana, he won't and we won't. Oh Govinda, I believe out of all the Samanas out there, perhaps not a single one, not a single one, will reach the nirvana. We find comfort, we find numbness, we learn feats, to deceive others. But the most important thing, the path of paths, we will not find."

"If you only," spoke Govinda, "wouldn't speak such terrible words, Siddhartha! How could it be that among so many learned men, among so many Brahmans, among so many austere and venerable Samanas, among so many who are searching, so many who are eagerly trying, so many holy men, no one will find the path of paths?"

But Siddhartha said in a voice which contained just as much sadness as mockery, with a quiet, a slightly sad, a slightly mocking voice: "Soon, Govinda, your friend will leave the path of the Samanas, he has walked along your side for so long. I'm suffering of thirst, oh Govinda, and on this long path of a Samana, my thirst has remained as strong as ever. I always thirsted for knowledge, I have always been full of questions. I have asked the Brahmans, year after year, and I have asked the holy Vedas, year after year, and I have asked the devote Samanas, year after year. Perhaps, oh Govinda, it had been just as well, had been just as smart and just as profitable, if I had asked the hornbill-bird or the chimpanzee. It took me a long time and am not finished learning this yet, oh Govinda: that there is nothing to be learned! There is indeed no such thing, so I believe, as what we refer to as 'learning'. There is, oh my friend, just one knowledge, this is everywhere, this is Atman, this is within me and within you and within every creature. And so I'm starting to believe that this knowledge has no worser enemy than the desire to know it, than learning."

At this, Govinda stopped on the path, rose his hands, and spoke: "If you, Siddhartha, only would not bother your friend with this kind of talk! Truly, you words stir up fear in my heart. And just consider: what would become of the sanctity of prayer, what of the venerability of the Brahmans' caste, what of the holiness of the Samanas, if it was as you say, if there was no learning?! What, oh Siddhartha, what would then become of all of this what is holy, what is precious, what is venerable on earth?!"

And Govinda mumbled a verse to himself, a verse from an Upanishad:

He who ponderingly, of a purified spirit, loses himself in the meditation of Atman, unexpressable by words is his blissfulness of his heart.

But Siddhartha remained silent. He thought about the words which Govinda had said to him and thought the words through to their end.

Yes, he thought, standing there with his head low, what would remain of all that which seemed to us to be holy? What remains? What can stand the test? And he shook his head.

At one time, when the two young men had lived among the Samanas for about three years and had shared their exercises, some news, a rumour, a myth reached them after being retold many times: A man had appeared,

Gotama by name, the exalted one, the Buddha, he had overcome the suffering of the world in himself and had halted the cycle of rebirths. He was said to wander through the land, teaching, surrounded by disciples, without possession, without home, without a wife, in the yellow cloak of an ascetic, but with a cheerful brow, a man of bliss, and Brahmans and princes would bow down before him and would become his students.

This myth, this rumour, this legend resounded, its fragrance rose up, here and there; in the towns, the Brahmans spoke of it and in the forest, the Samanas; again and again, the name of Gotama, the Buddha reached the ears of the young men, with good and with bad talk, with praise and with defamation.

It was as if the plague had broken out in a country and news had been spreading around that in one or another place there was a man, a wise man, a knowledgeable one, whose word and breath was enough to heal everyone who had been infected with the pestilence, and as such news would go through the land and everyone would talk about it, many would believe, many would doubt, but many would get on their way as soon as possible, to seek the wise man, the helper, just like this myth ran through the land, that fragrant myth of Gotama, the Buddha, the wise man of the family of Sakya. He possessed, so the believers said, the highest enlightenment, he remembered his previous lives, he had reached the nirvana and never returned into the cycle, was never again submerged in the murky river of physical forms. Many wonderful and unbelievable things were reported of him, he had performed miracles, had overcome the devil, had spoken to the gods. But his enemies and disbelievers said, this Gotama was a vain seducer, who spent his days in luxury, scorned the offerings, was without learning, and knew neither exercises nor self-castigation.

The myth of Buddha sounded sweet. The scent of magic flowed from these reports. After all, the world was sick, life was hard to bear—and behold, here a source seemed to spring forth, here a messenger seemed to call out, comforting, mild, full of noble promises. Everywhere where the rumour of Buddha was heard, everywhere in the lands of India, the young men listened up, felt a longing, felt hope, and among the Brahmans' sons of the towns and villages every pilgrim and stranger was welcome, when he brought news of him, the exalted one, the Sakyamuni.

The myth had also reached the Samanas in the forest, and also Siddhartha, and also Govinda, slowly, drop by drop, every drop laden with hope, every drop laden with doubt. They rarely talked about it, because the oldest one of the Samanas did not like this myth. He had heard that this alleged Buddha used to be an ascetic before and had lived in the forest, but had then turned back to luxury and worldly pleasures, and he had no high opinion of this Gotama.

"Oh Siddhartha," Govinda spoke one day to his friend. "Today, I was in the village, and a Brahman invited me into his house, and in his house, there was the son of a Brahman from Magadha, who has seen the Buddha with his own eyes and has heard him teach. Verily, this made my chest ache when I breathed, and thought to myself: If only I would too, if only we both would too, Siddhartha and me, live to see the hour when we will hear the teachings from the mouth of this perfected man! Speak, friend, wouldn't we want to go there too and listen to the teachings from the Buddha's mouth?"

Quoth Siddhartha: "Always, oh Govinda, I had thought, Govinda would stay with the Samanas, always I had believed his goal was to live to be sixty and seventy years of age and to keep on practising those feats and exercises, which are becoming a Samana. But behold, I had not known Govinda well enough, I knew little of his heart. So now you, my faithful friend, want to take a new path and go there, where the Buddha spreads his teachings."

Quoth Govinda: "You're mocking me. Mock me if you like, Siddhartha! But have you not also developed a desire, an eagerness, to hear these teachings? And have you not at one time said to me, you would not walk the path of the Samanas for much longer?"

At this, Siddhartha laughed in his very own manner, in which his voice assumed a touch of sadness and a touch of mockery, and said: "Well, Govinda, you've spoken well, you've remembered correctly. If you only remembered the other thing as well, you've heard from me, which is that I have grown distrustful and tired against teachings and learning, and that my faith in words, which are brought to us by teachers, is small. But let's do it, my dear, I am willing to listen to these teachings—though in my heart I believe that we've already tasted the best fruit of these teachings."

Quoth Govinda: "Your willingness delights my heart. But tell me, how should this be possible? How should the Gotama's teachings, even before we have heard them, have already revealed their best fruit to us?"

Quoth Siddhartha: "Let us eat this fruit and wait for the rest, oh Govinda! But this fruit, which we already now received thanks to the Gotama, consisted in him calling us away from the Samanas! Whether he has also other and better things to give us, oh friend, let us await with calm hearts."

On this very same day, Siddhartha informed the oldest one of the Samanas of his decision, that he wanted to leave him. He informed the oldest one with all the courtesy and modesty becoming to a younger one and a student. But the Samana became angry, because the two young men wanted to leave him, and talked loudly and used crude swearwords.

Govinda was startled and became embarrassed. But Siddhartha put his mouth close to Govinda's ear and whispered to him: "Now, I want to show the old man that I've learned something from him."

Positioning himself closely in front of the Samana, with a concentrated soul, he captured the old man's glance with his glances, deprived him of his power, made him mute, took away his free will, subdued him under his own will, commanded him, to do silently, whatever he demanded him to do. The old man became mute, his eyes became motionless, his will was paralysed, his arms were hanging down; without power, he had fallen victim to Siddhartha's spell. But Siddhartha's thoughts brought the Samana under their control, he had to carry out, what they commanded. And thus, the old man made several bows, performed gestures of blessing, spoke stammeringly a godly wish for a good journey. And the young men returned the bows with thanks, returned the wish, went on their way with salutations.

On the way, Govinda said: "Oh Siddhartha, you have learned more from the Samanas than I knew. It is hard, it is very hard to cast a spell on an old Samana. Truly, if you had stayed there, you would soon have learned to walk on water."

"I do not seek to walk on water," said Siddhartha. "Let old Samanas be content with such feats!"

GOTAMA

In the town of Savathi, every child knew the name of the exalted Buddha, and every house was prepared to fill the alms-dish of Gotama's disciples, the silently begging ones. Near the town was Gotama's favourite place to stay, the grove of Jetavana, which the rich merchant Anathapindika, an obedient worshipper of the exalted one, had given him and his people for a gift.

All tales and answers, which the two young ascetics had received in their search for Gotama's abode, had pointed them towards this area. And arriving at Savathi, in the very first house, before the door of which they stopped to beg, food has been offered to them, and they accepted the food, and Siddhartha asked the woman, who handed them the food:

"We would like to know, oh charitable one, where the Buddha dwells, the most venerable one, for we are two Samanas from the forest and have come, to see him, the perfected one, and to hear the teachings from his mouth."

Quoth the woman: "Here, you have truly come to the right place, you Samanas from the forest. You should know, in Jetavana, in the garden of Anathapindika is where the exalted one dwells. There you pilgrims shall spend the night, for there is enough space for the innumerable, who flock here, to hear the teachings from his mouth."

This made Govinda happy, and full of joy he exclaimed: "Well so, thus we have reached our destination, and our path has come to an end! But tell us, oh mother of the pilgrims, do you know him, the Buddha, have you seen him with your own eyes?"

Quoth the woman: "Many times I have seen him, the exalted one. On many days, I have seen him, walking through the alleys in silence, wearing his yellow cloak, presenting his alms-dish in silence at the doors of the houses, leaving with a filled dish."

Delightedly, Govinda listened and wanted to ask and hear much more. But Siddhartha urged him to walk on. They thanked and left and hardly had to ask for directions, for rather many pilgrims and monks as well from Gotama's community were on their way to the Jetavana. And since they reached it at night, there were constant arrivals, shouts, and talk of those who sought shelter and got it. The two Samanas, accustomed to life in the forest, found quickly and without making any noise a place to stay and rested there until the morning.

At sunrise, they saw with astonishment what a large crowd of believers and curious people had spent the night here. On all paths of the marvellous grove, monks walked in yellow robes, under the trees they sat here and there, in deep contemplation—or in a conversation about spiritual matters, the shady gardens looked like a city, full of people, bustling like bees. The majority of the monks went out with their alms-dish, to collect food in town for their lunch, the only meal of the day. The Buddha himself, the enlightened one, was also in the habit of taking this walk to beg in the morning.

Siddhartha saw him, and he instantly recognised him, as if a god had pointed him out to him. He saw him, a simple man in a yellow robe, bearing the alms-dish in his hand, walking silently.

"Look here!" Siddhartha said quietly to Govinda. "This one is the Buddha."

Attentively, Govinda looked at the monk in the yellow robe, who seemed to be in no way different from the hundreds of other monks. And soon, Govinda also realized: This is the one. And they followed him and observed him.

The Buddha went on his way, modestly and deep in his thoughts, his calm face was neither happy nor sad, it seemed to smile quietly and inwardly. With a hidden smile, quiet, calm, somewhat resembling a healthy child, the Buddha walked, wore the robe and placed his feet just as all of his monks did, according to a precise rule. But his face and his walk, his quietly lowered glance, his quietly dangling hand and even every finger of his quietly dangling hand expressed peace, expressed perfection, did not search, did not imitate, breathed softly in an unwhithering calm, in an unwhithering light, an untouchable peace.

Thus Gotama walked towards the town, to collect alms, and the two Samanas recognised him solely by the perfection of his calm, by the quietness of his appearance, in which there was no searching, no desire, no imitation, no effort to be seen, only light and peace.

"Today, we'll hear the teachings from his mouth," said Govinda.

Siddhartha did not answer. He felt little curiosity for the teachings, he did not believe that they would teach him anything new, but he had, just as Govinda had, heard the contents of this Buddha's teachings again and again, though these reports only represented second- or third-hand information. But attentively he looked at Gotama's head, his shoulders, his feet, his quietly dangling hand, and it seemed to him as if every joint of every finger of this hand was of these teachings, spoke of, breathed of, exhaled the fragrant of, glistened of truth. This man, this Buddha was truthful down to the gesture of his last finger. This man was holy. Never before, Siddhartha had venerated a person so much, never before he had loved a person as much as this one.

They both followed the Buddha until they reached the town and then returned in silence, for they themselves intended to abstain from on this day. They saw Gotama returning—what he ate could not even have satisfied a bird's appetite, and they saw him retiring into the shade of the mango-trees.

But in the evening, when the heat cooled down and everyone in the camp started to bustle about and gathered around, they heard the Buddha teaching. They heard his voice, and it was also perfected, was of perfect calmness, was full of peace. Gotama taught the teachings of suffering, of the origin of suffering, of the way to relieve suffering. Calmly and clearly his quiet speech flowed on. Suffering was life, full of suffering was the world, but salvation from suffering had been found: salvation was obtained by him who would walk the path of the Buddha. With a soft, yet firm voice the exalted one spoke, taught the four main doctrines, taught the eightfold path, patiently he went the usual path of the teachings, of the examples, of the repetitions, brightly and quietly his voice hovered over the listeners, like a light, like a starry sky.

When the Buddha—night had already fallen—ended his speech, many a pilgrim stepped forward and asked to be accepted into the community, sought refuge in the teachings. And Gotama accepted them by speaking: "You have heard the teachings well, it has come to you well. Thus join us and walk in holiness, to put an end to all suffering."

Behold, then Govinda, the shy one, also stepped forward and spoke: "I also take my refuge in the exalted one and his teachings," and he asked to be accepted into the community of his disciples and was accepted.

Right afterwards, when the Buddha had retired for the night, Govinda turned to Siddhartha and spoke eagerly: "Siddhartha, it is not my place to scold you. We have both heard the exalted one, we have both perceived the teachings. Govinda has heard the teachings, he has taken refuge in it. But you, my honoured friend, don't you also want to walk the path of salvation? Would you want to hesitate, do you want to wait any longer?"

Siddhartha awakened as if he had been asleep, when he heard Govinda's words. For a long time, he looked into Govinda's face. Then he spoke quietly, in a voice without mockery: "Govinda, my friend, now you have taken this step, now you have chosen this path. Always, oh Govinda, you've been my friend, you've always walked one step behind me. Often I have thought: Won't Govinda for once also take a step by himself, without me, out of his own soul? Behold, now you've turned into a man and are choosing your path for yourself. I wish that you would go it up to its end, oh my friend, that you shall find salvation!"

Govinda, not completely understanding it yet, repeated his question in an impatient tone: "Speak up, I beg you, my dear! Tell me, since it could not be any other way, that you also, my learned friend, will take your refuge with the exalted Buddha!"

Siddhartha placed his hand on Govinda's shoulder: "You failed to hear my good wish for you, oh Govinda. I'm repeating it: I wish that you would go this path up to its end, that you shall find salvation!"

In this moment, Govinda realized that his friend had left him, and he started to weep.

"Siddhartha!" he exclaimed lamentingly.

Siddhartha kindly spoke to him: "Don't forget, Govinda, that you are now one of the Samanas of the Buddha! You have renounced your home and your parents, renounced your birth and possessions, renounced your free will, renounced all friendship. This is what the teachings require, this is what the exalted one wants. This is what you wanted for yourself. Tomorrow, oh Govinda, I'll leave you."

For a long time, the friends continued walking in the grove; for a long time, they lay there and found no sleep. And over and over again, Govinda urged his friend, he should tell him why he would not want to seek refuge in Gotama's teachings, what fault he would find in these teachings. But Siddhartha turned him away every time and said: "Be content, Govinda! Very good are the teachings of the exalted one, how could I find a fault in them?"

Very early in the morning, a follower of Buddha, one of his oldest monks, went through the garden and called all those to him who had as novices taken their refuge in the teachings, to dress them up in the yellow robe and to instruct them in the first teachings and duties of their position. Then Govinda broke loose, embraced once again his childhood friend and left with the novices.

But Siddhartha walked through the grove, lost in thought.

Then he happened to meet Gotama, the exalted one, and when he greeted him with respect and the Buddha's glance was so full of kindness and calm, the young man summoned his courage and asked the venerable one for the permission to talk to him. Silently the exalted one nodded his approval.

Quoth Siddhartha: "Yesterday, oh exalted one, I had been privileged to hear your wondrous teachings. Together with my friend, I had come from afar, to hear your teachings. And now my friend is going to stay with your people, he has taken his refuge with you. But I will again start on my pilgrimage."

"As you please," the venerable one spoke politely.

"Too bold is my speech," Siddhartha continued, "but I do not want to leave the exalted one without having honestly told him my thoughts. Does it please the venerable one to listen to me for one moment longer?"

Silently, the Buddha nodded his approval.

Quoth Siddhartha: "One thing, oh most venerable one, I have admired in your teachings most of all. Everything in your teachings is perfectly clear, is proven; you are presenting the world as a perfect chain, a chain which is never and nowhere broken, an eternal chain the links of which are causes and effects. Never before, this has been seen so clearly; never before, this has been presented so irrefutably; truly, the heart of every Brahman has to beat stronger with love, once he has seen the world through your teachings perfectly connected, without gaps, clear as a crystal, not depending on chance, not depending on gods. Whether it may be good or bad, whether living according to it would be suffering or joy, I do not wish to discuss, possibly this is not essential—but the uniformity of the world, that everything which happens is connected, that the great and the small things are all encompassed by the same forces of time, by the same law of causes, of coming into being and of dying, this is what shines brightly out of your exalted teachings, oh perfected one. But according to your very own teachings, this unity and necessary sequence of all things is nevertheless broken in one place, through a small gap, this world of unity is invaded by something alien, something new, something which had not been there before, and which cannot be demonstrated and cannot be proven: these are your teachings of overcoming the world, of salvation. But with this small gap, with this small breach, the entire eternal and uniform law of the world is breaking apart again and becomes void. Please forgive me for expressing this objection."

Quietly, Gotama had listened to him, unmoved. Now he spoke, the perfected one, with his kind, with his polite and clear voice: "You've heard the teachings, oh son of a Brahman, and good for you that you've thought about it thus deeply. You've found a gap in it, an error. You should think about this further. But be warned, oh seeker of knowledge, of the thicket of opinions and of arguing about words. There is nothing to opinions, they may be beautiful or ugly, smart or foolish, everyone can support them or discard them. But the teachings, you've heard from me, are no opinion, and their goal is not to explain the world to those who seek knowledge. They have a different goal; their goal is salvation from suffering. This is what Gotama teaches, nothing else."

"I wish that you, oh exalted one, would not be angry with me," said the young man. "I have not spoken to you like this to argue with you, to argue about words. You are truly right, there is little to opinions. But let me say this one more thing: I have not doubted in you for a single moment. I have not doubted for a single moment that you are Buddha, that you have reached the goal, the highest goal towards which so many thousands of Brahmans and sons of Brahmans are on their way. You have found salvation from death. It has come to you in the course of your own search, on your own path, through thoughts, through meditation, through realizations, through enlightenment. It has not come to you by means of teachings! And—thus is my thought, oh exalted one—nobody will obtain salvation by means of teachings! You will not be able to convey and say to anybody, oh venerable one, in words and through teachings what has happened to you in the hour of enlightenment! The teachings of the enlightened Buddha contain much, it teaches many to live righteously, to avoid evil. But there is one thing which these so clear, these so venerable teachings do not contain: they do not contain the mystery of what the exalted one has experienced for himself, he alone among hundreds of thousands. This is what I have thought and realized, when I have heard the teachings. This is why I am continuing my travels—not to seek other, better teachings, for I know there are none, but to depart from all teachings and all teachers and to reach my goal by myself or to die. But often, I'll think of this day, oh exalted one, and of this hour, when my eyes beheld a holy man."

The Buddha's eyes quietly looked to the ground; quietly, in perfect equanimity his inscrutable face was smiling.

"I wish," the venerable one spoke slowly, "that your thoughts shall not be in error, that you shall reach the goal! But tell me: Have you seen the multitude of my Samanas, my many brothers, who have taken refuge in the teachings? And do you believe, oh stranger, oh Samana, do you believe that it would be better for them all the abandon the teachings and to return into the life the world and of desires?"

"Far is such a thought from my mind," exclaimed Siddhartha. "I wish that they shall all stay with the teachings, that they shall reach their goal! It is not my place to judge another person's life. Only for myself, for myself alone, I must decide, I must chose, I must refuse. Salvation from the self is what we Samanas search for, oh exalted one. If I merely were one of your disciples, oh venerable one, I'd fear that it might happen to me that only seemingly, only deceptively my self would be calm and be redeemed, but that in truth it would live on and grow, for then I had replaced my self with the teachings, my duty to follow you, my love for you, and the community of the monks!"

With half of a smile, with an unwavering openness and kindness, Gotama looked into the stranger's eyes and bid him to leave with a hardly noticeable gesture.

"You are wise, oh Samana," the venerable one spoke. "You know how to talk wisely, my friend. Be aware of too much wisdom!"

The Buddha turned away, and his glance and half of a smile remained forever etched in Siddhartha's memory.

I have never before seen a person glance and smile, sit and walk this way, he thought; truly, I wish to be able to glance and smile, sit and walk this way, too, thus free, thus venerable, thus concealed, thus open, thus childlike and mysterious. Truly, only a person who has succeeded in reaching the innermost part of his self would glance and walk this way. Well so, I also will seek to reach the innermost part of my self.

I saw a man, Siddhartha thought, a single man, before whom I would have to lower my glance. I do not want to lower my glance before any other, not before any other. No teachings will entice me any more, since this man's teachings have not enticed me.

I am deprived by the Buddha, thought Siddhartha, I am deprived, and even more he has given to me. He has deprived me of my friend, the one who had believed in me and now believes in him, who had been my shadow and is now Gotama's shadow. But he has given me Siddhartha, myself.

AWAKENING

When Siddhartha left the grove, where the Buddha, the perfected one, stayed behind, where Govinda stayed behind, then he felt that in this grove his past life also stayed behind and parted from him. He pondered about this sensation, which filled him completely, as he was slowly walking along. He pondered deeply, like diving into a deep water he let himself sink down to the ground of the sensation, down to the place where the causes lie, because to identify the causes, so it seemed to him, is the very essence of thinking, and by this alone sensations turn into realizations and are not lost, but become entities and start to emit like rays of light what is inside of them.

Slowly walking along, Siddhartha pondered. He realized that he was no youth any more, but had turned into a man. He realized that one thing had left him, as a snake is left by its old skin, that one thing no longer existed in him, which had accompanied him throughout his youth and used to be a part of him: the wish to have teachers and to listen to teachings. He had also left the last teacher who had appeared on his path, even him, the highest and wisest teacher, the most holy one, Buddha, he had left him, had to part with him, was not able to accept his teachings.

Slower, he walked along in his thoughts and asked himself: "But what is this, what you have sought to learn from teachings and from teachers, and what they, who have taught you much, were still unable to teach you?" And he found: "It was the self, the purpose and essence of which I sought to learn. It was the self, I wanted to free myself from, which I sought to overcome. But I was not able to overcome it, could only deceive it, could only flee from it, only hide from it. Truly, no thing in this world has kept my thoughts thus busy, as this my very own self, this mystery of me being alive, of me being one and being separated and isolated from all others, of me being Siddhartha! And there is no thing in this world I know less about than about me, about Siddhartha!"

Having been pondering while slowly walking along, he now stopped as these thoughts caught hold of him, and right away another thought sprang forth from these, a new thought, which was: "That I know nothing about myself, that Siddhartha has remained thus alien and unknown to me, stems from one cause, a single cause: I was afraid of myself, I was fleeing from myself! I searched Atman, I searched Brahman, I was willing to dissect my self and peel off all of its layers, to find the core of all peels in its unknown interior, the Atman, life, the divine part, the ultimate part. But I have lost myself in the process."

Siddhartha opened his eyes and looked around, a smile filled his face and a feeling of awakening from long dreams flowed through him from his head down to his toes. And it was not long before he walked again, walked quickly like a man who knows what he has got to do.

"Oh," he thought, taking a deep breath, "now I would not let Siddhartha escape from me again! No longer, I want to begin my thoughts and my life with Atman and with the suffering of the world. I do not want to kill and dissect myself any longer, to find a secret behind the ruins. Neither Yoga-Veda shall teach me any more, nor Atharva-Veda, nor the ascetics, nor any kind of teachings. I want to learn from myself, want to be my student, want to get to know myself, the secret of Siddhartha."

He looked around, as if he was seeing the world for the first time. Beautiful was the world, colourful was the world, strange and mysterious was the world! Here was blue, here was yellow, here was green, the sky and the river flowed, the forest and the mountains were rigid, all of it was beautiful, all of it was mysterious and magical, and in its midst was he, Siddhartha, the awakening one, on the path to himself. All of this, all this yellow and blue, river and forest, entered Siddhartha for the first time through the eyes, was no longer a spell of Mara, was no longer the veil of Maya, was no longer a pointless and coincidental diversity of mere appearances, despicable to the deeply thinking Brahman, who scorns diversity, who seeks unity. Blue was blue, river was river, and if also in the blue and the river, in Siddhartha, the singular and divine lived hidden, so it was still that very divinity's way and purpose, to be here yellow, here blue, there sky, there forest, and here Siddhartha. The purpose and the essential properties were not somewhere behind the things, they were in them, in everything.

"How deaf and stupid have I been!" he thought, walking swiftly along. "When someone reads a text, wants to discover its meaning, he will not scorn the symbols and letters and call them deceptions, coincidence, and worthless hull, but he will read them, he will study and love them, letter by letter. But I, who wanted to read the book of the world and the book of my own being, I have, for the sake of a meaning I had anticipated before I read, scorned the symbols and letters, I called the visible world a deception, called my eyes and my tongue coincidental and worthless forms without substance. No, this is over, I have awakened, I have indeed awakened and have not been born before this very day."

In thinking these thoughts, Siddhartha stopped once again, suddenly, as if there was a snake lying in front of him on the path.

Because suddenly, he had also become aware of this: He, who was indeed like someone who had just woken up or like a new-born baby, he had to start his life anew and start again at the very beginning. When he had left in this very morning from the grove Jetavana, the grove of that exalted one, already awakening, already on the path towards himself, he had every intention, regarded as natural and took for granted, that he, after years as an ascetic, would return to his home and his father. But now, only in this moment, when he stopped as if a snake was lying on his path, he also awoke to this realization: "But I am no longer the one I was, I am no ascetic any more, I am not a priest any more, I am no Brahman any more. Whatever should I do at home and at my father's place? Study? Make offerings? Practise meditation? But all this is over, all of this is no longer alongside my path."

Motionless, Siddhartha remained standing there, and for the time of one moment and breath, his heart felt cold, he felt a cold in his chest, as a small animal, a bird or a rabbit, would when seeing how alone he was. For many years, he had been without home and had felt nothing. Now, he felt it. Still, even in the deepest meditation, he had been his father's son, had been a Brahman, of a high caste, a cleric. Now, he was nothing but Siddhartha, the awoken one, nothing else was left. Deeply, he inhaled, and for a moment, he felt cold and shivered. Nobody was thus alone as he was. There was no nobleman who did not belong to the noblemen, no worker that did not belong to the workers, and found refuge with them, shared their life, spoke their language. No Brahman, who would not be regarded as Brahmans and lived with them, no ascetic who would not find his refuge in the caste of the Samanas, and even the most forlorn hermit in the forest was not just one and alone, he was also surrounded by a place he belonged to, he also belonged to a caste, in which he was at home. Govinda had become a monk, and a thousand monks were his brothers, wore the same robe as he, believed in his faith, spoke his language. But he, Siddhartha, where did he belong to? With whom would he share his life? Whose language would he speak?

Out of this moment, when the world melted away all around him, when he stood alone like a star in the sky, out of this moment of a cold and despair, Siddhartha emerged, more a self than before, more firmly concentrated. He felt: This had been the last tremor of the awakening, the last struggle of this birth. And it was not long until he walked again in long strides, started to proceed swiftly and impatiently, heading no longer for home, no longer to his father, no longer back.

SECOND PART

Dedicated to Wilhelm Gundert, my cousin in Japan

KAMALA

Siddhartha learned something new on every step of his path, for the world was transformed, and his heart was enchanted. He saw the sun rising over the mountains with their forests and setting over the distant beach with its palm-trees. At night, he saw the stars in the sky in their fixed positions and the crescent of the moon floating like a boat in the blue. He saw trees, stars, animals, clouds, rainbows, rocks, herbs, flowers, stream and river, the glistening dew in the bushes in the morning, distant high mountains which were blue and pale, birds sang and bees, wind silverishly blew through the rice-field. All of this, a thousand-fold and colourful, had always been there, always the sun and the moon had shone, always rivers had roared and bees had buzzed, but in former times all of this had been nothing more to Siddhartha than a fleeting, deceptive veil before his eyes, looked upon in distrust, destined to be penetrated and destroyed by thought, since it was not the essential existence, since this essence lay beyond, on the other side of, the visible. But now, his liberated eyes stayed on this side, he saw and became aware of the visible, sought to be at home in this world, did not search for the true essence, did not aim at a world beyond. Beautiful was this world, looking at it thus, without searching, thus simply, thus childlike. Beautiful were the moon and the stars, beautiful was the stream and the banks, the forest and the rocks, the goat and the gold-beetle, the flower and the butterfly. Beautiful and lovely it was, thus to walk through the world, thus childlike, thus awoken, thus open to what is near, thus without distrust. Differently the sun burnt the head, differently the shade of the forest cooled him down, differently the stream and the cistern, the pumpkin and the banana tasted. Short were the days, short the nights, every hour sped swiftly away like a sail on the sea, and under the sail was a ship full of treasures, full of joy. Siddhartha saw a group of apes moving through the high canopy of the forest, high in the branches, and heard their savage, greedy song. Siddhartha saw a male sheep following a female one and mating with her. In a lake of reeds, he saw the pike hungrily hunting for its dinner; propelling themselves away from it, in fear, wiggling and sparkling, the young fish jumped in droves out of the water; the scent of strength and passion came forcefully out of the hasty eddies of the water, which the pike stirred up, impetuously hunting.

All of this had always existed, and he had not seen it; he had not been with it. Now he was with it, he was part of it. Light and shadow ran through his eyes, stars and moon ran through his heart.

On the way, Siddhartha also remembered everything he had experienced in the Garden Jetavana, the teaching he had heard there, the divine Buddha, the farewell from Govinda, the conversation with the exalted one. Again he remembered his own words, he had spoken to the exalted one, every word, and with astonishment he became aware of the fact that there he had said things which he had not really known yet at this time. What he had said to Gotama: his, the Buddha's, treasure and secret was not the teachings, but the unexpressable and not teachable, which he had experienced in the hour of his enlightenment—it was nothing but this very thing which he had now gone to experience, what he now began to experience. Now, he had to experience his self. It is true that he had already known for a long time that his self was Atman, in its essence bearing the same eternal characteristics as Brahman. But never, he had really found this self, because he had wanted to capture it in the net of thought. With the body definitely not being the self, and not the spectacle of the senses, so it also was not the thought, not the rational mind, not the learned wisdom, not the learned ability to draw conclusions and to develop previous thoughts in to new ones. No, this world of thought was also still on this side, and nothing could be achieved by killing the random self of the senses, if the random self of thoughts and learned knowledge was fattened on the other hand. Both, the thoughts as well as the senses, were pretty things, the ultimate meaning was hidden behind both of them, both had to be listened to, both had to be played with, both neither had to be scorned nor overestimated, from both the secret voices of the innermost truth had to be attentively perceived. He wanted to strive for nothing, except for what the voice commanded him to strive for, dwell on nothing, except where the voice would advise him to do so. Why had Gotama, at that time, in the hour of all hours, sat down under the bo-tree, where the enlightenment hit him? He had heard a voice, a voice in his own heart, which had commanded him to seek rest under this tree, and he had neither preferred self-castigation, offerings, ablutions, nor prayer, neither food nor drink, neither sleep nor dream, he had obeyed the voice. To obey like this, not to an external command, only to the voice, to be ready like this, this was good, this was necessary, nothing else was necessary.

In the night when he slept in the straw hut of a ferryman by the river, Siddhartha had a dream: Govinda was standing in front of him, dressed in the yellow robe of an ascetic. Sad was how Govinda looked like, sadly he asked: Why have you forsaken me? At this, he embraced Govinda, wrapped his arms around him, and as he was pulling him close to his chest and kissed him, it was not Govinda any more, but a woman, and a full breast popped out of the woman's dress, at which Siddhartha lay and drank, sweetly and strongly tasted the milk from this breast. It tasted of woman and man, of sun and forest, of animal and flower, of every fruit, of every joyful desire. It intoxicated him and rendered him unconscious.

* * * *

When Siddhartha woke up, the pale river shimmered through the door of the hut, and in the forest, a dark call of an owl resounded deeply and pleasantly.

When the day began, Siddhartha asked his host, the ferryman, to get him across the river. The ferryman got him across the river on his bamboo-raft, the wide water shimmered reddishly in the light of the morning.

"This is a beautiful river," he said to his companion.

"Yes," said the ferryman, "a very beautiful river, I love it more than anything. Often I have listened to it, often I have looked into its eyes, and always I have learned from it. Much can be learned from a river."

"I thank you, my benefactor," spoke Siddhartha, disembarking on the other side of the river. "I have no gift I could give you for your hospitality, my dear, and also no payment for your work. I am a man without a home, a son of a Brahman and a Samana."

"I did see it," spoke the ferryman, "and I haven't expected any payment from you and no gift which would be the custom for guests to bear. You will give me the gift another time."

"Do you think so?" asked Siddhartha amusedly.

"Surely. This too, I have learned from the river: everything is coming back! You too, Samana, will come back. Now farewell! Let your friendship be my reward. Commemorate me, when you'll make offerings to the gods."

Smiling, they parted. Smiling, Siddhartha was happy about the friendship and the kindness of the ferryman. "He is like Govinda," he thought with a smile, "all I meet on my path are like Govinda. All are thankful, though they are the ones who would have a right to receive thanks. All are submissive, all would like to be friends, like to obey, think little. Like children are all people."

At about noon, he came through a village. In front of the mud cottages, children were rolling about in the street, were playing with pumpkin-seeds and sea-shells, screamed and wrestled, but they all timidly fled from the unknown Samana. In the end of the village, the path led through a stream, and by the side of the stream, a young woman was kneeling and washing clothes. When Siddhartha greeted her, she lifted her head and looked up to him with a smile, so that he saw the white in her eyes glistening. He called out a blessing to her, as it is the custom among travellers, and asked how far he still had to go to reach the large city. Then she got up and came to him, beautifully her wet mouth was shimmering in her young face. She exchanged humorous banter with him, asked whether he had eaten already, and whether it was true that the Samanas slept alone in the forest at night and were not allowed to have any women with them. While talking, she put her left foot on his right one and made a movement as a woman does who would want to initiate that kind of sexual pleasure with a man, which the textbooks call "climbing a tree". Siddhartha felt his blood heating up, and since in this moment he had to think of his dream again, he bend slightly down to the woman and kissed with his lips the brown nipple of her breast. Looking up, he saw her face smiling full of lust and her eyes, with contracted pupils, begging with desire.

Siddhartha also felt desire and felt the source of his sexuality moving; but since he had never touched a woman before, he hesitated for a moment, while his hands were already prepared to reach out for her. And in this moment he heard, shuddering with awe, the voice of his innermost self, and this voice said No. Then, all charms disappeared from the young woman's smiling face, he no longer saw anything else but the damp glance of a female animal in heat. Politely, he petted her cheek, turned away from her and disappeared away from the disappointed woman with light steps into the bamboo-wood.

On this day, he reached the large city before the evening, and was happy, for he felt the need to be among people. For a long time, he had lived in the forests, and the straw hut of the ferryman, in which he had slept that night, had been the first roof for a long time he had had over his head.

Before the city, in a beautifully fenced grove, the traveller came across a small group of servants, both male and female, carrying baskets. In their midst, carried by four servants in an ornamental sedan-chair, sat a woman, the mistress, on red pillows under a colourful canopy. Siddhartha stopped at the entrance to the pleasure-garden and watched the parade, saw the servants, the maids, the baskets, saw the sedan-chair and saw the lady in it.

Under black hair, which made to tower high on her head, he saw a very fair, very delicate, very smart face, a brightly red mouth, like a freshly cracked fig, eyebrows which were well tended and painted in a high arch, smart and watchful dark eyes, a clear, tall neck rising from a green and golden garment, resting fair hands, long and thin, with wide golden bracelets over the wrists.

Siddhartha saw how beautiful she was, and his heart rejoiced. He bowed deeply, when the sedan-chair came closer, and straightening up again, he looked at the fair, charming face, read for a moment in the smart eyes with the high arcs above, breathed in a slight fragrant, he did not know. With a smile, the beautiful woman nodded for a moment and disappeared into the grove, and then the servants as well.

Thus I am entering this city, Siddhartha thought, with a charming omen. He instantly felt drawn into the grove, but he thought about it, and only now he became aware of how the servants and maids had looked at him at the entrance, how despicable, how distrustful, how rejecting.

I am still a Samana, he thought, I am still an ascetic and beggar. I must not remain like this, I will not be able to enter the grove like this. And he laughed.

The next person who came along this path he asked about the grove and for the name of the woman, and was told that this was the grove of Kamala, the famous courtesan, and that, aside from the grove, she owned a house in the city.

Then, he entered the city. Now he had a goal.

Pursuing his goal, he allowed the city to suck him in, drifted through the flow of the streets, stood still on the squares, rested on the stairs of stone by the river. When the evening came, he made friends with barber's assistant, whom he had seen working in the shade of an arch in a building, whom he found again praying in a temple of Vishnu, whom he told about stories of Vishnu and the Lakshmi. Among the boats by the river, he slept this night, and early in the morning, before the first customers came into his shop, he had the barber's assistant shave his beard and cut his hair, comb his hair and anoint it with fine oil. Then he went to take his bath in the river.

When late in the afternoon, beautiful Kamala approached her grove in her sedan-chair, Siddhartha was standing at the entrance, made a bow and received the courtesan's greeting. But that servant who walked at the very end of her train he motioned to him and asked him to inform his mistress that a young Brahman would wish to talk to her. After a while, the servant returned, asked him, who had been waiting, to follow him, conducted him, who was following him, without a word into a pavilion, where Kamala was lying on a couch, and left him alone with her.

"Weren't you already standing out there yesterday, greeting me?" asked Kamala.

"It's true that I've already seen and greeted you yesterday."

"But didn't you yesterday wear a beard, and long hair, and dust in your hair?"

"You have observed well, you have seen everything. You have seen Siddhartha, the son of a Brahman, who has left his home to become a Samana, and who has been a Samana for three years. But now, I have left that path and came into this city, and the first one I met, even before I had entered the city, was you. To say this, I have come to you, oh Kamala! You are the first woman whom Siddhartha is not addressing with his eyes turned to the ground. Never again I want to turn my eyes to the ground, when I'm coming across a beautiful woman."

Kamala smiled and played with her fan of peacocks' feathers. And asked: "And only to tell me this, Siddhartha has come to me?"

"To tell you this and to thank you for being so beautiful. And if it doesn't displease you, Kamala, I would like to ask you to be my friend and teacher, for I know nothing yet of that art which you have mastered in the highest degree."

At this, Kamala laughed aloud.

"Never before this has happened to me, my friend, that a Samana from the forest came to me and wanted to learn from me! Never before this has happened to me, that a Samana came to me with long hair and an old, torn loincloth! Many young men come to me, and there are also sons of Brahmans among them, but they come in beautiful clothes, they come in fine shoes, they have perfume in their hair and money in their pouches. This is, oh Samana, how the young men are like who come to me."

Quoth Siddhartha: "Already I am starting to learn from you. Even yesterday, I was already learning. I have already taken off my beard, have combed the hair, have oil in my hair. There is little which is still missing in me, oh excellent one: fine clothes, fine shoes, money in my pouch. You shall know, Siddhartha has set harder goals for himself than such trifles, and he has reached them. How shouldn't I reach that goal, which I have set for myself yesterday: to be your friend and to learn the joys of love from you! You'll see that I'll learn quickly, Kamala, I have already learned harder things than what you're supposed to teach me. And now let's get to it: You aren't satisfied with Siddhartha as he is, with oil in his hair, but without clothes, without shoes, without money?"

Laughing, Kamala exclaimed: "No, my dear, he doesn't satisfy me yet. Clothes are what he must have, pretty clothes, and shoes, pretty shoes, and lots of money in his pouch, and gifts for Kamala. Do you know it now, Samana from the forest? Did you mark my words?"

"Yes, I have marked your words," Siddhartha exclaimed. "How should I not mark words which are coming from such a mouth! Your mouth is like a freshly cracked fig, Kamala. My mouth is red and fresh as well, it will be a suitable match for yours, you'll see. —But tell me, beautiful Kamala, aren't you at all afraid of the Samana from the forest, who has come to learn how to make love?"

"Whatever for should I be afraid of a Samana, a stupid Samana from the forest, who is coming from the jackals and doesn't even know yet what women are?"

"Oh, he's strong, the Samana, and he isn't afraid of anything. He could force you, beautiful girl. He could kidnap you. He could hurt you."

"No, Samana, I am not afraid of this. Did any Samana or Brahman ever fear, someone might come and grab him and steal his learning, and his religious devotion, and his depth of thought? No, for they are his very own, and he would only give away from those whatever he is willing to give and to whomever he is willing to give. Like this it is, precisely like this it is also with Kamala and with the pleasures of love. Beautiful and red is Kamala's mouth, but just try to kiss it against Kamala's will, and you will not obtain a single drop of sweetness from it, which knows how to give so many sweet things! You are learning easily, Siddhartha, thus you should also learn this: love can be obtained by begging, buying, receiving it as a gift, finding it in the street, but it cannot be stolen. In this, you have come up with the wrong path. No, it would be a pity, if a pretty young man like you would want to tackle it in such a wrong manner."

Siddhartha bowed with a smile. "It would be a pity, Kamala, you are so right! It would be such a great pity. No, I shall not lose a single drop of sweetness from your mouth, nor you from mine! So it is settled: Siddhartha will return, once he'll have what he still lacks: clothes, shoes, money. But speak, lovely Kamala, couldn't you still give me one small advice?"

"An advice? Why not? Who wouldn't like to give an advice to a poor, ignorant Samana, who is coming from the jackals of the forest?"

"Dear Kamala, thus advise me where I should go to, that I'll find these three things most quickly?"

"Friend, many would like to know this. You must do what you've learned and ask for money, clothes, and shoes in return. There is no other way for a poor man to obtain money. What might you be able to do?"

"I can think. I can wait. I can fast."

"Nothing else?"

"Nothing. But yes, I can also write poetry. Would you like to give me a kiss for a poem?"

"I would like to, if I'll like your poem. What would be its title?"

Siddhartha spoke, after he had thought about it for a moment, these verses:

Into her shady grove stepped the pretty Kamala, At the grove's entrance stood the brown Samana. Deeply, seeing the lotus's blossom, Bowed that man, and smiling Kamala thanked. More lovely, thought the young man, than offerings for gods, More lovely is offering to pretty Kamala.

Kamala loudly clapped her hands, so that the golden bracelets clanged.

"Beautiful are your verses, oh brown Samana, and truly, I'm losing nothing when I'm giving you a kiss for them."

She beckoned him with her eyes, he tilted his head so that his face touched hers and placed his mouth on that mouth which was like a freshly cracked fig. For a long time, Kamala kissed him, and with a deep astonishment Siddhartha felt how she taught him, how wise she was, how she controlled him, rejected him, lured him, and how after this first one there was to be a long, a well ordered, well tested sequence of kisses, every one different from the others, he was still to receive. Breathing deeply, he remained standing where he was, and was in this moment astonished like a child about the cornucopia of knowledge and things worth learning, which revealed itself before his eyes.

"Very beautiful are your verses," exclaimed Kamala, "if I was rich, I would give you pieces of gold for them. But it will be difficult for you to earn thus much money with verses as you need. For you need a lot of money, if you want to be Kamala's friend."

"The way you're able to kiss, Kamala!" stammered Siddhartha.

"Yes, this I am able to do, therefore I do not lack clothes, shoes, bracelets, and all beautiful things. But what will become of you? Aren't you able to do anything else but thinking, fasting, making poetry?"

"I also know the sacrificial songs," said Siddhartha, "but I do not want to sing them any more. I also know magic spells, but I do not want to speak them any more. I have read the scriptures—"

"Stop," Kamala interrupted him. "You're able to read? And write?"

"Certainly, I can do this. Many people can do this."

"Most people can't. I also can't do it. It is very good that you're able to read and write, very good. You will also still find use for the magic spells."

In this moment, a maid came running in and whispered a message into her mistress's ear.

"There's a visitor for me," exclaimed Kamala. "Hurry and get yourself away, Siddhartha, nobody may see you in here, remember this! Tomorrow, I'll see you again."

But to the maid she gave the order to give the pious Brahman white upper garments. Without fully understanding what was happening to him, Siddhartha found himself being dragged away by the maid, brought into a garden-house avoiding the direct path, being given upper garments as a gift, led into the bushes, and urgently admonished to get himself out of the grove as soon as possible without being seen.

Contently, he did as he had been told. Being accustomed to the forest, he managed to get out of the grove and over the hedge without making a sound. Contently, he returned to the city, carrying the rolled up garments under his arm. At the inn, where travellers stay, he positioned himself by the door, without words he asked for food, without a word he accepted a piece of rice-cake. Perhaps as soon as tomorrow, he thought, I will ask no one for food any more.

Suddenly, pride flared up in him. He was no Samana any more, it was no longer becoming to him to beg. He gave the rice-cake to a dog and remained without food.

"Simple is the life which people lead in this world here," thought Siddhartha. "It presents no difficulties. Everything was difficult, toilsome, and ultimately hopeless, when I was still a Samana. Now, everything is easy, easy like that lesson in kissing, which Kamala is giving me. I need clothes and money, nothing else; these are small, near goals, they won't make a person lose any sleep."

He had already discovered Kamala's house in the city long before, there he turned up the following day.

"Things are working out well," she called out to him. "They are expecting you at Kamaswami's, he is the richest merchant of the city. If he'll like you, he'll accept you into his service. Be smart, brown Samana. I had others tell him about you. Be polite towards him, he is very powerful. But don't be too modest! I do not want you to become his servant, you shall become his equal, or else I won't be satisfied with you. Kamaswami is starting to get old and lazy. If he'll like you, he'll entrust you with a lot."

Siddhartha thanked her and laughed, and when she found out that he had not eaten anything yesterday and today, she sent for bread and fruits and treated him to it.

"You've been lucky," she said when they parted, "I'm opening one door after another for you. How come? Do you have a spell?"

Siddhartha said: "Yesterday, I told you I knew how to think, to wait, and to fast, but you thought this was of no use. But it is useful for many things, Kamala, you'll see. You'll see that the stupid Samanas are learning and able to do many pretty things in the forest, which the likes of you aren't capable of. The day before yesterday, I was still a shaggy beggar, as soon as yesterday I have kissed Kamala, and soon I'll be a merchant and have money and all those things you insist upon."

"Well yes," she admitted. "But where would you be without me? What would you be, if Kamala wasn't helping you?"

"Dear Kamala," said Siddhartha and straightened up to his full height, "when I came to you into your grove, I did the first step. It was my resolution to learn love from this most beautiful woman. From that moment on when I had made this resolution, I also knew that I would carry it out. I knew that you would help me, at your first glance at the entrance of the grove I already knew it."

"But what if I hadn't been willing?"

"You were willing. Look, Kamala: When you throw a rock into the water, it will speed on the fastest course to the bottom of the water. This is how it is when Siddhartha has a goal, a resolution. Siddhartha does nothing, he waits, he thinks, he fasts, but he passes through the things of the world like a rock through water, without doing anything, without stirring; he is drawn, he lets himself fall. His goal attracts him, because he doesn't let anything enter his soul which might oppose the goal. This is what Siddhartha has learned among the Samanas. This is what fools call magic and of which they think it would be effected by means of the daemons. Nothing is effected by daemons, there are no daemons. Everyone can perform magic, everyone can reach his goals, if he is able to think, if he is able to wait, if he is able to fast."

Kamala listened to him. She loved his voice, she loved the look from his eyes.

"Perhaps it is so," she said quietly, "as you say, friend. But perhaps it is also like this: that Siddhartha is a handsome man, that his glance pleases the women, that therefore good fortune is coming towards him."

With one kiss, Siddhartha bid his farewell. "I wish that it should be this way, my teacher; that my glance shall please you, that always good fortune shall come to me out of your direction!"

WITH THE CHILDLIKE PEOPLE

Siddhartha went to Kamaswami the merchant, he was directed into a rich house, servants led him between precious carpets into a chamber, where he awaited the master of the house.

Kamaswami entered, a swiftly, smoothly moving man with very gray hair, with very intelligent, cautious eyes, with a greedy mouth. Politely, the host and the guest greeted one another.

"I have been told," the merchant began, "that you were a Brahman, a learned man, but that you seek to be in the service of a merchant. Might you have become destitute, Brahman, so that you seek to serve?"

"No," said Siddhartha, "I have not become destitute and have never been destitute. You should know that I'm coming from the Samanas, with whom I have lived for a long time."

"If you're coming from the Samanas, how could you be anything but destitute? Aren't the Samanas entirely without possessions?"

"I am without possessions," said Siddhartha, "if this is what you mean. Surely, I am without possessions. But I am so voluntarily, and therefore I am not destitute."

"But what are you planning to live of, being without possessions?"

"I haven't thought of this yet, sir. For more than three years, I have been without possessions, and have never thought about of what I should live."

"So you've lived of the possessions of others."

"Presumable this is how it is. After all, a merchant also lives of what other people own."

"Well said. But he wouldn't take anything from another person for nothing; he would give his merchandise in return."

"So it seems to be indeed. Everyone takes, everyone gives, such is life."

"But if you don't mind me asking: being without possessions, what would you like to give?"

"Everyone gives what he has. The warrior gives strength, the merchant gives merchandise, the teacher teachings, the farmer rice, the fisher fish."

"Yes indeed. And what is it now what you've got to give? What is it that you've learned, what you're able to do?"

"I can think. I can wait. I can fast."

"That's everything?"

"I believe, that's everything!"

"And what's the use of that? For example, the fasting—what is it good for?"

"It is very good, sir. When a person has nothing to eat, fasting is the smartest thing he could do. When, for example, Siddhartha hadn't learned to fast, he would have to accept any kind of service before this day is up, whether it may be with you or wherever, because hunger would force him to do so. But like this, Siddhartha can wait calmly, he knows no impatience, he knows no emergency, for a long time he can allow hunger to besiege him and can laugh about it. This, sir, is what fasting is good for."

"You're right, Samana. Wait for a moment."

Kamaswami left the room and returned with a scroll, which he handed to his guest while asking: "Can you read this?"

Siddhartha looked at the scroll, on which a sales-contract had been written down, and began to read out its contents.

"Excellent," said Kamaswami. "And would you write something for me on this piece of paper?"

He handed him a piece of paper and a pen, and Siddhartha wrote and returned the paper.

Kamaswami read: "Writing is good, thinking is better. Being smart is good, being patient is better."

"It is excellent how you're able to write," the merchant praised him. "Many a thing we will still have to discuss with one another. For today, I'm asking you to be my guest and to live in this house."

Siddhartha thanked and accepted, and lived in the dealer's house from now on. Clothes were brought to him, and shoes, and every day, a servant prepared a bath for him. Twice a day, a plentiful meal was served, but Siddhartha only ate once a day, and ate neither meat nor did he drink wine. Kamaswami told him about his trade, showed him the merchandise and storage-rooms, showed him calculations. Siddhartha got to know many new things, he heard a lot and spoke little. And thinking of Kamala's words, he was never subservient to the merchant, forced him to treat him as an equal, yes even more than an equal. Kamaswami conducted his business with care and often with passion, but Siddhartha looked upon all of this as if it was a game, the rules of which he tried hard to learn precisely, but the contents of which did not touch his heart.

He was not in Kamaswami's house for long, when he already took part in his landlord's business. But daily, at the hour appointed by her, he visited beautiful Kamala, wearing pretty clothes, fine shoes, and soon he brought her gifts as well. Much he learned from her red, smart mouth. Much he learned from her tender, supple hand. Him, who was, regarding love, still a boy and had a tendency to plunge blindly and insatiably into lust like into a bottomless pit, him she taught, thoroughly starting with the basics, about that school of thought which teaches that pleasure cannot be taken without giving pleasure, and that every gesture, every caress, every touch, every look, every spot of the body, however small it was, had its secret, which would bring happiness to those who know about it and unleash it. She taught him, that lovers must not part from one another after celebrating love, without one admiring the other, without being just as defeated as they have been victorious, so that none of them should start feeling fed up or bored and get that evil feeling of having abused or having been abused. Wonderful hours he spent with the beautiful and smart artist, became her student, her lover, her friend. Here with Kamala was the worth and purpose of his present life, not with the business of Kamaswami.

The merchant passed duties of writing important letters and contracts on to him and got into the habit of discussing all important affairs with him. He soon saw that Siddhartha knew little about rice and wool, shipping and trade, but that he acted in a fortunate manner, and that Siddhartha surpassed him, the merchant, in calmness and equanimity, and in the art of listening and deeply understanding previously unknown people. "This Brahman," he said to a friend, "is no proper merchant and will never be one, there is never any passion in his soul when he conducts our business. But he has that mysterious quality of those people to whom success comes all by itself, whether this may be a good star of his birth, magic, or something he has learned among Samanas. He always seems to be merely playing with our business-affairs, they never fully become a part of him, they never rule over him, he is never afraid of failure, he is never upset by a loss."

The friend advised the merchant: "Give him from the business he conducts for you a third of the profits, but let him also be liable for the same amount of the losses, when there is a loss. Then, he'll become more zealous."

Kamaswami followed the advice. But Siddhartha cared little about this. When he made a profit, he accepted it with equanimity; when he made losses, he laughed and said: "Well, look at this, so this one turned out badly!"

It seemed indeed, as if he did not care about the business. At one time, he travelled to a village to buy a large harvest of rice there. But when he got there, the rice had already been sold to another merchant. Nevertheless, Siddhartha stayed for several days in that village, treated the farmers for a drink, gave copper-coins to their children, joined in the celebration of a wedding, and returned extremely satisfied from his trip. Kamaswami held against him that he had not turned back right away, that he had wasted time and money. Siddhartha answered: "Stop scolding, dear friend! Nothing was ever achieved by scolding. If a loss has occurred, let me bear that loss. I am very satisfied with this trip. I have gotten to know many kinds of people, a Brahman has become my friend, children have sat on my knees, farmers have shown me their fields, nobody knew that I was a merchant."

"That's all very nice," exclaimed Kamaswami indignantly, "but in fact, you are a merchant after all, one ought to think! Or might you have only travelled for your amusement?"

"Surely," Siddhartha laughed, "surely I have travelled for my amusement. For what else? I have gotten to know people and places, I have received kindness and trust, I have found friendship. Look, my dear, if I had been Kamaswami, I would have travelled back, being annoyed and in a hurry, as soon as I had seen that my purchase had been rendered impossible, and time and money would indeed have been lost. But like this, I've had a few good days, I've learned, had joy, I've neither harmed myself nor others by annoyance and hastiness. And if I'll ever return there again, perhaps to buy an upcoming harvest, or for whatever purpose it might be, friendly people will receive me in a friendly and happy manner, and I will praise myself for not showing any hurry and displeasure at that time. So, leave it as it is, my friend, and don't harm yourself by scolding! If the day will come, when you will see: this Siddhartha is harming me, then speak a word and Siddhartha will go on his own path. But until then, let's be satisfied with one another."

Futile were also the merchant's attempts, to convince Siddhartha that he should eat his bread. Siddhartha ate his own bread, or rather they both ate other people's bread, all people's bread. Siddhartha never listened to Kamaswami's worries and Kamaswami had many worries. Whether there was a business-deal going on which was in danger of failing, or whether a shipment of merchandise seemed to have been lost, or a debtor seemed to be unable to pay, Kamaswami could never convince his partner that it would be useful to utter a few words of worry or anger, to have wrinkles on the forehead, to sleep badly. When, one day, Kamaswami held against him that he had learned everything he knew from him, he replied: "Would you please not kid me with such jokes! What I've learned from you is how much a basket of fish costs and how much interest may be charged on loaned money. These are your areas of expertise. I haven't learned to think from you, my dear Kamaswami, you ought to be the one seeking to learn from me."

Indeed his soul was not with the trade. The business was good enough to provide him with the money for Kamala, and it earned him much more than he needed. Besides from this, Siddhartha's interest and curiosity was only concerned with the people, whose businesses, crafts, worries, pleasures, and acts of foolishness used to be as alien and distant to him as the moon. However easily he succeeded in talking to all of them, in living with all of them, in learning from all of them, he was still aware that there was something which separated him from them and this separating factor was him being a Samana. He saw mankind going through life in a childlike or animallike manner, which he loved and also despised at the same time. He saw them toiling, saw them suffering, and becoming gray for the sake of things which seemed to him entirely unworthy of this price, for money, for little pleasures, for being slightly honoured, he saw them scolding and insulting each other, he saw them complaining about pain at which a Samana would only smile, and suffering because of deprivations which a Samana would not feel.

He was open to everything these people brought his way. Welcome was the merchant who offered him linen for sale, welcome was the debtor who sought another loan, welcome was the beggar who told him for one hour the story of his poverty and who was not half as poor as any given Samana. He did not treat the rich foreign merchant any different than the servant who shaved him and the street-vendor whom he let cheat him out of some small change when buying bananas. When Kamaswami came to him, to complain about his worries or to reproach him concerning his business, he listened curiously and happily, was puzzled by him, tried to understand him, consented that he was a little bit right, only as much as he considered indispensable, and turned away from him, towards the next person who would ask for him. And there were many who came to him, many to do business with him, many to cheat him, many to draw some secret out of him, many to appeal to his sympathy, many to get his advice. He gave advice, he pitied, he made gifts, he let them cheat him a bit, and this entire game and the passion with which all people played this game occupied his thoughts just as much as the gods and Brahmans used to occupy them.

At times he felt, deep in his chest, a dying, quiet voice, which admonished him quietly, lamented quietly; he hardly perceived it. And then, for an hour, he became aware of the strange life he was leading, of him doing lots of things which were only a game, of, though being happy and feeling joy at times, real life still passing him by and not touching him. As a ball-player plays with his balls, he played with his business-deals, with the people around him, watched them, found amusement in them; with his heart, with the source of his being, he was not with them. The source ran somewhere, far away from him, ran and ran invisibly, had nothing to do with his life any more. And at several times he suddenly became scared on account of such thoughts and wished that he would also be gifted with the ability to participate in all of these childlike-naive occupations of the daytime with passion and with his heart, really to live, really to act, really to enjoy and to live instead of just standing by as a spectator. But again and again, he came back to beautiful Kamala, learned the art of love, practised the cult of lust, in which more than in anything else giving and taking becomes one, chatted with her, learned from her, gave her advice, received advice. She understood him better than Govinda used to understand him, she was more similar to him.

Once, he said to her: "You are like me, you are different from most people. You are Kamala, nothing else, and inside of you, there is a peace and refuge, to which you can go at every hour of the day and be at home at yourself, as I can also do. Few people have this, and yet all could have it."

"Not all people are smart," said Kamala.

"No," said Siddhartha, "that's not the reason why. Kamaswami is just as smart as I, and still has no refuge in himself. Others have it, who are small children with respect to their mind. Most people, Kamala, are like a falling leaf, which is blown and is turning around through the air, and wavers, and tumbles to the ground. But others, a few, are like stars, they go on a fixed course, no wind reaches them, in themselves they have their law and their course. Among all the learned men and Samanas, of which I knew many, there was one of this kind, a perfected one, I'll never be able to forget him. It is that Gotama, the exalted one, who is spreading those teachings. Thousands of followers are listening to his teachings every day, follow his instructions every hour, but they are all falling leaves, not in themselves they have teachings and a law."

Kamala looked at him with a smile. "Again, you're talking about him," she said, "again, you're having a Samana's thoughts."

Siddhartha said nothing, and they played the game of love, one of the thirty or forty different games Kamala knew. Her body was flexible like that of a jaguar and like the bow of a hunter; he who had learned from her how to make love, was knowledgeable of many forms of lust, many secrets. For a long time, she played with Siddhartha, enticed him, rejected him, forced him, embraced him: enjoyed his masterful skills, until he was defeated and rested exhausted by her side.

The courtesan bent over him, took a long look at his face, at his eyes, which had grown tired.

"You are the best lover," she said thoughtfully, "I ever saw. You're stronger than others, more supple, more willing. You've learned my art well, Siddhartha. At some time, when I'll be older, I'd want to bear your child. And yet, my dear, you've remained a Samana, and yet you do not love me, you love nobody. Isn't it so?"

"It might very well be so," Siddhartha said tiredly. "I am like you. You also do not love—how else could you practise love as a craft? Perhaps, people of our kind can't love. The childlike people can; that's their secret."

SANSARA

For a long time, Siddhartha had lived the life of the world and of lust, though without being a part of it. His senses, which he had killed off in hot years as a Samana, had awoken again, he had tasted riches, had tasted lust, had tasted power; nevertheless he had still remained in his heart for a long time a Samana; Kamala, being smart, had realized this quite right. It was still the art of thinking, of waiting, of fasting, which guided his life; still the people of the world, the childlike people, had remained alien to him as he was alien to them.

Years passed by; surrounded by the good life, Siddhartha hardly felt them fading away. He had become rich, for quite a while he possessed a house of his own and his own servants, and a garden before the city by the river. The people liked him, they came to him, whenever they needed money or advice, but there was nobody close to him, except Kamala.

That high, bright state of being awake, which he had experienced that one time at the height of his youth, in those days after Gotama's sermon, after the separation from Govinda, that tense expectation, that proud state of standing alone without teachings and without teachers, that supple willingness to listen to the divine voice in his own heart, had slowly become a memory, had been fleeting; distant and quiet, the holy source murmured, which used to be near, which used to murmur within himself. Nevertheless, many things he had learned from the Samanas, he had learned from Gotama, he had learned from his father the Brahman, had remained within him for a long time afterwards: moderate living, joy of thinking, hours of meditation, secret knowledge of the self, of his eternal entity, which is neither body nor consciousness. Many a part of this he still had, but one part after another had been submerged and had gathered dust. Just as a potter's wheel, once it has been set in motion, will keep on turning for a long time and only slowly lose its vigour and come to a stop, thus Siddhartha's soul had kept on turning the wheel of asceticism, the wheel of thinking, the wheel of differentiation for a long time, still turning, but it turned slowly and hesitantly and was close to coming to a standstill. Slowly, like humidity entering the dying stem of a tree, filling it slowly and making it rot, the world and sloth had entered Siddhartha's soul, slowly it filled his soul, made it heavy, made it tired, put it to sleep. On the other hand, his senses had become alive, there was much they had learned, much they had experienced.

Siddhartha had learned to trade, to use his power over people, to enjoy himself with a woman, he had learned to wear beautiful clothes, to give orders to servants, to bathe in perfumed waters. He had learned to eat tenderly and carefully prepared food, even fish, even meat and poultry, spices and sweets, and to drink wine, which causes sloth and forgetfulness. He had learned to play with dice and on a chess-board, to watch dancing girls, to have himself carried about in a sedan-chair, to sleep on a soft bed. But still he had felt different from and superior to the others; always he had watched them with some mockery, some mocking disdain, with the same disdain which a Samana constantly feels for the people of the world. When Kamaswami was ailing, when he was annoyed, when he felt insulted, when he was vexed by his worries as a merchant, Siddhartha had always watched it with mockery. Just slowly and imperceptibly, as the harvest seasons and rainy seasons passed by, his mockery had become more tired, his superiority had become more quiet. Just slowly, among his growing riches, Siddhartha had assumed something of the childlike people's ways for himself, something of their childlikeness and of their fearfulness. And yet, he envied them, envied them just the more, the more similar he became to them. He envied them for the one thing that was missing from him and that they had, the importance they were able to attach to their lives, the amount of passion in their joys and fears, the fearful but sweet happiness of being constantly in love. These people were all of the time in love with themselves, with women, with their children, with honours or money, with plans or hopes. But he did not learn this from them, this out of all things, this joy of a child and this foolishness of a child; he learned from them out of all things the unpleasant ones, which he himself despised. It happened more and more often that, in the morning after having had company the night before, he stayed in bed for a long time, felt unable to think and tired. It happened that he became angry and impatient, when Kamaswami bored him with his worries. It happened that he laughed just too loud when he lost a game of dice. His face was still smarter and more spiritual than others, but it rarely laughed, and assumed, one after another, those features which are so often found in the faces of rich people, those features of discontent, of sickliness, of ill-humour, of sloth, of a lack of love. Slowly the disease of the soul, which rich people have, grabbed hold of him.

Like a veil, like a thin mist, tiredness came over Siddhartha, slowly, getting a bit denser every day, a bit murkier every month, a bit heavier every year. As a new dress becomes old in time, loses its beautiful colour in time, gets stains, gets wrinkles, gets worn off at the seams, and starts to show threadbare spots here and there, thus Siddhartha's new life, which he had started after his separation from Govinda, had grown old, lost colour and splendour as the years passed by, was gathering wrinkles and stains, and hidden at bottom, already showing its ugliness here and there, disappointment and disgust were waiting. Siddhartha did not notice it. He only noticed that this bright and reliable voice inside of him, which had awoken in him at that time and had ever guided him in his best times, had become silent.

He had been captured by the world, by lust, covetousness, sloth, and finally also by that vice which he had used to despise and mock the most as the most foolish one of all vices: greed. Property, possessions, and riches also had finally captured him; they were no longer a game and trifles to him, had become a shackle and a burden. In a strange and devious way, Siddhartha had gotten into this final and most base of all dependencies, by means of the game of dice. It was since that time, when he had stopped being a Samana in his heart, that Siddhartha began to play the game for money and precious things, which he at other times only joined with a smile and casually as a custom of the childlike people, with an increasing rage and passion. He was a feared gambler, few dared to take him on, so high and audacious were his stakes. He played the game due to a pain of his heart, losing and wasting his wretched money in the game brought him an angry joy, in no other way he could demonstrate his disdain for wealth, the merchants' false god, more clearly and more mockingly. Thus he gambled with high stakes and mercilessly, hating himself, mocking himself, won thousands, threw away thousands, lost money, lost jewelry, lost a house in the country, won again, lost again. That fear, that terrible and petrifying fear, which he felt while he was rolling the dice, while he was worried about losing high stakes, that fear he loved and sought to always renew it, always increase it, always get it to a slightly higher level, for in this feeling alone he still felt something like happiness, something like an intoxication, something like an elevated form of life in the midst of his saturated, lukewarm, dull life.

And after each big loss, his mind was set on new riches, pursued the trade more zealously, forced his debtors more strictly to pay, because he wanted to continue gambling, he wanted to continue squandering, continue demonstrating his disdain of wealth. Siddhartha lost his calmness when losses occurred, lost his patience when he was not paid on time, lost his kindness towards beggars, lost his disposition for giving away and loaning money to those who petitioned him. He, who gambled away tens of thousands at one roll of the dice and laughed at it, became more strict and more petty in his business, occasionally dreaming at night about money! And whenever he woke up from this ugly spell, whenever he found his face in the mirror at the bedroom's wall to have aged and become more ugly, whenever embarrassment and disgust came over him, he continued fleeing, fleeing into a new game, fleeing into a numbing of his mind brought on by sex, by wine, and from there he fled back into the urge to pile up and obtain possessions. In this pointless cycle he ran, growing tired, growing old, growing ill.

Then the time came when a dream warned him. He had spent the hours of the evening with Kamala, in her beautiful pleasure-garden. They had been sitting under the trees, talking, and Kamala had said thoughtful words, words behind which a sadness and tiredness lay hidden. She had asked him to tell her about Gotama, and could not hear enough of him, how clear his eyes, how still and beautiful his mouth, how kind his smile, how peaceful his walk had been. For a long time, he had to tell her about the exalted Buddha, and Kamala had sighed and had said: "One day, perhaps soon, I'll also follow that Buddha. I'll give him my pleasure-garden for a gift and take my refuge in his teachings." But after this, she had aroused him, and had tied him to her in the act of making love with painful fervour, biting and in tears, as if, once more, she wanted to squeeze the last sweet drop out of this vain, fleeting pleasure. Never before, it had become so strangely clear to Siddhartha, how closely lust was akin to death. Then he had lain by her side, and Kamala's face had been close to him, and under her eyes and next to the corners of her mouth he had, as clearly as never before, read a fearful inscription, an inscription of small lines, of slight grooves, an inscription reminiscent of autumn and old age, just as Siddhartha himself, who was only in his forties, had already noticed, here and there, gray hairs among his black ones. Tiredness was written on Kamala's beautiful face, tiredness from walking a long path, which has no happy destination, tiredness and the beginning of withering, and concealed, still unsaid, perhaps not even conscious anxiety: fear of old age, fear of the autumn, fear of having to die. With a sigh, he had bid his farewell to her, the soul full of reluctance, and full of concealed anxiety.

Then, Siddhartha had spent the night in his house with dancing girls and wine, had acted as if he was superior to them, towards the fellow-members of his caste, though this was no longer true, had drunk much wine and gone to bed a long time after midnight, being tired and yet excited, close to weeping and despair, and had for a long time sought to sleep in vain, his heart full of misery which he thought he could not bear any longer, full of a disgust which he felt penetrating his entire body like the lukewarm, repulsive taste of the wine, the just too sweet, dull music, the just too soft smile of the dancing girls, the just too sweet scent of their hair and breasts. But more than by anything else, he was disgusted by himself, by his perfumed hair, by the smell of wine from his mouth, by the flabby tiredness and listlessness of his skin. Like when someone, who has eaten and drunk far too much, vomits it back up again with agonising pain and is nevertheless glad about the relief, thus this sleepless man wished to free himself of these pleasures, these habits and all of this pointless life and himself, in an immense burst of disgust. Not until the light of the morning and the beginning of the first activities in the street before his city-house, he had slightly fallen asleep, had found for a few moments a half unconsciousness, a hint of sleep. In those moments, he had a dream:

Kamala owned a small, rare singing bird in a golden cage. Of this bird, he dreamt. He dreamt: this bird had become mute, who at other times always used to sing in the morning, and since this arose his attention, he stepped in front of the cage and looked inside; there the small bird was dead and lay stiff on the ground. He took it out, weighed it for a moment in his hand, and then threw it away, out in the street, and in the same moment, he felt terribly shocked, and his heart hurt, as if he had thrown away from himself all value and everything good by throwing out this dead bird.

Starting up from this dream, he felt encompassed by a deep sadness. Worthless, so it seemed to him, worthless and pointless was the way he had been going through life; nothing which was alive, nothing which was in some way delicious or worth keeping he had left in his hands. Alone he stood there and empty like a castaway on the shore.

With a gloomy mind, Siddhartha went to the pleasure-garden he owned, locked the gate, sat down under a mango-tree, felt death in his heart and horror in his chest, sat and sensed how everything died in him, withered in him, came to an end in him. By and by, he gathered his thoughts, and in his mind, he once again went the entire path of his life, starting with the first days he could remember. When was there ever a time when he had experienced happiness, felt a true bliss? Oh yes, several times he had experienced such a thing. In his years as a boy, he had had a taste of it, when he had obtained praise from the Brahmans, he had felt it in his heart: "There is a path in front of the one who has distinguished himself in the recitation of the holy verses, in the dispute with the learned ones, as an assistant in the offerings." Then, he had felt it in his heart: "There is a path in front of you, you are destined for, the gods are awaiting you." And again, as a young man, when the ever rising, upward fleeing, goal of all thinking had ripped him out of and up from the multitude of those seeking the same goal, when he wrestled in pain for the purpose of Brahman, when every obtained knowledge only kindled new thirst in him, then again he had, in the midst of the thirst, in the midst of the pain felt this very same thing: "Go on! Go on! You are called upon!" He had heard this voice when he had left his home and had chosen the life of a Samana, and again when he had gone away from the Samanas to that perfected one, and also when he had gone away from him to the uncertain. For how long had he not heard this voice any more, for how long had he reached no height any more, how even and dull was the manner in which his path had passed through life, for many long years, without a high goal, without thirst, without elevation, content with small lustful pleasures and yet never satisfied! For all of these many years, without knowing it himself, he had tried hard and longed to become a man like those many, like those children, and in all this, his life had been much more miserable and poorer than theirs, and their goals were not his, nor their worries; after all, that entire world of the Kamaswami-people had only been a game to him, a dance he would watch, a comedy. Only Kamala had been dear, had been valuable to him—but was she still thus? Did he still need her, or she him? Did they not play a game without an ending? Was it necessary to live for this? No, it was not necessary! The name of this game was Sansara, a game for children, a game which was perhaps enjoyable to play once, twice, ten times—but forever and ever over again?

Then, Siddhartha knew that the game was over, that he could not play it any more. Shivers ran over his body, inside of him, so he felt, something had died.

That entire day, he sat under the mango-tree, thinking of his father, thinking of Govinda, thinking of Gotama. Did he have to leave them to become a Kamaswami? He still sat there, when the night had fallen. When, looking up, he caught sight of the stars, he thought: "Here I'm sitting under my mango-tree, in my pleasure-garden." He smiled a little—was it really necessary, was it right, was it not as foolish game, that he owned a mango-tree, that he owned a garden?

He also put an end to this, this also died in him. He rose, bid his farewell to the mango-tree, his farewell to the pleasure-garden. Since he had been without food this day, he felt strong hunger, and thought of his house in the city, of his chamber and bed, of the table with the meals on it. He smiled tiredly, shook himself, and bid his farewell to these things.

In the same hour of the night, Siddhartha left his garden, left the city, and never came back. For a long time, Kamaswami had people look for him, thinking that he had fallen into the hands of robbers. Kamala had no one look for him. When she was told that Siddhartha had disappeared, she was not astonished. Did she not always expect it? Was he not a Samana, a man who was at home nowhere, a pilgrim? And most of all, she had felt this the last time they had been together, and she was happy, in spite of all the pain of the loss, that she had pulled him so affectionately to her heart for this last time, that she had felt one more time to be so completely possessed and penetrated by him.

When she received the first news of Siddhartha's disappearance, she went to the window, where she held a rare singing bird captive in a golden cage. She opened the door of the cage, took the bird out and let it fly. For a long time, she gazed after it, the flying bird. From this day on, she received no more visitors and kept her house locked. But after some time, she became aware that she was pregnant from the last time she was together with Siddhartha.

BY THE RIVER

Siddhartha walked through the forest, was already far from the city, and knew nothing but that one thing, that there was no going back for him, that this life, as he had lived it for many years until now, was over and done away with, and that he had tasted all of it, sucked everything out of it until he was disgusted with it. Dead was the singing bird he had dreamt of. Dead was the bird in his heart. Deeply, he had been entangled in Sansara, he had sucked up disgust and death from all sides into his body, like a sponge sucks up water until it is full. And full he was, full of the feeling of been sick of it, full of misery, full of death, there was nothing left in this world which could have attracted him, given him joy, given him comfort.

Passionately he wished to know nothing about himself anymore, to have rest, to be dead. If there only was a lightning-bolt to strike him dead! If there only was a tiger to devour him! If there only was a wine, a poison which would numb his senses, bring him forgetfulness and sleep, and no awakening from that! Was there still any kind of filth he had not soiled himself with, a sin or foolish act he had not committed, a dreariness of the soul he had not brought upon himself? Was it still at all possible to be alive? Was it possible to breathe in again and again, to breathe out, to feel hunger, to eat again, to sleep again, to sleep with a woman again? Was this cycle not exhausted and brought to a conclusion for him?

Siddhartha reached the large river in the forest, the same river over which a long time ago, when he had still been a young man and came from the town of Gotama, a ferryman had conducted him. By this river he stopped, hesitantly he stood at the bank. Tiredness and hunger had weakened him, and whatever for should he walk on, wherever to, to which goal? No, there were no more goals, there was nothing left but the deep, painful yearning to shake off this whole desolate dream, to spit out this stale wine, to put an end to this miserable and shameful life.

A hang bent over the bank of the river, a coconut-tree; Siddhartha leaned against its trunk with his shoulder, embraced the trunk with one arm, and looked down into the green water, which ran and ran under him, looked down and found himself to be entirely filled with the wish to let go and to drown in these waters. A frightening emptiness was reflected back at him by the water, answering to the terrible emptiness in his soul. Yes, he had reached the end. There was nothing left for him, except to annihilate himself, except to smash the failure into which he had shaped his life, to throw it away, before the feet of mockingly laughing gods. This was the great vomiting he had longed for: death, the smashing to bits of the form he hated! Let him be food for fishes, this dog Siddhartha, this lunatic, this depraved and rotten body, this weakened and abused soul! Let him be food for fishes and crocodiles, let him be chopped to bits by the daemons!

With a distorted face, he stared into the water, saw the reflection of his face and spit at it. In deep tiredness, he took his arm away from the trunk of the tree and turned a bit, in order to let himself fall straight down, in order to finally drown. With his eyes closed, he slipped towards death.

Then, out of remote areas of his soul, out of past times of his now weary life, a sound stirred up. It was a word, a syllable, which he, without thinking, with a slurred voice, spoke to himself, the old word which is the beginning and the end of all prayers of the Brahmans, the holy "Om", which roughly means "that what is perfect" or "the completion". And in the moment when the sound of "Om" touched Siddhartha's ear, his dormant spirit suddenly woke up and realized the foolishness of his actions.

Siddhartha was deeply shocked. So this was how things were with him, so doomed was he, so much he had lost his way and was forsaken by all knowledge, that he had been able to seek death, that this wish, this wish of a child, had been able to grow in him: to find rest by annihilating his body! What all agony of these recent times, all sobering realizations, all desperation had not brought about, this was brought on by this moment, when the Om entered his consciousness: he became aware of himself in his misery and in his error.

Om! he spoke to himself: Om! and again he knew about Brahman, knew about the indestructibility of life, knew about all that is divine, which he had forgotten.

But this was only a moment, flash. By the foot of the coconut-tree, Siddhartha collapsed, struck down by tiredness, mumbling Om, placed his head on the root of the tree and fell into a deep sleep.

Deep was his sleep and without dreams, for a long time he had not known such a sleep any more. When he woke up after many hours, he felt as if ten years had passed, he heard the water quietly flowing, did not know where he was and who had brought him here, opened his eyes, saw with astonishment that there were trees and the sky above him, and he remembered where he was and how he got here. But it took him a long while for this, and the past seemed to him as if it had been covered by a veil, infinitely distant, infinitely far away, infinitely meaningless. He only knew that his previous life (in the first moment when he thought about it, this past life seemed to him like a very old, previous incarnation, like an early pre-birth of his present self)—that his previous life had been abandoned by him, that, full of disgust and wretchedness, he had even intended to throw his life away, but that by a river, under a coconut-tree, he had come to his senses, the holy word Om on his lips, that then he had fallen asleep and had now woken up and was looking at the world as a new man. Quietly, he spoke the word Om to himself, speaking which he had fallen asleep, and it seemed to him as if his entire long sleep had been nothing but a long meditative recitation of Om, a thinking of Om, a submergence and complete entering into Om, into the nameless, the perfected.

What a wonderful sleep had this been! Never before by sleep, he had been thus refreshed, thus renewed, thus rejuvenated! Perhaps, he had really died, had drowned and was reborn in a new body? But no, he knew himself, he knew his hands and his feet, knew the place where he lay, knew this self in his chest, this Siddhartha, the eccentric, the weird one, but this Siddhartha was nevertheless transformed, was renewed, was strangely well rested, strangely awake, joyful and curious.

Siddhartha straightened up, then he saw a person sitting opposite to him, an unknown man, a monk in a yellow robe with a shaven head, sitting in the position of pondering. He observed the man, who had neither hair on his head nor a beard, and he had not observed him for long when he recognised this monk as Govinda, the friend of his youth, Govinda who had taken his refuge with the exalted Buddha. Govinda had aged, he too, but still his face bore the same features, expressed zeal, faithfulness, searching, timidness. But when Govinda now, sensing his gaze, opened his eyes and looked at him, Siddhartha saw that Govinda did not recognise him. Govinda was happy to find him awake; apparently, he had been sitting here for a long time and been waiting for him to wake up, though he did not know him.

"I have been sleeping," said Siddhartha. "However did you get here?"

"You have been sleeping," answered Govinda. "It is not good to be sleeping in such places, where snakes often are and the animals of the forest have their paths. I, oh sir, am a follower of the exalted Gotama, the Buddha, the Sakyamuni, and have been on a pilgrimage together with several of us on this path, when I saw you lying and sleeping in a place where it is dangerous to sleep. Therefore, I sought to wake you up, oh sir, and since I saw that your sleep was very deep, I stayed behind from my group and sat with you. And then, so it seems, I have fallen asleep myself, I who wanted to guard your sleep. Badly, I have served you, tiredness has overwhelmed me. But now that you're awake, let me go to catch up with my brothers."

"I thank you, Samana, for watching out over my sleep," spoke Siddhartha. "You're friendly, you followers of the exalted one. Now you may go then."

"I'm going, sir. May you, sir, always be in good health."

"I thank you, Samana."

Govinda made the gesture of a salutation and said: "Farewell."

"Farewell, Govinda," said Siddhartha.

The monk stopped.

"Permit me to ask, sir, from where do you know my name?"

Now, Siddhartha smiled.

"I know you, oh Govinda, from your father's hut, and from the school of the Brahmans, and from the offerings, and from our walk to the Samanas, and from that hour when you took your refuge with the exalted one in the grove Jetavana."

"You're Siddhartha," Govinda exclaimed loudly. "Now, I'm recognising you, and don't comprehend any more how I couldn't recognise you right away. Be welcome, Siddhartha, my joy is great, to see you again."

"It also gives me joy, to see you again. You've been the guard of my sleep, again I thank you for this, though I wouldn't have required any guard. Where are you going to, oh friend?"

"I'm going nowhere. We monks are always travelling, whenever it is not the rainy season, we always move from one place to another, live according to the rules of the teachings passed on to us, accept alms, move on. It is always like this. But you, Siddhartha, where are you going to?"

Quoth Siddhartha: "With me too, friend, it is as it is with you. I'm going nowhere. I'm just travelling. I'm on a pilgrimage."

Govinda spoke: "You're saying: you're on a pilgrimage, and I believe you. But, forgive me, oh Siddhartha, you do not look like a pilgrim. You're wearing a rich man's garments, you're wearing the shoes of a distinguished gentleman, and your hair, with the fragrance of perfume, is not a pilgrim's hair, not the hair of a Samana."

"Right so, my dear, you have observed well, your keen eyes see everything. But I haven't said to you that I was a Samana. I said: I'm on a pilgrimage. And so it is: I'm on a pilgrimage."

"You're on a pilgrimage," said Govinda. "But few would go on a pilgrimage in such clothes, few in such shoes, few with such hair. Never I have met such a pilgrim, being a pilgrim myself for many years."

"I believe you, my dear Govinda. But now, today, you've met a pilgrim just like this, wearing such shoes, such a garment. Remember, my dear: Not eternal is the world of appearances, not eternal, anything but eternal are our garments and the style of our hair, and our hair and bodies themselves. I'm wearing a rich man's clothes, you've seen this quite right. I'm wearing them, because I have been a rich man, and I'm wearing my hair like the worldly and lustful people, for I have been one of them."

"And now, Siddhartha, what are you now?"

"I don't know it, I don't know it just like you. I'm travelling. I was a rich man and am no rich man any more, and what I'll be tomorrow, I don't know."

"You've lost your riches?"

"I've lost them or they me. They somehow happened to slip away from me. The wheel of physical manifestations is turning quickly, Govinda. Where is Siddhartha the Brahman? Where is Siddhartha the Samana? Where is Siddhartha the rich man? Non-eternal things change quickly, Govinda, you know it."

Govinda looked at the friend of his youth for a long time, with doubt in his eyes. After that, he gave him the salutation which one would use on a gentleman and went on his way.

With a smiling face, Siddhartha watched him leave, he loved him still, this faithful man, this fearful man. And how could he not have loved everybody and everything in this moment, in the glorious hour after his wonderful sleep, filled with Om! The enchantment, which had happened inside of him in his sleep and by means of the Om, was this very thing that he loved everything, that he was full of joyful love for everything he saw. And it was this very thing, so it seemed to him now, which had been his sickness before, that he was not able to love anybody or anything.

With a smiling face, Siddhartha watched the leaving monk. The sleep had strengthened him much, but hunger gave him much pain, for by now he had not eaten for two days, and the times were long past when he had been tough against hunger. With sadness, and yet also with a smile, he thought of that time. In those days, so he remembered, he had boasted of three things to Kamala, had been able to do three noble and undefeatable feats: fasting—waiting—thinking. These had been his possessions, his power and strength, his solid staff; in the busy, laborious years of his youth, he had learned these three feats, nothing else. And now, they had abandoned him, none of them was his any more, neither fasting, nor waiting, nor thinking. For the most wretched things, he had given them up, for what fades most quickly, for sensual lust, for the good life, for riches! His life had indeed been strange. And now, so it seemed, now he had really become a childlike person.

Siddhartha thought about his situation. Thinking was hard on him, he did not really feel like it, but he forced himself.

Now, he thought, since all these most easily perishing things have slipped from me again, now I'm standing here under the sun again just as I have been standing here a little child, nothing is mine, I have no abilities, there is nothing I could bring about, I have learned nothing. How wondrous is this! Now, that I'm no longer young, that my hair is already half gray, that my strength is fading, now I'm starting again at the beginning and as a child! Again, he had to smile. Yes, his fate had been strange! Things were going downhill with him, and now he was again facing the world void and naked and stupid. But he could not feel sad about this, no, he even felt a great urge to laugh, to laugh about himself, to laugh about this strange, foolish world.

"Things are going downhill with you!" he said to himself, and laughed about it, and as he was saying it, he happened to glance at the river, and he also saw the river going downhill, always moving on downhill, and singing and being happy through it all. He liked this well, kindly he smiled at the river. Was this not the river in which he had intended to drown himself, in past times, a hundred years ago, or had he dreamed this?

Wondrous indeed was my life, so he thought, wondrous detours it has taken. As a boy, I had only to do with gods and offerings. As a youth, I had only to do with asceticism, with thinking and meditation, was searching for Brahman, worshipped the eternal in the Atman. But as a young man, I followed the penitents, lived in the forest, suffered of heat and frost, learned to hunger, taught my body to become dead. Wonderfully, soon afterwards, insight came towards me in the form of the great Buddha's teachings, I felt the knowledge of the oneness of the world circling in me like my own blood. But I also had to leave Buddha and the great knowledge. I went and learned the art of love with Kamala, learned trading with Kamaswami, piled up money, wasted money, learned to love my stomach, learned to please my senses. I had to spend many years losing my spirit, to unlearn thinking again, to forget the oneness. Isn't it just as if I had turned slowly and on a long detour from a man into a child, from a thinker into a childlike person? And yet, this path has been very good; and yet, the bird in my chest has not died. But what a path has this been! I had to pass through so much stupidity, through so much vice, through so many errors, through so much disgust and disappointments and woe, just to become a child again and to be able to start over. But it was right so, my heart says "Yes" to it, my eyes smile to it. I've had to experience despair, I've had to sink down to the most foolish one of all thoughts, to the thought of suicide, in order to be able to experience divine grace, to hear Om again, to be able to sleep properly and awake properly again. I had to become a fool, to find Atman in me again. I had to sin, to be able to live again. Where else might my path lead me to? It is foolish, this path, it moves in loops, perhaps it is going around in a circle. Let it go as it likes, I want to take it.

Wonderfully, he felt joy rolling like waves in his chest.

Wherever from, he asked his heart, where from did you get this happiness? Might it come from that long, good sleep, which has done me so good? Or from the word Om, which I said? Or from the fact that I have escaped, that I have completely fled, that I am finally free again and am standing like a child under the sky? Oh how good is it to have fled, to have become free! How clean and beautiful is the air here, how good to breathe! There, where I ran away from, there everything smelled of ointments, of spices, of wine, of excess, of sloth. How I hated this world of the rich, of those who revel in fine food, of the gamblers! How I hated myself for staying in this terrible world for so long! How I hated myself, have deprived, poisoned, tortured myself, have made myself old and evil! No, never again I will, as I used to like doing so much, delude myself into thinking that Siddhartha was wise! But this one thing I have done well, this I like, this I must praise, that there is now an end to that hatred against myself, to that foolish and dreary life! I praise you, Siddhartha, after so many years of foolishness, you have once again had an idea, have done something, have heard the bird in your chest singing and have followed it!

Thus he praised himself, found joy in himself, listened curiously to his stomach, which was rumbling with hunger. He had now, so he felt, in these recent times and days, completely tasted and spit out, devoured up to the point of desperation and death, a piece of suffering, a piece of misery. Like this, it was good. For much longer, he could have stayed with Kamaswami, made money, wasted money, filled his stomach, and let his soul die of thirst; for much longer he could have lived in this soft, well upholstered hell, if this had not happened: the moment of complete hopelessness and despair, that most extreme moment, when he hung over the rushing waters and was ready to destroy himself. That he had felt this despair, this deep disgust, and that he had not succumbed to it, that the bird, the joyful source and voice in him was still alive after all, this was why he felt joy, this was why he laughed, this was why his face was smiling brightly under his hair which had turned gray.

"It is good," he thought, "to get a taste of everything for oneself, which one needs to know. That lust for the world and riches do not belong to the good things, I have already learned as a child. I have known it for a long time, but I have experienced only now. And now I know it, don't just know it in my memory, but in my eyes, in my heart, in my stomach. Good for me, to know this!"

For a long time, he pondered his transformation, listened to the bird, as it sang for joy. Had not this bird died in him, had he not felt its death? No, something else from within him had died, something which already for a long time had yearned to die. Was it not this what he used to intend to kill in his ardent years as a penitent? Was this not his self, his small, frightened, and proud self, he had wrestled with for so many years, which had defeated him again and again, which was back again after every killing, prohibited joy, felt fear? Was it not this, which today had finally come to its death, here in the forest, by this lovely river? Was it not due to this death, that he was now like a child, so full of trust, so without fear, so full of joy?

Now Siddhartha also got some idea of why he had fought this self in vain as a Brahman, as a penitent. Too much knowledge had held him back, too many holy verses, too many sacrificial rules, to much self-castigation, so much doing and striving for that goal! Full of arrogance, he had been, always the smartest, always working the most, always one step ahead of all others, always the knowing and spiritual one, always the priest or wise one. Into being a priest, into this arrogance, into this spirituality, his self had retreated, there it sat firmly and grew, while he thought he would kill it by fasting and penance. Now he saw it and saw that the secret voice had been right, that no teacher would ever have been able to bring about his salvation. Therefore, he had to go out into the world, lose himself to lust and power, to woman and money, had to become a merchant, a dice-gambler, a drinker, and a greedy person, until the priest and Samana in him was dead. Therefore, he had to continue bearing these ugly years, bearing the disgust, the teachings, the pointlessness of a dreary and wasted life up to the end, up to bitter despair, until Siddhartha the lustful, Siddhartha the greedy could also die. He had died, a new Siddhartha had woken up from the sleep. He would also grow old, he would also eventually have to die, mortal was Siddhartha, mortal was every physical form. But today he was young, was a child, the new Siddhartha, and was full of joy.

He thought these thoughts, listened with a smile to his stomach, listened gratefully to a buzzing bee. Cheerfully, he looked into the rushing river, never before he had liked a water so well as this one, never before he had perceived the voice and the parable of the moving water thus strongly and beautifully. It seemed to him, as if the river had something special to tell him, something he did not know yet, which was still awaiting him. In this river, Siddhartha had intended to drown himself, in it the old, tired, desperate Siddhartha had drowned today. But the new Siddhartha felt a deep love for this rushing water, and decided for himself, not to leave it very soon.

THE FERRYMAN

By this river I want to stay, thought Siddhartha, it is the same which I have crossed a long time ago on my way to the childlike people, a friendly ferryman had guided me then, he is the one I want to go to, starting out from his hut, my path had led me at that time into a new life, which had now grown old and is dead—my present path, my present new life, shall also take its start there!

Tenderly, he looked into the rushing water, into the transparent green, into the crystal lines of its drawing, so rich in secrets. Bright pearls he saw rising from the deep, quiet bubbles of air floating on the reflecting surface, the blue of the sky being depicted in it. With a thousand eyes, the river looked at him, with green ones, with white ones, with crystal ones, with sky-blue ones. How did he love this water, how did it delight him, how grateful was he to it! In his heart he heard the voice talking, which was newly awaking, and it told him: Love this water! Stay near it! Learn from it! Oh yes, he wanted to learn from it, he wanted to listen to it. He who would understand this water and its secrets, so it seemed to him, would also understand many other things, many secrets, all secrets.

But out of all secrets of the river, he today only saw one, this one touched his soul. He saw: this water ran and ran, incessantly it ran, and was nevertheless always there, was always at all times the same and yet new in every moment! Great be he who would grasp this, understand this! He understood and grasped it not, only felt some idea of it stirring, a distant memory, divine voices.

Siddhartha rose, the workings of hunger in his body became unbearable. In a daze he walked on, up the path by the bank, upriver, listened to the current, listened to the rumbling hunger in his body.

When he reached the ferry, the boat was just ready, and the same ferryman who had once transported the young Samana across the river, stood in the boat, Siddhartha recognised him, he had also aged very much.

"Would you like to ferry me over?" he asked.

The ferryman, being astonished to see such an elegant man walking along and on foot, took him into his boat and pushed it off the bank.

"It's a beautiful life you have chosen for yourself," the passenger spoke. "It must be beautiful to live by this water every day and to cruise on it."

With a smile, the man at the oar moved from side to side: "It is beautiful, sir, it is as you say. But isn't every life, isn't every work beautiful?"

"This may be true. But I envy you for yours."

"Ah, you would soon stop enjoying it. This is nothing for people wearing fine clothes."

Siddhartha laughed. "Once before, I have been looked upon today because of my clothes, I have been looked upon with distrust. Wouldn't you, ferryman, like to accept these clothes, which are a nuisance to me, from me? For you must know, I have no money to pay your fare."

"You're joking, sir," the ferryman laughed.

"I'm not joking, friend. Behold, once before you have ferried me across this water in your boat for the immaterial reward of a good deed. Thus, do it today as well, and accept my clothes for it."

"And do you, sir, intent to continue travelling without clothes?"

"Ah, most of all I wouldn't want to continue travelling at all. Most of all I would rather you, ferryman, gave me an old loincloth and kept me with you as your assistant, or rather as your trainee, for I'll have to learn first how to handle the boat."

For a long time, the ferryman looked at the stranger, searching.

"Now I recognise you," he finally said. "At one time, you've slept in my hut, this was a long time ago, possibly more than twenty years ago, and you've been ferried across the river by me, and we parted like good friends. Haven't you been a Samana? I can't think of your name any more."

"My name is Siddhartha, and I was a Samana, when you've last seen me."

"So be welcome, Siddhartha. My name is Vasudeva. You will, so I hope, be my guest today as well and sleep in my hut, and tell me, where you're coming from and why these beautiful clothes are such a nuisance to you."

They had reached the middle of the river, and Vasudeva pushed the oar with more strength, in order to overcome the current. He worked calmly, his eyes fixed in on the front of the boat, with brawny arms. Siddhartha sat and watched him, and remembered, how once before, on that last day of his time as a Samana, love for this man had stirred in his heart. Gratefully, he accepted Vasudeva's invitation. When they had reached the bank, he helped him to tie the boat to the stakes; after this, the ferryman asked him to enter the hut, offered him bread and water, and Siddhartha ate with eager pleasure, and also ate with eager pleasure of the mango fruits Vasudeva offered him.

Afterwards, it was almost the time of the sunset, they sat on a log by the bank, and Siddhartha told the ferryman about where he originally came from and about his life, as he had seen it before his eyes today, in that hour of despair. Until late at night, lasted his tale.

Vasudeva listened with great attention. Listening carefully, he let everything enter his mind, birthplace and childhood, all that learning, all that searching, all joy, all distress. This was among the ferryman's virtues one of the greatest: like only a few, he knew how to listen. Without him having spoken a word, the speaker sensed how Vasudeva let his words enter his mind, quiet, open, waiting, how he did not lose a single one, awaited not a single one with impatience, did not add his praise or rebuke, was just listening. Siddhartha felt, what a happy fortune it is, to confess to such a listener, to bury in his heart his own life, his own search, his own suffering.

But in the end of Siddhartha's tale, when he spoke of the tree by the river, and of his deep fall, of the holy Om, and how he had felt such a love for the river after his slumber, the ferryman listened with twice the attention, entirely and completely absorbed by it, with his eyes closed.

But when Siddhartha fell silent, and a long silence had occurred, then Vasudeva said: "It is as I thought. The river has spoken to you. It is your friend as well, it speaks to you as well. That is good, that is very good. Stay with me, Siddhartha, my friend. I used to have a wife, her bed was next to mine, but she has died a long time ago, for a long time, I have lived alone. Now, you shall live with me, there is space and food for both."

"I thank you," said Siddhartha, "I thank you and accept. And I also thank you for this, Vasudeva, for listening to me so well! These people are rare who know how to listen. And I did not meet a single one who knew it as well as you did. I will also learn in this respect from you."

"You will learn it," spoke Vasudeva, "but not from me. The river has taught me to listen, from it you will learn it as well. It knows everything, the river, everything can be learned from it. See, you've already learned this from the water too, that it is good to strive downwards, to sink, to seek depth. The rich and elegant Siddhartha is becoming an oarsman's servant, the learned Brahman Siddhartha becomes a ferryman: this has also been told to you by the river. You'll learn that other thing from it as well."

Quoth Siddhartha after a long pause: "What other thing, Vasudeva?"

Vasudeva rose. "It is late," he said, "let's go to sleep. I can't tell you that other thing, oh friend. You'll learn it, or perhaps you know it already. See, I'm no learned man, I have no special skill in speaking, I also have no special skill in thinking. All I'm able to do is to listen and to be godly, I have learned nothing else. If I was able to say and teach it, I might be a wise man, but like this I am only a ferryman, and it is my task to ferry people across the river. I have transported many, thousands; and to all of them, my river has been nothing but an obstacle on their travels. They travelled to seek money and business, and for weddings, and on pilgrimages, and the river was obstructing their path, and the ferryman's job was to get them quickly across that obstacle. But for some among thousands, a few, four or five, the river has stopped being an obstacle, they have heard its voice, they have listened to it, and the river has become sacred to them, as it has become sacred to me. Let's rest now, Siddhartha."

Siddhartha stayed with the ferryman and learned to operate the boat, and when there was nothing to do at the ferry, he worked with Vasudeva in the rice-field, gathered wood, plucked the fruit off the banana-trees. He learned to build an oar, and learned to mend the boat, and to weave baskets, and was joyful because of everything he learned, and the days and months passed quickly. But more than Vasudeva could teach him, he was taught by the river. Incessantly, he learned from it. Most of all, he learned from it to listen, to pay close attention with a quiet heart, with a waiting, opened soul, without passion, without a wish, without judgement, without an opinion.

In a friendly manner, he lived side by side with Vasudeva, and occasionally they exchanged some words, few and at length thought about words. Vasudeva was no friend of words; rarely, Siddhartha succeeded in persuading him to speak.

"Did you," so he asked him at one time, "did you too learn that secret from the river: that there is no time?"

Vasudeva's face was filled with a bright smile.

"Yes, Siddhartha," he spoke. "It is this what you mean, isn't it: that the river is everywhere at once, at the source and at the mouth, at the waterfall, at the ferry, at the rapids, in the sea, in the mountains, everywhere at once, and that there is only the present time for it, not the shadow of the past, not the shadow of the future?"

"This it is," said Siddhartha. "And when I had learned it, I looked at my life, and it was also a river, and the boy Siddhartha was only separated from the man Siddhartha and from the old man Siddhartha by a shadow, not by something real. Also, Siddhartha's previous births were no past, and his death and his return to Brahma was no future. Nothing was, nothing will be; everything is, everything has existence and is present."

Siddhartha spoke with ecstasy; deeply, this enlightenment had delighted him. Oh, was not all suffering time, were not all forms of tormenting oneself and being afraid time, was not everything hard, everything hostile in the world gone and overcome as soon as one had overcome time, as soon as time would have been put out of existence by one's thoughts? In ecstatic delight, he had spoken, but Vasudeva smiled at him brightly and nodded in confirmation; silently he nodded, brushed his hand over Siddhartha's shoulder, turned back to his work.

And once again, when the river had just increased its flow in the rainy season and made a powerful noise, then said Siddhartha: "Isn't it so, oh friend, the river has many voices, very many voices? Hasn't it the voice of a king, and of a warrior, and of a bull, and of a bird of the night, and of a woman giving birth, and of a sighing man, and a thousand other voices more?"

"So it is," Vasudeva nodded, "all voices of the creatures are in its voice."

"And do you know," Siddhartha continued, "what word it speaks, when you succeed in hearing all of its ten thousand voices at once?"

Happily, Vasudeva's face was smiling, he bent over to Siddhartha and spoke the holy Om into his ear. And this had been the very thing which Siddhartha had also been hearing.

And time after time, his smile became more similar to the ferryman's, became almost just as bright, almost just as thoroughly glowing with bliss, just as shining out of thousand small wrinkles, just as alike to a child's, just as alike to an old man's. Many travellers, seeing the two ferrymen, thought they were brothers. Often, they sat in the evening together by the bank on the log, said nothing and both listened to the water, which was no water to them, but the voice of life, the voice of what exists, of what is eternally taking shape. And it happened from time to time that both, when listening to the river, thought of the same things, of a conversation from the day before yesterday, of one of their travellers, the face and fate of whom had occupied their thoughts, of death, of their childhood, and that they both in the same moment, when the river had been saying something good to them, looked at each other, both thinking precisely the same thing, both delighted about the same answer to the same question.

There was something about this ferry and the two ferrymen which was transmitted to others, which many of the travellers felt. It happened occasionally that a traveller, after having looked at the face of one of the ferrymen, started to tell the story of his life, told about pains, confessed evil things, asked for comfort and advice. It happened occasionally that someone asked for permission to stay for a night with them to listen to the river. It also happened that curious people came, who had been told that there were two wise men, or sorcerers, or holy men living by that ferry. The curious people asked many questions, but they got no answers, and they found neither sorcerers nor wise men, they only found two friendly little old men, who seemed to be mute and to have become a bit strange and gaga. And the curious people laughed and were discussing how foolishly and gullibly the common people were spreading such empty rumours.

The years passed by, and nobody counted them. Then, at one time, monks came by on a pilgrimage, followers of Gotama, the Buddha, who were asking to be ferried across the river, and by them the ferrymen were told that they were most hurriedly walking back to their great teacher, for the news had spread the exalted one was deadly sick and would soon die his last human death, in order to become one with the salvation. It was not long, until a new flock of monks came along on their pilgrimage, and another one, and the monks as well as most of the other travellers and people walking through the land spoke of nothing else than of Gotama and his impending death. And as people are flocking from everywhere and from all sides, when they are going to war or to the coronation of a king, and are gathering like ants in droves, thus they flocked, like being drawn on by a magic spell, to where the great Buddha was awaiting his death, where the huge event was to take place and the great perfected one of an era was to become one with the glory.

Often, Siddhartha thought in those days of the dying wise man, the great teacher, whose voice had admonished nations and had awoken hundreds of thousands, whose voice he had also once heard, whose holy face he had also once seen with respect. Kindly, he thought of him, saw his path to perfection before his eyes, and remembered with a smile those words which he had once, as a young man, said to him, the exalted one. They had been, so it seemed to him, proud and precocious words; with a smile, he remembered them. For a long time he knew that there was nothing standing between Gotama and him any more, though he was still unable to accept his teachings. No, there was no teaching a truly searching person, someone who truly wanted to find, could accept. But he who had found, he could approve of any teachings, every path, every goal, there was nothing standing between him and all the other thousand any more who lived in that what is eternal, who breathed what is divine.

On one of these days, when so many went on a pilgrimage to the dying Buddha, Kamala also went to him, who used to be the most beautiful of the courtesans. A long time ago, she had retired from her previous life, had given her garden to the monks of Gotama as a gift, had taken her refuge in the teachings, was among the friends and benefactors of the pilgrims. Together with Siddhartha the boy, her son, she had gone on her way due to the news of the near death of Gotama, in simple clothes, on foot. With her little son, she was travelling by the river; but the boy had soon grown tired, desired to go back home, desired to rest, desired to eat, became disobedient and started whining.

Kamala often had to take a rest with him, he was accustomed to having his way against her, she had to feed him, had to comfort him, had to scold him. He did not comprehend why he had to go on this exhausting and sad pilgrimage with his mother, to an unknown place, to a stranger, who was holy and about to die. So what if he died, how did this concern the boy?

The pilgrims were getting close to Vasudeva's ferry, when little Siddhartha once again forced his mother to rest. She, Kamala herself, had also become tired, and while the boy was chewing a banana, she crouched down on the ground, closed her eyes a bit, and rested. But suddenly, she uttered a wailing scream, the boy looked at her in fear and saw her face having grown pale from horror; and from under her dress, a small, black snake fled, by which Kamala had been bitten.

Hurriedly, they now both ran along the path, in order to reach people, and got near to the ferry, there Kamala collapsed, and was not able to go any further. But the boy started crying miserably, only interrupting it to kiss and hug his mother, and she also joined his loud screams for help, until the sound reached Vasudeva's ears, who stood at the ferry. Quickly, he came walking, took the woman on his arms, carried her into the boat, the boy ran along, and soon they all reached the hut, where Siddhartha stood by the stove and was just lighting the fire. He looked up and first saw the boy's face, which wondrously reminded him of something, like a warning to remember something he had forgotten. Then he saw Kamala, whom he instantly recognised, though she lay unconscious in the ferryman's arms, and now he knew that it was his own son, whose face had been such a warning reminder to him, and the heart stirred in his chest.

Kamala's wound was washed, but had already turned black and her body was swollen, she was made to drink a healing potion. Her consciousness returned, she lay on Siddhartha's bed in the hut and bent over her stood Siddhartha, who used to love her so much. It seemed like a dream to her; with a smile, she looked at her friend's face; just slowly she, realized her situation, remembered the bite, called timidly for the boy.

"He's with you, don't worry," said Siddhartha.

Kamala looked into his eyes. She spoke with a heavy tongue, paralysed by the poison. "You've become old, my dear," she said, "you've become gray. But you are like the young Samana, who at one time came without clothes, with dusty feet, to me into the garden. You are much more like him than you were like him at that time when you had left me and Kamaswami. In the eyes, you're like him, Siddhartha. Alas, I have also grown old, old— could you still recognise me?"

Siddhartha smiled: "Instantly, I recognised you, Kamala, my dear."

Kamala pointed to her boy and said: "Did you recognise him as well? He is your son."

Her eyes became confused and fell shut. The boy wept, Siddhartha took him on his knees, let him weep, petted his hair, and at the sight of the child's face, a Brahman prayer came to his mind, which he had learned a long time ago, when he had been a little boy himself. Slowly, with a singing voice, he started to speak; from his past and childhood, the words came flowing to him. And with that singsong, the boy became calm, was only now and then uttering a sob and fell asleep. Siddhartha placed him on Vasudeva's bed. Vasudeva stood by the stove and cooked rice. Siddhartha gave him a look, which he returned with a smile.

"She'll die," Siddhartha said quietly.

Vasudeva nodded; over his friendly face ran the light of the stove's fire.

Once again, Kamala returned to consciousness. Pain distorted her face, Siddhartha's eyes read the suffering on her mouth, on her pale cheeks. Quietly, he read it, attentively, waiting, his mind becoming one with her suffering. Kamala felt it, her gaze sought his eyes.

Looking at him, she said: "Now I see that your eyes have changed as well. They've become completely different. By what do I still recognise that you're Siddhartha? It's you, and it's not you."

Siddhartha said nothing, quietly his eyes looked at hers.

"You have achieved it?" she asked. "You have found peace?"

He smiled and placed his hand on hers.

"I'm seeing it," she said, "I'm seeing it. I too will find peace."

"You have found it," Siddhartha spoke in a whisper.

Kamala never stopped looking into his eyes. She thought about her pilgrimage to Gotama, which she wanted to take, in order to see the face of the perfected one, to breathe his peace, and she thought that she had now found him in his place, and that it was good, just as good, as if she had seen the other one. She wanted to tell this to him, but the tongue no longer obeyed her will. Without speaking, she looked at him, and he saw the life fading from her eyes. When the final pain filled her eyes and made them grow dim, when the final shiver ran through her limbs, his finger closed her eyelids.

For a long time, he sat and looked at her peacefully dead face. For a long time, he observed her mouth, her old, tired mouth, with those lips, which had become thin, and he remembered, that he used to, in the spring of his years, compare this mouth with a freshly cracked fig. For a long time, he sat, read in the pale face, in the tired wrinkles, filled himself with this sight, saw his own face lying in the same manner, just as white, just as quenched out, and saw at the same time his face and hers being young, with red lips, with fiery eyes, and the feeling of this both being present and at the same time real, the feeling of eternity, completely filled every aspect of his being. Deeply he felt, more deeply than ever before, in this hour, the indestructibility of every life, the eternity of every moment.

When he rose, Vasudeva had prepared rice for him. But Siddhartha did not eat. In the stable, where their goat stood, the two old men prepared beds of straw for themselves, and Vasudeva lay himself down to sleep. But Siddhartha went outside and sat this night before the hut, listening to the river, surrounded by the past, touched and encircled by all times of his life at the same time. But occasionally, he rose, stepped to the door of the hut and listened, whether the boy was sleeping.

Early in the morning, even before the sun could be seen, Vasudeva came out of the stable and walked over to his friend.

"You haven't slept," he said.

"No, Vasudeva. I sat here, I was listening to the river. A lot it has told me, deeply it has filled me with the healing thought, with the thought of oneness."

"You've experienced suffering, Siddhartha, but I see: no sadness has entered your heart."

"No, my dear, how should I be sad? I, who have been rich and happy, have become even richer and happier now. My son has been given to me."

"Your son shall be welcome to me as well. But now, Siddhartha, let's get to work, there is much to be done. Kamala has died on the same bed on which my wife had died a long time ago. Let us also build Kamala's funeral pile on the same hill on which I had then built my wife's funeral pile."

While the boy was still asleep, they built the funeral pile.

THE SON

Timid and weeping, the boy had attended his mother's funeral; gloomy and shy, he had listened to Siddhartha, who greeted him as his son and welcomed him at his place in Vasudeva's hut. Pale, he sat for many days by the hill of the dead, did not want to eat, gave no open look, did not open his heart, met his fate with resistance and denial.

Siddhartha spared him and let him do as he pleased, he honoured his mourning. Siddhartha understood that his son did not know him, that he could not love him like a father. Slowly, he also saw and understood that the eleven-year-old was a pampered boy, a mother's boy, and that he had grown up in the habits of rich people, accustomed to finer food, to a soft bed, accustomed to giving orders to servants. Siddhartha understood that the mourning, pampered child could not suddenly and willingly be content with a life among strangers and in poverty. He did not force him, he did many a chore for him, always picked the best piece of the meal for him. Slowly, he hoped to win him over, by friendly patience.

Rich and happy, he had called himself, when the boy had come to him. Since time had passed on in the meantime, and the boy remained a stranger and in a gloomy disposition, since he displayed a proud and stubbornly disobedient heart, did not want to do any work, did not pay his respect to the old men, stole from Vasudeva's fruit-trees, then Siddhartha began to understand that his son had not brought him happiness and peace, but suffering and worry. But he loved him, and he preferred the suffering and worries of love over happiness and joy without the boy. Since young Siddhartha was in the hut, the old men had split the work. Vasudeva had again taken on the job of the ferryman all by himself, and Siddhartha, in order to be with his son, did the work in the hut and the field.

For a long time, for long months, Siddhartha waited for his son to understand him, to accept his love, to perhaps reciprocate it. For long months, Vasudeva waited, watching, waited and said nothing. One day, when Siddhartha the younger had once again tormented his father very much with spite and an unsteadiness in his wishes and had broken both of his rice-bowls, Vasudeva took in the evening his friend aside and talked to him.

"Pardon me," he said, "from a friendly heart, I'm talking to you. I'm seeing that you are tormenting yourself, I'm seeing that you're in grief. Your son, my dear, is worrying you, and he is also worrying me. That young bird is accustomed to a different life, to a different nest. He has not, like you, run away from riches and the city, being disgusted and fed up with it; against his will, he had to leave all this behind. I asked the river, oh friend, many times I have asked it. But the river laughs, it laughs at me, it laughs at you and me, and is shaking with laughter at our foolishness. Water wants to join water, youth wants to join youth, your son is not in the place where he can prosper. You too should ask the river; you too should listen to it!"

Troubled, Siddhartha looked into his friendly face, in the many wrinkles of which there was incessant cheerfulness.

"How could I part with him?" he said quietly, ashamed. "Give me some more time, my dear! See, I'm fighting for him, I'm seeking to win his heart, with love and with friendly patience I intend to capture it. One day, the river shall also talk to him, he also is called upon."

Vasudeva's smile flourished more warmly. "Oh yes, he too is called upon, he too is of the eternal life. But do we, you and me, know what he is called upon to do, what path to take, what actions to perform, what pain to endure? Not a small one, his pain will be; after all, his heart is proud and hard, people like this have to suffer a lot, err a lot, do much injustice, burden themselves with much sin. Tell me, my dear: you're not taking control of your son's upbringing? You don't force him? You don't beat him? You don't punish him?"

"No, Vasudeva, I don't do anything of this."

"I knew it. You don't force him, don't beat him, don't give him orders, because you know that 'soft' is stronger than 'hard', water stronger than rocks, love stronger than force. Very good, I praise you. But aren't you mistaken in thinking that you wouldn't force him, wouldn't punish him? Don't you shackle him with your love? Don't you make him feel inferior every day, and don't you make it even harder on him with your kindness and patience? Don't you force him, the arrogant and pampered boy, to live in a hut with two old banana-eaters, to whom even rice is a delicacy, whose thoughts can't be his, whose hearts are old and quiet and beat in a different pace than his? Isn't he forced, isn't he punished by all this?"

Troubled, Siddhartha looked to the ground. Quietly, he asked: "What do you think should I do?"

Quoth Vasudeva: "Bring him into the city, bring him into his mother's house, there'll still be servants around, give him to them. And when there aren't any around any more, bring him to a teacher, not for the teachings' sake, but so that he shall be among other boys, and among girls, and in the world which is his own. Have you never thought of this?"

"You're seeing into my heart," Siddhartha spoke sadly. "Often, I have thought of this. But look, how shall I put him, who had no tender heart anyhow, into this world? Won't he become exuberant, won't he lose himself to pleasure and power, won't he repeat all of his father's mistakes, won't he perhaps get entirely lost in Sansara?"

Brightly, the ferryman's smile lit up; softly, he touched Siddhartha's arm and said: "Ask the river about it, my friend! Hear it laugh about it! Would you actually believe that you had committed your foolish acts in order to spare your son from committing them too? And could you in any way protect your son from Sansara? How could you? By means of teachings, prayer, admonition? My dear, have you entirely forgotten that story, that story containing so many lessons, that story about Siddhartha, a Brahman's son, which you once told me here on this very spot? Who has kept the Samana Siddhartha safe from Sansara, from sin, from greed, from foolishness? Were his father's religious devotion, his teacher's warnings, his own knowledge, his own search able to keep him safe? Which father, which teacher had been able to protect him from living his life for himself, from soiling himself with life, from burdening himself with guilt, from drinking the bitter drink for himself, from finding his path for himself? Would you think, my dear, anybody might perhaps be spared from taking this path? That perhaps your little son would be spared, because you love him, because you would like to keep him from suffering and pain and disappointment? But even if you would die ten times for him, you would not be able to take the slightest part of his destiny upon yourself."

Never before, Vasudeva had spoken so many words. Kindly, Siddhartha thanked him, went troubled into the hut, could not sleep for a long time. Vasudeva had told him nothing he had not already thought and known for himself. But this was a knowledge he could not act upon, stronger than the knowledge was his love for the boy, stronger was his tenderness, his fear to lose him. Had he ever lost his heart so much to something, had he ever loved any person thus, thus blindly, thus sufferingly, thus unsuccessfully, and yet thus happily?

Siddhartha could not heed his friend's advice, he could not give up the boy. He let the boy give him orders, he let him disregard him. He said nothing and waited; daily, he began the mute struggle of friendliness, the silent war of patience. Vasudeva also said nothing and waited, friendly, knowing, patient. They were both masters of patience.

At one time, when the boy's face reminded him very much of Kamala, Siddhartha suddenly had to think of a line which Kamala a long time ago, in the days of their youth, had once said to him. "You cannot love," she had said to him, and he had agreed with her and had compared himself with a star, while comparing the childlike people with falling leaves, and nevertheless he had also sensed an accusation in that line. Indeed, he had never been able to lose or devote himself completely to another person, to forget himself, to commit foolish acts for the love of another person; never he had been able to do this, and this was, as it had seemed to him at that time, the great distinction which set him apart from the childlike people. But now, since his son was here, now he, Siddhartha, had also become completely a childlike person, suffering for the sake of another person, loving another person, lost to a love, having become a fool on account of love. Now he too felt, late, once in his lifetime, this strongest and strangest of all passions, suffered from it, suffered miserably, and was nevertheless in bliss, was nevertheless renewed in one respect, enriched by one thing.

He did sense very well that this love, this blind love for his son, was a passion, something very human, that it was Sansara, a murky source, dark waters. Nevertheless, he felt at the same time, it was not worthless, it was necessary, came from the essence of his own being. This pleasure also had to be atoned for, this pain also had to be endured, these foolish acts also had to be committed.

Through all this, the son let him commit his foolish acts, let him court for his affection, let him humiliate himself every day by giving in to his moods. This father had nothing which would have delighted him and nothing which he would have feared. He was a good man, this father, a good, kind, soft man, perhaps a very devout man, perhaps a saint, all these were no attributes which could win the boy over. He was bored by this father, who kept him prisoner here in this miserable hut of his, he was bored by him, and for him to answer every naughtiness with a smile, every insult with friendliness, every viciousness with kindness, this very thing was the hated trick of this old sneak. Much more the boy would have liked it if he had been threatened by him, if he had been abused by him.

A day came when what young Siddhartha had on his mind came bursting forth, and he openly turned against his father. The latter had given him a task, he had told him to gather brushwood. But the boy did not leave the hut, in stubborn disobedience and rage he stayed where he was, thumped on the ground with his feet, clenched his fists, and screamed in a powerful outburst his hatred and contempt into his father's face.

"Get the brushwood for yourself!" he shouted, foaming at the mouth, "I'm not your servant. I do know that you won't hit me, you don't dare; I do know that you constantly want to punish me and put me down with your religious devotion and your indulgence. You want me to become like you, just as devout, just as soft, just as wise! But I, listen up, just to make you suffer, I rather want to become a highway-robber and murderer, and go to hell, than to become like you! I hate you, you're not my father, and if you've ten times been my mother's fornicator!"

Rage and grief boiled over in him, foamed at the father in a hundred savage and evil words. Then the boy ran away and only returned late at night.

But the next morning, he had disappeared. What had also disappeared was a small basket, woven out of bast of two colours, in which the ferrymen kept those copper and silver coins which they received as a fare. The boat had also disappeared, Siddhartha saw it lying by the opposite bank. The boy had run away.

"I must follow him," said Siddhartha, who had been shivering with grief since those ranting speeches the boy had made yesterday. "A child can't go through the forest all alone. He'll perish. We must build a raft, Vasudeva, to get over the water."

"We will build a raft," said Vasudeva, "to get our boat back, which the boy has taken away. But him, you shall let run along, my friend, he is no child any more, he knows how to get around. He's looking for the path to the city, and he is right, don't forget that. He's doing what you've failed to do yourself. He's taking care of himself, he's taking his course. Alas, Siddhartha, I see you suffering, but you're suffering a pain at which one would like to laugh, at which you'll soon laugh for yourself."

Siddhartha did not answer. He already held the axe in his hands and began to make a raft of bamboo, and Vasudeva helped him to tie the canes together with ropes of grass. Then they crossed over, drifted far off their course, pulled the raft upriver on the opposite bank.

"Why did you take the axe along?" asked Siddhartha.

Vasudeva said: "It might have been possible that the oar of our boat got lost."

But Siddhartha knew what his friend was thinking. He thought, the boy would have thrown away or broken the oar in order to get even and in order to keep them from following him. And in fact, there was no oar left in the boat. Vasudeva pointed to the bottom of the boat and looked at his friend with a smile, as if he wanted to say: "Don't you see what your son is trying to tell you? Don't you see that he doesn't want to be followed?" But he did not say this in words. He started making a new oar. But Siddhartha bid his farewell, to look for the run-away. Vasudeva did not stop him.

When Siddhartha had already been walking through the forest for a long time, the thought occurred to him that his search was useless. Either, so he thought, the boy was far ahead and had already reached the city, or, if he should still be on his way, he would conceal himself from him, the pursuer. As he continued thinking, he also found that he, on his part, was not worried for his son, that he knew deep inside that he had neither perished nor was in any danger in the forest. Nevertheless, he ran without stopping, no longer to save him, just to satisfy his desire, just to perhaps see him one more time. And he ran up to just outside of the city.

When, near the city, he reached a wide road, he stopped, by the entrance of the beautiful pleasure-garden, which used to belong to Kamala, where he had seen her for the first time in her sedan-chair. The past rose up in his soul, again he saw himself standing there, young, a bearded, naked Samana, the hair full of dust. For a long time, Siddhartha stood there and looked through the open gate into the garden, seeing monks in yellow robes walking among the beautiful trees.

For a long time, he stood there, pondering, seeing images, listening to the story of his life. For a long time, he stood there, looked at the monks, saw young Siddhartha in their place, saw young Kamala walking among the high trees. Clearly, he saw himself being served food and drink by Kamala, receiving his first kiss from her, looking proudly and disdainfully back on his Brahmanism, beginning proudly and full of desire his worldly life. He saw Kamaswami, saw the servants, the orgies, the gamblers with the dice, the musicians, saw Kamala's song-bird in the cage, lived through all this once again, breathed Sansara, was once again old and tired, felt once again disgust, felt once again the wish to annihilate himself, was once again healed by the holy Om.

After having been standing by the gate of the garden for a long time, Siddhartha realised that his desire was foolish, which had made him go up to this place, that he could not help his son, that he was not allowed to cling to him. Deeply, he felt the love for the run-away in his heart, like a wound, and he felt at the same time that this wound had not been given to him in order to turn the knife in it, that it had to become a blossom and had to shine.

That this wound did not blossom yet, did not shine yet, at this hour, made him sad. Instead of the desired goal, which had drawn him here following the run-away son, there was now emptiness. Sadly, he sat down, felt something dying in his heart, experienced emptiness, saw no joy any more, no goal. He sat lost in thought and waited. This he had learned by the river, this one thing: waiting, having patience, listening attentively. And he sat and listened, in the dust of the road, listened to his heart, beating tiredly and sadly, waited for a voice. Many an hour he crouched, listening, saw no images any more, fell into emptiness, let himself fall, without seeing a path. And when he felt the wound burning, he silently spoke the Om, filled himself with Om. The monks in the garden saw him, and since he crouched for many hours, and dust was gathering on his gray hair, one of them came to him and placed two bananas in front of him. The old man did not see him.

From this petrified state, he was awoken by a hand touching his shoulder. Instantly, he recognised this touch, this tender, bashful touch, and regained his senses. He rose and greeted Vasudeva, who had followed him. And when he looked into Vasudeva's friendly face, into the small wrinkles, which were as if they were filled with nothing but his smile, into the happy eyes, then he smiled too. Now he saw the bananas lying in front of him, picked them up, gave one to the ferryman, ate the other one himself. After this, he silently went back into the forest with Vasudeva, returned home to the ferry. Neither one talked about what had happened today, neither one mentioned the boy's name, neither one spoke about him running away, neither one spoke about the wound. In the hut, Siddhartha lay down on his bed, and when after a while Vasudeva came to him, to offer him a bowl of coconut-milk, he already found him asleep.

OM

For a long time, the wound continued to burn. Many a traveller Siddhartha had to ferry across the river who was accompanied by a son or a daughter, and he saw none of them without envying him, without thinking: "So many, so many thousands possess this sweetest of good fortunes—why don't I? Even bad people, even thieves and robbers have children and love them, and are being loved by them, all except for me." Thus simply, thus without reason he now thought, thus similar to the childlike people he had become.

Differently than before, he now looked upon people, less smart, less proud, but instead warmer, more curious, more involved. When he ferried travellers of the ordinary kind, childlike people, businessmen, warriors, women, these people did not seem alien to him as they used to: he understood them, he understood and shared their life, which was not guided by thoughts and insight, but solely by urges and wishes, he felt like them. Though he was near perfection and was bearing his final wound, it still seemed to him as if those childlike people were his brothers, their vanities, desires for possession, and ridiculous aspects were no longer ridiculous to him, became understandable, became lovable, even became worthy of veneration to him. The blind love of a mother for her child, the stupid, blind pride of a conceited father for his only son, the blind, wild desire of a young, vain woman for jewelry and admiring glances from men, all of these urges, all of this childish stuff, all of these simple, foolish, but immensely strong, strongly living, strongly prevailing urges and desires were now no childish notions for Siddhartha any more, he saw people living for their sake, saw them achieving infinitely much for their sake, travelling, conducting wars, suffering infinitely much, bearing infinitely much, and he could love them for it, he saw life, that what is alive, the indestructible, the Brahman in each of their passions, each of their acts. Worthy of love and admiration were these people in their blind loyalty, their blind strength and tenacity. They lacked nothing, there was nothing the knowledgeable one, the thinker, had to put him above them except for one little thing, a single, tiny, small thing: the consciousness, the conscious thought of the oneness of all life. And Siddhartha even doubted in many an hour, whether this knowledge, this thought was to be valued thus highly, whether it might not also perhaps be a childish idea of the thinking people, of the thinking and childlike people. In all other respects, the worldly people were of equal rank to the wise men, were often far superior to them, just as animals too can, after all, in some moments, seem to be superior to humans in their tough, unrelenting performance of what is necessary.

Slowly blossomed, slowly ripened in Siddhartha the realisation, the knowledge, what wisdom actually was, what the goal of his long search was. It was nothing but a readiness of the soul, an ability, a secret art, to think every moment, while living his life, the thought of oneness, to be able to feel and inhale the oneness. Slowly this blossomed in him, was shining back at him from Vasudeva's old, childlike face: harmony, knowledge of the eternal perfection of the world, smiling, oneness.

But the wound still burned, longingly and bitterly Siddhartha thought of his son, nurtured his love and tenderness in his heart, allowed the pain to gnaw at him, committed all foolish acts of love. Not by itself, this flame would go out.

And one day, when the wound burned violently, Siddhartha ferried across the river, driven by a yearning, got off the boat and was willing to go to the city and to look for his son. The river flowed softly and quietly, it was the dry season, but its voice sounded strange: it laughed! It laughed clearly. The river laughed, it laughed brightly and clearly at the old ferryman. Siddhartha stopped, he bent over the water, in order to hear even better, and he saw his face reflected in the quietly moving waters, and in this reflected face there was something, which reminded him, something he had forgotten, and as he thought about it, he found it: this face resembled another face, which he used to know and love and also fear. It resembled his father's face, the Brahman. And he remembered how he, a long time ago, as a young man, had forced his father to let him go to the penitents, how he had bid his farewell to him, how he had gone and had never come back. Had his father not also suffered the same pain for him, which he now suffered for his son? Had his father not long since died, alone, without having seen his son again? Did he not have to expect the same fate for himself? Was it not a comedy, a strange and stupid matter, this repetition, this running around in a fateful circle?

The river laughed. Yes, so it was, everything came back, which had not been suffered and solved up to its end, the same pain was suffered over and over again. But Siddhartha went back into the boat and ferried back to the hut, thinking of his father, thinking of his son, laughed at by the river, at odds with himself, tending towards despair, and not less tending towards laughing along at himself and the entire world.

Alas, the wound was not blossoming yet, his heart was still fighting his fate, cheerfulness and victory were not yet shining from his suffering. Nevertheless, he felt hope, and once he had returned to the hut, he felt an undefeatable desire to open up to Vasudeva, to show him everything, the master of listening, to say everything.

Vasudeva was sitting in the hut and weaving a basket. He no longer used the ferry-boat, his eyes were starting to get weak, and not just his eyes; his arms and hands as well. Unchanged and flourishing was only the joy and the cheerful benevolence of his face.

Siddhartha sat down next to the old man, slowly he started talking. What they had never talked about, he now told him of, of his walk to the city, at that time, of the burning wound, of his envy at the sight of happy fathers, of his knowledge of the foolishness of such wishes, of his futile fight against them. He reported everything, he was able to say everything, even the most embarrassing parts, everything could be said, everything shown, everything he could tell. He presented his wound, also told how he fled today, how he ferried across the water, a childish run-away, willing to walk to the city, how the river had laughed.

While he spoke, spoke for a long time, while Vasudeva was listening with a quiet face, Vasudeva's listening gave Siddhartha a stronger sensation than ever before, he sensed how his pain, his fears flowed over to him, how his secret hope flowed over, came back at him from his counterpart. To show his wound to this listener was the same as bathing it in the river, until it had cooled and become one with the river. While he was still speaking, still admitting and confessing, Siddhartha felt more and more that this was no longer Vasudeva, no longer a human being who was listening to him, that this motionless listener was absorbing his confession into himself like a tree the rain, that this motionless man was the river itself, that he was God himself, that he was the eternal itself. And while Siddhartha stopped thinking of himself and his wound, this realisation of Vasudeva's changed character took possession of him, and the more he felt it and entered into it, the less wondrous it became, the more he realised that everything was in order and natural, that Vasudeva had already been like this for a long time, almost forever, that only he had not quite recognised it, yes, that he himself had almost reached the same state. He felt, that he was now seeing old Vasudeva as the people see the gods, and that this could not last; in his heart, he started bidding his farewell to Vasudeva. Throughout all this, he talked incessantly.

When he had finished talking, Vasudeva turned his friendly eyes, which had grown slightly weak, at him, said nothing, let his silent love and cheerfulness, understanding and knowledge, shine at him. He took Siddhartha's hand, led him to the seat by the bank, sat down with him, smiled at the river.

"You've heard it laugh," he said. "But you haven't heard everything. Let's listen, you'll hear more."

They listened. Softly sounded the river, singing in many voices. Siddhartha looked into the water, and images appeared to him in the moving water: his father appeared, lonely, mourning for his son; he himself appeared, lonely, he also being tied with the bondage of yearning to his distant son; his son appeared, lonely as well, the boy, greedily rushing along the burning course of his young wishes, each one heading for his goal, each one obsessed by the goal, each one suffering. The river sang with a voice of suffering, longingly it sang, longingly, it flowed towards its goal, lamentingly its voice sang.

"Do you hear?" Vasudeva's mute gaze asked. Siddhartha nodded.

"Listen better!" Vasudeva whispered.

Siddhartha made an effort to listen better. The image of his father, his own image, the image of his son merged, Kamala's image also appeared and was dispersed, and the image of Govinda, and other images, and they merged with each other, turned all into the river, headed all, being the river, for the goal, longing, desiring, suffering, and the river's voice sounded full of yearning, full of burning woe, full of unsatisfiable desire. For the goal, the river was heading, Siddhartha saw it hurrying, the river, which consisted of him and his loved ones and of all people he had ever seen, all of these waves and waters were hurrying, suffering, towards goals, many goals, the waterfall, the lake, the rapids, the sea, and all goals were reached, and every goal was followed by a new one, and the water turned into vapour and rose to the sky, turned into rain and poured down from the sky, turned into a source, a stream, a river, headed forward once again, flowed on once again. But the longing voice had changed. It still resounded, full of suffering, searching, but other voices joined it, voices of joy and of suffering, good and bad voices, laughing and sad ones, a hundred voices, a thousand voices.

Siddhartha listened. He was now nothing but a listener, completely concentrated on listening, completely empty, he felt, that he had now finished learning to listen. Often before, he had heard all this, these many voices in the river, today it sounded new. Already, he could no longer tell the many voices apart, not the happy ones from the weeping ones, not the ones of children from those of men, they all belonged together, the lamentation of yearning and the laughter of the knowledgeable one, the scream of rage and the moaning of the dying ones, everything was one, everything was intertwined and connected, entangled a thousand times. And everything together, all voices, all goals, all yearning, all suffering, all pleasure, all that was good and evil, all of this together was the world. All of it together was the flow of events, was the music of life. And when Siddhartha was listening attentively to this river, this song of a thousand voices, when he neither listened to the suffering nor the laughter, when he did not tie his soul to any particular voice and submerged his self into it, but when he heard them all, perceived the whole, the oneness, then the great song of the thousand voices consisted of a single word, which was Om: the perfection.

"Do you hear," Vasudeva's gaze asked again.

Brightly, Vasudeva's smile was shining, floating radiantly over all the wrinkles of his old face, as the Om was floating in the air over all the voices of the river. Brightly his smile was shining, when he looked at his friend, and brightly the same smile was now starting to shine on Siddhartha's face as well. His wound blossomed, his suffering was shining, his self had flown into the oneness.

In this hour, Siddhartha stopped fighting his fate, stopped suffering. On his face flourished the cheerfulness of a knowledge, which is no longer opposed by any will, which knows perfection, which is in agreement with the flow of events, with the current of life, full of sympathy for the pain of others, full of sympathy for the pleasure of others, devoted to the flow, belonging to the oneness.

When Vasudeva rose from the seat by the bank, when he looked into Siddhartha's eyes and saw the cheerfulness of the knowledge shining in them, he softly touched his shoulder with his hand, in this careful and tender manner, and said: "I've been waiting for this hour, my dear. Now that it has come, let me leave. For a long time, I've been waiting for this hour; for a long time, I've been Vasudeva the ferryman. Now it's enough. Farewell, but, farewell, river, farewell, Siddhartha!"

Siddhartha made a deep bow before him who bid his farewell.

"I've known it," he said quietly. "You'll go into the forests?"

"I'm going into the forests, I'm going into the oneness," spoke Vasudeva with a bright smile.

With a bright smile, he left; Siddhartha watched him leaving. With deep joy, with deep solemnity he watched him leave, saw his steps full of peace, saw his head full of lustre, saw his body full of light.

GOVINDA

Together with other monks, Govinda used to spend the time of rest between pilgrimages in the pleasure-grove, which the courtesan Kamala had given to the followers of Gotama for a gift. He heard talk of an old ferryman, who lived one day's journey away by the river, and who was regarded as a wise man by many. When Govinda went back on his way, he chose the path to the ferry, eager to see the ferryman. Because, though he had lived his entire life by the rules, though he was also looked upon with veneration by the younger monks on account of his age and his modesty, the restlessness and the searching still had not perished from his heart.

He came to the river and asked the old man to ferry him over, and when they got off the boat on the other side, he said to the old man: "You're very good to us monks and pilgrims, you have already ferried many of us across the river. Aren't you too, ferryman, a searcher for the right path?"

Quoth Siddhartha, smiling from his old eyes: "Do you call yourself a searcher, oh venerable one, though you are already well on in years and are wearing the robe of Gotama's monks?"

"It's true, I'm old," spoke Govinda, "but I haven't stopped searching. Never I'll stop searching, this seems to be my destiny. You too, so it seems to me, have been searching. Would you like to tell me something, oh honourable one?"

Quoth Siddhartha: "What should I possibly have to tell you, oh venerable one? Perhaps that you're searching far too much? That in all that searching, you don't find the time for finding?"

"How come?" asked Govinda.

"When someone is searching," said Siddhartha, "then it might easily happen that the only thing his eyes still see is that what he searches for, that he is unable to find anything, to let anything enter his mind, because he always thinks of nothing but the object of his search, because he has a goal, because he is obsessed by the goal. Searching means: having a goal. But finding means: being free, being open, having no goal. You, oh venerable one, are perhaps indeed a searcher, because, striving for your goal, there are many things you don't see, which are directly in front of your eyes."

"I don't quite understand yet," asked Govinda, "what do you mean by this?"

Quoth Siddhartha: "A long time ago, oh venerable one, many years ago, you've once before been at this river and have found a sleeping man by the river, and have sat down with him to guard his sleep. But, oh Govinda, you did not recognise the sleeping man."

Astonished, as if he had been the object of a magic spell, the monk looked into the ferryman's eyes.

"Are you Siddhartha?" he asked with a timid voice. "I wouldn't have recognised you this time as well! From my heart, I'm greeting you, Siddhartha; from my heart, I'm happy to see you once again! You've changed a lot, my friend. —And so you've now become a ferryman?"

In a friendly manner, Siddhartha laughed. "A ferryman, yes. Many people, Govinda, have to change a lot, have to wear many a robe, I am one of those, my dear. Be welcome, Govinda, and spend the night in my hut."

Govinda stayed the night in the hut and slept on the bed which used to be Vasudeva's bed. Many questions he posed to the friend of his youth, many things Siddhartha had to tell him from his life.

When in the next morning the time had come to start the day's journey, Govinda said, not without hesitation, these words: "Before I'll continue on my path, Siddhartha, permit me to ask one more question. Do you have a teaching? Do you have a faith or a knowledge you follow, which helps you to live and to do right?"

Quoth Siddhartha: "You know, my dear, that I already as a young man, in those days when we lived with the penitents in the forest, started to distrust teachers and teachings and to turn my back to them. I have stuck with this. Nevertheless, I have had many teachers since then. A beautiful courtesan has been my teacher for a long time, and a rich merchant was my teacher, and some gamblers with dice. Once, even a follower of Buddha, travelling on foot, has been my teacher; he sat with me when I had fallen asleep in the forest, on the pilgrimage. I've also learned from him, I'm also grateful to him, very grateful. But most of all, I have learned here from this river and from my predecessor, the ferryman Vasudeva. He was a very simple person, Vasudeva, he was no thinker, but he knew what is necessary just as well as Gotama, he was a perfect man, a saint."

Govinda said: "Still, oh Siddhartha, you love a bit to mock people, as it seems to me. I believe in you and know that you haven't followed a teacher. But haven't you found something by yourself, though you've found no teachings, you still found certain thoughts, certain insights, which are your own and which help you to live? If you would like to tell me some of these, you would delight my heart."

Quoth Siddhartha: "I've had thoughts, yes, and insight, again and again. Sometimes, for an hour or for an entire day, I have felt knowledge in me, as one would feel life in one's heart. There have been many thoughts, but it would be hard for me to convey them to you. Look, my dear Govinda, this is one of my thoughts, which I have found: wisdom cannot be passed on. Wisdom which a wise man tries to pass on to someone always sounds like foolishness."

"Are you kidding?" asked Govinda.

"I'm not kidding. I'm telling you what I've found. Knowledge can be conveyed, but not wisdom. It can be found, it can be lived, it is possible to be carried by it, miracles can be performed with it, but it cannot be expressed in words and taught. This was what I, even as a young man, sometimes suspected, what has driven me away from the teachers. I have found a thought, Govinda, which you'll again regard as a joke or foolishness, but which is my best thought. It says: The opposite of every truth is just as true! That's like this: any truth can only be expressed and put into words when it is one-sided. Everything is one-sided which can be thought with thoughts and said with words, it's all one-sided, all just one half, all lacks completeness, roundness, oneness. When the exalted Gotama spoke in his teachings of the world, he had to divide it into Sansara and Nirvana, into deception and truth, into suffering and salvation. It cannot be done differently, there is no other way for him who wants to teach. But the world itself, what exists around us and inside of us, is never one-sided. A person or an act is never entirely Sansara or entirely Nirvana, a person is never entirely holy or entirely sinful. It does really seem like this, because we are subject to deception, as if time was something real. Time is not real, Govinda, I have experienced this often and often again. And if time is not real, then the gap which seems to be between the world and the eternity, between suffering and blissfulness, between evil and good, is also a deception."

"How come?" asked Govinda timidly.

"Listen well, my dear, listen well! The sinner, which I am and which you are, is a sinner, but in times to come he will be Brahma again, he will reach the Nirvana, will be Buddha—and now see: these 'tis?mes to come' are a deception, are only a parable! The sinner is not on his way to become a Buddha, he is not in the process of developing, though our capacity for thinking does not know how else to picture these things. No, within the sinner is now and today already the future Buddha, his future is already all there, you have to worship in him, in you, in everyone the Buddha which is coming into being, the possible, the hidden Buddha. The world, my friend Govinda, is not imperfect, or on a slow path towards perfection: no, it is perfect in every moment, all sin already carries the divine forgiveness in itself, all small children already have the old person in themselves, all infants already have death, all dying people the eternal life. It is not possible for any person to see how far another one has already progressed on his path; in the robber and dice-gambler, the Buddha is waiting; in the Brahman, the robber is waiting. In deep meditation, there is the possibility to put time out of existence, to see all life which was, is, and will be as if it was simultaneous, and there everything is good, everything is perfect, everything is Brahman. Therefore, I see whatever exists as good, death is to me like life, sin like holiness, wisdom like foolishness, everything has to be as it is, everything only requires my consent, only my willingness, my loving agreement, to be good for me, to do nothing but work for my benefit, to be unable to ever harm me. I have experienced on my body and on my soul that I needed sin very much, I needed lust, the desire for possessions, vanity, and needed the most shameful despair, in order to learn how to give up all resistance, in order to learn how to love the world, in order to stop comparing it to some world I wished, I imagined, some kind of perfection I had made up, but to leave it as it is and to love it and to enjoy being a part of it. —These, oh Govinda, are some of the thoughts which have come into my mind."

Siddhartha bent down, picked up a stone from the ground, and weighed it in his hand.

"This here," he said playing with it, "is a stone, and will, after a certain time, perhaps turn into soil, and will turn from soil into a plant or animal or human being. In the past, I would have said: This stone is just a stone, it is worthless, it belongs to the world of the Maya; but because it might be able to become also a human being and a spirit in the cycle of transformations, therefore I also grant it importance. Thus, I would perhaps have thought in the past. But today I think: this stone is a stone, it is also animal, it is also god, it is also Buddha, I do not venerate and love it because it could turn into this or that, but rather because it is already and always everything—and it is this very fact, that it is a stone, that it appears to me now and today as a stone, this is why I love it and see worth and purpose in each of its veins and cavities, in the yellow, in the gray, in the hardness, in the sound it makes when I knock at it, in the dryness or wetness of its surface. There are stones which feel like oil or soap, and others like leaves, others like sand, and every one is special and prays the Om in its own way, each one is Brahman, but simultaneously and just as much it is a stone, is oily or juicy, and this is the very fact which I like and regard as wonderful and worthy of worship. —But let me speak no more of this. The words are not good for the secret meaning, everything always becomes a bit different, as soon as it is put into words, gets distorted a bit, a bit silly—yes, and this is also very good, and I like it a lot, I also very much agree with this, that this what is one man's treasure and wisdom always sounds like foolishness to another person."

Govinda listened silently.

"Why have you told me this about the stone?" he asked hesitantly after a pause.

"I did it without any specific intention. Or perhaps what I meant was, that I love this very stone, and the river, and all these things we are looking at and from which we can learn. I can love a stone, Govinda, and also a tree or a piece of bark. These are things, and things can be loved. But I cannot love words. Therefore, teachings are no good for me, they have no hardness, no softness, no colours, no edges, no smell, no taste, they have nothing but words. Perhaps it is these which keep you from finding peace, perhaps it is the many words. Because salvation and virtue as well, Sansara and Nirvana as well, are mere words, Govinda. There is no thing which would be Nirvana; there is just the word Nirvana."

Quoth Govinda: "Not just a word, my friend, is Nirvana. It is a thought."

Siddhartha continued: "A thought, it might be so. I must confess to you, my dear: I don't differentiate much between thoughts and words. To be honest, I also have no high opinion of thoughts. I have a better opinion of things. Here on this ferry-boat, for instance, a man has been my predecessor and teacher, a holy man, who has for many years simply believed in the river, nothing else. He had noticed that the river spoke to him, he learned from it, it educated and taught him, the river seemed to be a god to him, for many years he did not know that every wind, every cloud, every bird, every beetle was just as divine and knows just as much and can teach just as much as the worshipped river. But when this holy man went into the forests, he knew everything, knew more than you and me, without teachers, without books, only because he had believed in the river."

Govinda said: "But is that what you call 'things', actually something real, something which has existence? Isn't it just a deception of the Maya, just an image and illusion? Your stone, your tree, your river—are they actually a reality?"

"This too," spoke Siddhartha, "I do not care very much about. Let the things be illusions or not, after all I would then also be an illusion, and thus they are always like me. This is what makes them so dear and worthy of veneration for me: they are like me. Therefore, I can love them. And this is now a teaching you will laugh about: love, oh Govinda, seems to me to be the most important thing of all. To thoroughly understand the world, to explain it, to despise it, may be the thing great thinkers do. But I'm only interested in being able to love the world, not to despise it, not to hate it and me, to be able to look upon it and me and all beings with love and admiration and great respect."

"This I understand," spoke Govinda. "But this very thing was discovered by the exalted one to be a deception. He commands benevolence, clemency, sympathy, tolerance, but not love; he forbade us to tie our heart in love to earthly things."

"I know it," said Siddhartha; his smile shone golden. "I know it, Govinda. And behold, with this we are right in the middle of the thicket of opinions, in the dispute about words. For I cannot deny, my words of love are in a contradiction, a seeming contradiction with Gotama's words. For this very reason, I distrust in words so much, for I know, this contradiction is a deception. I know that I am in agreement with Gotama. How should he not know love, he, who has discovered all elements of human existence in their transitoriness, in their meaninglessness, and yet loved people thus much, to use a long, laborious life only to help them, to teach them! Even with him, even with your great teacher, I prefer the thing over the words, place more importance on his acts and life than on his speeches, more on the gestures of his hand than his opinions. Not in his speech, not in his thoughts, I see his greatness, only in his actions, in his life."

For a long time, the two old men said nothing. Then spoke Govinda, while bowing for a farewell: "I thank you, Siddhartha, for telling me some of your thoughts. They are partially strange thoughts, not all have been instantly understandable to me. This being as it may, I thank you, and I wish you to have calm days."

(But secretly he thought to himself: This Siddhartha is a bizarre person, he expresses bizarre thoughts, his teachings sound foolish. So differently sound the exalted one's pure teachings, clearer, purer, more comprehensible, nothing strange, foolish, or silly is contained in them. But different from his thoughts seemed to me Siddhartha's hands and feet, his eyes, his forehead, his breath, his smile, his greeting, his walk. Never again, after our exalted Gotama has become one with the Nirvana, never since then have I met a person of whom I felt: this is a holy man! Only him, this Siddhartha, I have found to be like this. May his teachings be strange, may his words sound foolish; out of his gaze and his hand, his skin and his hair, out of every part of him shines a purity, shines a calmness, shines a cheerfulness and mildness and holiness, which I have seen in no other person since the final death of our exalted teacher.)

As Govinda thought like this, and there was a conflict in his heart, he once again bowed to Siddhartha, drawn by love. Deeply he bowed to him who was calmly sitting.

"Siddhartha," he spoke, "we have become old men. It is unlikely for one of us to see the other again in this incarnation. I see, beloved, that you have found peace. I confess that I haven't found it. Tell me, oh honourable one, one more word, give me something on my way which I can grasp, which I can understand! Give me something to be with me on my path. It is often hard, my path, often dark, Siddhartha."

Siddhartha said nothing and looked at him with the ever unchanged, quiet smile. Govinda stared at his face, with fear, with yearning, suffering, and the eternal search was visible in his look, eternal not-finding.

Siddhartha saw it and smiled.

"Bend down to me!" he whispered quietly in Govinda's ear. "Bend down to me! Like this, even closer! Very close! Kiss my forehead, Govinda!"

But while Govinda with astonishment, and yet drawn by great love and expectation, obeyed his words, bent down closely to him and touched his forehead with his lips, something miraculous happened to him. While his thoughts were still dwelling on Siddhartha's wondrous words, while he was still struggling in vain and with reluctance to think away time, to imagine Nirvana and Sansara as one, while even a certain contempt for the words of his friend was fighting in him against an immense love and veneration, this happened to him:

He no longer saw the face of his friend Siddhartha, instead he saw other faces, many, a long sequence, a flowing river of faces, of hundreds, of thousands, which all came and disappeared, and yet all seemed to be there simultaneously, which all constantly changed and renewed themselves, and which were still all Siddhartha. He saw the face of a fish, a carp, with an infinitely painfully opened mouth, the face of a dying fish, with fading eyes—he saw the face of a new-born child, red and full of wrinkles, distorted from crying—he saw the face of a murderer, he saw him plunging a knife into the body of another person—he saw, in the same second, this criminal in bondage, kneeling and his head being chopped off by the executioner with one blow of his sword—he saw the bodies of men and women, naked in positions and cramps of frenzied love—he saw corpses stretched out, motionless, cold, void—he saw the heads of animals, of boars, of crocodiles, of elephants, of bulls, of birds—he saw gods, saw Krishna, saw Agni—he saw all of these figures and faces in a thousand relationships with one another, each one helping the other, loving it, hating it, destroying it, giving re-birth to it, each one was a will to die, a passionately painful confession of transitoriness, and yet none of them died, each one only transformed, was always reborn, received evermore a new face, without any time having passed between the one and the other face—and all of these figures and faces rested, flowed, generated themselves, floated along and merged with each other, and they were all constantly covered by something thin, without individuality of its own, but yet existing, like a thin glass or ice, like a transparent skin, a shell or mold or mask of water, and this mask was smiling, and this mask was Siddhartha's smiling face, which he, Govinda, in this very same moment touched with his lips. And, Govinda saw it like this, this smile of the mask, this smile of oneness above the flowing forms, this smile of simultaneousness above the thousand births and deaths, this smile of Siddhartha was precisely the same, was precisely of the same kind as the quiet, delicate, impenetrable, perhaps benevolent, perhaps mocking, wise, thousand-fold smile of Gotama, the Buddha, as he had seen it himself with great respect a hundred times. Like this, Govinda knew, the perfected ones are smiling.

Not knowing any more whether time existed, whether the vision had lasted a second or a hundred years, not knowing any more whether there existed a Siddhartha, a Gotama, a me and a you, feeling in his innermost self as if he had been wounded by a divine arrow, the injury of which tasted sweet, being enchanted and dissolved in his innermost self, Govinda still stood for a little while bent over Siddhartha's quiet face, which he had just kissed, which had just been the scene of all manifestations, all transformations, all existence. The face was unchanged, after under its surface the depth of the thousand-foldness had closed up again, he smiled silently, smiled quietly and softly, perhaps very benevolently, perhaps very mockingly, precisely as he used to smile, the exalted one.

Deeply, Govinda bowed; tears he knew nothing of, ran down his old face; like a fire burned the feeling of the most intimate love, the humblest veneration in his heart. Deeply, he bowed, touching the ground, before him who was sitting motionlessly, whose smile reminded him of everything he had ever loved in his life, what had ever been valuable and holy to him in his life.

STEPPENWOLF

Translated from the German by Basil Creighton.

PREFACE

This book contains the records left us by a man whom, according to the expression he often used himself, we called the Steppenwolf. Whether this manuscript needs any introductory remarks may be open to question. I, however, feel the need of adding a few pages to those of the Steppenwolf in which I try to record my recollections of him. What I know of him is little enough. Indeed, of his past life and origins I know nothing at all. Yet the impression left by his personality has remained, in spite of all, a deep and sympathetic one.

Some years ago the Steppenwolf, who was then approaching fifty, called on my aunt to inquire for a furnished room. He took the attic room on the top floor and the bedroom next it, returned a day or two later with two trunks and a big case of books and stayed nine or ten months with us. He lived by himself very quietly, and but for the fact that our bedrooms were next door to each other—which occasioned a good many chance encounters on the stairs and in the passage—we should have remained practically unacquainted. For he was not a sociable man. Indeed, he was unsociable to a degree I had never before experienced in anybody. He was, in fact, as he called himself, a real wolf of the Steppes, a strange, wild, shy—very shy—being from another world than mine. How deep the loneliness into which his life had drifted on account of his disposition and destiny and how consciously he accepted this loneliness as his destiny, I certainly did not know until I read the records he left behind him. Yet, before that, from our occasional talks and encounters, I became gradually acquainted with him, and I found that the portrait in his records was in substantial agreement with the paler and less complete one that our personal acquaintance had given me.

By chance I was there at the very moment when the Steppenwolf entered our house for the first time and became my aunt's lodger. He came at noon. The table had not been cleared and I still had half an hour before going back to the office. I have never forgotten the odd and very conflicting impressions he made on me at this first encounter. He came through the glazed door, having just rung the bell and my aunt asked him in the dim light of the hall what he wanted. The Steppenwolf, however, first threw up his sharp, closely cropped head and sniffed around nervously before he either made any answer or announced his name.

"Oh, it smells good here," he said, and at that he smiled and my aunt smiled too. For my part, I found this manner of introducing himself ridiculous and was not favourably impressed.

"However," said he, "I've come about the room you have to let."

I did not get a good look at him until we were all three on our way up to the top floor. Though not very big, he had the bearing of a big man. He wore a fashionable and comfortable winter overcoat and he was well, though carelessly, dressed, clean-shaven, and his cropped head showed here and there a streak of grey. He carried himself in a way I did not at all like at first. There was something weary and undecided about it that did not go with his keen and striking profile nor with the tone of his voice. Later, I found out that his health was poor and that walking tired him. With a peculiar smile—at that time equally unpleasant to me—he contemplated the stairs, the walls, and windows, and the tall old cupboards on the staircase. All this seemed to please and at the same time to amuse him. Altogether he gave the impression of having come out of an alien world, from another continent perhaps. He found it all very charming and a little odd. I cannot deny that he was polite, even friendly. He agreed at once and without objection to the terms for lodging and breakfast and so forth, and yet about the whole man there was a foreign and, as I chose to think, disagreeable or hostile atmosphere. He took the room and the bedroom too, listened attentively and amiably to all he was told about the heating, the water, the service and the rules of the household, agreed to everything, offered at once to pay a sum in advance—and yet he seemed at the same time to be outside it all, to find it comic to be doing as he did and not to take it seriously. It was as though it were a very odd and new experience for him, occupied as he was with quite other concerns, to be renting a room and talking to people in German. Such more or less was my impression and it would certainly not have been a good one if it had not been revised and corrected by many small instances. Above all, his face pleased me from the first, in spite of the foreign air it had. It was a rather original face and perhaps a sad one, but alert, thoughtful, strongly marked and highly intellectual. And then, to reconcile me further, there was his polite and friendly manner, which though it seemed to cost him some pains, was all the same quite without pretention; on the contrary, there was something almost touching, imploring in it. The explanation of it I found later, but it disposed me at once in his favour.

* * * *

Before we had done inspecting the rooms and going into the arrangements, my luncheon hour was up and I had to go back to business. I took my leave and left him to my aunt. When I got back at night, she told me that he had taken the rooms and was coming in in a day or two. The only request he had made was that his arrival should not be notified to the police, as in his poor state of health he found these formalities and the standing about in official waiting-rooms more than he could tolerate. I remember very well how this surprised me and how I warned my aunt against giving in to his stipulation. This fear of the police seemed to me to agree only too well with the mysterious and alien air man had and struck me as suspicious. I explained to my aunt that she ought not on any account to put herself in this equivocal and in any case rather peculiar position for a complete stranger; it might well turn out to have very unpleasant consequences for her. But it then came out that my aunt had already granted his request, and, indeed, had let herself be altogether captivated and charmed by the strange gentleman. For she never took a lodger with whom she did not contrive to stand in some human, friendly, and as it were auntlike or, rather, motherly relation; and many a one has made full use of this weakness of hers. And thus for the first weeks things went on; I had many a fault to find with the new lodger, while my aunt every time warmly took his part.

As I was not at all pleased about this business of neglecting to notify the police, I wanted at least to know what my aunt had learnt about him; what sort of family he came of and what his intentions were. And, of course, she had learnt one thing and another, although he had only stayed a short while after I left at noon. He had told her that he thought of spending some months in our town to avail himself of the libraries and to see its antiquities. I may say it did not please my aunt that he was only taking the rooms for so short a time, but he had clearly quite won her heart in spite of his rather peculiar way of presenting himself. In short, the rooms were let and my objections came too late.

"Why on earth did he say that it smelt so good here?" I asked.

"I know well enough," she replied, with her usual insight. "There's a smell of cleanliness and good order here, of comfort and respectability. It was that that pleased him. He looks as if he weren't used to that of late and missed it."

Just so, thought I to myself.

"But," I said aloud, "if he isn't used to an orderly and respectable life, what is going to happen? What will you say if he has filthy habits and makes dirt everywhere, or comes home drunk at all hours of the night?"

"We shall see, we shall see," she said, and laughed; and I left it at that.

And in the upshot my fears proved groundless. The lodger, though he certainly did not live a very orderly or rational life, was no worry or trouble to us. Yet my aunt and I bothered our heads a lot about him, and I confess I have not by a long way done with him even now. I often dream of him at night, and the mere existence of such a man, much as I got to like him, has had a thoroughly disturbing and disquieting effect on me.

* * * *

Two days after this the stranger's luggage—his name was Harry Haller—was brought in by a porter. He had a very fine leather trunk, which made a good impression on me, and a big flat cabin-trunk that showed signs of having travelled far—at least it was plastered with labels of hotels and travel agencies of various countries, some overseas.

Then he himself appeared, and the time began during which I gradually got acquainted with this strange man. At first I did nothing on my side to encourage it. Although Haller interested me from the moment I saw him I took no steps for the first two or three weeks to run across him or to get into conversation with him. On the other hand I confess that I did, all the same and from the very first, keep him under observation a little and also went into his room now and again when he was out and my curiosity drove me to do a little spy-work.

I have already given some account of the Steppenwolf's outward appearance. He gave at the very first glance the impression of a significant, an uncommon, and unusually gifted man. His face was intellectual, and the abnormally delicate and mobile play of his features reflected a soul of extremely emotional and unusually delicate sensibility. When one spoke to him and he, as was not always the case, dropped conventionalities and said personal and individual things that came out of his own alien world, then a man like myself came under his spell on the spot. He had thought more than other men, and in matters of the intellect he had that calm objectivity, that certainty of thought and knowledge, such as only really intellectual men have, who have no axe to grind, who never wish to shine, or to talk others down, or to appear always in the right.

I remember an instance of this in the last days he was here, if I can call a mere fleeting glance he gave me an example of what I mean. It was when a celebrated historian and art critic, a man of European fame, had announced a lecture in the Aula. I had succeeded in persuading the Steppenwolf to attend it, though at first he had little desire to do so. We went together and sat next to each other. When the lecturer ascended the platform and began his address, many of his hearers, who had expected a sort of prophet, were disappointed by his rather spruce and conceited air. And when he proceeded, by way of introduction, to say a few flattering things to the audience, thanking them for their attendance in such numbers, the Steppenwolf threw me a quick look, a look which criticised both the words and the speaker of them—an unforgettable and frightful look which spoke volumes! It was a look that did not simply criticise that lecturer, annihilating the celebrated man with its crushing yet delicate irony. That was the least of it. It was more sad than ironical; it was indeed utterly and hopelessly sad; it conveyed a quiet despair, born partly of conviction, partly of a mode of thought which had become habitual with him. This despair of his not only unmasked the conceited lecturer and dismissed with its irony the matter at hand, the expectant attitude of the public, the somewhat presumptuous title under which the lecture was announced—no, the Steppenwolf's look pierced our whole epoch, its whole overwrought activity, the whole surge and strife, the whole vanity, the whole superficial play of a shallow, opinionated intellectuality. And alas! The look went still deeper, went far below the faults, defects and hopelessness of our time, our intellect, our culture alone. It went right to the heart of all humanity, it bespoke eloquently in a single second the whole despair of a thinker, of one who knew the full worth and meaning of man's life. It said: "See what monkeys we are! Look, such is man!" and at once all renown, all intelligence, all the attainments of the spirit, all progress towards the sublime, the great and the enduring in man fell away and became a monkey's trick!

With this I have gone far ahead and, contrary to my actual plan and intention, already conveyed what Haller essentially meant to me; whereas my original aim was to uncover his picture by degrees while telling the course of my gradual acquaintance with him.

Now that I have gone so far ahead it will save time to say a little more about Haller's puzzling "strangeness" and to tell in detail how I gradually guessed and became aware of the causes and meaning of this strangeness, this extraordinary and frightful loneliness. It will be better so, for I wish to leave my own personality as far as possible in the background. I do not want to put down my own confessions, to tell a story or to write an essay on psychology, but simply as an eye-witness to contribute something to the picture of the peculiar individual who left this Steppenwolf manuscript behind him.

At the very first sight of him, when he came into my aunt's home, craning his head like a bird and praising the smell of the house, I was at once astonished by something curious about him; and my first natural reaction was repugnance. I suspected (and my aunt, who unlike me is the very reverse of an intellectual person, suspected very much the same thing)—I suspected that the man was ailing, ailing in the spirit in some way, or in his temperament or character, and I shrank from him with the instinct of the healthy. This shrinking was in course of time replaced by a sympathy inspired by pity for one who had suffered so long and deeply, and whose loneliness and inward death I witnessed. In course of time I was more and more conscious, too, that this affliction was not due to any defects of nature, but rather to a profusion of gifts and powers which had not attained to harmony. I saw that Haller was a genius of suffering and that in the meaning of many sayings of Nietzsche he had created within himself with positive genius a boundless and frightful capacity for pain. I saw at the same time that the root of his pessimism was not world-contempt but self-contempt; for however mercilessly he might annihilate institutions and persons in his talk he never spared himself. It was always at himself first and foremost that he aimed the shaft, himself first and foremost whom he hated and despised.

And here I cannot refrain from a psychological observation. Although I know very little of the Steppenwolf's life, I have all the same good reason to suppose that he was brought up by devoted but severe and very pious parents and teachers in accordance with that doctrine, that makes the breaking of the will the corner-stone of education and up-bringing. But in this case the attempt to destroy the personality and to break the will did not succeed. He was much too strong and hardy, too proud and spirited. Instead of destroying his personality they succeeded only in teaching him to hate himself. It was against himself that, innocent and noble as he was, he directed during his whole life the whole wealth of his fancy, the whole of his thought; and in so far as he let loose upon himself every barbed criticism, every anger and hate he could command, he was, in spite of all, a real Christian and a real martyr. As for others and the world around him he never ceased in his heroic and earnest endeavour to love them, to be just to them, to do them no harm, for the love of his neighbour was as deeply in him as the hatred of himself, and so his whole life was an example that love of one's neighbour is not possible without love of oneself, and that self-hate is really the same thing as sheer egoism, and in the long run breeds the same cruel isolation and despair.

It is now time, however, to put my own thoughts aside and to get to facts. What I first discovered about Haller, partly through my espionage, partly from my aunt's remarks, concerned his way of living. It was soon obvious that his days were spent with his thoughts and his books, and that he pursued no practical calling. He lay always very late in bed. Often he was not up much before noon and went across from his bedroom to his sitting-room in his dressing-gown. This sitting-room, a large and comfortable attic room with two windows, after a few days was not at all the same as when occupied by other tenants. It filled up; and as time went on it was always fuller. Pictures were hung on the walls, drawings tacked up—sometimes illustrations cut out from magazines and often changed. A southern landscape, photographs of a little German country town, apparently Haller's home, hung there, and between them were some brightly painted water-colours, which, as we discovered later, he had painted himself. Then there were photographs of a pretty young woman, or—rather—girl. For a long while a Siamese Buddha hung on the wall, to be replaced first by Michelangelo's "Night," then by a portrait of the Mahatma Gandhi. Books filled the large book-case and lay everywhere else as well, on the table, on the pretty old bureau, on the sofa, on the chairs and all about on the floor, books with notes slipped into them which were continually changing. The books constantly increased, for besides bringing whole armfuls back with him from the libraries he was always getting parcels of them by post. The occupant of this room might well be a learned man; and to this the all-pervading smell of cigar-smoke might testify as well as the stumps and ash of cigars all about the room. A great part of the books, however, were not books of learning. The majority were works of the poets of all times and peoples. For a long while there lay about on the sofa where he often spent whole days all six volumes of a work with the title *Sophia's Journey from Memel to Saxony*—a work of the latter part of the eighteenth century. A complete edition of Goethe and one of Jean Paul showed signs of wear, also Novalis, while Lessing, Jacobi and Lichtenberg were in the same condition. A few volumes of Dostoievski bristled with pencilled slips. On the big table among the books and papers there was often a vase of flowers. There, too, a paint box, generally full of dust, reposed among flakes of cigar ash and (to leave nothing out) sundry bottles of wine. There was a straw-covered bottle usually containing Italian red wine, which he procured from a little shop in the neighbourhood; often, too, a bottle of Burgundy as well as Malaga; and a squat bottle of Cherry brandy was, as I saw, nearly emptied in a very brief space—after which it disappeared in a corner of the room, there to collect the dust without further diminution of its contents. I will not pretend to justify this espionage I carried on, and I will say openly that all these signs of a life full of intellectual curiosity, but thoroughly slovenly and disorderly all the same, inspired me at first with aversion and mistrust. I am not only a middle-class man, living a regular life, fond of work and punctuality; I am also an abstainer and non-smoker, and these bottles in Haller's room pleased me even less than the rest of his artistic disorder.

He was just as irregular and irresponsible about his meal times as he was about his hours of sleep and work. There were days when he did not go out at all and had nothing but his coffee in the morning. Sometimes my aunt found nothing but a banana peel to show that he had dined. Other days, however, he took his meals in restaurants, sometimes in the best and most fashionable, sometimes in little out-lying taverns. His health did not seem good. Besides his limping gait that often made the stairs fatiguing to him, he seemed to be plagued with other troubles and he once said to me that it was years since he had had either a good digestion or sound sleep. I put it down first and last to his drinking. When, later on, I accompanied him sometimes to his haunts I often saw with my own eyes how he drank when the mood was on him, though neither I nor anyone else ever saw him really drunk.

I have never forgotten our first encounter. We knew each other then only as fellow-lodgers whose rooms were adjoining ones. Then one evening I came home from business and to my astonishment found Haller seated on the landing between the first and second floors. He was sitting on the top step and he moved to one side to let me pass. I asked him if he was all right and offered to take him up to the top.

Haller looked at me and I could see that I had awoken him from a kind of trance. Slowly he began to smile his delightful sad smile that has so often filled my heart with pity. Then he invited me to sit beside him. I thanked him, but said it was not my custom to sit on the stairs at other people's doors.

"Ah, yes," he said, and smiled the more. "You're quite right. But wait a moment, for I really must tell you what it was made me sit here for a bit."

He pointed as he spoke to the entrance of the first floor flat, where a widow lived. In the little space with parquet flooring between the stairs, the window and the glazed front door there stood a tall cupboard of mahogany, with some old pewter on it, and in front of the cupboard on the floor there were two plants, an azalea and an araucaria, in large pots which stood on low stands. The plants looked very pretty and were always kept spotlessly neat and clean, as I had often noticed with pleasure.

"Look at this little vestibule," Haller went on, "with the araucaria and its wonderful smell. Many a time I can't go by without pausing a moment. At your aunt's too, there reigns a wonderful smell of order and extreme cleanliness, but this little place of the araucaria, why, it's so shiningly clean, so dusted and polished and scoured, so inviolably clean that it positively glitters. I always have to take a deep breath of it as I go by; don't you smell it too? What a fragrance there is here—the scent of floor polish with a fainter echo of turpentine blending with the mahogany and the washed leaves of the plants, of superlative bourgeois cleanliness, of care and precision, of duty done and devotion to little things. I don't know who lives here, but behind that glazed door there must be a paradise of cleanliness and spotless mediocrity, of ordered ways, a touching and anxious devotion to life's little habits and tasks."

"Do not, please, think for a moment," he went on when I said nothing in reply, "that I speak with irony. My dear sir, I would not for the world laugh at the bourgeois life. It is true that I live myself in another world, and perhaps I could not endure to live a single day in a house with araucarias. But though I am a shabby old Steppenwolf, still I'm the son of a mother and my mother too was a middle-class man's wife and raised plants and took care to have her house and home as clean and neat and tidy as ever she could make it. All that is brought back to me by this breath of turpentine and by the araucaria, and so here I sat me down then and there; and I look into this quiet little garden of order and rejoice that such things still are."

He wanted to get up, but found it difficult; and he did not repulse me when I offered him a little help. I was silent, but I submitted just as my aunt had done before me to a certain charm the strange man could sometimes exercise. We went slowly up the stairs together, and at his door, the key in his hand, he looked me once more in the eyes in a friendly way and said: "You've come from business? Well, of course, I know little of all that. I live a bit to one side, on the edge of things, you see. But you too, I believe, interest yourself in books and such matters. Your aunt told me one day that you had been through the Gymnasium and were a good Greek scholar. Now, this morning I came on a passage in Novalis. May I show it you? It would delight you, I know."

He took me into his room, which smelt strongly of tobacco, and took out a book from one of the heaps, turned the leaves and looked for the passage.

"This is good too, very good," he said, "listen to this: 'A man should be proud of suffering. All suffering is a reminder of our high estate.' Fine! Eighty years before Nietzsche. But that is not the sentence I meant. Wait a moment, here I have it. This: 'Most men will not swim before they are able to.' Is not that witty? Naturally, they won't swim! They are born for the solid earth, not for the water. And naturally they won't think. They are made for life, not for thought. Yes, and he who thinks, what's more, he who makes thought his business, he may go far in it, but he has bartered the solid earth for the water all the same, and one day he will drown."

He had got hold of me now. I was interested; and I stayed on a short while with him; and after that we often talked when we met on the stairs or in the street. On such occasions I always had at first the feeling that he was being ironical with me. But it was not so. He had a real respect for me, just as he had for the araucaria. He was so convinced and conscious of his isolation, his swimming in the water, his uprootedness, that a glimpse now and then of the orderly daily round—the punctuality, for example, that kept me to my office hours, or an expression let fall by a servant or tramway-conductor—acted on him literally as a stimulus without in the least arousing his scorn. At first all this seemed to me a ridiculous exaggeration, the affectation of a gentleman of leisure, a playful sentimentality. But I came to see more and more that from the empty spaces of his lone wolfishness he actually really admired and loved our little bourgeois world as something solid and secure, as the home and peace which must ever remain far and unattainable, with no road leading from him to them. He took off his hat to our charwoman, a worthy person, every time he met her, with genuine respect; and when my aunt had any little occasion to talk to him, to draw his attention, it might be, to some mending of his linen or to warn him of a button hanging loose on his coat, he listened to her with an air of great attention and consequence, as though it were only with an extreme and desperate effort that he could force his way through any crack into our little peaceful world and be at home there if only for an hour.

During that very first conversation, about the araucaria, he called himself the Steppenwolf, and this too estranged and disturbed me a little. What an expression! However, custom did not only reconcile me to it, but soon I never thought of him by any other name; nor could I today hit on a better description of him. A wolf of the Steppes that had lost its way and strayed into the towns and the life of the herd, a more striking image could not be found for his shy loneliness, his savagery, his restlessness, his homesickness, his homelessness.

I was able once to observe him for a whole evening. It was at a Symphony concert, where to my surprise I found him seated near me. He did not see me. First some Handel was played, noble and lovely music. But the Steppenwolf sat absorbed in his own thoughts, detached alike from the music and his surroundings. Unheeding and alone, he sat with downcast eyes, and a cold but sorrowful expression. After the Handel came a little Symphony of Friedman Bach and after a few notes I was astonished to see him begin to smile and give himself up to the music. He was abstracted—but happily so—and lost in such pleasant dreams, that for at least ten minutes I paid more attention to him than to the music. When the piece ended he woke up, and made a movement to go; but after all he kept his seat and heard the last piece too. It was *Variations* by Reger, a composition that many found rather long and tiresome. The Steppenwolf, too, who at first made up his mind to listen, wandered again, put his hands into his pockets and sank once more into his own thoughts, not happily and dreamily as before, but sadly and finally irritated. His face was once more vacant and grey. The light in it was quenched and he looked old, ill and discontented.

I saw him again after the concert in the street and walked along behind him. Wrapped in his cloak he went his way joylessly and wearily in the direction of our quarter, but stopped in front of a small old-fashioned inn, and after looking irresolutely at the time, went in. I obeyed a momentary impulse and followed him; and there he sat at a table in the backroom of the bar, greeted by hostess and waitress as a well-known guest. Greeting him, too, I took my seat beside him. We sat there for an hour, and while I drank two glasses of mineral water, he accounted for a pint of red wine and then called for another half. I remarked that I had been to the concert, but he did not follow up this topic. He read the label on my bottle and asked whether I would not drink some wine. When I declined his offer and said that I never drank it, the old helpless expression came over his face.

"You're quite right there," he said. "I have practised abstinence myself for years, and had my time of fasting, too, but now I find myself once more beneath the sign of Aquarius, a dark and humid constellation."

And then, when I playfully took up his allusion and remarked how unlikely it seemed to me that he really believed in astrology, he promptly resumed the too polite tone which often hurt me and said: "You are right. Unfortunately, I cannot believe in that science either."

I took my leave and went. It was very late before he came in, but his step was as usual, and as always, instead of going straight to bed, he stayed up an hour longer in his sitting-room, as I from my neighbouring room could hear plainly enough.

There was another evening which I have not forgotten. My aunt was out and I was alone in the house, when the doorbell rang. I opened the door and there stood a young and very pretty woman, whom, as soon as she asked for Mr. Haller, I recognised from the photograph in his room. I showed her his door and withdrew. She stayed a short while above, but soon I heard them both come down stairs and go out, talking and laughing together very happily. I was much astonished that the hermit had his love, and one so young and pretty and elegant; and all my conjectures about him and his life were upset once more. But before an hour had gone he came back alone and dragged himself wearily upstairs with his sad and heavy tread. For hours together he paced softly to and fro in his sitting-room, exactly like a wolf in its cage. The whole night till close on morning there was light in his room. I know nothing at all about this occasion, and have only this to add. On one other occasion I saw him in this lady's company. It was in one of the streets of the town. They were arm in arm and he looked very happy; and again I wondered to see how much charm—what an even child-like expression—his care-ridden face had sometimes. It explained the young lady to me, also the predilection my aunt had for him. That day, too, however, he came back in the evening, sad and wretched as usual. I met him at the door and under his cloak, as many a time before, he had the bottle of Italian wine, and he sat with it half the night in his hell upstairs. It grieved me. What a comfortless, what a forlorn and shiftless life he led!

And now I have gossiped enough. No more is needed to show that the Steppenwolf lived a suicidal existence. But all the same I do not believe that he took his own life when, after paying all he owed but without a word of warning or farewell, he left our town one day and vanished. We have not heard from him since and we are still keeping some letters that came for him after he had left. He left nothing behind but his manuscript. It was written during the time he was here, and he left it with a few lines to say that I might do what I liked with it.

It was not in my power to verify the truth of the experiences related in Haller's manuscript. I have no doubt that they are for the most part fictitious, not, however, in the sense of arbitrary invention. They are rather the deeply lived spiritual events which he has attempted to express by giving them the form of tangible experiences. The partly fantastic occurrences in Haller's fiction come presumably from the later period of his stay here, and I have no doubt that even they have some basis in real occurrence. At that time our guest did in fact alter very much in behaviour and in appearance. He was out a great deal, for whole nights sometimes; and his books lay untouched. On the rare occasions when I saw him at that time I was very much struck by his air of vivacity and youth. Sometimes, indeed, he seemed positively happy. This does not mean that a new and heavy depression did not follow immediately. All day long he lay in bed. He had no desire for food. At that time the young lady appeared once more on the scene, and an extremely violent, I may even say brutal, quarrel occurred which upset the whole house and for which Haller begged my aunt's pardon for days after.

No, I am sure he has not taken his life. He is still alive, and somewhere wearily goes up and down the stairs of strange houses, stares somewhere at clean-scoured parquet floors and carefully tended araucarias, sits for days in libraries and nights in taverns, or lying on a hired sofa, listens to the world beneath his window and the hum of human life from which he knows that he is excluded. But he has not killed himself, for a glimmer of belief still tells him that he is to drink this frightful suffering in his heart to the dregs, and that it is of this suffering he must die. I think of him often. He has not made life lighter for me. He had not the gift of fostering strength and joy in me. Oh, on the contrary! But I am not he, and I live my own life, a narrow, middle-class life, but a solid one, filled with duties. And so we can think of him peacefully and affectionately, my aunt and I. She would have more to say of him than I have, but that lies buried in her good heart.

* * * *

And now that we come to these records of Haller's, these partly diseased, partly beautiful and thoughtful fantasies, I must confess that if they had fallen into my hands by chance and if I had not known their author, I should most certainly have thrown them away in disgust. But owing to my acquaintance with Haller I have been able, to some extent, to understand them, and even to appreciate them. I should hesitate to share them with others if I saw in them nothing but the pathological fancies of a single and isolated case of a diseased temperament. But I see something more in them. I see them as a document of the times, for Haller's sickness of the soul, as I now know, is not the eccentricity of a single individual, but the sickness of the times themselves, the neurosis of that generation to which Haller belongs, a sickness, it seems, that by no means attacks the weak and worthless only but, rather, precisely those who are strongest in spirit and richest in gifts.

These records, however much or however little of real life may lie at the back of them, are not an attempt to disguise or to palliate this widespread sickness of our times. They are an attempt to present the sickness itself in its actual manifestation. They mean, literally, a journey through hell, a sometimes fearful, sometimes courageous journey through the chaos of a world whose souls dwell in darkness, a journey undertaken with the determination to go through hell from one end to the other, to give battle to chaos, and to suffer torture to the full.

It was some remembered conversation with Haller that gave me the key to this interpretation. He said to me once when we were talking of the so-called horrors of the Middle Ages: "These horrors were really non-existent. A man of the Middle Ages would detest the whole mode of our present day life as something far more than horrible, far more than barbarous. Every age, every culture, every custom and tradition has its own character, its own weakness and its own strength, its beauties and ugliness; accepts certain sufferings as matters of course, puts up patiently with certain evils. Human life is reduced to real suffering, to hell, only when two ages, two cultures and religions overlap. A man of the Classical Age who had to live in medieval times would suffocate miserably just as a savage does in the midst of our civilisation. Now there are times when a whole generation is caught in this way between two ages, two modes of life, with the consequence that it loses all power to understand itself and has no standard, no security, no simple acquiescence. Naturally, every one does not feel this equally strongly. A nature such as Nietzsche's had to suffer our present ills more than a generation in advance. What he had to go through alone and misunderstood, thousands suffer today."

I often had to think of these words while reading the records. Haller belongs to those who have been caught between two ages, who are outside of all security and simple acquiescence. He belongs to those whose fate it is to live the whole riddle of human destiny heightened to the pitch of a personal torture, a personal hell.

There, as it seems to me, lies the meaning these records can have for us, and because of this I decided to publish them. For the rest, I neither approve nor condemn them. Let every reader do as his conscience bids him.

HARRY HALLER'S RECORDS

"FOR MADMEN ONLY"

The day had gone by just as days go by. I had killed it in accordance with my primitive and retiring way of life. I had worked for an hour or two and perused the pages of old books. I had had pains for two hours, as elderly people do. I had taken a powder and been very glad when the pains consented to disappear. I had lain in a hot bath and absorbed its kindly warmth. Three times the post had come with undesired letters and circulars to look through. I had done my breathing exercises, but found it convenient today to omit the thought exercises. I had been for an hour's walk and seen the loveliest feathery cloud patterns pencilled against the sky. That was very delightful. So was the reading of the old books. So was the lying in the warm bath. But, taken all in all, it had not been exactly a day of rapture. No, it had not even been a day brightened with happiness and joy. Rather, it had been just one of those days which for a long while now had fallen to my lot; the moderately pleasant, the wholly bearable and tolerable, lukewarm days of a discontented middle-aged man; days without special pains, without special cares, without particular worry, without despair; days which put the question quietly of their own accord whether the time has not come to follow the example of Adalbert Stifter and have a fatal accident while shaving.

He who has known the other days, the angry ones of gout attacks, or those with that wicked headache rooted behind the eyeballs that casts a spell on every nerve of eye and ear with a fiendish delight in torture, or soul-destroying, evil days of inward vacancy and despair, when, on this distracted earth, sucked dry by the vampires of finance, the world of men and of so-called culture grins back at us with the lying, vulgar, brazen glamour of a Fair and dogs us with the persistence of an emetic, and when all is concentrated and focussed to the last pitch of the intolerable upon your own sick self—he who has known these days of hell may be content indeed with normal half-and-half days like today. Thankfully you sit by the warm stove, thankfully you assure yourself as you read your morning paper that another day has come and no war broken out, no new dictatorship has been set up, no peculiarly disgusting scandal been unveiled in the worlds of politics or finance. Thankfully you tune the strings of your mouldering lyre to a moderated, to a passably joyful, nay, to an even delighted psalm of thanksgiving and with it bore your quiet, flabby and slightly muzzy half-and-half god of contentment; and in the thick warm air of a contented boredom and very welcome painlessness the nodding mandarin of a half-and-half god and the nodding middle-aged gentleman who sings his muffled psalm look as like each other as two peas.

There is much to be said for contentment and painlessness, for these bearable and submissive days, on which neither pain nor pleasure is audible, but pass by whispering and on tip-toe. But the worst of it is that it is just this contentment that I cannot endure. After a short time it fills me with irrepressible hatred and nausea. In desperation I have to escape and throw myself on the road to pleasure, or, if that cannot be, on the road to pain. When I have neither pleasure nor pain and have been breathing for a while the lukewarm insipid air of these so-called good and tolerable days, I feel so bad in my childish soul that I smash my mouldering lyre of thanksgiving in the face of the slumbering god of contentment and would rather feel the very devil burn in me than this warmth of a well-heated room. A wild longing for strong emotions and sensations seethes in me, a rage against this toneless, flat, normal and sterile life. I have a mad impulse to smash something, a warehouse, perhaps, or a cathedral, or myself, to commit outrages, to pull off the wigs of a few revered idols, to provide a few rebellious schoolboys with the longed-for ticket to Hamburg, or to stand one or two representatives of the established order on their heads. For what I always hated and detested and cursed above all things was this contentment, this healthiness and comfort, this carefully preserved optimism of the middle classes, this fat and prosperous brood of mediocrity.

It was in such a mood then that I finished this not intolerable and very ordinary day as dusk set in. I did not end it in a manner becoming a rather ailing man and go to bed tempted by a hot water bottle. Instead I put on my shoes ill-humouredly, discontented and disgusted with the little work I had done, and went out into the dark and foggy streets to drink what men according to an old convention call "a glass of wine," at the sign of the Steel Helmet.

In this plight then, I went down the steep stairs from my attic-cell among strangers, those smug and well-brushed stairs of a three-storey house, let as three flats to highly respectable families. I don't know how it comes about, but I, the homeless Steppenwolf, the solitary, the hater of life's petty conventions, always take up my quarters in just such houses as this. It is an old weakness of mine. I live neither in palatial houses nor in those of the humble poor, but instead and deliberately in these respectable and wearisome and spotless middle class homes, which smell of turpentine and soap and where there is a panic if you bang the door or come in with dirty shoes. The love of this atmosphere comes, no doubt, from the days of my childhood, and a secret yearning I have for something homelike drives me, though with little hope, to follow the same old stupid road. Then again, I like the contrast between my lonely, loveless, hunted, and thoroughly disorderly existence and this middle-class family-life. I like to breathe in on the stairs this odour of quiet and order, of cleanliness and respectable domesticity. There is something in it that touches me in spite of my hatred for all it stands for. I like to step across the threshold of my room and leave it suddenly behind; to see, instead, cigar-ash and wine-bottles among the heaped-up books and there is nothing but disorder and neglect; and where everything—books, manuscript, thoughts—is marked and saturated with the plight of lonely men, with the problem of existence and with the yearning after a new orientation for an age that has lost its bearings.

And now I came to the araucaria. I must tell you that on the first floor of this house the stairs pass by a little vestibule at the entrance to a flat which, I am convinced, is even more spotlessly swept and garnished than the others; for this little vestibule shines with a super-human housewifery. It is a little temple of order. On the parquet floor, where it seems desecration to tread, are two elegant stands and on each a large pot. In the one grows an azalea. In the other a stately araucaria, a thriving, straight-grown baby-tree, a perfect specimen, which to the last needle of the topmost twig reflects the pride of frequent ablutions. Sometimes, when I know that I am unobserved, I use this place as a temple. I take my seat on a step of the stairs above the araucaria and, resting awhile with folded hands, I contemplate this little garden of order and let the touching air it has and its somewhat ridiculous loneliness move me to the depths of my soul. I imagine behind this vestibule, in the sacred shadow, one may say, of the araucaria, a home full of shining mahogany, and a life full of sound respectability—early rising, attention to duty, restrained but cheerful family gatherings, Sunday church-going, early to bed.

Affecting lightheartedness, I trod the moist pavements of the narrow streets. As though in tears and veiled, the lamps glimmered through the chill gloom and sucked their reflections slowly from the wet ground. The forgotten years of my youth came back to me. How I used to love the dark, sad evenings of late autumn and winter, how eagerly I imbibed their moods of loneliness and melancholy when wrapped in my cloak I strode for half the night through rain and storm, through the leafless winter landscape, lonely enough then too, but full of deep joy, and full of poetry which later I wrote down by candle-light sitting on the edge of my bed! All that was past now. The cup was emptied and would never be filled again. Was that a matter for regret? No, I did not regret the past. My regret was for the present day, for all the countless hours and days that I lost in mere passivity and that brought me nothing, not even the shocks of awakening. But, thank God, there were exceptions. There were now and then, though rarely, the hours that brought the welcome shock, pulled down the walls and brought me back again from my wanderings to the living heart of the world. Sadly and yet deeply moved, I set myself to recall the last of these experiences. It was at a concert of lovely old music. After two or three notes of the piano the door was opened of a sudden to the other world. I sped through heaven and saw God at work. I suffered holy pains. I dropped all my defences and was afraid of nothing in the world. I accepted all things and to all things I gave up my heart. It did not last very long, a quarter of an hour perhaps; but it returned to me in a dream at night, and since, through all the barren days, I caught a glimpse of it now and then. Sometimes for a minute or two I saw it clearly, threading my life like a divine and golden track. But nearly always it was blurred in dirt and dust. Then again it gleamed out in golden sparks as though never to be lost again and yet was soon quite lost once more. Once it happened, as I lay awake at night, that I suddenly spoke in verses, in verses so beautiful and strange that I did not venture to think of writing them down, and then in the morning they vanished; and yet they lay hidden within me like the hard kernel within an old brittle husk. Once it came to me while reading a poet, while pondering a thought of Descartes, of Pascal; again it shone out and drove its gold track far into the sky while I was in the presence of my beloved. Ah, but it is hard to find this track of the divine in the midst of this life we lead, in this besotted humdrum age of spiritual blindness, with its architecture, its business, its politics, its men! How could I fail to be a lone wolf, and an uncouth hermit, as I did not share one of its aims nor understand one of its pleasures? I cannot remain for long in either theatre or picture-house. I can scarcely read a paper, seldom a modern book. I cannot understand what pleasures and joys they are that drive people to the overcrowded railways and hotels, into the packed cafés with the suffocating and oppressive music, to the Bars and variety entertainments, to World Exhibitions, to the Corsos. I cannot understand nor share these joys, though they are within my reach, for which thousands of others strive. On the other hand, what happens to me in my rare hours of joy, what for me is bliss and life and ecstasy and exaltation, the world in general seeks at most in imagination; in life it finds it absurd. And in fact, if the world is right, if this music of the cafés, these mass-enjoyments and these Americanised men who are pleased with so little are right, then I am wrong, I am crazy. I am in truth the Steppenwolf that I often call myself; that beast astray who finds neither home nor joy nor nourishment in a world that is strange and incomprehensible to him.

With these familiar thoughts I went along the wet street through one of the quietest and oldest quarters of the town. On the opposite side there stood in the darkness an old stone wall which I always noticed with pleasure. Old and serene, it stood between a little church and an old hospital and often during the day I let my eyes rest on its rough surface. There were few such quiet and peaceful spaces in the centre of the town where from every square foot some lawyer, or quack, or doctor, or barber, or chiropodist shouted his name at you. This time, too, the wall was peaceful, and serene and yet something was altered in it. I was amazed to see a small and pretty doorway with a Gothic arch in the middle of the wall, for I could not make up my mind whether this doorway had always been there or whether it had just been made. It looked old without a doubt, very old; apparently this closed portal with its door of blackened wood had opened hundreds of years ago onto a sleepy convent yard, and did so still, even though the convent was no longer there. Probably I had seen it a hundred times and simply not noticed it. Perhaps it had been painted afresh and caught my eye for that reason. I paused to examine it from where I stood without crossing over, as the street between was so deep in mud and water. From the sidewalk where I stood and looked across it seemed to me in the dim light that a garland, or something gaily coloured, was festooned round the doorway, and now that I looked more closely I saw over the portal a bright shield, on which, it seemed to me, there was something written. I strained my eyes and at last, in spite of the mud and puddles, went across, and there over the door I saw a stain showing up faintly on the grey-green of the wall, and over the stain bright letters dancing and then disappearing, returning and vanishing once more. So that's it, thought I. They've disfigured this good old wall with an electric sign. Meanwhile I deciphered one or two of the letters as they appeared again for an instant; but they were hard to read even by guess work, for they came with very irregular spaces between them and very faintly, and then abruptly vanished. Whoever hoped for any result from a display like that was not very smart. He was a Steppenwolf, poor fellow. Why have his letters playing on this old wall in the darkest alley of the Old Town on a wet night with not a soul passing by, and why were they so fleeting, so fitful and illegible? But wait, at last I succeeded in catching several words on end. They were:

MAGIC THEATRE
ENTRANCE NOT FOR EVERYBODY

I tried to open the door, but the heavy old latch would not stir. The display too was over. It had suddenly ceased, sadly convinced of its uselessness. I took a few steps back, landing deep into the mud, but no more letters came. The display was over. For a long time I stood waiting in the mud, but in vain.

Then, when I had given up and gone back to the alley, a few coloured letters were dropped here and there, reflected on the asphalt in front of me. I read:

FOR MADMEN ONLY!

My feet were wet and I was chilled to the bone. Nevertheless, I stood waiting. Nothing more. But while I waited, thinking how prettily the letters had danced in their ghostly fashion over the damp wall and the black sheen of the asphalt, a fragment of my former thoughts came suddenly to my mind; the similarity to the track of shining gold which suddenly vanishes and cannot be found.

I was freezing and walked on following that track in my dreams, longing too for that doorway to an enchanted theatre, which was for madmen only. Meanwhile I had reached the Market Place, where there is never a lack of evening entertainments. At every other step were placards and posters with their various attractions, Ladies' Orchestra, Variété, Cinema, Ball. But none of these were for me. They were for "everybody," for those normal persons whom I saw crowding every entrance. In spite of that my sadness was a little lightened. I had had a greeting from another world, and a few dancing, coloured letters had played upon my soul and sounded its secret strings. A glimmer of the golden track had been visible once again.

I sought out the little ancient tavern where nothing had altered since my first visit to this town a good twenty-five years before. Even the landlady was the same as then and many of the patrons who sat there in those days sat there still at the same places before the same glasses. There I took refuge. True, it was only a refuge, something like the one on the stairs opposite the araucaria. Here, too, I found neither home nor company, nothing but a seat from which to view a stage where strange people played strange parts. None the less, the quiet of the place was worth something; no crowds, no music; only a few peaceful townsfolk at bare wooden tables (no marble, no enamel, no plush, no brass) and before each his evening glass of good old wine. Perhaps this company of habitués, all of whom I knew by sight, were all regular Philistines and had in their Philistine dwellings their altars of the home dedicated to sheepish idols of contentment; perhaps, too, they were solitary fellows who had been sidetracked, quiet, thoughtful topers of bankrupt ideals, lone wolves and poor devils like me. I could not say. Either homesickness or disappointment, or need of change drew them there, the married to recover the atmosphere of his bachelor days, the old official to recall his student years. All of them were silent, and all were drinkers who would rather, like me, sit before a pint of Elsasser than listen to a Ladies' Orchestra. Here I cast anchor, for an hour, or it might be two. With the first sip of Elsasser I realised that I had eaten nothing that day since my morning roll.

It is remarkable, all that men can swallow. For a good ten minutes I read a newspaper. I allowed the spirit of an irresponsible man who chews and munches another's words in his mouth, and gives them out again undigested, to enter into me through my eyes. I absorbed a whole column of it. And then I devoured a large piece cut from the liver of a slaughtered calf. Odd indeed! The best was the Elsasser. I am not fond, for everyday at least, of racy, heady wines that diffuse a potent charm and have their own particular flavour. What I like the best is a clean, light, modest country vintage of no special name. One can carry plenty of it and it has the good and homely flavour of the land, and of earth and sky and woods. A pint of Elsasser and a piece of good bread is the best of all meals. By this time, however, I had already eaten my portion of liver (an unusual indulgence for me, as I seldom eat meat) and the second pint had been set before me. And this too was odd: that somewhere in a green valley vines were tended by good, strong fellows and the wine pressed so that here and there in the world, far away, a few disappointed, quietly drinking townsfolk and feckless Steppenwolves could sip a little heart and courage from their glasses.

For me, at least, the charm worked. As I thought again of that newspaper article and its jumble of words, a refreshing laughter rose in me, and suddenly the forgotten melody of those notes of the piano came back to me again. It soared aloft like a soap-bubble, reflecting the whole world in miniature on its rainbow surface, and then softly burst. Could I be altogether lost when that heavenly little melody had been secretly rooted within me and now put forth its lovely bloom with all its tender hues? I might be a beast astray, with no sense of its environment, yet there was some meaning in my foolish life, something in me gave an answer and was the receiver of those distant calls from worlds far above. In my brain were stored a thousand pictures:

Giotto's flock of angels from the blue vaulting of a little church in Padua, and near them walked Hamlet and the garlanded Ophelia, fair similitudes of all sadness and misunderstanding in the world, and there stood Gianozzo, the aeronaut, in his burning balloon and blew a blast on his horn, Attila carrying his new headgear in his hand, and the Borobudur reared its soaring sculpture in the air. And though all these figures lived in a thousand other hearts as well, there were ten thousand more unknown pictures and tunes there which had no dwelling place but in me, no eyes to see, no ears to hear them but mine. The old hospital wall with its grey-green weathering, its cracks and stains in which a thousand frescoes could be fancied, who responded to it, who looked into its soul, who loved it, who found the charm of its colours ever delicately dying away? The old books of the monks, softly illumined with their miniatures, and the books of the German poets of two hundred and a hundred years ago whom their own folk have forgotten, all the thumbed and dampstained volumes, and the works in print and manuscripts of the old composers, the stout and yellowing music sheets dreaming their music through a winter sleep—who heard their spirited, their roguish and yearning tones, who carried through a world estranged from them a heart full of their spirit and their charm? Who still remembered that slender cypress on a hill over Gubbio, that though split and riven by a fall of stone yet held fast to life and put forth with its last resources a new sparse tuft at top? Who read by night above the Rhine the cloud-script of the drifting mists? It was the Steppenwolf. And who over the ruins of his life pursued its fleeting, fluttering significance, while he suffered its seeming meaninglessness and lived its seeming madness, and who hoped in secret at the last turn of the labyrinth of Chaos for revelation and God's presence?

I held my hand over my glass when the landlady wanted to fill it once more, and got up. I needed no more wine. The golden trail was blazed and I was reminded of the eternal, and of Mozart, and the stars. For an hour I could breathe once more and live and face existence, without the need to suffer torment, fear or shame.

A cold wind was sifting the fine rain as I went out into the deserted street. It drove the drops with a patter against the street-lamps where they glimmered with a glassy sparkle. And now, whither? If I had had a magic wand at this moment I should have conjured up a small and charming Louis Seize music-room where a few musicians would have played me two or three pieces of Handel and Mozart. I was in the very mood for it, and would have sipped the cool and noble music as gods sip nectar. Oh, if I had had a friend at this moment, a friend in an attic room, dreaming by candle light and with a violin lying ready at his hand! How I should have slipped up to him in his quiet hour, noiselessly climbing the winding stair to take him by surprise, and then with talk and music we should have held heavenly festival throughout the night! Once, in years gone by, I had often known such happiness, but this too time had taken away. Withered years lay between those days and now.

I loitered as I wended my way homeward; turned up my collar and struck my stick on the wet pavement. However long I lingered outside I should find myself all too soon in my top-floor room, my makeshift home, which I could neither love nor do without; for the time had gone by when I could spend a wet winter's night in the open. And now my prayer was not to let the good mood the evening had given me be spoilt, neither by the rain, nor by gout, nor by the araucaria; and though there was no chamber-music to be had nor a lonely friend with his violin, still that lovely melody was in my head and I could play it through to myself after a fashion, humming the rhythm of it as I drew my breath. Reflecting thus, I walked on and on. Yes, even without the chamber-music and the friend. How foolish to wear oneself out in vain longing for warmth! Solitude is independence. It had been my wish and with the years I had attained it. It was cold. Oh, cold enough! But it was also still, wonderfully still and vast like the cold stillness of space in which the stars revolve.

From a dance-hall there met me as I passed by the strains of lively jazz music, hot and raw as the steam of raw flesh. I stopped a moment. This kind of music, much as I detested it, had always had a secret charm for me. It was repugnant to me, and yet ten times preferable to all the academic music of the day. For me too, its raw and savage gaiety reached an underworld of instinct and breathed a simple honest sensuality.

I stood for a moment on the scent, smelling this shrill and blood-raw music, sniffing the atmosphere of the hall angrily, and hankering after it a little too. One half of this music, the melody, was all pomade and sugar and sentimentality. The other half was savage, temperamental and vigorous. Yet the two went artlessly well together and made a whole. It was the music of decline. There must have been such music in Rome under the later emperors. Compared with Bach and Mozart and real music it was, naturally, a miserable affair; but so was all our art, all our thought, all our makeshift culture in comparison with real culture. And this music had the merit of a great sincerity. Amiably and unblushingly negroid, it had the mood of childlike happiness. There was something of the negro in it, something of the American, who with all his strength seems so boyishly fresh and childlike to us Europeans. Was Europe to become the same? Was it on the way already? Were we, the old connoisseurs, the reverers of Europe as it used to be, of genuine music and poetry as once they were, nothing but a pigheaded minority suffering from a complex neurosis, whom tomorrow would forget or deride? Was all that we called culture, spirit, soul, all that we called beautiful and sacred, nothing but a ghost long dead, which only a few fools like us took for true and living? Had it perhaps indeed never been true and living? Had all that we poor fools bothered our heads about never been anything but a phantom?

I was now in the old quarter of the town. The little church stood up dim and grey and unreal. At once the experience of the evening came back to me, the mysterious Gothic doorway, the mysterious tablet above it and the illuminated letters dancing in mockery. How did the writing run? "Entrance not for Everybody." And: "For madmen only." I scrutinised the old wall opposite in the secret hope that the magic night might begin again; the writing invite me, the madman; the little doorway give me admittance. There perhaps lay my desire, and there perhaps would my music be played.

The dark stone wall looked back at me with composure, shut off in a deep twilight, sunk in a dream of its own. And there was no gateway anywhere and no pointed arch; only the dark unbroken masonry. With a smile I went on, giving it a friendly nod. "Sleep well. I will not awake you. The time will come when you will be pulled down or plastered with covetous advertisements. But for the present, there you stand, beautiful and quiet as ever, and I love you for it."

From the black mouth of an alley a man appeared with startling suddenness at my elbow, a lone man going his homeward way with weary step. He wore a cap and a blue blouse, and above his shoulders he carried a signboard fixed on a pole, and in front of him an open tray suspended by straps such as pedlars carry at fairs. He walked on wearily in front of me without looking round. Otherwise I should have bidden him a good evening and given him a cigar. I tried to read the device on his standard—a red signboard on a pole—in the light of the next lamp; but it swayed to and fro and I could decipher nothing. Then I called out and asked him to let me read his placard. He stopped and held his pole a little steadier. Then I could read the dancing reeling letters:

ANARCHIST EVENING ENTERTAINMENT
MAGIC THEATRE
ENTRANCE NOT FOR EVERYBODY

"I've been looking for you," I shouted with delight. "What is this Evening Entertainment? Where is it? When?"

He was already walking on.

"Not for everybody," he said dully with a sleepy voice. He had had enough. He was for home, and on he went.

"Stop," I cried, and ran after him. "What have you got there in your box? I want to buy something from you."

Without stopping, the man felt mechanically in his box, pulled out a little book and held it out to me. I took it quickly and put it in my pocket. While I felt for the buttons of my coat to get out some money, he turned in at a doorway, shut the door behind him and disappeared. His heavy steps rang on a flagged yard, then on wooden stairs; and then I heard no more. And suddenly I too felt very tired. It came over me that it must be very late—and high time to go home. I walked on faster and, following the road to the suburb, I was soon in my own neighbourhood among the well-kept gardens, where in clean little apartment houses behind lawn and ivy are the dwellings of officialdom and people of modest means. Passing the ivy and the grass and the little fir tree I reached the door of the house, found the keyhole and the switch, slipped past the glazed doors, and the polished cupboards and the potted plants and unlocked the door of my room, my little pretence of a home, where the armchair and the stove, the ink-pot and the paint-box, Novalis and Dostoievski, awaited me just as do the mother, or the wife, the children, maids, dogs and cats in the case of more sensible people.

As I threw off my wet coat I came upon the little book, and took it out. It was one of those little books wretchedly printed on wretched paper that are sold at fairs, "Were you born in January?" or "How to be twenty years younger in a week."

However, when I settled myself in my armchair and put on my glasses, it was with great astonishment and a sudden sense of impending fate that I read the title on the cover of this companion volume to fortune-telling booklets. *"Treatise on the Steppenwolf. Not for Everybody."*

I read the contents at a sitting with an engrossing interest that deepened page by page.

TREATISE ON THE STEPPENWOLF

There was once a man, Harry, called the Steppenwolf. He went on two legs, wore clothes and was a human being, but nevertheless he was in reality a wolf of the Steppes. He had learnt a good deal of all that people of a good intelligence can, and was a fairly clever fellow. What he had not learnt, however, was this: to find contentment in himself and his own life. The cause of this apparently was that at the bottom of his heart he knew all the time (or thought he knew) that he was in reality not a man, but a wolf of the Steppes. Clever men might argue the point whether he truly was a wolf, whether, that is, he had been changed, before birth perhaps, from a wolf into a human being, or had been given the soul of a wolf, though born as a human being; or whether, on the other hand, this belief that he was a wolf was no more than a fancy or a disease of his. It might, for example, be possible that in his childhood he was a little wild and disobedient and disorderly, and that those who brought him up had declared a war of extinction against the beast in him; and precisely this had given him the idea and the belief that he was in fact actually a beast with only a thin covering of the human. On this point one could speak at length and entertainingly, and indeed write a book about it. The Steppenwolf, however, would be none the better for it, since for him it was all one whether the wolf had been bewitched or beaten into him, or whether it was merely an idea of his own. What others chose to think about it or what he chose to think himself was no good to him at all. It left the wolf inside him just the same.

And so the Steppenwolf had two natures, a human and a wolfish one. This was his fate, and it may well be that it was not a very exceptional one. There must have been many men who have had a good deal of the dog or the fox, of the fish or the serpent in them without experiencing any extraordinary difficulties on that account. In such cases, the man and the fish lived on together and neither did the other any harm. The one even helped the other. Many a man indeed has carried this condition to such enviable lengths that he has owed his happiness more to the fox or the ape in him than to the man. So much for common knowledge. In the case of Harry, however, it was just the opposite. In him the man and the wolf did not go the same way together, but were in continual and deadly enmity. The one existed simply and solely to harm the other, and when there are two in one blood and in one soul who are at deadly enmity, then life fares ill. Well, to each his lot, and none is light.

Now with our Steppenwolf it was so that in his conscious life he lived now as a wolf, now as a man, as indeed the case is with all mixed beings. But, when he was a wolf, the man in him lay in ambush, ever on the watch to interfere and condemn, while at those times that he was man the wolf did just the same. For example, if Harry, as man, had a beautiful thought, felt a fine and noble emotion, or performed a so-called good act, then the wolf bared his teeth at him and laughed and showed him with bitter scorn how laughable this whole pantomime was in the eyes of a beast, of a wolf who knew well enough in his heart what suited him, namely, to trot alone over the Steppes and now and then to gorge himself with blood or to pursue a female wolf. Then, wolfishly seen, all human activities became horribly absurd and misplaced, stupid and vain. But it was exactly the same when Harry felt and behaved as a wolf and showed others his teeth and felt hatred and enmity against all human beings and their lying and degenerate manners and customs. For then the human part of him lay in ambush and watched the wolf, called him brute and beast, and spoiled and embittered for him all pleasure in his simple and healthy and wild wolf's being.

Thus it was then with the Steppenwolf, and one may well imagine that Harry did not have an exactly pleasant and happy life of it. This does not mean, however, that he was unhappy in any extraordinary degree (although it may have seemed so to himself all the same, inasmuch as every man takes the sufferings that fall to his share as the greatest). That cannot be said of any man. Even he who has no wolf in him, may be none the happier for that. And even the unhappiest life has its sunny moments and its little flowers of happiness between sand and stone. So it was, then, with the Steppenwolf too. It cannot be denied that he was generally very unhappy; and he could make others unhappy also, that is, when he loved them or they him. For all who got to love him, saw always only the one side in him. Many loved him as a refined and clever and interesting man, and were horrified and disappointed when they had come upon the wolf in him. And they had to because Harry wished, as every sentient being does, to be loved as a whole and therefore it was just with those whose love he most valued that he could least of all conceal and belie the wolf. There were those, however, who loved precisely the wolf in him, the free, the savage, the untamable, the dangerous and strong, and these found it peculiarly disappointing and deplorable when suddenly the wild and wicked wolf was also a man, and had hankerings after goodness and refinement, and wanted to hear Mozart, to read poetry and to cherish human ideals. Usually these were the most disappointed and angry of all; and so it was that the Steppenwolf brought his own dual and divided nature into the destinies of others besides himself whenever he came into contact with them.

Now, whoever thinks that he knows the Steppenwolf and that he can imagine to himself his lamentably divided life is nevertheless in error. He does not know all by a long way. He does not know that, as there is no rule without an exception and as one sinner may under certain circumstances be dearer to God than ninety and nine righteous persons, with Harry too there were now and then exceptions and strokes of good luck, and that he could breathe and think and feel sometimes as the wolf, sometimes as the man, clearly and without confusion of the two; and even on very rare occasions, they made peace and lived for one another in such fashion that not merely did one keep watch whilst the other slept but each strengthened and confirmed the other. In the life of this man, too, as well as in all things else in the world, daily use and the accepted and common knowledge seemed sometimes to have no other aim than to be arrested now and again for an instant, and broken through, in order to yield the place of honour to the exceptional and miraculous. Now whether these short and occasional hours of happiness balanced and alleviated the lot of the Steppenwolf in such a fashion that in the upshot happiness and suffering held the scales even, or whether perhaps the short but intense happiness of those few hours outweighed all suffering and left a balance over is again a question over which idle persons may meditate to their hearts' content. Even the wolf brooded often thereover, and those were his idle and unprofitable days.

In this connection one thing more must be said. There are a good many people of the same kind as Harry. Many artists are of his kind. These persons all have two souls, two beings within them. There is God and the devil in them; the mother's blood and the father's; the capacity for happiness and the capacity for suffering; and in just such a state of enmity and entanglement towards and within each other as were the wolf and man in Harry. And these men, for whom life has no repose, live at times in their rare moments of happiness with such strength and indescribable beauty, the spray of their moment's happiness is flung so high and dazzlingly over the wide sea of suffering, that the light of it, spreading its radiance, touches others too with its enchantment. Thus, like a precious, fleeting foam over the sea of suffering arise all those works of art, in which a single individual lifts himself for an hour so high above his personal destiny that his happiness shines like a star and appears to all who see it as something eternal and as a happiness of their own. All these men, whatever their deeds and works may be, have really no life; that is to say, their lives are not their own and have no form. They are not heroes, artists or thinkers in the same way that other men are judges, doctors, shoemakers, or schoolmasters. Their life consists of a perpetual tide, unhappy and torn with pain, terrible and meaningless, unless one is ready to see its meaning in just those rare experiences, acts, thoughts and works that shine out above the chaos of such a life. To such men the desperate and horrible thought has come that perhaps the whole of human life is but a bad joke, a violent and ill-fated abortion of the primal mother, a savage and dismal catastrophe of nature. To them, too, however, the other thought has come that man is perhaps not merely a half-rational animal but a child of the gods and destined to immortality.

Men of every kind have their characteristics, their features, their virtues and vices and their deadly sins. It was part of the sign manual of the Steppenwolf that he was a night prowler. The morning was a bad time of day for him. He feared it and it never brought him any good. On no morning of his life has he ever been in good spirits nor done any good before midday, nor ever had a happy idea, nor devised any pleasure for himself or others. By degrees during the afternoon he warmed and became alive, and only towards evening, on his good days, was he productive, active and, sometimes, aglow with joy. With this was bound up his need for loneliness and independence. There was never a man with a deeper and more passionate craving for independence than he. In his youth when he was poor and had difficulty in earning his bread, he preferred to go hungry and in torn clothes rather than endanger his narrow limit of independence. He never sold himself for money or an easy life or to women or to those in power; and had thrown away a hundred times what in the world's eyes was his advantage and happiness in order to safeguard his liberty. No prospect was more hateful and distasteful to him than that he should have to go to an office and conform to daily and yearly routine and obey others. He hated all kinds of offices, governmental or commercial, as he hated death, and his worst nightmare was confinement in barracks. He contrived, often at great sacrifice, to avoid all such predicaments. It was here that his strength and his virtue rested. On this point he could neither be bent nor bribed. Here his character was firm and indeflectable. Only, through this virtue, he was bound the closer to his destiny of suffering. It happened to him as it does to all; what he strove for with the deepest and stubbornest instinct of his being fell to his lot, but more than is good for men. In the beginning his dream and his happiness, in the end it was his bitter fate. The man of power is ruined by power, the man of money by money, the submissive man by subservience, the pleasure seeker by pleasure. He achieved his aim. He was ever more independent. He took orders from no man and ordered his ways to suit no man. Independently and alone, he decided what to do and to leave undone. For every strong man attains to that which a genuine impulse bids him seek. But in the midst of the freedom he had attained Harry suddenly became aware that his freedom was a death and that he stood alone. The world in an uncanny fashion left him in peace. Other men concerned him no longer. He was not even concerned about himself. He began to suffocate slowly in the more and more rarefied atmosphere of remoteness and solitude. For now it was his wish no longer, nor his aim, to be alone and independent, but rather his lot and his sentence. The magic wish had been fulfilled and could not be cancelled, and it was no good now to open his arms with longing and goodwill to welcome the bonds of society. People left him alone now. It was not, however, that he was an object of hatred and repugnance. On the contrary, he had many friends. A great many people liked him. But it was no more than sympathy and friendliness. He received invitations, presents, pleasant letters; but no more. No one came near to him. There was no link left, and no one could have had any part in his life even had anyone wished it. For the air of lonely men surrounded him now, a still atmosphere in which the world around him slipped away, leaving him incapable of relationship, an atmosphere again which neither will nor longing availed. This was one of the significant earmarks of his life.

Another was that he was numbered among the suicides. And here it must be said that to call suicides only those who actually destroy themselves is false. Among these, indeed, there are many who in a sense are suicides only by accident and in whose being suicide has no necessary place. Among the common run of men there are many of little personality and stamped with no deep impress of fate, who find their end in suicide without belonging on that account to the type of the suicide by inclination; while on the other hand, of those who are to be counted as suicides by the very nature of their beings are many, perhaps a majority, who never in fact lay hands on themselves. The "suicide," and Harry was one, need not necessarily live in a peculiarly close relationship to death. One may do this without being a suicide. What is peculiar to the suicide is that his ego, rightly or wrongly, is felt to be an extremely dangerous, dubious, and doomed germ of nature; that he is always in his own eyes exposed to an extraordinary risk, as though he stood with the slightest foothold on the peak of a crag whence a slight push from without or an instant's weakness from within suffices to precipitate him into the void. The line of fate in the case of these men is marked by the belief they have that suicide is their most probable manner of death. It might be presumed that such temperaments, which usually manifest themselves in early youth and persist through life, show a singular defect of vital force. On the contrary, among the "suicides" are to be found unusually tenacious and eager and also hardy natures. But just as there are those who at the least indisposition develop a fever, so do those whom we call suicides, and who are always very emotional and sensitive, develop at the least shock the notion of suicide. Had we a science with the courage and authority to concern itself with mankind, instead of with the mechanism merely of vital phenomena, had we something of the nature of an anthropology, or a psychology, these matters of fact would be familiar to every one.

What was said above on the subject of suicides touches obviously nothing but the surface. It is psychology, and, therefore, partly physics. Metaphysically considered, the matter has a different and a much clearer aspect. In this aspect suicides present themselves as those who are overtaken by the sense of guilt inherent in individuals, those souls that find the aim of life not in the perfecting and moulding of the self, but in liberating themselves by going back to the mother, back to God, back to the all. Many of these natures are wholly incapable of ever having recourse to real suicide, because they have a profound consciousness of the sin of doing so. For us they are suicides none the less; for they see death and not life as the releaser. They are ready to cast themselves away in surrender, to be extinguished and to go back to the beginning.

As every strength may become a weakness (and under some circumstances must) so, on the contrary, may the typical suicide find a strength and a support in his apparent weakness. Indeed, he does so more often than not. The case of Harry, the Steppenwolf, is one of these. As thousands of his like do, he found consolation and support, and not merely the melancholy play of youthful fancy, in the idea that the way to death was open to him at any moment. It is true that with him, as with all men of his kind, every shock, every pain, every untoward predicament at once called forth the wish to find an escape in death. By degrees, however, he fashioned for himself out of this tendency a philosophy that was actually serviceable to life. He gained strength through familiarity with the thought that the emergency exit stood always open, and became curious, too, to taste his suffering to the dregs. If it went too badly with him he could feel sometimes with a grim malicious pleasure: "I am curious to see all the same just how much a man can endure. If the limit of what is bearable is reached, I have only to open the door to escape." There are a great many suicides to whom this thought imparts an uncommon strength.

On the other hand, all suicides have the responsibility of fighting against the temptation of suicide. Every one of them knows very well in some corner of his soul that suicide, though a way out, is rather a mean and shabby one, and that it is nobler and finer to be conquered by life than to fall by one's own hand. Knowing this, with a morbid conscience whose source is much the same as that of the militant conscience of so-called self-contented persons, the majority of suicides are left to a protracted struggle against their temptation. They struggle as the kleptomaniac against his own vice. The Steppenwolf was not unfamiliar with this struggle. He had engaged in it with many a change of weapons. Finally, at the age of forty-seven or thereabouts, a happy and not unhumorous idea came to him from which he often derived some amusement. He appointed his fiftieth birthday as the day on which he might allow himself to take his own life. On this day, according to his mood, so he agreed with himself, it should be open to him to employ the emergency exit or not. Let happen to him what might, illness, poverty, suffering and bitterness, there was a time-limit. It could not extend beyond these few years, months, days whose number daily diminished. And in fact he bore much adversity, which previously would have cost him severer and longer tortures and shaken him perhaps to the roots of his being, very much more easily. When for any reason it went particularly badly with him, when peculiar pains and penalties were added to the desolateness and loneliness and savagery of his life, he could say to his tormentors: "Only wait, two years and I am your master." And with this he cherished the thought of the morning of his fiftieth birthday. Letters of congratulation would arrive, while he, relying on his razor, took leave of all his pains and closed the door behind him. Then gout in the joints, depression of spirits, and all pains of head and body could look for another victim.

* * * *

It still remains to elucidate the Steppenwolf as an isolated phenomenon, in his relation, for example, to the bourgeois world, so that his symptoms may be traced to their source. Let us take as a starting point, since it offers itself, his relation to the bourgeoisie.

To take his own view of the matter, the Steppenwolf stood entirely outside the world of convention, since he had neither family life nor social ambitions. He felt himself to be single and alone, whether as a strange fellow and a hermit in poor health, or as a person removed from the common run of men by the prerogative of talents that had something of genius in them. Deliberately, he looked down upon the ordinary man and was proud that he was not one. Nevertheless his life in many aspects was thoroughly ordinary. He had money in the bank and supported poor relations. He was dressed respectably and inconspicuously, even though without particular care. He was glad to live on good terms with the police and the tax collectors and other such powers. Besides this, he was secretly and persistently attracted to the little bourgeois world, to those quiet and respectable homes with tidy gardens, irreproachable stair-cases and their whole modest air of order and comfort. It pleased him to set himself outside it, with his little vices and ex-travagances, as a strange fellow or a genius, but he never had his domicile in those provinces of life where the bourgeoisie had ceased to exist. He was not at ease with violent and exceptional persons nor with criminals and out-laws, and he took up his abode always among the middle classes, with whose habits and standards and atmosphere he stood in a constant relation, even though it might be one of contrast and revolt. Moreover, he had been brought up in a provincial and conventional home and many of the notions and much of the examples of those days had never left him. In theory he had nothing whatever against the servant class; yet in practice it would have been beyond him to take a servant quite seriously as his equal. He was capable of loving the political criminal, the revolutionary or intellectual seducer, the outlaw of state and society, as his brother, but as for theft and robbery, murder and rape, he would not have known how to deplore them otherwise than in a thoroughly bourgeois manner.

In this way he was always recognising and affirming with one half of himself, in thought and act, what with the other half he fought against and denied. Brought up, as he was, in a cultivated home in the approved manner, he never tore part of his soul loose from its conventionalities even after he had long since individualised himself to a degree beyond its scope and freed himself from the substance of its ideals and beliefs.

Now what we call "bourgeois," when regarded as an element always to be found in human life, is nothing else than the search for a balance. It is the striving after a mean between the countless extremes and opposites that arise in human conduct. If we take anyone of these coupled opposites, such as piety and profligacy, the analogy is immediately comprehensible. It is open to a man to give himself up wholly to spiritual views, to seeking after God, to the ideal of saintliness. On the other hand, he can equally give himself up entirely to the life of instinct, to the lusts of the flesh, and so direct all his efforts to the attainment of momentary pleasures. The one path leads to the saint, to the martyrdom of the spirit and surrender to God. The other path leads to the profligate, to the martyrdom of the flesh, the surrender to corruption. Now it is between the two, in the middle of the road, that the bourgeois seeks to walk. He will never surrender himself either to lust or to asceticism. He will never be a martyr nor agree to his own destruction. On the contrary, his ideal is not to give up but to maintain his own identity. He strives neither for the saintly nor its opposite. The absolute is his abhorrence. He may be ready to serve God, but not by giving up the flesh-pots. He is ready to be virtuous, but likes to be easy and comfortable in this world as well. In short, his aim is to make a home for himself between two extremes in a temperate zone without violent storms and tempests; and in this he succeeds though it be at the cost of that intensity of life and feeling which an extreme life affords. A man cannot live intensely except at the cost of the self. Now the bourgeois treasures nothing more highly than the self (rudimentary as his may be). And so at the cost of intensity he achieves his own preservation and security. His harvest is a quiet mind which he prefers to being possessed by God, as he does comfort to pleasure, convenience to liberty, and a pleasant temperature to that deathly inner consuming fire. The bourgeois is consequently by nature a creature of weak impulses, anxious, fearful of giving himself away and easy to rule. Therefore, he has substituted majority for power, law for force, and the polling booth for responsibility.

It is clear that this weak and anxious being, in whatever numbers he exists, cannot maintain himself, and that qualities such as his can play no other rôle in the world than that of a herd of sheep among free roving wolves. Yet we see that, though in times when commanding natures are uppermost, the bourgeois goes at once to the wall, he never goes under; indeed at times he even appears to rule the world. How is this possible? Neither the great numbers of the herd, nor virtue, nor common sense, nor organisation could avail to save it from destruction. No medicine in the world can keep a pulse beating that from the outset was so weak. Nevertheless the bourgeoisie prospers. Why?

The answer runs: Because of the Steppenwolves. In fact, the vital force of the bourgeoisie resides by no means in the qualities of its normal members, but in those of its extremely numerous "outsiders" who by virtue of the extensiveness and elasticity of its ideals it can embrace. There is always a large number of strong and wild natures who share the life of the fold. Our Steppenwolf, Harry, is a characteristic example. He who is developed far beyond the level possible to the bourgeois, he who knows the bliss of meditation no less than the gloomy joys of hatred and self-hatred, he who despises law, virtue and common sense, is nevertheless captive to the bourgeoisie and cannot escape it. And so all through the mass of the real bourgeoisie are interposed numerous layers of humanity, many thousands of lives and minds, every one of whom, it is true, would have outgrown it and have obeyed the call to unconditioned life, were they not fastened to it by sentiments of their childhood and infected for the most part with its less intense life; and so they are kept lingering, obedient and bound by obligation and service. For with the bourgeoisie the opposite of the formula for the great is true: He who is not against me is with me.

If we now pause to test the soul of the Steppenwolf, we find him distinct from the bourgeois in the higher development of his individuality—for all extensions of the individuality revolve upon the self and tend to destroy it. We see that he had in him a strong impulse both to the saint and the profligate; and yet he could not, owing to some weakness or inertia, make the plunge into the untrammelled realms of space. The parent constellation of the bourgeoisie binds him with its spell. This is his place in the universe and this his bondage. Most intellectuals and most artists belong to the same type. Only the strongest of them force their way through the atmosphere of the Bourgeois-Earth and attain to the cosmic. The others all resign themselves, or make compromises. Despising the bourgeoisie, and yet belonging to it, they add to its strength and glory; for in the last resort they have to share their beliefs in order to live. The lives of these infinitely numerous persons make no claim to the tragic; but they live under an evil star in a quite considerable affliction; and in this hell their talents ripen and bear fruit. The few who break free seek their reward in the unconditioned and go down in splendour. They wear the thorn crown and their number is small. The others, however, who remain in the fold and from whose talents the bourgeoisie reaps much gain, have a third kingdom left open to them, an imaginary and yet a sovereign world, humour. The lone wolves who know no peace, these victims of unceasing pain to whom the urge for tragedy has been denied and who can never break through the starry space, who feel themselves summoned thither and yet cannot survive in its atmosphere—for them is reserved, provided suffering has made their spirits tough and elastic enough, a way of reconcilement and an escape into humour. Humour has always something bourgeois in it, although the true bourgeois is incapable of understanding it. In its imaginary realm the intricate and many-faceted ideal of all Steppenwolves finds its realisation. Here it is possible not only to extol the saint and the profligate in one breath and to make the poles meet, but to include the bourgeois, too, in the same affirmation. Now it is possible to be possessed by God and to affirm the sinner, and vice versa, but it is not possible for either saint or sinner (nor for any other of the unconditioned) to affirm as well that lukewarm mean, the bourgeois. Humour alone, that magnificent discovery of those who are cut short in their calling to highest endeavour, those who falling short of tragedy are yet as rich in gifts as in affliction, humour alone (perhaps the most inborn and brilliant achievement of the spirit) attains to the impossible and brings every aspect of human existence within the rays of its prism. To live in the world as though it were not the world, to respect the law and yet to stand above it, to have possessions as though "one possessed nothing," to renounce as though it were no renunciation, all these favourite and often formulated propositions of an exalted worldly wisdom, it is in the power of humour alone to make efficacious.

And supposing the Steppenwolf were to succeed, and he has gifts and resources in plenty, in decocting this magic draught in the sultry mazes of his hell, his rescue would be assured. Yet there is much lacking. The possibility, the hope only are there. Whoever loves him and takes his part may wish him this rescue. It would, it is true, keep him forever tied to the bourgeois world, but his suffering would be bearable and productive. His relation to the bourgeois world would lose its sentimentality both in its love and its hatred, and his bondage to it would cease to cause him the continual torture of shame.

To attain to this, or, perhaps it may be, to be able at last to dare the leap into the unknown, a Steppenwolf must once have a good look at himself. He must look deeply into the chaos of his own soul and plumb its depths. The riddle of his existence would then be revealed to him at once in all its change-lessness, and it would be impossible for him ever after to escape first from the hell of the flesh to the comforts of a sentimental philosophy and then back to the blind orgy of his wolfishness. Man and wolf would then be compelled to recognise one another without the masks of false feeling and to look one another straight in the eye. Then they would either explode and separate for-ever, and there would be no more Steppenwolf, or else they would come to terms in the dawning light of humour.

It is possible that Harry will one day be led to this latter alternative. It is possible that he will learn one day to know himself. He may get hold of one of our little mirrors. He may encounter the Immortals. He may find in one of our magic theatres the very thing that is needed to free his neglected soul. A thousand such possibilities await him. His fate brings them on, leaving him no choice; for those outside of the bourgeoisie live in the atmosphere of these magic possibilities. A mere nothing suffices—and the lightning strikes.

And all this is very well known to the Steppenwolf, even though his eye may never fall on this fragment of his inner biography. He has a suspicion of his allotted place in the world, a suspicion of the Immortals, a suspicion that he may meet himself face to face; and he is aware of the existence of that mirror in which he has such bitter need to look and from which he shrinks in such deathly fear.

* * * *

For the close of our study there is left one last fiction, a fundamental de-lusion to make clear. All interpretation, all psychology, all attempts to make things comprehensible, require the medium of theories, mythologies and lies; and a self-respecting author should not omit, at the close of an exposition, to dissipate these lies so far as may be in his power. If I say "above" or "below," that is already a statement that requires explanation, since an above and a below exist only in thought, only as abstractions. The world itself knows nothing of above or below.

So too, to come to the point, is the Steppenwolf a fiction. When Harry feels himself to be a were-wolf, and chooses to consist of two hostile and opposed beings, he is merely availing himself of a mythological simplification. He is no were-wolf at all, and if we appeared to accept without scrutiny this lie which he invented for himself and believes in, and tried to regard him literally as a two-fold being and a Steppenwolf, and so designated him, it was merely in the hope of being more easily understood with the assistance of a delusion, which we must now endeavour to put in its true light.

The division into wolf and man, flesh and spirit, by means of which Harry tries to make his destiny more comprehensible to himself is a very great simplification. It is a forcing of the truth to suit a plausible, but erroneous, explanation of that contradiction which this man discovers in himself and which appears to himself to be the source of his by no means negligible sufferings. Harry finds in himself a "human being," that is to say, a world of thoughts and feelings, of culture and tamed or sublimated nature, and besides this he finds within himself also a "wolf," that is to say, a dark world of instinct, of savagery and cruelty, of unsublimated or raw nature. In spite of this apparently clear division of his being between two spheres, hostile to one another, he has known happy moments now and then when the man and the wolf for a short while were reconciled with one another. Suppose that Harry tried to ascertain in any single moment of his life, any single act, what part the man had in it and what part the wolf, he would find himself at once in a dilemma, and his whole beautiful wolf-theory would go to pieces. For there is not a single human being, not even the primitive negro, not even the idiot, who is so conveniently simple that his being can be explained as the sum of two or three principal elements; and to explain so complex a man as Harry by the artless division into wolf and man is a hopelessly childish attempt. Harry consists of a hundred or a thousand selves, not of two. His life oscillates, as everyone's does, not merely between two poles, such as the body and the spirit, the saint and the sinner, but between thousand and thousands.

We need not be surprised that even so intelligent and educated a man as Harry should take himself for a Steppenwolf and reduce the rich and complex organism of his life to a formula so simple, so rudimentary and primitive. Man is not capable of thought in any high degree, and even the most spiritual and highly cultivated of men habitually sees the world and himself through the lenses of delusive formulas and artless simplifications—and most of all himself. For it appears to be an inborn and imperative need of all men to regard the self as a unit. However often and however grievously this illusion is shattered, it always mends again. The judge who sits over the murderer and looks into his face, and at one moment recognises all the emotions and potentialities and possibilities of the murderer in his own soul and hears the murderer's voice as his own is at the next moment one and indivisible as the judge, and scuttles back into the shell of his cultivated self and does his duty and condemns the murderer to death. And if ever the suspicion of their manifold being dawns upon men of unusual powers and of unusually delicate perceptions, so that, as all genius must, they break through the illusion of the unity of the personality and perceive that the self is made up of a bundle of selves, they have only to say so and at once the majority puts them under lock and key, calls science to aid, establishes schizomania and protects humanity from the necessity of hearing the cry of truth from the lips of these unfortunate persons. Why then waste words, why utter a thing that every thinking man accepts as self-evident, when the mere utterance of it is a breach of taste? A man, therefore, who gets so far as making the supposed unity of the self two-fold is already almost a genius, in any case a most exceptional and interesting person. In reality, however, every ego, so far from being a unity is in the highest degree a manifold world, a constellated heaven, a chaos of forms, of states and stages, of inheritances and potentialities. It appears to be a necessity as imperative as eating and breathing for everyone to be forced to regard this chaos as a unity and to speak of his ego as though it were a one-fold and clearly detached and fixed phenomenon. Even the best of us share the delusion.

The delusion rests simply upon a false analogy. As a body everyone is single, as a soul never. In literature, too, even in its ultimate achievement, we find this customary concern with apparently whole and single personalities. Of all literature up to our days the drama has been the most highly prized by writers and critics, and rightly, since it offers (or might offer) the greatest possibilities of representing the ego as a manifold entity, but for the optical illusion which makes us believe that the characters of the play are one-fold entities by lodging each one in an undeniable body, singly, separately and once and for all. An artless æsthetic criticism, then, keeps its highest praise for this so-called character-drama in which each character makes his appearance unmistakably as a separate and single entity. Only from afar and by degrees the suspicion dawns here and there that all this is perhaps a cheap and superficial æsthetic philosophy; and that we make a mistake in attributing to our great dramatists those magnificent conceptions of beauty that come to us from antiquity. These conceptions are not native to us, but are merely picked up at second hand, and it is in them, with their common source in the visible body, that the origin of the fiction of an ego, an individual, is really to be found. There is no trace of such a notion in the poems of ancient India. The heroes of the epics of India are not individuals, but whole reels of individualities in a series incarnations. And in modern times there are poems, in which, behind the veil of a concern with individuality and character that is scarcely, indeed, in the author's mind, the motive is to present a manifold activity of soul. Whoever wishes to recognise this must resolve once and for all not to regard the characters of such a poem as separate beings, but as the various facets and aspects of a higher unity, in my opinion, of the poet's soul. If "Faust," is treated in this way, Faust, Mephistopheles, Wagner and the rest form a unity and a supreme individuality; and it is in this higher unity alone, not in the several characters, that something of the true nature of the soul is revealed. When Faust, in a line immortalised among schoolmasters and greeted with a shudder of astonishment by the Philistine, says: "Two souls, alas, inhabit in my breast!" he has forgotten Mephisto and a whole crowd of other souls that he has in his breast likewise. The Steppenwolf, too, believes that he bears two souls (wolf and man) in his breast and even so finds his breast disagreeably cramped because of them. The breast and the body are indeed one, but the souls that dwell in it are not two, nor five, but countless in number. Man is an onion made up of a hundred integuments, a texture made up of many threads. The ancient Asiatics knew this well enough, and in the Buddhist Yoga an exact technique was devised for unmasking the illusion of the personality. The human merry-go-round sees many changes: the illusion that cost India the efforts of thousands of years to unmask is the same illusion that the West has laboured just as hard to maintain and strengthen.

If we consider the Steppenwolf from this standpoint it will be clear to us why he suffered so much under his ludicrous dual personality. He believes, like Faust, that two souls are far too many for a single breast and must tear the breast asunder. They are on the contrary far too few, and Harry does shocking violence to his poor soul when he endeavours to apprehend it by means of so primitive an image. Although he is a most cultivated person, he proceeds like a savage that cannot count further than two. He calls himself part wolf, part man, and with that he thinks he has come to an end and exhausted the matter. With the "man" he packs in everything spiritual and sublimated or even cultivated to be found in himself, and with the wolf all that is instinctive, savage and chaotic. But things are not so simple in life as in our thoughts, nor so rough and ready as in our poor idiotic language; and Harry lies about himself twice over when he employs this niggardly wolf-theory. He assigns, we fear, whole provinces of his soul to the "man" which are a long way from being human, and parts of his being to the wolf that long ago have left the wolf behind.

Like all men Harry believes that he knows very well what man is and yet does not know at all, although in dreams and other states not subject to control he often has his suspicions. If only he might not forget them, but keep them, as far as possible at least, for his own. Man is not by any means of fixed and enduring form (this, in spite of suspicions to the contrary on the part of their wise men, was the ideal of the ancients). He is much more an experiment and a transition. He is nothing else than the narrow and perilous bridge between nature and spirit. His innermost destiny drives him on to the spirit and to God. His innermost longing draws him back to nature, the mother. Between the two forces his life hangs tremulous and irresolute. What is commonly meant, meanwhile, by the word "man" is never anything more than a transient agreement, a bourgeois compromise. Certain of the more naked instincts are excluded and penalised by this concordat; a degree of human consciousness and culture are won from the beast; and a small modicum of spirit is not only permitted but even encouraged. The "man" of this concordat, like every other bourgeois ideal, is a compromise, a timid and artlessly sly experiment, with the aim of cheating both the angry primal mother Nature and the troublesome primal father Spirit of their pressing claims, and of living in a temperate zone between the two of them. For this reason the bourgeois today burns as heretics and hangs as criminals those to whom he erects monuments tomorrow.

That man is not yet a finished creation but rather a challenge of the spirit; a distant possibility dreaded as much as it is desired; that the way towards it has only been covered for a very short distance and with terrible agonies and ecstasies even by those few for whom it is the scaffold today and the monument tomorrow—all this the Steppenwolf, too, suspected. What, however, he calls the "man" in himself, as opposed to the wolf, is to a great extent nothing else than this very same average man of the bourgeois convention.

As for the way to true manhood, the way to the immortals, he has, it is true, an inkling of it and starts upon it now and then for a few hesitating steps and pays for them with much suffering and many pangs of loneliness. But as for striving with assurance, in response to that supreme demand, towards the genuine manhood of the spirit, and going the one narrow way to immortality, he is deeply afraid of it. He knows too well that it leads to still greater sufferings, to proscription, to the last renunciation, perhaps to the scaffold, and even though the enticement of immortality lies at the journey's end, he is still unwilling to suffer all these sufferings and to die all these deaths. Though the end of manhood is better known to him than to the bourgeois, still he shuts his eyes. He is resolved to forget that the desperate clinging to the self and the desperate clinging to life are the surest way to eternal death, while the power to die, to strip one's self naked, and the eternal surrender of the self bring immortality with them. When he worships his favourites among the immortals, Mozart, it may be, he regards him always in the long run with the bourgeois eye. His tendency is to explain Mozart's perfected being, just as a schoolmaster would, as a supreme and special gift rather than as the outcome of his immense powers of surrender and suffering, of his indifference to the ideals of the bourgeois, and of his patience under that last extremity of loneliness which rarefies the atmosphere of the bourgeois world to an ice-cold ether, around those who suffer to become men, that loneliness of the garden of Gethsemane.

This Steppenwolf of ours has always been aware of at least the Faustian two-fold nature within him. He has discovered that the one-fold of the body is not inhabited by a one-fold of the soul, and that at best he is only at the beginning of a long pilgrimage towards this ideal harmony. He would like either to overcome the wolf and become wholly man or to renounce mankind and at last to live wholly a wolf's life. It may be presumed that he has never carefully watched a real wolf. Had he done so he would have seen, perhaps, that even animals are not undivided in spirit. With them, too, the well-knit beauty of the body hides a being of manifold states and strivings. The wolf, too, has his abysses. The wolf, too, suffers. No, back to nature is a false track that leads nowhere but to suffering and despair. Harry can never turn back again and become wholly wolf, and could he do so he would find that even the wolf is not of primeval simplicity, but already a creature of manifold complexity. Even the wolf has two, and more than two, souls in his wolf's breast, and he who desires to be a wolf falls into the same forgetfulness as the man who sings: "If I could be a child once more!" He who sentimentally sings of blessed childhood is thinking of the return to nature and innocence and the origin of things, and has quite forgotten that these blessed children are beset with conflict and complexities and capable of all suffering.

There is, in fact, no way back either to the wolf or to the child. From the very start there is no innocence and no singleness. Every created thing, even the simplest, is already guilty, already multiple. It has been thrown into the muddy stream of being and may never more swim back again to its source. The way to innocence, to the uncreated and to God leads on, not back, not back to the wolf or to the child, but ever further into sin, ever deeper into human life. Suicide, even, unhappy Steppenwolf, will not seriously serve your turn. You will find yourself embarked on the longer and wearier and harder road to human life. You will have to multiply many times your two-fold being and complicate your complexities still further. Instead of narrowing your world and simplifying your soul, you will at last take the whole world into your soul, cost what it may, before you are through and come to rest. This is the road that Buddha and every great man has gone, whether consciously or not, in so far as fortune favoured his quest. All births betoken the parting from the All, the confinement within limitation, the separation from God, the pangs of being born ever anew. The return into the All betokens the lifting of the personality through suffering till it reaches God, the expansion of the soul until it is able once more to embrace the All.

We are not dealing here with man as he is known to economics and statistics, as he is seen thronging the streets by the million, and of whom no more account can be made than of the sand of the sea or the spray of its waves. We are not concerned with the few millions less or more. They are a stock-in-trade, nothing else. No, we are speaking of man in the highest sense, of the end of the long road to true manhood, of kingly men, of the immortals. Genius is not so rare as we sometimes think; nor, certainly, so frequent as may appear from history books or, indeed, from the newspapers. Harry has, we should say, genius enough to attempt the quest of true manhood instead of discoursing pitifully about his stupid Steppenwolf at every difficulty encountered.

It is as much a matter for surprise and sorrow that men of such possibilities should fall back on Steppenwolves and "Two souls, alas!" as that they reveal so often that pitiful love for the bourgeoisie. A man who can understand Buddha and has an intuition of the heaven and hell of humanity ought not to live in a world ruled by "common sense" and democracy and bourgeois standards. It is only from cowardice that he lives in it; and if its dimensions are too cramping for him and the bourgeois parlour too confined, he lays it at the wolf's door, and refuses to see that the wolf is as often as not the best part of him. All that is wild in himself he calls wolf and considers it wicked and dangerous and the bugbear of all decent life. He cannot see, even though he thinks himself an artist and possessed of delicate perceptions, that a great deal else exists in him besides and behind the wolf. He cannot see that not all that bites is wolf and that fox, dragon, tiger, ape and bird of paradise are there also. Yet he allows this whole world, a garden of Eden in which are manifestations of beauty and terror, of greatness and meanness, of strength and tenderness, to be huddled together and shut away by the wolf-legend, just as is the real man in him by the shams and pretences of a bourgeois existence.

Man designs for himself a garden with a hundred kinds of trees, a thousand kinds of flowers, a hundred kinds of fruit and vegetables. Suppose, then, that the gardener of this garden knew no other distinction than between edible and inedible, nine-tenths of this garden would be useless to him. He would pull up the most enchanting flowers and hew down the noblest trees and even regard them with a loathing and envious eye. This is what the Steppenwolf does with the thousand flowers of his soul. What does not stand classified as either man or wolf he does not see at all. And consider all that he imputes to "man"! All that is cowardly and apish, stupid and mean—while to the wolf, only because he has not succeeded in making himself its master, is set down all that is strong and noble.

Now we bid Harry good-bye and leave him to go on his way alone. Were he already among the immortals—were he already there at the goal to which his difficult path seems to be taking him, with what amazement he would look back to all this coming and going, all this indecision and wild zig-zag trail. With what a mixture of encouragement and blame, pity and joy, he would smile at this Steppenwolf.

When I had read to the end it came to my mind that some weeks before I had written one night a rather peculiar poem, likewise about the Steppenwolf. I made a search among the snow-drift of papers on my writing table, found it, and read:

> *The Wolf trots to and fro,*
> *The world lies deep in snow,*
> *The raven from the birch tree flies,*
> *But nowhere a hare, nowhere a roe.*
> *The roe—she is so dear, so sweet—*
> *If such a thing I might surprise*
> *In my embrace, my teeth would meet,*
> *What else is there beneath the skies?*
> *The lovely creature I would so treasure,*
> *And feast myself deep on her tender thigh,*
> *I would drink of her red blood full measure,*
> *Then howl till the night went by.*
> *Even a hare I would not despise;*
> *Sweet enough its warm flesh in the night.*
> *Is everything to be denied*
> *That could make life a little bright?*
> *The hair on my brush is getting grey.*
> *The sight is failing from my eyes.*
> *Years ago my dear mate died.*
> *And now I trot and dream of a roe.*
> *I trot and dream of a hare.*
> *I hear the wind of midnight howl.*
> *I cool with the snow my burning jowl,*
> *And on to the devil my wretched soul I bear.*

So now I had two portraits of myself before me, one a self-portrait in doggerel verse, as sad and sorry as myself; the other painted with the air of a lofty impartiality by one who stood outside and who knew more and yet less of me than I did myself. And both these pictures of myself, my dispirited and halting poem and the clever study by an unknown hand, equally afflicted me. Both were right. Both gave the unvarnished truth about my shiftless existence. Both showed clearly how unbearable and untenable my situation was. Death was decreed for this Steppenwolf. He must with his own hand make an end of his detested existence—unless, molten in the fire of a renewed self-knowledge, he underwent a change and passed over to a self, new and undisguised. Alas! This transition was not unknown to me. I had often experienced it already, and always in times of the utmost despair. On each occasion of this terribly uprooting experience myself, as it then was, was shattered to fragments. Each time deep-seated powers had shaken and destroyed it; each time there had followed the loss of a cherished and particularly beloved part of my life that was true to me no more. Once, I had lost my profession and livelihood. I had had to forfeit the esteem of those who before had touched their caps to me. Next, my family life fell in ruins over night, when my wife, whose mind was disordered, drove me from house and home. Love and confidence had changed of a sudden to hate and deadly enmity and the neighbours saw me go with pitying scorn. It was then that my solitude had its beginning. Years of hardship and bitterness went by. I had built up the ideal of a new life, inspired by the asceticism of the intellect. I had attained a certain serenity and elevation of life once more, submitting myself to the practice of abstract thought and to a rule of austere meditation. But this mould, too, was broken and lost at one blow all its exalted and noble intent. A whirl of travel drove me afresh over the earth; fresh sufferings were heaped up, and fresh guilt. And every occasion when a mask was torn off, an ideal broken, was preceded by this hateful vacancy and stillness, this deathly constriction and loneliness and unrelatedness, this waste and empty hell of lovelessness and despair, such as I had now to pass through once more.

It is true that every time my life was shattered in this way I had in the end gained something, some increase in liberty and in spiritual growth and depth, but with it went an increased loneliness, an increasing chill of severance and estrangement. Looked at with the bourgeois eye, my life had been a continuous descent from one shattering to the next that left me more remote at every step from all that was normal, permissible and healthful. The passing years had stripped me of my calling, my family, my home. I stood outside all social circles, alone, beloved by none, mistrusted by many, in unceasing and bitter conflict with public opinion and morality; and though I lived in a bourgeois setting, I was all the same an utter stranger to this world in all I thought and felt. Religion, country, family, state all lost their value and meant nothing to me any more. The pomposity of the sciences, societies, and arts disgusted me. My views and tastes and all that I thought, once the shining adornments of a gifted and sought-after person, had run to seed in neglect and were looked at askance. Granting that I had in the course of all my painful transmutations made some invisible and unaccountable gain, I had had to pay dearly for it; and at every turn my life was harsher, more difficult, lonely and perilous. In truth, I had little cause to wish to continue in that way which led on into ever thinner air, like the smoke in Nietzsche's harvest song.

Oh, yes, I had experienced all these changes and transmutations that fate reserves for her difficult children, her ticklish customers. I knew them only too well. I knew them as well as a zealous but unsuccessful sportsman knows the stands at a shoot; as an old gambler on the Exchange knows each stage of speculation, the scoop, the weakening market, the break and bankruptcy. Was I really to live through all this again? All this torture, all this pressing need, all these glimpses into the paltriness and worthlessness of my own self, the frightful dread lest I succumb, and the fear of death. Wasn't it better and simpler to prevent a repetition of so many sufferings and to quit the stage? Certainly, it was simpler and better. Whatever the truth of all that was said in the little book on the Steppenwolf about "suicides," no one could forbid me the satisfaction of invoking the aid of a gas-stove or a razor or revolver, and so sparing myself this repetition of a process whose bitter agony I had had to drink often enough, surely, and to the dregs. No, in all conscience, there was no power in the world that could prevail with me to go through the mortal terror of another encounter with myself, to face another reorganisation, a new incarnation, when at the end of the road there was no peace or quiet— but forever destroying the self, in order to renew the self. Let suicide be as stupid, cowardly, shabby as you please, call it an infamous and ignominious escape; still, any escape, even the most ignominious, from this treadmill of suffering was the only thing to wish for. No stage was left for the noble and heroic heart. Nothing was left but the simple choice between a slight and swift pang and an unthinkable, a devouring and endless suffering. I had played Don Quixote often enough in my difficult, crazed life, had put honour before comfort, and heroism before reason. There was an end of it!

Daylight was dawning through the window panes, the leaden, infernal daylight of a rainy winter's day, when at last I got to bed. I took my resolution to bed with me. At the very last, however, on the last verge of consciousness in the moment of falling asleep, the remarkable passage in the Steppenwolf pamphlet which deals with the immortals flashed through me. With it came the enchanting recollection that several times, the last quite recently, I had felt near enough to the immortals to share in one measure of old music their cool, bright, austere and yet smiling wisdom. The memory of it soared, shone out, then died away; and heavy as a mountain, sleep descended on my brain.

I woke about midday, and at once the situation, as I had disentangled it, came back to me. There lay the little book on my bed-side table, and my poem. My resolution, too, was there. After the night's sleep it had taken shape and looked at me out of the confusion of my youth with a calm and friendly greeting. Haste makes no speed. My resolve to die was not the whim of an hour. It was the ripe, sound fruit that had grown slowly to full size, lightly rocked by the winds of fate whose next breath would bring it to the ground.

I had in my medicine-chest an excellent means of stilling pain—an unusually strong tincture of laudanum. I indulged very rarely in it and often refrained from using it for months at a time. I had recourse to the drug only when physical pain plagued me beyond endurance. Unfortunately, it was of no use in putting an end to myself. I had proved this some years before. Once when despair had again got the better of me I had swallowed a big dose of it—enough to kill six men, and yet it had not killed me. I fell asleep, it is true, and lay for several hours completely stupefied; but then to my frightful disappointment I was half awakened by violent convulsions of the stomach and fell asleep once more. It was the middle of the next day when I woke up in earnest in a state of dismal sobriety. My empty brain was burning and I had almost lost my memory. Apart from a spell of insomnia and severe pains in the stomach no trace of the poison was left.

This expedient, then, was no good. But I put my resolution in this way: the next time I felt that I must have recourse to the opium, I might allow myself to use big means instead of small, that is, a death of absolute certainty with a bullet or a razor. Then I could be sure. As for waiting till my fiftieth birthday, as the little book wittily prescribed—this seemed to me much too long a delay. There were still two years till then. Whether it were a year hence or a month, were it even the following day, the door stood open.

I cannot say that the resolution altered my life very profoundly. It made me a little more indifferent to my afflictions, a little freer in the use of opium and wine, a little more inquisitive to know the limits of endurance, but that was all. The other experiences of that evening had a stronger after-effect. I read the Steppenwolf treatise through again many times, now submitting gratefully to an invisible magician because of his wise conduct of my destiny, now with scorn and contempt for its futility, and the little understanding it showed of my actual disposition and predicament. All that was written there of Steppenwolves and suicides was very good, no doubt, and very clever. It might do for the species, the type; but it was too wide a mesh to catch my own individual soul, my unique and unexampled destiny.

What, however, occupied my thoughts more than all else was the hallucination, or vision, of the church wall. The announcement made by the dancing illuminated letters promised much that was hinted at in the treatise, and the voices of that strange world had powerfully aroused my curiosity. For hours I pondered deeply over them. On these occasions I was more and more impressed by the warning of that inscription—"Not for everybody!" and "For madmen only!" Madman, then, I must certainly be and far from the mould of "everybody" if those voices reached me and that world spoke to me. In heaven's name, had I not long ago been remote from the life of everybody and from normal thinking and normal existence? Had I not long ago given ample margin to isolation and madness? All the same, I understood the summons well enough in my innermost heart. Yes, I understood the invitation to madness and the jettison of reason and the escape from the clogs of convention in surrender to the unbridled surge of spirit and fantasy.

One day after I had made one more vain search through streets and squares for the man with the signboard and prowled several times past the wall of the invisible door with watchful eye, I met a funeral procession in St. Martin's. While I was contemplating the faces of the mourners who followed the hearse with halting step, I thought to myself, "Where in this town or in the whole world is the man whose death would be a loss to me? And where is the man to whom my death would mean anything?" There was Erica, it is true, but for a long while we had lived apart. We rarely saw one another without quarreling and at the moment I did not even know her address. She came to see me now and then, or I made the journey to her, and since both of us were lonely, difficult people related somehow to one another in soul, and sickness of soul, there was a link between us that held in spite of all. But would she not perhaps breathe more freely if she heard of my death? I did not know. I did not know either how far my own feeling for her was to be relied upon. To know anything of such matters one needs to live in a world of practical possibilities.

Meanwhile, obeying my fancy, I had fallen in at the rear of the funeral procession and jogged along behind the mourners to the cemetery, an up-to-date affair all of concrete, and complete with crematorium. The deceased in question was not however to be cremated. His coffin was set down before a simple hole in the ground, and I saw the clergyman and the other vultures and functionaries of a burial establishment going through their performances, to which they endeavoured to give all the appearance of great ceremony and sorrow and with such effect that they outdid themselves and from pure play-acting they got caught in their own lies and ended by being comic. I saw how their black professional robes fell in folds, and what pains they took to work up the company of mourners and to force them to bend the knee before the majesty of death. It was labour in vain. Nobody wept. The deceased did not appear to have been indispensable. Nor could anyone be talked into a pious frame of mind; and when the clergyman addressed the company repeatedly as "dear fellow-Christians," all the silent faces of these shop-people and master-bakers and their wives were turned down in embarrassment and expressed nothing but the wish that this uncomfortable function might soon be over. When the end came, the two foremost of the fellow-Christians shook the clergyman's hand, scraped the moist clay in which the dead had been laid from their shoes at the next scraper and without hesitation their faces again showed their natural expression; and then it was that one of them seemed suddenly familiar. It was, so it seemed to me, the man who had carried the signboard and thrust the little book into my hands.

At the moment when I thought I recognised him he stopped and, stooping down, carefully turned up his black trousers, and then walked away at a smart pace with his umbrella clipped under his arm. I walked after him, but when I overtook him and gave him a nod, he did not appear to recognise me.

"Is there no show tonight?" I asked with an attempt at a wink such as two conspirators give each other. But it was long ago that such pantomime was familiar to me. Indeed, living as I did, I had almost lost the habit of speech, and I felt myself that I only made a silly grimace.

"Show tonight?" he growled, and looked at me as though he had never set eyes on me before. "Go to the Black Eagle, man, if that's what you want."

And, in fact, I was no longer certain it was he. I was disappointed and feeling the disappointment I walked on aimlessly. I had no motives, no incentives to exert myself, no duties. Life tasted horribly bitter. I felt that the long-standing disgust was coming to a crisis and that life pushed me out and cast me aside. I walked through the grey streets in a rage and everything smelt of moist earth and burial. I swore that none of these death-vultures should stand at my grave, with cassocks and fellow-christianly murmurings. Ah, look where I might and think what I might, there was no cause for rejoicing and nothing beckoned me. There was nothing to charm me or tempt me. Everything was old, withered, grey, limp and spent, and stank of staleness and decay. Dear God, how was it possible? How had I, with the wings of youth and poetry, come to this? Art and travel and the glow of ideals—and now this! How had this paralysis of hatred against myself and every one else, this obstruction of all feeling, this mud-hell of an empty heart and despair crept over me so softly and so slowly?

Passing by the Library I met a young professor of whom in earlier years I used occasionally to see a good deal. When I last stayed in the town, some years before, I had even been several times to his house to talk oriental mythology, a study in which I was then very much interested. He came in my direction walking stiffly and with a short-sighted air and only recognised me at the last moment as I was passing by. In my lamentable state I was half-thankful for the cordiality with which he threw himself on me. His pleasure in seeing me became quite lively as he recalled the talks we had had together and assured me that he owed a great deal to the stimulus they had given him and that he often thought of me. He had rarely had such stimulating and productive discussions with any colleague since. He asked how long I had been in the town (I lied and said "a few days") and why I had not looked him up. The learned man held me with his friendly eye and, though I really found it all ridiculous, I could not help enjoying these crumbs of warmth and kindliness, and was lapping them up like a starved dog. Harry, the Steppenwolf, was moved to a grin. Saliva collected in his parched throat and against his will he bowed down to sentiment. Yes, zealously piling lie upon lie, I said that I was only here in passing, for the purpose of research, and should of course have paid him a visit but that I had not been feeling very fit. And when he went on to invite me very heartily to spend the evening with him, I accepted with thanks and sent my greetings to his wife, until my cheeks fairly ached with the unaccustomed efforts of all these forced smiles and speeches. And while I, Harry Haller, stood there in the street, flattered and surprised and studiously polite and smiling into the good fellow's kindly, short-sighted face, there stood the other Harry, too, at my elbow and grinned likewise. He stood there and grinned as he thought what a funny, crazy, dishonest fellow I was to show my teeth in rage and curse the whole world one moment and, the next, to be falling all over myself in the eagerness of my response to the first amiable greeting of the first good honest fellow who came my way, to be wallowing like a suckling-pig in the luxury of a little pleasant feeling and friendly esteem. Thus stood the two Harrys, neither playing a very pretty part, over against the worthy professor, mocking one another, watching one another, and spitting at one another, while as always in such predicaments, the eternal question presented itself whether all this was simple stupidity and human frailty, a common depravity, or whether this sentimental egoism and perversity, this slovenliness and two-facedness of feeling was merely a personal idiosyncrasy of the Steppenwolves. And if this nastiness was common to men in general, I could rebound from it with renewed energy into hatred of all the world, but if it was a personal frailty, it was good occasion for an orgy of hatred of myself.

While my two selves were thus locked in conflict, the professor was almost forgotten; and when the oppressiveness of his presence came suddenly back to me, I made haste to be relieved of it. I looked after him for a long while as he disappeared into the distance along the leafless avenue with the good-natured and slightly comic gait of an ingenuous idealist. Within me, the battle raged furiously. Mechanically I bent and unbent my stiffened fingers as though to fight the ravages of a secret poison, and at the same time had to realise that I had been nicely framed. Round my neck was the invitation for 8:30, with all its obligations of politeness, of talking shop and of contemplating another's domestic bliss. And so home—in wrath. Once there, I poured myself out some brandy and water, swallowed some of my gout pills with it, and, lying on the sofa, tried to read. No sooner had I succeeded in losing myself for a moment in *Sophia's Journey from Memel to Saxony*, a delightful old book of the eighteenth century, than the invitation came over me of a sudden and reminded me that I was neither shaved nor dressed. Why, in heaven's name, had I brought all this on myself? Well, get up, so I told myself, lather yourself, scrape your chin till it bleeds, dress and show an amiable disposition towards your fellow-men. And while I lathered my face, I thought of that sordid hole in the clay of the cemetery into which some unknown person had been lowered that day. I thought of the pinched faces of the bored fellow-Christians and I could not even laugh. There in that sordid hole in the clay, I thought, to the accompaniment of stupid and insincere ministrations and the no less stupid and insincere demeanour of the group of mourners, in the discomforting sight of all the metal crosses and marble slabs and artificial flowers of wire and glass, ended not only that unknown man, and, tomorrow or the day after, myself as well, buried in the soil with a hypocritical show of sorrow—no, there and so ended everything; all our striving, all our culture, all our beliefs, all our joy and pleasure in life—already sick and soon to be buried there too. Our whole civilization was a cemetery where Jesus Christ and Socrates, Mozart and Haydn, Dante and Goethe were but the indecipherable names on mouldering stones; and the mourners who stood round affecting a pretence of sorrow would give much to believe in these inscriptions which once were holy, or at least to utter one heart-felt word of grief and despair about this world that is no more. And nothing was left them but the embarrassed grimaces of a company round a grave. As I raged on like this I cut my chin in the usual place and had to apply a caustic to the wound; and even so there was my clean collar, scarce put on, to change again, and all this for an invitation that did not give me the slightest pleasure. And yet a part of me began play-acting again, calling the professor a sympathetic fellow, yearning after a little talk and intercourse with my fellow men, reminding me of the professor's pretty wife, prompting me to believe that an evening spent with my pleasant host and hostess would be in reality positively cheering, helping me to clap some court plaster to my chin, to put on my clothes and tie my tie well, and gently putting me, in fact, far from my genuine desire of staying at home. Whereupon it occurred to me—so it is with every one. Just as I dress and go out to visit the professor and exchange a few more or less insincere compliments with him, without really wanting to at all, so it is with the majority of men day by day and hour by hour in their daily lives and affairs. Without really wanting to at all, they pay calls and carry on conversations, sit out their hours at desks and on office chairs; and it is all compulsory, mechanical and against the grain, and it could all be done or left undone just as well by machines; and indeed it is this never-ceasing machinery that prevents their being, like me, the critics of their own lives and recognising the stupidity and shallowness, the hopeless tragedy and waste of the lives they lead, and the awful ambiguity grinning over it all. And they are right, right a thousand times to live as they do, playing their games and pursuing their business, instead of resisting the dreary machine and staring into the void as I do who have left the track. Let no one think that I blame other men, though now and then in these pages I scorn and even deride them, or that I accuse them of the responsibility of my personal misery. But now that I have come so far, and standing as I do on the extreme verge of life where the ground falls away before me into bottomless darkness, I should do wrong and I should lie if I pretended to myself or to others that that machine still revolved for me and that I was still obedient to the eternal child's play of that charming world.

On all this the evening before me afforded a remarkable commentary. I paused a moment in front of the house and looked up at the windows. There he lives, I thought, and carries on his labours year by year, reads and annotates texts, seeks for analogies between western Asiatic and Indian mythologies, and it satisfies him, because he believes in the value of it all. He believes in the studies whose servant he is; he believes in the value of mere knowledge and its acquisition, because he believes in progress and evolution. He has not been through the war, nor is he acquainted with the shattering of the foundations of thought by Einstein (that, thinks he, only concerns the mathematicians). He sees nothing of the preparations for the next war that are going on all round him. He hates Jews and Communists. He is a good, unthinking, happy child, who takes himself seriously; and, in fact, he is much to be envied. And so, pulling myself together, I entered the house. A maid in cap and apron opened the door. Warned by some premonition, I noticed with care where she laid my hat and coat, and was then shown into a warm and well-lighted room and requested to wait. Instead of saying a prayer or taking a nap, I followed a wayward impulse and picked up the first thing I saw. It chanced to be a small picture in a frame that stood on the round table leaning back on its paste-board support. It was an engraving and it represented the poet Goethe as an old man full of character, with a finely chiseled face and a genius' mane. Neither the renowned fire of his eyes nor the lonely and tragic expression beneath the courtly whitewash was lacking. To this the artist had given special care, and he had succeeded in combining the elemental force of the old man with a somewhat professional make-up of self-discipline and righteousness, without prejudice to his profundity; and had made of him, all in all, a really charming old gentleman, fit to adorn any drawing room. No doubt this portrait was no worse than others of its description. It was much the same as all those representations by careful craftsmen of saviours, apostles, heroes, thinkers and statesmen. Perhaps I found it exasperating only because of a certain pretentious virtuosity. In any case, and whatever the cause, this empty and self-satisfied presentation of the aged Goethe shrieked at me at once as a fatal discord, exasperated and oppressed as I was already. It told me that I ought never to have come. Here fine Old Masters and the Nation's Great Ones were at home, not Steppenwolves.

If only the master of the house had come in now, I might have had the luck to find some favourable opportunity for finding my way out. As it was, his wife came in, and I surrendered to fate though I scented danger. We shook hands and to the first discord there succeeded nothing but new ones. The lady complimented me on my looks, though I knew only too well how sadly the years had aged me since our last meeting. The clasp of her hand on my gouty fingers had reminded me of it already. Then she went on to ask after my dear wife, and I had to say that my wife had left me and that we were divorced. We were glad enough when the professor came in. He too gave me a hearty welcome and the awkward comedy came to a beautiful climax. He was holding a newspaper to which he subscribed, an organ of the militarist and jingoist party, and after shaking hands he pointed to it and commented on a paragraph about a namesake of mine—a publicist called Haller, a bad fellow and a rotten patriot—who had been making fun of the Kaiser and expressing the view that his own country was no less responsible for the outbreak of war than the enemy nations. There was a man for you! The editor had given him his deserts and put him in the pillory. However, when the professor saw that I was not interested, we passed to other topics, and the possibility that this horrid fellow might be sitting in front of them did not even remotely occur to either of them. Yet so it was, I myself was that horrid fellow. Well, why make a fuss and upset people? I laughed to myself, but gave up all hope now of a pleasant evening.

I have a clear recollection of the moment when the professor spoke of Haller as a traitor to his country. It was then that the horrid feeling of depression and despair which had been mounting in me and growing stronger and stronger ever since the burial scene condensed to a dreary dejection. It rose to the pitch of a bodily anguish, arousing within me a dread and suffocating foreboding. I had the feeling that something lay in wait for me, that a danger stalked me from behind. Fortunately the announcement that dinner was on the table supervened. We went into the dining room, and while I racked my brains again and again for something harmless to say, I ate more than I was accustomed to do and felt myself growing more wretched with every moment. Good heavens, I thought all the while, why do we put ourselves to such exertions? I felt distinctly that my hosts were not at their ease either and that their liveliness was forced, whether it was that I had a paralysing effect on them or because of some other and domestic embarrassment. There was not a question they put to me that I could answer frankly, and I was soon fairly entangled in my lies and wrestling with my nausea at every word. At last, for the sake of changing the subject, I began to tell them of the funeral which I had witnessed earlier in the day. But I could not hit the right note. My efforts at humour fell entirely flat and we were more than ever at odds. Within me the Steppenwolf bared his teeth in a grin. By the time we had reached dessert, silence had descended on all three of us.

We went back to the room we had come from to invoke the aid of coffee and cognac. There, however, my eye fell once more on the magnate of poetry, although he had been put on a chest of drawers at one side of the room. Unable to get away from him, I took him once more in my hands, though warning voices were plainly audible, and proceeded to attack him. I was as though obsessed by the feeling that the situation was intolerable and that the time had come either to warm my hosts up, to carry them off their feet and put them in tune with myself, or else to bring about a final explosion.

"Let us hope," said I, "that Goethe did not really look like this. This conceited air of nobility, the great man ogling the distinguished company, and beneath the manly exterior what a world of charming sentimentality! Certainly, there is much to be said against him. I have a good deal against his venerable pomposity myself. But to represent him like this—no, that is going too far."

The lady of the house finished pouring out the coffee with a deeply wounded expression and then hurriedly left the room; and her husband explained to me with mingled embarrassment and reproach that the picture of Goethe belonged to his wife and was one of her dearest possessions. "And even if, objectively speaking, you are right, though I don't agree with you, you need not have been so outspoken."

"There you are right," I admitted. "Unfortunately it is a habit, a vice of mine, always to speak my mind as much as possible, as indeed Goethe did, too, in his better moments. In this chaste drawing-room Goethe would certainly never have allowed himself to use an outrageous, a genuine and unqualified expression. I sincerely beg your wife's pardon and your own. Tell her, please, that I am a schizomaniac. And now, if you will allow me, I will take my leave."

To this he made objections in spite of his perplexity. He even went back to the subject of our former discussions and said once more how interesting and stimulating they had been and how deep an impression my theories about Mithras and Krishna had made on him at the time. He had hoped that the present occasion would have been an opportunity to renew these discussions. I thanked him for speaking as he did. Unfortunately, my interest in Krishna had vanished and also my pleasure in learned discussions. Further, I had told him several lies that day. For example, I had been many months in the town, and not a few days, as I had said. I lived, however, quite by myself, and was no longer fit for decent society; for in the first place, I was nearly always in a bad temper and afflicted with the gout, and in the second place, usually drunk. Lastly, to make a clean slate, and not to go away, at least, as a liar, it was my duty to inform him that he had grievously insulted me that evening. He had endorsed the attitude taken up by a reactionary paper towards Haller's opinions; a stupid bull-necked paper, fit for an officer on half-pay, not for a man of learning. This bad fellow and rotten patriot, Haller, however, and myself were one and the same person, and it would be better for our country and the world in general, if at least the few people who were capable of thought stood for reason and the love of peace instead of heading wildly with a blind obsession for a new war. And so I would bid him good-bye.

With that I got up and took leave of Goethe and of the professor. I seized my hat and coat from the rack outside and left the house. Loud in my soul the wolf howled his glee, and between my two selves there opened an immense field of operations. For it was at once clear to me that this disagreeable evening had much more significance for me than for the indignant professor. For him, it was a disillusionment and a petty outrage. For me, it was a final failure and flight. It was my leave-taking from the respectable, moral and learned world, and a complete triumph for the Steppenwolf. I was sent flying and beaten from the field, bankrupt in my own eyes, dismissed without a shred of credit or a ray of humour to comfort me. I had taken leave of the world in which I had once found a home, the world of convention and culture, in the manner of the man with a weak stomach who has given up pork. In a rage I went on my way beneath the street lamps, in a rage and sick unto death. What a hideous day of shame and wretchedness it had been from morning to night, from the cemetery to the scene with the professor. For what? And why? Was there any sense in taking up the burden of more such days as this or of sitting out any more such suppers? There was not. This very night I would make an end of the comedy, go home and cut my throat. No more tarrying.

I paced the streets in all directions, driven on by wretchedness. Naturally it was stupid of me to bespatter the drawing-room ornaments of the worthy folk, stupid and ill-mannered, but I could not help it; and even now I could not help it. I could not bear this tame, lying, well-mannered life any longer. And since it appeared that I could not bear my loneliness any longer either, since my own company had become so unspeakably hateful and nauseous, since I struggled for breath in a vacuum and suffocated in hell, what way out was left me? There was none. I thought of my father and mother, of the sacred flame of my youth long extinct, of the thousand joys and labours and aims of my life. Nothing of them all was left me, not even repentance, nothing but agony and nausea. Never had the clinging to mere life seemed so grievous as now.

I rested a moment in a tavern in an outlying part of the town and drank some brandy and water; then to the streets once more, with the devil at my heels, up and down the steep and winding streets of the Old Town, along the avenues, across the station square. The thought of going somewhere took me into the station. I scanned the time-tables on the walls; drank some wine and tried to come to my senses. Then the spectre that I went in dread of came nearer, till I saw it plain. It was the dread of returning to my room and coming to a halt there, faced by my despair. There was no escape from this moment though I walked the streets for hours. Sooner or later I should be at my door, at the table with my books, on the sofa with the photograph of Erica above it. Sooner or later the moment would come to take out my razor and cut my throat. More and more plainly the picture rose before me. More and more plainly, with a wildly beating heart, I felt the dread of all dreads, the fear of death. Yes, I was horribly afraid of death. Although I saw no other way out, although nausea, agony and despair threatened to engulf me; although life had no allurement and nothing to give me either of joy or hope, I shuddered all the same with an unspeakable horror of a gaping wound in a condemned man's flesh.

I saw no other way of escape from this dreadful spectre. Suppose that today cowardice won a victory over despair, tomorrow and each succeeding day I would again face despair heightened by self-contempt. It was merely taking up and throwing down the knife till at last it was done. Better today then. I reasoned with myself as though with a frightened child. But the child would not listen. It ran away. It wanted to live. I renewed my fitful wanderings through the town, making many detours not to return to the house which I had always in my mind and always deferred. Here and there I came to a stop and lingered, drinking a glass or two, and then, as if pursued, ran around in a circle whose centre had the razor as a goal, and meant death. Sometimes from utter weariness I sat on a bench, on a fountain's rim, or a curb-stone and wiped the sweat from my forehead and listened to the beating of my heart. Then on again in mortal dread and an intense yearning for life.

Thus it was I found myself late at night in a distant and unfamiliar part of the town; and there I went into a public house from which there came the lively sound of dance music. Over the entrance as I went in I read "The Black Eagle" on the old signboard. Within I found it was a free night— crowds, smoke, the smell of wine, and the clamour of voices, with dancing in a room at the back, whence issued the frenzy of music. I stayed in the nearer room where there were none but simple folk, some of them poorly dressed, whereas behind in the dance-hall smart people were also to be seen. Carried forward by the crowd, I soon found myself near the bar, wedged against a table at which sat a pale and pretty girl against the wall. She wore a thin dance-frock cut very low and a withered flower in her hair. She gave me a friendly and observant look as I came up and with a smile moved to one side to make room for me.

"May I?" I asked and sat down beside her.

"Of course, you may," she said. "But who are you?"

"Thanks," I replied. "I cannot possibly go home, cannot, cannot. I'll stay here with you if you'll let me. No, I can't go back home."

She nodded as though to humour me, and as she nodded I observed the curl that fell from her temple to her ear, and I saw that the withered flower was a camellia. From within crashed the music and at the buffet the waitresses hurriedly shouted their orders.

"Well, stay here then," she said with a voice that comforted me. "Why can't you go home?"

"I can't. There's something waiting for me there. No, I can't—it's too frightful."

"Let it wait then and stay here. First wipe your glasses. You can see nothing like that. Give me your handkerchief. What shall we drink? Burgundy?"

While she wiped my glasses, I had the first clear impression of her pale, firm face, with its clear grey eyes and smooth forehead, and the short, tight curl in front of her ear. Good-naturedly and with a touch of mockery she began to take me in hand. She ordered the wine, and as she clinked her glass with mine, her eyes fell on my shoes.

"Good Lord, wherever have you come from? You look as though you had come from Paris on foot. That's no state to come to a dance in."

I answered "yes" and "no," laughed now and then, and let her talk. I found her charming, very much to my surprise, for I had always avoided girls of her kind and regarded them with suspicion. And she treated me exactly in the way that was best for me at that moment, and so she has since without an exception. She took me under her wing just as I needed, and mocked me, too, just as I needed. She ordered me a sandwich and told me to eat it. She filled my glass and bade me sip it and not drink too fast. Then she commended my docility.

"That's fine," she said to encourage me. "You're not difficult. I wouldn't mind betting it's a long while since you have had to obey anyone."

"You'd win the bet. How did you know it?"

"Nothing in that. Obeying is like eating and drinking. There's nothing like it if you've been without it too long. Isn't it so, you're glad to do as I tell you?"

"Very glad. You know everything."

"You make it easy to. Perhaps, my friend, I could tell you, too, what it is that's waiting for you at home and what you dread so much. But you know that for yourself. We needn't talk about it, eh? Silly business! Either a man goes and hangs himself, and then he hangs sure enough, and he'll have his reasons for it, or else he goes on living and then he has only living to bother himself with. Simple enough."

"Oh," I cried, "if only it were so simple. I've bothered myself enough with life, God knows, and little use it has been to me. To hang oneself is hard, perhaps. I don't know. But to live is far, far harder. God, how hard it is!"

"You'll see it's child's play. We've made a start already. You've polished your glasses, eaten something and had a drink. Now we'll go and give your shoes and trousers a brush and then you'll dance a shimmy with me."

"Now that shows," I cried in a fluster, "that I was right! Nothing could grieve me more than not to be able to carry out any command of yours, but I can dance no shimmy, nor waltz, nor polka, nor any of the rest of them. I've never danced in my life. Now you can see it isn't all as easy as you think."

Her bright red lips smiled and she firmly shook her waved and shingled head; and as I looked at her, I thought I could see a resemblance to Rosa Kreisler, with whom I had been in love as a boy. But she had a dark complexion and dark hair. I could not tell of whom it was she reminded me. I knew only that it was of someone in my early youth and boyhood.

"Wait a bit," she cried. "So you can't dance? Not at all? Not even a one-step? And yet you talk of the trouble you've taken to live? You told a fib there, my boy, and you shouldn't do that at your age. How can you say that you've taken any trouble to live when you won't even dance?"

"But if I can't—I've never learnt!"

She laughed.

"But you learnt reading and writing and arithmetic, I suppose, and French and Latin and a lot of other things? I don't mind betting you were ten or twelve years at school and studied whatever else you could as well. Perhaps you've even got your doctor's degree and know Chinese or Spanish. Am I right? Very well then. But you couldn't find the time and money for a few dancing lessons! No, indeed!"

"It was my parents," I said to justify myself. "They let me learn Latin and Greek and all the rest of it. But they didn't let me learn to dance. It wasn't the thing with us. My parents had never danced themselves."

She looked at me quite coldly, with real contempt, and again something in her face reminded me of my youth.

"So your parents must take the blame then. Did you ask them whether you might spend the evening at the Black Eagle? Did you? They're dead a long while ago, you say? So much for that. And now supposing you were too obedient to learn to dance when you were young (though I don't believe you were such a model child), what have you been doing with yourself all these years?"

"Well," I confessed, "I scarcely know myself—studied, played music, read books, written books, travelled—"

"Fine views of life, you have. You have always done the difficult and complicated things and the simple ones you haven't even learnt. No time, of course. More amusing things to do. Well, thank God, I'm not your mother. But to do as you do and then say you've tested life to the bottom and found nothing in it is going a bit too far."

"Don't scold me," I implored. "It isn't as if I didn't know I was mad."

"Oh, don't make a song of your sufferings. You are no madman, Professor. You're not half mad enough to please me. It seems to me you're much too clever in a silly way, just like a professor. Have another roll. You can tell me some more later."

She got another roll for me, put a little salt and mustard on it, cut a piece for herself and told me to eat it. I did all she told me except dance. It did me a prodigious lot of good to do as I was told and to have someone sitting by me who asked me things and ordered me about and scolded me. If the professor or his wife had done so an hour or two earlier, it would have spared me a lot. But no, it was well as it was. I should have missed much.

"What's your name?" she asked suddenly.

"Harry."

"Harry? A babyish sort of name. And a baby you are, Harry, in spite of your few grey hairs. You're a baby and you need someone to look after you. I'll say no more of dancing. But look at your hair! Have you no wife, no sweetheart?"

"I haven't a wife any longer. We are divorced. A sweetheart, yes, but she doesn't live here. I don't see her very often. We don't get on very well."

She whistled softly.

"You must be difficult if nobody sticks to you. But now tell me what was up in particular this evening? What sent you chasing round out of your wits? Down on your luck? Lost at cards?"

This was not easy to explain.

"Well," I began, "you see, it was really a small matter. I had an invitation to dinner with a professor—I'm not one myself, by the way—and really I ought not to have gone. I've lost the habit of being in company and making conversation. I've forgotten how it's done. As soon as I entered the house I had the feeling something would go wrong, and when I hung my hat on the peg I thought to myself that perhaps I should want it sooner than I expected. Well, at the professor's there was a picture that stood on the table, a stupid picture. It annoyed me—"

"What sort of picture? Annoyed you—why?" she broke in.

"Well, it was a picture representing Goethe, the poet Goethe, you know. But it was not in the least as he really looked. That, of course, nobody can know exactly. He has been dead a hundred years. However, some artist of today had painted his portrait as he imagined him to have been and prettified him, and this picture annoyed me. It made me perfectly sick. I don't know whether you can understand that."

"I understand all right. Don't you worry. Go on."

"Before this in any case I didn't see eye to eye with the professor. Like nearly all professors, he is a great patriot, and during the war did his bit in the way of deceiving the public, with the best intentions, of course. I, however, am opposed to war. But that's all one. To continue my story, there was not the least need for me to look at the picture—"

"Certainly not."

"But in the first place it made me sorry because of Goethe, whom I love very dearly, and then, besides, I thought—well, I had better say just how I thought, or felt. There I was, sitting with people as one of themselves and believing that they thought of Goethe as I did and had the same picture of him in their minds as I, and there stood that tasteless, false and sickly affair and they thought it lovely and had not the least idea that the spirit of that picture and the spirit of Goethe were exact opposites. They thought the picture splendid, and so they might for all I cared, but for me it ended, once and for all, any confidence, any friendship, any feeling of affinity I could have for these people. In any case, my friendship with them did not amount to very much. And so I got furious, and sad, too, when I saw that I was quite alone with no one to understand me. Do you see what I mean?"

"It is very easy to see. And next? Did you throw the picture at them?"

"No, but I was rather insulting and left the house. I wanted to go home, but—"

"But you'd have found no mummy there to comfort the silly baby or scold it. I must say, Harry, you make me almost sorry for you. I never knew such a baby."

So it seemed to me, I must own. She gave me a glass of wine to drink. In fact, she was like a mother to me. In a glimpse, though, now and then I saw how young and beautiful she was.

"And so," she began again, "Goethe has been dead a hundred years, and you're very fond of him, and you have a wonderful picture in your head of what he must have looked like, and you have the right to, I suppose. But the artist who adores Goethe too, and makes a picture of him, has no right to do it, nor the professor either, nor anybody else—because you don't like it. You find it intolerable. You have to be insulting and leave the house. If you had sense, you would laugh at the artist and the professor—laugh and be done with it. If you were out of your senses, you'd smash the picture in their faces. But as you're only a little baby, you run home and want to hang yourself. I've understood your story very well, Harry. It's a funny story. You make me laugh. But don't drink so fast. Burgundy should be sipped. Otherwise you'll get hot. But you have to be told everything—like a little child."

She admonished me with the look of a severe governess of sixty.

"Oh, I know," I said contentedly. "Only tell me everything."

"What shall I tell you?"

"Whatever you feel like telling me."

"Good. Then I'll tell you something. For an hour I've been saying 'thou' to you, and you have been saying 'you' to me. Always Latin and Greek, always as complicated as possible. When a girl addresses you intimately and she isn't disagreeable to you, then you should address her in the same way. So now you've learnt something. And secondly—for half an hour I've known that you're called Harry. I know it because I asked you. But you don't care to know my name."

"Oh, but indeed—I'd like to know very much."

"You're too late! If we meet again, you can ask me again. Today I shan't tell you. And now I'm going to dance."

At the first sign she made of getting up, my heart sank like lead. I dreaded her going and leaving me alone, for then it would all come back as it was before. In a moment, the old dread and wretchedness took hold of me like a toothache that has passed off and then comes back of a sudden and burns like fire. Oh, God, had I forgotten, then, what was waiting for me? Had anything altered?

"Stop," I implored, "don't go. You can dance of course, as much as you please, but don't stay away too long. Come back again, come back again."

She laughed as she got up. I expected that she would have been taller. She was slender, but not tall. Again I was reminded of someone. Of whom? I could not make out.

"You're coming back?"

"I'm coming back, but it may be half an hour or an hour, perhaps. I want to tell you something. Shut your eyes and sleep for a little. That's what you need."

I made room for her to pass. Her skirt brushed my knees and she looked, as she went, in a little pocket mirror, lifted her eyebrows, and powdered her chin; then she disappeared into the dance hall. I looked round me; strange faces, smoking men, spilt beer on marble-tops, clatter and clamour everywhere, the dance music in my ear. I was to sleep, she had said. Ah, my good child, you know a lot about my sleep that is shyer than a weasel. Sleep in this hurly-burly, sitting at a table, amidst the clatter of beer-pots! I sipped the wine and, taking out a cigar, looked round for matches, but as I had after all no inclination to smoke, I put down the cigar on the table in front of me. "Shut your eyes," she had said. God knows where the girl got her voice; it was so deep and good and maternal. It was good to obey such a voice, I had found that out already. Obediently I shut my eyes, leant my head against the wall and heard the roar of a hundred mingled noises surge around me and smiled at the idea of sleep in such a place. I made up my mind to go to the door of the dance-hall and from there catch a glimpse of my beautiful girl as she danced. I made a movement to go, then felt at last how unutterably tired out I was from my hours of wandering and remained seated; and, thereupon I fell asleep as I had been told. I slept greedily, thankfully, and dreamt more lightly and pleasantly than I had for a long while.

I dreamt that I was waiting in an old-fashioned ante-room. At first I knew no more than that my audience was with some Excellency or other. Then it came to me that it was Goethe who was to receive me. Unfortunately I was not there quite on a personal call. I was a reporter, and this worried me a great deal and I could not understand how the devil I had got into such a fix. Besides this, I was upset by a scorpion that I had seen a moment before trying to climb up my leg. I had shaken myself free of the black crawling beast, but I did not know where it had got to next and did not dare make a grab after it.

Also I was not very sure whether I had been announced by a mistake to Matthisson instead of to Goethe, and him again I mixed up in my dream with Bürger, for I took him for the author of the poem to Molly. Moreover I would have liked extremely to meet Molly. I imagined her wonderful, tender, musical. If only I were not here at the orders of that cursed newspaper office. My ill-humour over this increased until by degrees it extended even to Goethe, whom I suddenly treated to all manner of reflections and reproaches. It was going to be a lively interview. The scorpion, however, dangerous though he was and hidden no doubt somewhere within an inch of me, was all the same not so bad perhaps. Possibly he might even betoken something friendly. It seemed to me extremely likely that he had something to do with Molly. He might be a kind of messenger from her—or an heraldic beast, dangerously and beautifully emblematic of woman and sin. Might not his name perhaps be Vulpius? But at that moment a flunkey threw open the door. I rose and went in.

There stood old Goethe, short and very erect, and on his classic breast, sure enough, was the corpulent star of some Order. Not for a moment did he relax his commanding attitude, his air of giving audience, and of controlling the world from that museum of his at Weimar. Indeed, he had scarcely looked at me before with a nod and a jerk like an old raven he began pompously: "Now, you young people have, I believe, very little appreciation of us and our efforts."

"You are quite right," said I, chilled by his ministerial glance. "We young people have, indeed, very little appreciation of you. You are too pompous for us, Excellency, too vain and pompous, and not outright enough. That is, no doubt, at the bottom of it—not outright enough."

The little old man bent his erect head forward, and as his hard mouth with its official folds relaxed in a little smile and became enchantingly alive, my heart gave a sudden bound; for all at once the poem came to my mind— "The dusk with folding wing"—and I remembered that it was from the lips of this man that the poem came. Indeed, at this moment I was entirely disarmed and overwhelmed and would have chosen of all things to kneel before him. But I held myself erect and heard him say with a smile: "Oh, so you accuse me of not being outright? What a thing to say! Will you explain yourself a little more fully?"

I was very glad indeed to do so.

"Like all great spirits, Herr von Goethe, you have clearly recognised and felt the riddle and the hopelessness of human life, with its moments of transcendence that sink again to wretchedness, and the impossibility of rising to one fair peak of feeling except at the cost of many days' enslavement to the daily round; and, then, the ardent longing for the realm of the spirit in eternal and deadly war with the equally ardent and holy love of the lost innocence of nature, the whole frightful suspense in vacancy and uncertainty, this condemnation to the transient that can never be valid, that is ever experimental and dilettantish; in short, the utter lack of purpose to which the human state is condemned—to its consuming despair. You have known all this, yes, and said as much over and over again; yet you gave up your whole life to preaching its opposite, giving utterance to faith and optimism and spreading before yourself and others the illusion that our spiritual strivings mean something and endure. You have lent a deaf ear to those that plumbed the depths and suppressed the voices that told the truth of despair, and not in yourself only, but also in Kleist and Beethoven. Year after year you lived on at Weimar accumulating knowledge and collecting objects, writing letters and gathering them in, as though in your old age you had found the real way to discover the eternal in the momentary, though you could only mummify it, and to spiritualise nature though you could only hide it with a pretty mask. This is why we reproach you with insincerity."

The old big-wig kept his eyes musingly on mine, smiling as before.

Then to my surprise, he asked, "You must have a strong objection, then, to the *Magic Flute* of Mozart?"

And before I could protest, he went on:

"The *Magic Flute* presents life to us as a wondrous song. It honours our feelings, transient, as they are, as something eternal and divine. It agrees neither with Herr von Kleist nor with Herr Beethoven. It preaches optimism and faith."

"I know, I know," I cried in a rage. "God knows why you hit of all things on the *Magic Flute* that is dearer to me than anything else in the world. But Mozart did not live to be eighty-two. He did not make pretensions in his own life to the enduring and the orderly and to exalted dignity as you did. He did not think himself so important! He sang his divine melodies and died. He died young—poor and misunderstood—"

I lost my breath. A thousand things ought to have been said in ten words. My forehead began to sweat.

Goethe, however, said very amiably: "It may be unforgivable that I lived to be eighty-two. My satisfaction on that account was, however, less than you may think. You are right that a great longing for survival possessed me continually. I was in continual fear of death and continually struggling with it. I believe that the struggle against death, the unconditional and self-willed determination to live, is the motive power behind the lives and activities of all outstanding men. My eighty-two years showed just as conclusively that we must all die in the end as if I had died as a schoolboy. If it helps to justify me I should like to say this too: there was much of the child in my nature—curiosity and love of wasting time in play. Well, and so it went on and on, till I saw that sooner or later there must be enough of play."

As he said this, his smile was quite cunning—a downright roguish leer. He had grown taller and his erect bearing and the constrained dignity of his face had disappeared. The air, too, around us was now ringing with melodies, all of them songs of Goethe's. I heard Mozart's *Violets* and Schubert's *Again thou fillest brake and vale* quite distinctly. And Goethe's face was rosy and youthful, and he laughed; and now he resembled Mozart like a brother, now Schubert, and the star on his breast was composed entirely of wild flowers. A yellow primrose blossomed luxuriantly in the middle of it.

It did not altogether suit me to have the old gentleman avoid my questions and accusations in this sportive manner, and I looked at him reproachfully. At that he bent forward and brought his mouth, which had now become quite like a child's, close to my ear and whispered softly into it: "You take the old Goethe much too seriously, my young friend. You should not take old people who are already dead seriously. It does them injustice. We immortals do not like things to be taken seriously. We like joking. Seriousness, young man, is an accident of time. It consists, I don't mind telling you in confidence, in putting too high a value on time. I, too, once put too high a value on time. For that reason I wished to be a hundred years old. In eternity, however, there is no time, you see. Eternity is a mere moment, just long enough for a joke."

And indeed there was no saying another serious word to the man. He capered joyfully and nimbly up and down and made the primrose shoot out from his star like a rocket and then he made it shrink and disappear. While he flickered to and fro with his dance-steps and figures, it was borne in upon me that he at least had not neglected learning to dance. He could do it wonderfully. Then I remembered the scorpion, or Molly, rather, and I called out to Goethe: "Tell me, is Molly there?"

Goethe laughed aloud. He went to his table and opened a drawer; took out a handsome leather or velvet box, and held it open under my eyes. There, small, faultless, and gleaming, lay a diminutive effigy of a woman's leg on the dark velvet, an enchanting leg, with the knee a little bent and the foot pointing downwards to end in the daintiest of toes.

I stretched out my hand, for I had quite fallen in love with the little leg and I wanted to have it, but just as I was going to take hold of it with my finger and thumb, the little toy seemed to move with a tiny start and it occurred to me suddenly that this might be the scorpion. Goethe seemed to read my thought, and even to have wanted to cause this deep timidity, this hectic struggle between desire and dread. He held the provoking little scorpion close to my face and watched me start forward with desire, then start back with dread; and this seemed to divert him exceedingly. While he was teasing me with the charming, dangerous thing, he became quite old once more, very, very old, a thousand years old, with hair as white as snow, and his withered greybeard's face laughed a still and soundless laughter that shook him to the depths with abysmal old man's humour.

When I woke I had forgotten the dream; it did not come back to me till later. I had slept for nearly an hour, as I never thought I could possibly have done at a café-table with the music and the bustle all round me. The dear girl stood in front of me with one hand on my shoulder.

"Give me two or three marks," she said. "I've spent something in there."

I gave her my purse. She took it and was soon back again.

"Well, now I can sit with you for a little and then I have to go. I have an engagement."

I was alarmed.

"With whom?" I asked quickly.

"With a man, my dear Harry. He has invited me to the Odéon Bar."

"Oh! I didn't think you would leave me alone."

"Then you should have invited me yourself. Some one has got in before you. Well, there's good money saved. Do you know the Odéon? Nothing but champagne after midnight. Armchairs like at a club, jaz band, jolly fine."

I had never considered all this.

"But let me invite you," I entreated her. "I thought it was an understood thing, now that we've made friends. Invite yourself wherever you like. Do, please, I beg you."

"That is nice of you. But, you see, a promise is a promise, and I've given my word and I shall keep it and go. Don't worry any more over that. Have another drink of wine. There's still some in the bottle. Drink it up and then go comfortably home and sleep. Promise me."

"No, you know that's just what I can't do—go home."

"Oh—you—with your tales! Will you never be done—with your Goethe?" (The dream about Goethe came back to me at that moment.) "But if you really can't go home, stay here. There are bedrooms. Shall I see about one for you?"

I was satisfied with that and asked where I could find her again? Where did she live? She would not tell me. I should find her in one place or another if I looked.

"Mayn't I invite you somewhere?"

"Where?"

"Where and when you like."

"Good. Tuesday for dinner at the old Franciscan. First floor. Good-bye."

She gave me her hand. I noticed for the first time how well it matched her voice—a beautiful hand, firm and intelligent and good-natured. She laughed at me when I kissed it.

Then at the last moment she turned once more and said: "I'll tell you something else—about Goethe. What you felt about him and finding the picture of him more than you could put up with, I often feel about the saints."

"The saints? Are you so religious?"

"No, I'm not religious, I'm sorry to say. But I was once and shall be again. There is no time now to be religious."

"No time. Does it need time to be religious?"

"Oh, yes. To be religious you must have time and, even more, independence of time. You can't be religious in earnest and at the same time live in actual things and still take them seriously, time and money and the Odéon Bar and all that."

"Yes, I understand. But what was that you said about the saints?"

"Well, there are many saints I'm particularly fond of—Stephen, St. Francis and others. I often see pictures of them and of the Saviour and the Virgin—such utterly lying and false and silly pictures—and I can put up with them just as little as you could with that picture of Goethe. When I see one of those sweet and silly Saviours or St. Francises and see how other people find them beautiful and edifying, I feel it is an insult to the real Saviour and it makes me think: Why did He live and suffer so terribly if people find a picture as silly as that satisfactory to them! But in spite of this I know that my own picture of the Saviour or St. Francis is only a human picture and falls short of the original, and that the Saviour Himself would find the picture I have of Him within me just as stupid as I do those sickly reproductions. I don't say this to justify you in your ill-temper and rage with the picture of Goethe. There's no justification. I say it simply to show you that I can understand you. You learned people and artists have, no doubt, all sorts of superior things in your heads; but you're human beings like the rest of us, and we, too, have our dreams and fancies. I noticed, for example, learned sir, that you felt a slight embarrassment when it came to telling me your Goethe story. You had to make a great effort to make your ideas comprehensible to a simple girl like me. Well, and so I wanted to show you that you needn't have made such an effort. I understand you all right. And now I've finished and your place is in bed."

She went away and an old house porter took me up two flights of stairs. But first he asked me where my luggage was, and when he heard that I hadn't any, I had to pay down what he called "sleep-money." Then he took me up an old dark staircase to a room upstairs and left me alone. There was a bleak wooden bedstead and on the wall hung a sabre and a coloured print of Garibaldi and also a withered wreath that had once figured in a club festival. I would have given much for pyjamas. At any rate there was water and a small towel and I could wash. Then I lay down on the bed in my clothes, and, leaving the light on, gave myself up to my reflections. So I had settled accounts with Goethe. It was splendid that he had come to me in a dream. And this wonderful girl—if only I had known her name! All of a sudden there was a human being, a living human being, to shatter the death that had come down over me like a glass case, and to put out a hand to me, a good and beautiful and warm hand. All of a sudden there were things that concerned me again, which I could think of with joy and eagerness. All of a sudden a door was thrown open through which life came in. Perhaps I could live once more and once more be a human being. My soul that had fallen asleep in the cold and nearly frozen breathed once more, and sleepily spread its weak and tiny wings. Goethe had been with me. A girl had bidden me eat and drink and sleep, and had shown me friendship and had laughed at me and had called me a silly little boy. And this wonderful friend had talked to me of the saints and shown me that even when I had outdone myself in absurdity I was not alone. I was not an incomprehensible and ailing exception. There were people akin to me. I was understood. Should I see her again? Yes, for certain. She could be relied upon. "A promise is a promise."

And before I knew, I was asleep once more and slept four or five hours. It had gone ten when I woke. My clothes were all creases. I felt utterly exhausted. And in my head was the memory of yesterday's half-forgotten horror; but I had life, hope and happy thoughts. As I returned to my room I experienced nothing of that terror that this return had had for me the day before. On the stairs above the araucaria I met the "aunt," my landlady. I saw her seldom but her kindly nature always delighted me. The meeting was not very propitious, for I was still unkempt and uncombed after my night out, and I had not shaved. I greeted her and would have passed on. As a rule, she always respected my desire to live alone and unobserved. Today, however, as it turned out, a veil between me and the outer world seemed to be torn aside, a barrier fallen. She laughed and stopped.

"You have been on a spree, Mr. Haller. You were not in bed last night. You must be pretty tired!"

"Yes," I said, and was forced to laugh too. "There was something lively going on last night, and as I did not like to shock you, I slept at an hotel. My respect for the repose and dignity of your house is great. I sometimes feel like a 'foreign body' in it."

"You are poking fun, Mr. Haller."

"Only at myself."

"You ought not to do that even. You ought not to feel like a 'foreign body' in my house. You should live as best pleases you and do as best you can. I have had before now many exceedingly respectable tenants, jewels of respectability, but not one has been quieter or disturbed us less than you. And now—would you like some tea?"

I did not refuse. Tea was brought me in her drawing-room with the old-fashioned pictures and furniture, and we had a little talk. In her friendly way she elicited this and that about my life and thoughts without actually asking questions and listened attentively to my confessions, while at the same time she did not give them more importance than an intelligent and motherly woman should to the peccadilloes of men. We talked, too, of her nephew and she showed me in a neighbouring room his latest hobby, a wireless set. There the industrious young man spent his evenings, fitting together the apparatus, a victim to the charms of wireless, and kneeling on pious knees before the god of applied science whose might had made it possible to discover after thousands of years a fact which every thinker has always known and put to better use than in this recent and very imperfect development. We spoke about this, for the aunt had a slight leaning to piety and religious topics were not unwelcome to her. I told her that the omnipresence of all forces and facts was well known to ancient India, and that science had merely brought a small fraction of this fact into general use by devising for it, that is, for sound waves, a receiver and transmitter which were still in their first stages and miserably defective. The principal fact known to that ancient knowledge was, I said, the unreality of time. This science had not yet observed. Finally, it would, of course, make this "discovery," also, and then the inventors would get busy over it. The discovery would be made—and perhaps very soon—that there were floating round us not only the pictures and events of the transient present in the same way that music from Paris or Berlin was now heard in Frankfurt or Zurich, but that all that had ever happened in the past could be registered and brought back likewise. We might well look for the day when, with wires or without, with or without the disturbance of other sounds, we should hear King Solomon speaking, or Walter von der Vogel-weide. And all this, I said, just as today was the case with the beginnings of wireless, would be of no more service to man than as an escape from himself and his true aims, and a means of surrounding himself with an ever closer mesh of distractions and useless activities. But instead of embarking on these familiar topics with my customary bitterness and scorn for the times and for science, I made a joke of them; and the aunt smiled, and we sat together for an hour or so and drank our tea with much content.

It was for Tuesday evening that I had invited the charming and remarkable girl of the Black Eagle, and I was a good deal put to it to know how to pass the time till then; and when at last Tuesday came, the importance of my relation to this unknown girl had become alarmingly clear to me. I thought of nothing but her. I expected everything from her. I was ready to lay everything at her feet. I was not in the least in love with her. Yet I had only to imagine that she might fail to keep the appointment, or forget it, to see where I stood. Then the world would be a desert once more, one day as dreary and worthless as the last, and the deathly stillness and wretchedness would surround me once more on all sides with no way out from this hell of silence except the razor. And these few days had not made me think any the more fondly of the razor. It had lost none of its terror. This was indeed the hateful truth: I dreaded to cut my throat with a dread that crushed my heart. My fear was as wild and obstinate as though I were the healthiest of men and my life a paradise. I realised my situation recklessly and without a single illusion. I realised that it was the unendurable tension between inability to live and inability to die that made the unknown girl, the pretty dancer of the Black Eagle, so important to me. She was the one window, the one tiny crack of light in my black hole of dread. She was my release and my way to freedom. She had to teach me to live or teach me to die. She had to touch my deadened heart with her firm and pretty hand, and at the touch of life it would either leap again to flame or subside in ashes. I could not imagine whence she derived these powers, what the source of her magic was, in what secret soil this deep meaning she had for me had grown up; nor did it matter. I did not care to know. There was no longer the least importance for me in any knowledge or perception I might have. Indeed it was just in that line that I was overstocked, for the ignominy under which I suffered lay just in this—that I saw my own situation so clearly and was so very conscious, too, of hers. I saw this wretch, this brute beast of a Steppenwolf as a fly in a web, and saw too the approaching decision of his fate. Entangled and defenceless he hung in the web. The spider was ready to devour him, and further off was the rescuing hand. I might have made the most intelligent and penetrating remarks about the ramifications and the causes of my sufferings, my sickness of soul, my general bedevilment of neurosis. The mechanism was transparent to me. But what I needed was not knowledge and understanding. What I longed for in my despair was life and resolution, action and reaction, impulse and impetus.

Although during the few days of waiting I never despaired of my friend keeping her word, this did not prevent my being in a state of acute suspense when the day arrived. Never in my life have I waited more impatiently for a day to end. And while the suspense and impatience were almost intolerable, they were at the same time of wonderful benefit to me. It was unimaginably beautiful and new for me who for a long while had been too listless to await anything or to find joy in anything—yes, it was wonderful to be running here and there all day long in restless anxiety and intense expectation, to be anticipating the meeting and the talk and the outcome that the evening had in store, to be shaving and dressing with peculiar care (new linen, new tie, new laces in my shoes). Whoever this intelligent and mysterious girl might be and however she got into this relation to myself was all one. She was there.

The miracle had happened. I had found a human being once more and a new interest in life. All that mattered was that the miracle should go on, that I should surrender myself to this magnetic power and follow this star.

Unforgettable moment when I saw her once more! I sat in the old-fashioned and comfortable restaurant at a small table that I had quite unnecessarily engaged by telephone, and studied the menu. In a tumbler were two orchids I had bought for my new acquaintance. I had a good while to wait, but I was sure she would come and was no longer agitated. And then she came. She stopped for a moment at the cloakroom and greeted me only by an observant and rather quizzical glance from her clear grey eyes. Distrustful, I took care to see how the waiter behaved towards her. No, there was nothing confidential, no lack of distance. He was scrupulously respectful. And yet they knew each other. She called him Emil.

She laughed with pleasure when I gave her the orchids.

"That's sweet of you, Harry. You wanted to make me a present, didn't you, and weren't sure what to choose. You weren't quite sure you would be right in making me a present. I might be insulted, and so you chose orchids, and though they're only flowers they're dear enough. So I thank you ever so much. And by the way I'll tell you now that I won't take presents from you. I live on men, but I won't live on you. But how you have altered! No one would know you. The other day you looked as if you had been cut down from a gallows, and now you're very nearly a man again. And now—have you carried out my orders?"

"What orders?"

"You've never forgotten? I mean, have you learnt the fox-trot? You said you wished nothing better than to obey my commands, that nothing was dearer to you than obeying me. Do you remember?"

"Indeed I do, and so it shall be. I meant it."

"And yet you haven't learnt to dance yet?"

"Can that be done so quickly—in a day or two?"

"Of course. The fox-trot you can learn in an hour. The Boston in two. The Tango takes longer, but that you don't need."

"But now I really must know your name."

She looked at me for a moment without speaking.

"Perhaps you can guess it. I should be so glad if you did. Pull yourself together and take a good look at me. Hasn't it ever occurred to you that sometimes my face is just like a boy's? Now, for example."

Yes, now that I looked at her face carefully, I had to admit she was right. It was a boy's face. And after a moment I saw something in her face that reminded me of my own boyhood and of my friend of those days. His name was Herman. For a moment it seemed that she had turned into this Herman.

"If you were a boy," said I in amazement, "I should say your name was Herman."

"Who knows, perhaps I am one and am simply in woman's clothing," she said, joking.

"Is your name Hermine?"

She nodded, beaming, delighted at my guess. At that moment the waiter brought the food and we began to eat. She was as happy as a child. Of all the things that pleased and charmed me about her, the prettiest and most characteristic was her rapid changes from the deepest seriousness to the drollest merriment, and this without doing herself the least violence, with the facility of a gifted child. Now for a while she was merry and chaffed me about the fox-trot, trod on my feet under the table, enthusiastically praised the meal, remarked on the care I had taken dressing, though she also had many criticisms to make on my appearance.

Meanwhile I asked her: "How did you manage to look like a boy and make me guess your name?"

"Oh, you did all that yourself. Doesn't your learning reveal to you that the reason why I please you and mean so much to you is because I am a kind of looking-glass for you, because there's something in me that answers you and understands you. Really, we ought all to be such looking-glasses to each other and answer and correspond to each other, but such owls as you are a bit peculiar. They give themselves on the slightest provocation over to the strangest notions that they can see nothing and read nothing any longer in the eyes of other men and then nothing seems right to them. And then when an owl like that after all finds a face that looks back into his and gives him a glimpse of understanding—well, then he's pleased, naturally."

"There's nothing you don't know, Hermine," I cried in amazement. "It's exactly as you say. And yet you're so entirely different from me. Why, you're my opposite. You have all that I lack."

"So you think," she said shortly, "and it's well you should."

And now a dark cloud of seriousness spread over her face. It was indeed like a magic mirror to me. Of a sudden her face bespoke seriousness and tragedy and it looked as fathomless as the hollow eyes of a mask. Slowly, as though it were dragged from her word for word, she said:

"Mind, don't forget what you said to me. You said that I was to command you and that it would be a joy to you to obey my commands. Don't forget that. You must know this, my little Harry—just as something in me corresponds to you and gives you confidence, so it is with me. The other day when I saw you come in to the Black Eagle, exhausted and beside yourself and scarcely in this world any longer, it came to me at once: This man will obey me. All he wants is that I should command him. And that's what I'm going to do. That's why I spoke to you and why we made friends."

She spoke so seriously from a deep impulse of her very soul that I scarcely liked to encourage her. I tried to calm her down. She shook her head with a frown and with a compelling look went on: "I tell you, you must keep your word, my boy. If you don't you'll regret it. You will have many commands from me and you will carry them out. Nice ones and agreeable ones that it will be a pleasure to you to obey. And at the last you will fulfil my last command as well, Harry."

"I will," I said, half giving in. "What will your last command be?"

I guessed it already—God knows why.

She shivered as though a passing chill went through her and seemed to be waking slowly from her trance. Her eyes did not release me. Suddenly she became still more sinister.

"If I were wise, I shouldn't tell you. But I won't be wise, Harry, not for this time. I'll be just the opposite. So now mind what I say! You will hear it and forget it again. You will laugh over it, and you will weep over it. So look out! I am going to play with you for life and death, little brother, and before we begin the game I'm going to lay my cards on the table."

How beautiful she looked, how unearthly, when she said that! Cool and clear, there swam in her eyes a conscious sadness. These eyes of hers seemed to have suffered all imaginable suffering and to have acquiesced in it. Her lips spoke with difficulty and as though something hindered them, as though a keen frost had numbed her face; but between her lips at the corners of her mouth where the tip of her tongue showed at rare intervals, there was but sweet sensuality and inward delight that contradicted the expression of her face and the tone of her voice. A short lock hung down over the smooth expanse of her forehead, and from this corner of her forehead whence fell the lock of hair, her boyishness welled up from time to time like a breath of life and cast the spell of an hermaphrodite. I listened with an eager anxiety and yet as though dazed and only half aware.

"You like me," she went on, "for the reason I said before, because I have broken through your isolation. I have caught you from the very gates of hell and wakened you to new life. But I want more from you—much more. I want to make you in love with me. No, don't interrupt me. Let me speak. You like me very much. I can see that. And you're grateful to me. But you're not in love with me. I mean to make you fall in love with me, and it is part of my calling. It is my living to be able to make men fall in love with me. But mind this, I don't do it because I find you exactly captivating. I'm as little in love with you as you with me. But I need you as you do me. You need me now, for the moment, because you're desperate. You're dying just for the lack of a push to throw you into the water and bring you to life again. You need me to teach you to dance and to laugh and to live. But I need you, not today—later, for something very important and beautiful too. When you are in love with me I will give you my last command and you will obey it, and it will be the better for both of us."

She pulled one of the brown and purple green-veined orchids up a little in the glass and bending over stared a moment at the bloom.

"You won't find it easy, but you will do it. You will carry out my command and—kill me. There—ask no more."

When she came to the end her eyes were still on the orchid, and her face relaxed, losing its strain like a flower-bud unfolding its petals. In an instant there was an enchanting smile on her lips while her eyes for a moment were still fixed and spell-bound. Then she gave a shake of her head with its little boyish lock, took a sip of water, and realising of a sudden that we were at a meal fell to eating again with appetite and enjoyment.

I had heard her uncanny communication clearly word for word. I had even guessed what her last command was before she said it and was horrified no longer. All that she said sounded as convincing to me as a decree of fate. I accepted it without protest. And yet in spite of the terrifying seriousness with which she had spoken I did not take it all as fully real and serious. While part of my soul drank in her words and believed in them, another part appeased me with a nod and took note that Hermine too, for all her wisdom and health and assurance, had her fantasies and twilight states. Scarcely was her last word spoken before a layer of unreality and ineffectuality settled over the whole scene.

All the same I could not get back to realities and probabilities with the same lightness as Hermine.

"And so I shall kill you one day?" I asked, still half in a dream while she laughed, and attacked her fowl with great relish.

"Of course," she nodded lightly. "Enough of that. It is time to eat. Harry, be an angel and order me a little more salad. Haven't you any appetite? It seems to me you've still to learn all the things that come naturally to other people, even the pleasure of eating. So look, my boy, I must tell you that this is the celebration of the duck, and when you pick the tender flesh from the bone it's a festal occasion and you must be just as eager and glad at heart and delighted as a lover when he unhooks his lady-love for the first time. Don't you understand? Oh, you're a sheep! Are you ready? I'm going to give you a piece off the little bone. So open your mouth. Oh, what a fright you are! There he goes, squinting round the room in case anyone sees him taking a bite from my fork. Don't be afraid, you prodigal son, I won't make a scandal. But it's a poor fellow who can't take his pleasure without asking other people's permission."

The scene that had gone before became more and more unreal. I was less and less able to believe that these were the same eyes that a moment before had been fixed in a dread obsession. But in this Hermine was like life itself, one moment succeeding to the next and not one to be foreseen. Now she was eating, and the duck and the salad, the sweet and the liqueur were the important thing, and each time the plates were changed a new chapter began. Yet though she played at being a child she had seen through me completely, and though she made me her pupil there and then in the game of living for each fleeting moment, she seemed to know more of life than is known to the wisest of the wise. It might be the highest wisdom or the merest artlessness. It is certain in any case that life is quite disarmed by the gift to live so entirely in the present, to treasure with such eager care every flower by the wayside and the light that plays on every passing moment. Was I to believe that this happy child with her hearty appetite and the air of a gourmet was at the same time a victim of hysterical visions who wished to die? or a careful calculating woman who, unmoved herself, had the conscious intention of making me her lover and her slave? I could not believe it. No, her surrender to the moment was so simple and complete that the fleeting shadows and agitation to the very depths of the soul came to her no less than every pleasurable impulse and were lived as fully.

Though I saw Hermine only for the second time that day, she knew everything about me and it seemed to me quite impossible that I could ever have a secret from her. Perhaps she might not understand everything of my spiritual life, might not perhaps follow me in my relation to music, to Goethe, to Novalis or Baudelaire. This too, however, was open to question. Probably it would give her as little trouble as the rest. And anyway, what was there left of my spiritual life? Hadn't all that gone to atoms and lost its meaning? As for the rest, my more personal problems and concerns, I had no doubt that she would understand them all. I should very soon be talking to her about the Steppenwolf and the treatise and all the rest of it, though till now it had existed for myself alone and never been mentioned to a single soul. Indeed, I could not resist the temptation of beginning forthwith.

"Hermine," I said, "an extraordinary thing happened to me the other day. An unknown man gave me a little book, the sort of thing you'd buy at a Fair, and inside I found my whole story and everything about me. Rather remarkable, don't you think?"

"What was it called," she asked lightly.

"Treatise on the Steppenwolf!"

"Oh, 'Steppenwolf' is magnificent! And are you the Steppenwolf? Is that meant for you?"

"Yes, it's me. I am one who is half-wolf and half-man, or thinks himself so at least."

She made no answer. She gave me a searching look in the eyes, then looked at my hands, and for a moment her face and expression had that deep seriousness and sinister passion of a few minutes before. Making a guess at her thoughts I felt she was wondering whether I were wolf enough to carry out her last command.

"That is, of course, your own fanciful idea," she said, becoming serene once more, "or a poetical one, if you like. But there's something in it. You're no wolf today, but the other day when you came in as if you had fallen from the moon there was really something of the beast about you. It is just what struck me at the time."

She broke off as though surprised by a sudden idea.

"How absurd those words are, such as beast and beast of prey. One should not speak of animals in that way. They may be terrible sometimes, but they're much more right than men."

"How do you mean—right?"

"Well, look at an animal, a cat, a dog, or a bird, or one of those beautiful great beasts in the Zoo, a puma or a giraffe. You can't help seeing that all of them are right. They're never in any embarrassment. They always know what to do and how to behave themselves. They don't flatter and they don't intrude. They don't pretend. They are as they are, like stones or flowers or stars in the sky. Don't you agree?"

I did.

"Animals are sad as a rule," she went on. "And when a man is sad—I don't mean because he has the toothache or has lost some money, but because he sees, for once in a way, how it all is with life and everything, and is sad in earnest—he always looks a little like an animal. He looks not only sad, but more right and more beautiful than usual. That's how it is, and that's how you looked, Steppenwolf, when I saw you for the first time."

"Well, Hermine, and what do you think about this book with a description of me in it?"

"Oh, I can't always be thinking. We'll talk about it another time. You can give it me to read one day. Or, no, if I ever start reading again, give me one of the books you've written yourself."

She asked for coffee and for a while seemed absent-minded and distraught. Then she suddenly beamed and seemed to have found the clue to her speculations.

"Hullo," she cried, delighted, "now I've got it!"

"What have you got?"

"The fox-trot. I've been thinking about it all the evening. Now tell me, have you a room where we two could dance sometimes? It doesn't matter if it's small, but there mustn't be anybody underneath to come up and play hell if his ceiling rocks a bit. Well, that's fine, you can learn to dance at home."

"Yes," I said in alarm, "so much the better. But I thought music was required."

"Of course it's required. You've got to buy that. At the most it won't cost as much as a course of lessons. You save that because I'll give them myself. This way we have the music whenever we like and at the end we have the gramophone into the bargain."

"The gramophone?"

"Of course. You can buy a small one and a few dance records—"

"Splendid," I cried, "and if you bring it off and teach me to dance, the gramophone is yours as an honorarium. Agreed?"

I brought it out very pat, but scarcely from the heart. I could not picture the detested instrument in my study among my books, and I was by no means reconciled to the dancing either. It had been in my mind that I might try how it went for a while, though I was convinced that I was too old and stiff and would never learn now. And to go at it hammer and tongs as she proposed seemed to me altogether too sudden and uncompromising. As an old and fastidious connoisseur of music, I could feel my gorge rising against the gramophone and jazz and modern dance-music. It was more than anyone could ask of me to have dance tunes that were the latest rage of America let loose upon the sanctum where I took refuge with Novalis and Jean Paul and to be made to dance to them. But it was not anyone who asked it of me. It was Hermine, and it was for her to command, and for me to obey. Of course, I obeyed.

We met at a café on the following afternoon. Hermine was there before me, drinking tea, and she pointed with a smile to my name which she had found in a newspaper. It was one of the reactionary jingo papers of my own district in which from time to time violently abusive references to me were circulated. During the war I had been opposed to it and, after, I had from time to time counselled quiet and patience and humanity and a criticism that began at home; and I had resisted the nationalist jingoism that became every day more pronounced, more insane and unrestrained. Here, then, was another attack of this kind, badly written, in part the work of the editor himself and in part stolen from articles of a similar kind in papers of similar tendencies to his own. It is common knowledge that no one writes worse than these defenders of decrepit ideas. No one plies his trade with less of decency and conscientious care. Hermine had read the article, and it had informed her that Harry Haller was a noxious insect and a man who disowned his native land, and that it stood to reason that no good could come to the country so long as such persons and such ideas were tolerated and the minds of the young turned to sentimental ideas of humanity instead of to revenge by arms upon the hereditary foe.

"Is that you?" asked Hermine, pointing to my name. "Well, you've made yourself some enemies and no mistake. Does it annoy you?"

I read a few lines. There was not a single line of stereotyped abuse that had not been drummed into me for years till I was sick and tired of it.

"No," I said, "it doesn't annoy me. I was used to it long ago. Now and again I have expressed the opinion that every nation, and even every person, would do better, instead of rocking himself to sleep with political catchwords about war-guilt, to ask himself how far his own faults and negligences and evil tendencies are guilty of the war and all the other wrongs of the world, and that there lies the only possible means of avoiding the next war. They don't forgive me that, for, of course, they are themselves all guiltless, the Kaiser, the generals, the trade magnates, the politicians, the papers. Not one of them has the least thing to blame himself for. Not one has any guilt. One might believe that everything was for the best, even though a few million men lie under the ground. And mind you, Hermine, even though such abusive articles cannot annoy me any longer, they often sadden me all the same. Two-thirds of my countrymen read this kind of newspaper, read things written in this tone every morning and every night, are every day worked up and admonished and incited, and robbed of their peace of mind and better feelings by them, and the end and aim of it all is to have the war over again, the next war that draws nearer and nearer, and it will be a good deal more horrible than the last. All that is perfectly clear and simple. Any one could comprehend it and reach the same conclusion after a moment's reflection. But nobody wants to. Nobody wants to avoid the next war, nobody wants to spare himself and his children the next holocaust if this be the cost. To reflect for one moment, to examine himself for a while and ask what share he has in the world's confusion and wickedness—look you, nobody wants to do that. And so there's no stopping it, and the next war is being pushed on with enthusiasm by thousands upon thousands day by day. It has paralysed me since I knew it, and brought me to despair. I have no country and no ideals left. All that comes to nothing but decorations for the gentlemen by whom the next slaughter is ushered in. There is no sense in thinking or saying or writing anything of human import, to bother one's head with thoughts of goodness—for two or three men who do that, there are thousands of papers, periodicals, speeches, meetings in public and in private, that make the opposite their daily endeavour and succeed in it too."

Hermine had listened attentively.

"Yes," she said now, "there you're right enough. Of course, there will be another war. One doesn't need to read the papers to know that. And of course one can be sad about it, but it isn't any use. It is just the same as when a man is sad to think that one day, in spite of his utmost efforts to prevent it, he will inevitably die. The war against death, dear Harry, is always a beautiful, noble and wonderful and glorious thing, and so, it follows, is the war against war. But it is always hopeless and quixotic too."

"That is perhaps true," I cried heatedly, "but truths like that—that we must all soon be dead and so it is all one and the same—make the whole of life flat and stupid. Are we then to throw everything up and renounce the spirit altogether and all effort and all that is human and let ambition and money rule forever while we await the next mobilisation over a glass of beer?"

Remarkable the look that Hermine now gave me, a look full of amusement, full of irony and roguishness and fellow-feeling, and at the same time so grave, so wise, so unfathomably serious.

"You shan't do that," she said in a voice that was quite maternal. "Your life will not be flat and dull even though you know that your war will never be victorious. It is far flatter, Harry, to fight for something good and ideal and to know all the time that you are bound to attain it. Are ideals attainable? Do we live to abolish death? No—we live to fear it and then again to love it, and just for death's sake it is that our spark of life glows for an hour now and then so brightly. You're a child, Harry. Now, do as I tell you and come along. We've a lot to get done today. I am not going to bother myself any more today about the war or the papers either. What about you?"

Oh, no, I had no wish to.

We went together—it was our first walk in the town—to a music shop and looked at gramophones. We turned them on and off and heard them play, and when we had found one that was very suitable and nice and cheap I wanted to buy it. Hermine, however, was not for such rapid transactions. She pulled me back and I had to go off with her in search of another shop and there, too, look at and listen to gramophones of every shape and size, from the dearest to the cheapest, before she finally agreed to return to the first shop and buy the machine we first thought of.

"You see," I said, "it would have been as simple to have taken it at once."

"Think so? And then perhaps tomorrow we should have seen the very same one in a shop window at twenty francs less. And besides, it's fun buying things and you have to pay for your fun. You've a lot to learn yet."

We got a porter to carry the purchase home.

Hermine made a careful inspection of my room. She commended the stove and the sofa, tried the chairs, picked up the books, stood a long while in front of the photograph of Erica. We had put the gramophone on a chest of drawers among piles of books. And now my instruction began. Hermine turned on a fox-trot and, after showing me the first steps, began to take me in hand. I trotted obediently round with her, colliding with chairs, hearing her directions and failing to understand them, treading on her toes, and being as clumsy as I was conscientious. After the second dance she threw herself on the sofa and laughed like a child.

"Oh! How stiff you are! Just go straight ahead as if you were walking. There's not the least need to exert yourself. Why, I should think you have made yourself positively hot, haven't you? No, let's rest five minutes! Dancing, don't you see, is every bit as easy as thinking, when you can do it, and much easier to learn. Now you can understand why people won't get the habit of thinking and prefer calling Herr Haller a traitor to his country and waiting quietly for the next war to come along."

In an hour she was gone, assuring me that it would go better next time. I had my own thoughts about that, and I was sorely disappointed over my stupidity and clumsiness. It did not seem to me that I had learnt anything whatever and I did not believe that it would go better next time. No, one had to bring certain qualities to dancing that I was entirely without, gaiety, innocence, frivolity, elasticity. Well, I had always thought so.

But there, the next time it did in fact go better. I even got some fun out of it, and at the end of the lesson Hermine announced that I was now proficient in the fox-trot. But when she followed it up by saying that I had to dance with her the next day at a restaurant, I was thrown into a panic and resisted the idea with vehemence. She reminded me coolly of my oath of obedience and arranged a meeting for tea on the following day at the Balance Hotel.

That evening I sat in my room and tried to read; but I could not. I was in dread of the morrow. It was a most horrible thought that I, an elderly, shy, touchy crank, was to frequent one of those modern deserts of jazz music, a *thé dansant*, and a far more horrible thought that I was to figure there as a dancer, though I did not in the least know how to dance. And I own I laughed at myself and felt shame in my own eyes when alone in the quiet of my studious room I turned on the machine and softly in stockinged feet went through the steps of my dance.

A small orchestra played every other day at the Balance Hotel and tea and whisky were served. I made an attempt at bribing Hermine, I put cakes before her and proposed a bottle of good wine, but she was inflexible.

"You're not here for your amusement today. It is a dancing lesson."

I had to dance with her two or three times, and during an interval she introduced me to the saxophone player, a dark and good-looking youth of Spanish or South American origin, who, she told me, could play on all instruments and talk every language in the world. This señor appeared to know Hermine well and to be on excellent terms with her. He had two saxophones of different sizes in front of him which he played on by turns, while his darkly gleaming eyes scrutinised the dancers and beamed with pleasure. I was surprised to feel something like jealousy of this agreeable and charming musician, not a lover's jealousy, for there was no question of love between Hermine and me, but a subtler jealousy of their friendship; for he did not seem to me so eminently worthy of the interest, and even reverence, with which she so conspicuously distinguished him. I apparently was to meet some strange people, I thought to myself in ill-humour. Then Hermine was asked to dance again, and I was left alone to drink tea and listen to the music, a kind of music that I had never till that day known how to endure. Good God, I thought, so now I am to be initiated, and made to feel at home in this world of idlers and pleasure seekers, a world that is utterly strange and repugnant to me and that to this day I have always carefully avoided and utterly despised, a smooth and stereotyped world of marble-topped tables, jazz music, cocottes and commercial travellers! Sadly, I swallowed my tea and stared at the crowd of second-rate elegance. Two beautiful girls caught my eye. They were both good dancers. I followed their movements with admiration and envy. How elastic, how beautiful and gay and certain their steps!

Soon Hermine appeared once more. She was not pleased with me. She scolded me and said that I was not there to wear such a face and sit idling at tea-tables. I was to pull myself together, please, and dance. What, I knew no one? That was not necessary. Were there, then, no girls there who met with my approval?

I pointed out one of the two, and the more attractive, who happened at the moment to be standing near us. She looked enchanting in her pretty velvet dress with her short luxuriant blonde hair and her rounded womanly arms. Hermine insisted that I should go up to her forthwith and ask her to dance. I shrank back in despair.

"Indeed, I cannot do it," I said in my misery. "Of course, if I were young and good-looking—but for a stiff old hack like me who can't dance for the life of him—she would laugh at me!"

Hermine looked at me contemptuously.

"And that I should laugh at you, of course, doesn't matter. What a coward you are! Every one risks being laughed at when he addresses a girl. That's always at stake. So take the risk, Harry, and if the worst come to the worst let yourself be laughed at. Otherwise it's all up with my belief in your obedience...."

She was obdurate. I got up automatically and approached the young beauty just as the music began again.

"As a matter of fact, I'm engaged for this one," she said and looked me up and down with her large clear eyes, "but my partner seems to have got stranded at the bar over there, so come along."

I grasped her and performed the first steps, still in amazement that she had not sent me about my business. She was not long in taking my measure and in taking charge of me. She danced wonderfully and I caught the infection. I forgot for the moment all the rules I had conscientiously learnt and simply floated along. I felt my partner's taut hips, her quick and pliant knees, and looking in her young and radiant face I owned to her that this was the first time in my life that I had ever really danced. She smiled encouragement and replied to my enchanted gaze and flattering words with a wonderful compliance, not of words, but of movements whose soft enchantment brought us more closely and delightfully in touch. My right hand held her waist firmly and I followed every movement of her feet and arms and shoulders with eager happiness. Not once, to my astonishment, did I step on her feet, and when the music stopped, we both stood where we were and clapped till the dance was played again; and then with all a lover's zeal I devoutly performed the rite once more.

When, too soon, the dance came to an end, my beautiful partner in velvet disappeared and I suddenly saw Hermine standing near me. She had been watching us.

"Now do you see?" she laughed approvingly. "Have you made the discovery that women's legs are not table legs? Well, bravo! You know the fox-trot now, thank the Lord. Tomorrow we'll get on to the Boston, and in three weeks there's the Masked Ball at the Globe Rooms."

We had taken seats for the interval when the charming young Herr Pablo, with a friendly nod, sat down beside Hermine. He seemed to be very intimate with her. As for myself, I must own that I was not by any means delighted with the gentleman at this first encounter. He was good-looking, I could not deny, both of face and figure, but I could not discover what further advantages he had. Even his linguistic accomplishments sat very lightly on him—to such an extent, indeed, that he did not speak at all beyond uttering such words as please, thanks, you bet, rather and hallo. These, certainly, he knew in several languages. No, he said nothing, this Señor Pablo, nor did he even appear to think much, this charming caballero. His business was with the saxophone in the jazz-band and to this calling he appeared to devote himself with love and passion. Often during the course of the music he would suddenly clap with his hands, or permit himself other expressions of enthusiasm, such as, singing out "O O O, Ha Ha, Hallo." Apart from this, however, he confined himself to being beautiful, to pleasing women, to wearing collars and ties of the latest fashion and a great number of rings on his fingers. His manner of entertaining us consisted in sitting beside us, in smiling upon us, in looking at his wrist watch and in rolling cigarettes—at which he was an expert. His dark and beautiful Creole eyes and his black locks hid no romance, no problems, no thoughts. Closely looked at, this beautiful demigod of love was no more than a complacent and rather spoilt young man with pleasant manners. I talked to him about his instrument and about tone-colours in jazz music, and he must have seen that he was confronted by one who had the enjoyment of a connoisseur for all that touched on music. But he made no response, and while I, in compliment to him, or rather, to Hermine, embarked upon a musicianly justification of jazz, he smiled amiably upon me and my efforts. Presumably, he had not the least idea that there was any music but jazz or that any music had ever existed before it. He was pleasant, certainly, pleasant and polite, and his large, vacant eyes smiled most charmingly. Between him and me, however, there appeared to be nothing whatever in common. Nothing of all that was, perhaps, important and sacred to him could be so for me as well. We came of contrasted races and spoke languages in which no two words were akin. (Later, nevertheless, Hermine told me a remarkable thing. She told me that Pablo, after a conversation about me, had said that she must treat me very nicely, for I was so very unhappy. And when she asked what brought him to that conclusion, he said: "Poor, poor fellow. Look at his eyes. Doesn't know how to laugh.")

When the dark-eyed young man had taken his leave of us and the music began again, Hermine stood up. "Now you might have another dance with me. Or don't you care to dance any more?"

With her, too, I danced more easily now, in a freer and more sprightly fashion, even though not so buoyantly and more self-consciously than with the other. Hermine had me lead, adapting herself as softly and lightly as the leaf of a flower, and with her, too, I now experienced all these delights that now advanced and now took wing. She, too, now exhaled the perfume of woman and love, and her dancing, too, sang with intimate tenderness the lovely and enchanting song of sex. And yet I could not respond to all this with warmth and freedom. I could not entirely forget myself in abandon. Hermine stood in too close a relation to me. She was my comrade and sister—my double, almost, in her resemblance not to me only, but to Herman, my boyhood friend, the enthusiast, the poet, who had shared with ardour all my intellectual pursuits and extravagances.

"I know," she said when I spoke of it. "I know that well enough. All the same, I shall make you fall in love with me, but there's no use hurrying. First of all we're comrades, two people who hope to be friends, because we have recognised each other. For the present we'll each learn from the other and amuse ourselves together. I show you my little stage, and teach you to dance and to have a little pleasure and be silly; and you show me your thoughts and something of all you know."

"There's little there to show you, Hermine, I'm afraid. You know far more than I do. You're a most remarkable person—and a woman. But do I mean anything to you? Don't I bore you?"

She looked down darkly to the floor.

"That's how I don't like to hear you talk. Think of that evening when you came broken from your despair and loneliness, to cross my path and be my comrade. Why was it, do you think, I was able to recognise you and understand you?"

"Why, Hermine? Tell me!"

"Because it's the same for me as for you, because I am alone exactly as you are, because I'm as little fond of life and men and myself as you are and can put up with them as little. There are always a few such people who demand the utmost of life and yet cannot come to terms with its stupidity and crudeness."

"You, you!" I cried in deep amazement. "I understand you, my comrade. No one understands you better than I. And yet you're a riddle. You are such a past-master at life. You have your wonderful reverence for its little details and enjoyments. You are such an artist in life. How can you suffer at life's hands? How can you despair?"

"I don't despair. As to suffering—oh, yes, I know all about that! You are surprised that I should be unhappy when I can dance and am so sure of myself in the superficial things of life. And I, my friend, am surprised that you are so disillusioned with life when you are at home with the very things in it that are the deepest and most beautiful, spirit, art, and thought! That is why we were drawn to one another and why we are brother and sister. I am going to teach you to dance and play and smile, and still not be happy. And you are going to teach me to think and to know and yet not be happy. Do you know that we are both children of the devil?"

"Yes, that is what we are. The devil is the spirit, and we are his unhappy children. We have fallen out of nature and hang suspended in space. And that reminds me of something. In the Steppenwolf treatise that I told you about, there is something to the effect that it is only a fancy of his to believe that he has one soul, or two, that he is made up of one or two personalities. Every human being, it says, consists of ten, or a hundred, or a thousand souls."

"I like that very much," cried Hermine. "In your case, for example, the spiritual part is very highly developed, and so you are very backward in all the little arts of living. Harry, the thinker, is a hundred years old, but Harry, the dancer, is scarcely half a day old. It's he we want to bring on, and all his little brothers who are just as little and stupid and stunted as he is."

She looked at me, smiling; and then asked softly in an altered voice:

"And how did you like Maria, then?"

"Maria? Who is she?"

"The girl you danced with. She is a lovely girl, a very lovely girl. You were a little smitten with her, as far as I could see."

"You know her then?"

"Oh, yes, we know each other well. Were you very much taken with her?"

"I liked her very much, and I was delighted that she was so indulgent about my dancing."

"As if that were the whole story! You ought to make love to her a little, Harry. She is very pretty and such a good dancer, and you are in love with her already, I know very well. You'll succeed with her, I'm sure."

"Believe me, I have no such aspiration."

"There you're lying a little. Of course, I know that you have an attach-ment. There is a girl somewhere or other whom you see once or twice a year in order to have a quarrel with her. Of course, it's very charming of you to wish to be true to this estimable friend of yours, but you must permit me not to take it so very seriously. I suspect you of taking love frightfully seriously. That is your own affair. You can love as much as you like in your ideal fash-ion for all I care. All I have to worry about is that you should learn to know a little more of the little arts and lighter sides of life. In this sphere, I am your teacher, and I shall be a better one than your ideal love ever was, you may be sure of that! It's high time you slept with a pretty girl again, Steppenwolf."

"Hermine," I cried in torment, "you have only to look at me, I am an old man!"

"You're a child. You were too lazy to learn to dance till it was nearly too late, and in the same way you were too lazy to learn to love. As for ideal and tragic love, that, I don't doubt, you can do marvellously—and all honour to you. Now you will learn to love a little in an ordinary human way. We have made a start. You will soon be fit to go to a ball, but you must know the Bos-ton first, and we'll begin on that tomorrow. I'll come at three. How did you like the music, by the way?"

"Very much indeed."

"Well, there's another step forward, you see. Up to now you couldn't stand all this dance and jazz music. It was too superficial and frivolous for you. Now you have seen that there's no need to take it seriously and that it can all the same be very agreeable and delightful. And, by the way, the whole orchestra would be nothing without Pablo. He conducts it and puts fire into it."

* * * *

Just as the gramophone contaminated the æsthetic and intellectual atmo-sphere of my study and just as the American dances broke in as strangers and disturbers, yes, and as destroyers, into my carefully tended garden of music, so, too, from all sides there broke in new and dreaded and disintegrating influences upon my life that, till now, had been so sharply marked off and so deeply secluded. The Steppenwolf treatise, and Hermine too, were right in their doctrine of the thousand souls. Every day new souls kept springing up beside the host of old ones, making clamorous demands and creating confu-sion; and now I saw as clearly as in a picture what an illusion my former personality had been. The few capacities and pursuits in which I had hap-pened to be strong had occupied all my attention, and I had painted a picture of myself as a person who was in fact nothing more than a most refined and educated specialist in poetry, music and philosophy; and as such I had lived, leaving all the rest of me to be a chaos of potentialities, instincts and impulses which I found an encumbrance and gave the label of Steppenwolf.

Meanwhile, though cured of an illusion, I found this disintegration of the personality by no means a pleasant and amusing adventure. On the contrary, it was often exceedingly painful, often almost intolerable. Often the sound of the gramophone was truly fiendish to my ears in the midst of surroundings where everything was tuned to so very different a key. And many a time, when I danced my one-step in a stylish restaurant among pleasure seekers and elegant rakes, I felt that I was a traitor to all that I was bound to hold most sacred. Had Hermine left me for one week alone I should have fled at once from this wearisome and laughable trafficking with the world of pleasure. Hermine, however, was always there. Though I might not see her every day, I was all the same continually under her eye, guided, guarded and counselled—besides, she read all my mad thoughts of rebellion and escape in my face, and smiled at them.

As the destruction of all that I had called my personality went on, I began to understand, too, why it was that I had feared death so horribly in spite of all my despair. I began to perceive that this ignoble horror in the face of death was a part of my old conventional and lying existence. The late Herr Haller, gifted writer, student of Mozart and Goethe, author of essays upon the metaphysics of art, upon genius and tragedy and humanity, the melancholy hermit in a cell encumbered with books, was given over bit by bit to self-criticism and at every point was found wanting. This gifted and interesting Herr Haller had, to be sure, preached reason and humanity and had protested against the barbarity of the war; but he had not let himself be stood against a wall and shot, as the proper consequence of his way of thinking would have been. He had found some way of accommodating himself; one, of course, that was outwardly reputable and noble, but still a compromise and no more. He was, further, opposed to the power of capital and yet he had industrial securities lying at his bank and spent the interest from them without a pang of conscience. And so it was all through. Harry Haller had, to be sure, rigged himself out finely as an idealist and contemner of the world, as a melancholy hermit and growling prophet. At bottom, however, he was a bourgeois who took exception to a life like Hermine's and fretted himself over the nights thrown away in a restaurant and the money squandered there, and had them on his conscience. Instead of longing to be freed and completed, he longed, on the contrary, most earnestly to get back to those happy times when his intellectual trifling had been his diversion and brought him fame. Just so those newspaper readers—whom he despised and scorned—longed to get back to the ideal time before the war, because it was so much more comfortable than taking a lesson from those who had gone through it. Oh, the devil, he made one sick, this Herr Haller! And yet I clung to him all the same, or to the mask of him that was already falling away, clung to his coquetting with the spiritual, to his bourgeois horror of the disorderly and accidental (to which death, too, belonged) and compared the new Harry—the somewhat timid and ludicrous dilettante of the dance rooms—scornfully and enviously with the old one in whose ideal and lying portrait he had since discovered all those fatal characteristics which had upset him that night so grievously in the professor's print of Goethe. He himself, the old Harry, had been just such a bourgeoise idealisation of Goethe, a spiritual champion whose all-too-noble gaze shone with the unction of elevated thought and humanity, until he was almost overcome by his own nobleness of mind! The devil! Now, at last, this fine picture stood badly in need of repairs! The ideal Herr Haller had been lamentably dismantled! He looked like a dignitary who had fallen among thieves—with his tattered breeches—and he would have shown sense if he had studied now the rôle that his rags appointed him instead of wearing them with an air of respectability and carrying on a whining pretence to lost repute.

I was constantly finding myself in the company of Pablo, the musician, and my estimate of him had to be revised if only because Hermine liked him so much and was so eager for his company. Pablo had left on me the impression of a pretty nonentity, a little beau, and somewhat empty at that, as happy as a child for whom there are no problems, whose joy it is to dribble into his toy trumpet and who is kept quiet with praises and chocolate. Pablo, however, was not interested in my opinions. They were as indifferent to him as my musical theories. He listened with friendly courtesy, smiling as he always did; but he refrained all the same from any actual reply. On the other hand, in spite of this, it seemed that I had aroused his interest. It was clear that he put himself out to please me and to show me goodwill. Once when I showed a certain irritation, and even ill-humour, over one of these fruitless attempts at conversation he looked in my face with a troubled and sorrowful air and, taking my left hand and stroking it, he offered me a pinch from his little gold snuff-box. It would do me good. I looked inquiringly at Hermine. She nodded and I took a pinch. The almost immediate effect was that I became clearer in the head and more cheerful. No doubt there was cocaine in the powder. Hermine told me that Pablo had many such drugs, and that he procured them through secret channels. He offered them to his friends now and then and was a master in the mixing and prescribing of them. He had drugs for stilling pain, for inducing sleep, for begetting beautiful dreams, lively spirits and the passion of love.

One day I met him in the street near the quay and he turned at once to accompany me. This time I succeeded at last in making him talk.

"Herr Pablo," I said to him as he played with his slender ebony and silver walking-stick, "you are a friend of Hermine's and that is why I take an interest in you. But I can't say you make it easy to get on with you. Several times

I have attempted to talk about music with you. It would have interested me to know your thoughts and opinions, whether they contradicted mine or not, but you have disdained to make me even the barest reply."

He gave me a most amiable smile and this time a reply was accorded me.

"Well," he said with equanimity, "you see, in my opinion there is no point at all in talking about music. I never talk about music. What reply, then, was I to make to your very able and just remarks? You were perfectly right in all you said. But, you see, I am a musician, not a professor, and I don't believe that, as regards music, there is the least point in being right. Music does not depend on being right, on having good taste and education and all that."

"Indeed. Then what does it depend on?"

"On making music, Herr Haller, on making music as well and as much as possible and with all the intensity of which one is capable. That is the point, Monsieur. Though I carried the complete works of Bach and Haydn in my head and could say the cleverest things about them not a soul would be the better for it. But when I take hold of my mouth-piece and play a lively shimmy, whether the shimmy be good or bad, it will give people pleasure. It gets into their legs and into their blood. That's the point and that alone. Look at the faces in a dance-hall at the moment when the music strikes up after a longish pause, how eyes sparkle, legs twitch and faces begin to laugh. *That* is why one makes music."

"Very good, Herr Pablo. But there is not only sensual music. There is spiritual also. Besides the music that is actually played at the moment, there is the immortal music that lives on even when it is not actually being played. It can happen to a man to lie alone in bed and to call to mind a melody from the *Magic Flute* or the *Matthew Passion*, and then there is music without anybody blowing into a flute or passing a bow across a fiddle."

"Certainly, Herr Haller. *Yearning* and *Valencia* are recalled every night by many a lonely dreamer. Even the poorest typist in her office has the latest one-step in her head and taps her keys in time to it. You are right. I don't grudge all those lonely persons their mute music, whether it's *Yearning* or the *Magic Flute* or *Valencia*. But where do they get their lonely and mute music from? They get it from us, the musicians. It must first have been played and heard, it must have got into the blood, before anyone at home in his room can think of it and dream of it."

"Granted," I said coolly, "all the same it won't do to put Mozart and the latest fox-trot on the same level. And it is not one and the same thing whether you play people divine and eternal music or cheap stuff of the day that is forgotten tomorrow."

When Pablo observed from my tone that I was getting heated, he at once put on his most amiable expression and touching my arm caressingly he gave an unbelievable softness to his voice.

"Ah, my dear sir, you may be perfectly right with your levels. I have nothing to say to your putting Mozart and Haydn and *Valencia* on what levels you please. It is all one to me. It is not for me to decide about levels. I shall never be asked about them. Mozart, perhaps, will still be played in a hundred years and *Valencia* in two will be played no more—we can well leave that, I think, in God's hands. God is good and has the span of all our days in his hands and that of every waltz and fox-trot too. He is sure to do what is right. We musicians, however, we must play our parts according to our duties and our gifts. We have to play what is actually in demand, and we have to play it as well and as beautifully and as expressively as ever we can."

With a sigh I gave it up. There was no getting past the fellow.

At many moments the old and the new, pain and pleasure, fear and joy were quite oddly mixed with one another. Now I was in heaven, now in hell, generally in both at once. The old Harry and the new lived at one moment in bitter strife, at the next in peace. Many a time the old Harry appeared to be dead and done with, to have died and been buried, and then of a sudden there he was again, giving orders and tyrannising and contradictory till the little new young Harry was silent for very shame and let himself be pushed to the wall. At other times the young Harry took the old by the throat and squeezed with all his might. There was many a groan, many a death-struggle, many a thought of the razor-blade.

Often, however, suffering and happiness broke over me in one wave. One such moment was when a few days after my first public exhibition of dancing, I went into my bedroom at night and to my indescribable astonishment, dismay, horror and enchantment found the lovely Maria lying in my bed.

Of all the surprises that Hermine had prepared for me this was the most violent. For I had not a moment's doubt that it was she who had sent me this bird of paradise. I had not, as usually, been with Hermine that evening. I had been to a recital of old church music in the Cathedral, a beautiful, though melancholy, excursion into my past life, to the fields of my youth, the territory of my ideal self. Beneath the lofty Gothic of the church whose netted vaulting swayed with a ghostly life in the play of the sparse lights, I heard pieces by Buxtehude, Pachelbel, Bach and Haydn. I had gone the old beloved way once more. I had heard the magnificent voice of a Bach singer with whom in the old days when we were friends I had enjoyed many a memorable musical occasion. The notes of the old music with its eternal dignity and sanctity had called to life all the exalted enchantment and enthusiasm of youth. I had sat in the lofty choir, sad and abstracted, a guest for an hour of this noble and blessed world which once had been my home. During a Haydn duet the tears had come suddenly to my eyes. I had not waited for the end of the concert. Dropping the thought I had had of seeing the singer again (what evenings I had once spent with the artistes after such concerts) and stealing away out of the Cathedral, I had wearily paced the dark and narrow streets, where here and there behind the windows of the restaurants jazz orchestras were playing the tunes of the life I had now come to live. Oh, what a dull maze of error I had made of my life!

For long during this night's walk I had reflected upon the significance of my relation to music, and not for the first time recognised this appealing and fatal relation as the destiny of the entire German spirit. In the German spirit the matriarchal link with nature rules in the form of the hegemony of music to an extent unknown in any other people. We intellectuals instead of opposing ourselves to this tendency like men, and rendering obedience to the spirit, the Logos, the Word, and gaining a hearing for it, are all dreaming of a speech without words that utters the inexpressible and gives form to the formless. Instead of playing his part as truly and honestly as he could, the German intellectual has constantly rebelled against the word and against reason and courted music. And so the German spirit, carousing in music, in wonderful creations of sound, and wonderful beauties of feeling and mood that were never pressed home to reality, has left the greater part of its practical gifts to decay. None of us intellectuals is at home in reality. We are strange to it and hostile. That is why the part played by intellect even in our own German reality, in our history and politics and public opinion, has been so lamentable a one. Well, I had often pondered all this, not without an intense longing sometimes to turn to and do something real for once, to be seriously and responsibly active instead of occupying myself forever with nothing but æsthetics and intellectual and artistic pursuits. It always ended, however, in resignation, in surrender to destiny. The generals and the captains of industry were quite right. There was nothing to be made of us intellectuals. We were a superfluous, irresponsible lot of talented chatterboxes for whom reality had no meaning. With a curse, I came back to the razor.

So, full of thoughts and the echoes of the music, my heart weighed down with sadness and the longing of despair for life and reality and sense and all that was irretrievably lost, I had got home at last; climbed my stairs; put on the light in my sitting room; tried in vain to read; thought of the appointment which compelled me to drink whisky and dance at the Cecil Bar on the following evening; thought with malice and bitterness not only of myself, but of Hermine too. She might be good and have the best and kindest intentions and she might be a wonderful person, but she would have done better all the same to let me go to perdition instead of sweeping me into this whirligig of frivolities where I should never be any other than an alien and where the best in me was demoralised and had been lowered.

And so I had sadly put out the light and taken myself to my bedroom and sadly begun to undress; and then I was surprised by an unaccustomed smell.

There was a faint aroma of scent, and looking round I saw the lovely Maria lying in my bed, smiling and a little startled, with large blue eyes.

"Maria!" I said. And my first thoughts were that my landlady would give me notice when she knew of it.

"I've come," she said softly. "Are you angry with me?"

"No, no. I see Hermine gave you the key. Isn't that it?"

"Oh, it does make you angry. I'll go again."

"No, lovely Maria, stay! Only, just tonight, I'm very sad. I can't be jolly tonight. Perhaps tomorrow I'll be better again."

I was bending over her and she took my head in her large firm hands and drawing it down gave me a long kiss. Then I sat down on the bed beside her and took her hands and asked her to speak low in case we were heard, and looked at her beautiful full rounded face that lay so strangely and wonderfully on my pillow like a large flower. She drew my hand slowly to her lips and laid it beneath the clothes on her warm and evenly breathing breast.

"You don't need to be jolly," she said. "Hermine told me that you had troubles. Any one can understand that. Tell me, then, do I please you still? The other day, when we were dancing, you were very much in love with me."

I kissed her eyes, her mouth and neck and breasts. A moment ago I had thought of Hermine with bitterness and reproach. Now I held her gift in my hands and was thankful. Maria's caresses did not harm the wonderful music I had heard that evening. They were its worthy fulfilment. Slowly I drew the clothes from her lovely body till my kisses reached her feet. When I lay down beside her, her flower-face smiled back at me omniscient and bountiful.

During this night by Maria's side I did not sleep much, but my sleep was as deep and peaceful as a child's. And between sleeping I drank of her beautiful warm youth and heard, as we talked softly, a number of curious tales about her life and Hermine's. I had never known much of this side of life. Only in the theatrical world, occasionally, in earlier years had I come across similar existences—women as well as men who lived half for art and half for pleasure. Now, for the first time, I had a glimpse into this kind of life, remarkable alike for its singular innocence and singular corruption. These girls, mostly from poor homes, but too intelligent and too pretty to give their whole lives to some ill-paid and joyless way of gaining their living, all lived sometimes on casual work, sometimes on their charm and easy virtue. Now and then, for a month or two, they sat at a typewriter; at times were the mistresses of well-to-do men of the world, receiving pocket money and presents; lived at times in furs and motorcars, at other times in attics, and though a good offer might under some circumstances induce them to marry, they were not at all eager for it. Many of them had little inclination for love and gave themselves very unwillingly, and then only for money and at the highest price. Others, and Maria was one of them, were unusually gifted in love and unable to do without it. They lived solely for love and besides their official and lucrative friends had other love affairs as well. Assiduous and busy, care-ridden and light-hearted, intelligent and yet thoughtless, these butterflies lived a life at once childlike and raffiné; independent, not to be bought by every one, finding their account in good luck and fine weather, in love with life and yet clinging to it far less than the bourgeois, always ready to follow a fairy prince to his castle, always certain, though scarcely conscious of it, that a difficult and sad end was in store for them.

During that wonderful first night and the days that followed Maria taught me much. She taught me the charming play and delights of the senses, but she gave me, also, new understanding, new insight, new love. The world of the dance and pleasure resorts, the cinemas, bars and hotel lounges that for me, the hermit and æsthete, had always about it something trivial, forbidden, and degrading, was for Maria and Hermine and their companions the world pure and simple. It was neither good nor bad, neither loved nor hated. In this world their brief and eager lives flowered and faded. They were at home in it and knew all its ways. They loved a champagne or a special dish at a restaurant as one of us might a composer or poet, and they lavished the same enthusiasm and rapture and emotion on the latest craze in dances or the sentimental cloying song of a jazz singer as one of us on Nietzsche or Hamsun. Maria talked to me about the handsome saxophone player, Pablo, and spoke of an American song that he had sung them sometimes, and she was so carried away with admiration and love as she spoke of it that I was far more moved and impressed than by the ecstasies of any highly cultured person over artistic pleasures of the rarest and most distinguished quality. I was ready to enthuse in sympathy, be the song what it might. Maria's glowing words and her eager effusive face made large rents in my æsthetics. There was to be sure a Beauty, one and indivisible, small and select, that seemed to me, with Mozart at the top, to be above all dispute and doubt, but where was the limit? Hadn't we all as connoisseurs and critics in our youth been consumed with love for works of art and for artists that today we regarded with doubt and dismay? Hadn't that happened to us with Liszt and Wagner, and, to many of us, even with Beethoven? Wasn't the blossoming of Maria's childish emotion over the song from America just as pure and beautiful an artistic experience and exalted as far beyond doubt as the rapture of any academic big-wig over Tristan, or the ecstasy of a conductor over the Ninth Symphony? And didn't this agree remarkably well with the views of Herr Pablo and prove him right?

Maria too appeared to love the beautiful Pablo extremely.

"He certainly is a beauty," said I. "I like him very much too. But tell me, Maria, how can you have a fondness for me as well, a tiresome old fellow with no looks, who even has grey hairs and doesn't play a saxophone and doesn't sing any English love-songs?"

"Don't talk so horribly," she scolded. "It is quite natural. I like you too. You, too, have something nice about you that endears you and marks you out. I wouldn't have you different. One oughtn't to talk of these things and want them accounted for. Listen, when you kiss my neck or my ear, I feel that I please you, that you like me. You have a way of kissing as though you were shy, and that tells me: 'You please him. He is grateful to you for being pretty.' That gives me great, great pleasure. And then again with another man it's just the opposite that pleases me, that he kisses me as though he thought little of me and conferred a favour."

Again we fell asleep and again I woke to find my arm still about her, my beautiful, beautiful flower.

And this beautiful flower, strange to say, continued to be none the less the gift that Hermine had made me. Hermine continued to stand in front of her and to hide her with a mask. Then suddenly the thought of Erica intervened—my distant, angry love, my poor friend. She was hardly less pretty than Maria, even though not so blooming; and she was more constrained, and not so richly endowed in the little arts of making love. She stood a moment before my eyes, clearly and painfully, loved and deeply woven into my destiny; then fell away again in a deep oblivion, at a half regretted distance.

And so in the tender beauty of the night many pictures of my life rose before me who for so long had lived in a poor pictureless vacancy. Now, at the magic touch of Eros, the source of them was opened up and flowed in plenty. For moments together my heart stood still between delight and sorrow to find how rich was the gallery of my life, and how thronged the soul of the wretched Steppenwolf with high eternal stars and constellations. My childhood and my mother showed in a tender transfiguration like a distant glimpse over mountains into the fathomless blue; the litany of my friendships, beginning with the legendary Herman, soul-brother of Hermine, rang out as clear as trumpets; the images of many women floated by me with an unearthly fragrance like moist sea-flowers on the surface of the water, women whom I had loved, desired and sung, whose love I had seldom won and seldom striven to win. My wife, too, appeared. I had lived with her many years and she had taught me comradeship, strife and resignation. In spite of all the shortcomings of our life, my confidence in her remained untouched up to the very day when she broke out against me and deserted me without warning, sick as I was in mind and body. And now, as I looked back, I saw how deep my love and trust must have been for her betrayal to have inflicted so deep and lifelong a wound.

These pictures—there were hundreds of them, with names and without—all came back. They rose fresh and new out of this night of love, and

I knew again, what in my wretchedness I had forgotten, that they were my life's possession and all its worth. Indestructible and abiding as the stars, these experiences, though forgotten, could never be erased. Their series was the story of my life, their starry light the undying value of my being. My life had become weariness. It had wandered in a maze of unhappiness that led to renunciation and nothingness; it was bitter with the salt of all human things; yet it had laid up riches, riches to be proud of. It had been for all its wretchedness a princely life. Let the little way to death be as it might, the kernel of this life of mine was noble. It had purpose and character and turned not on trifles, but on the stars.

Time has passed and much has happened, much has changed; and I can only remember a little of all that passed that night, a little of all we said and did in the deep tenderness of love, a few moments of clear awakening from the deep sleep of love's weariness. That night, however, for the first time since my downfall gave me back the unrelenting radiance of my own life and made me recognise chance as destiny once more and see the ruins of my being as fragments of the divine. My soul breathed once more. My eyes were opened. There were moments when I felt with a glow that I had only to snatch up my scattered images and raise my life as Harry Haller and as the Steppenwolf to the unity of one picture, in order to enter myself into the world of imagination and be immortal. Was not this, then, the goal set for the progress of every human life?

In the morning, after we had shared breakfast, I had to smuggle Maria from the house. Later in the same day I took a little room in a neighbouring quarter which was designed solely for our meetings.

True to her duties, Hermine, my dancing mistress, appeared and I had to learn the Boston. She was firm and inexorable and would not release me from a single lesson, for it was decided that I was to attend the Fancy Dress Ball in her company. She had asked me for money for her costume, but she refused to tell me anything about it. To visit her, or even to know where she lived, was still forbidden me.

This time, about three weeks before the Fancy Dress Ball, was remarkable for its wonderful happiness. Maria seemed to me to be the first woman I had ever really loved. I had always wanted mind and culture in the women I had loved, and I had never remarked that even the most intellectual and, comparatively speaking, educated woman never gave any response to the Logos in me, but rather constantly opposed it. I took my problems and my thoughts with me to the company of women and it would have seemed to me utterly impossible to love a girl for more than an hour who had scarcely read a book, scarcely knew what reading was, and could not have distinguished Tschaikovsky from Beethoven. Maria had no education. She had no need of these circuitous substitutes. Her problems all sprang directly from the senses.

All her art and the whole task she set herself lay in extracting the utmost delight from the senses she had been endowed with, and from her particular figure, her colour, her hair, her voice, her skin, her temperament; and in employing every faculty, every curve and line and every softest modelling of her body to find responsive perceptions in her lovers and to conjure up in them an answering quickness of delight. The first shy dance I had had with her had already told me this much. I had caught the scent and the charm of a brilliant and carefully cultivated sensibility and had been enchanted by it. Certainly, too, it was no accident that Hermine, the all-knowing, introduced me to this Maria. She had the scent and the very significance of summer and of roses.

It was not my fortune to be Maria's only lover, nor even her favourite one. I was one of many. Often she had no time for me, often only an hour at midday, seldom a night. She took no money from me. Hermine saw to that. She was glad of presents, however, and when I gave her, perhaps, a new little purse of red lacquered leather there might be two or three gold pieces inside it. As a matter of fact, she laughed at me over the red purse. It was charming, but a bargain, and no longer in fashion. In these matters, about which up to that time I was as little learned as in any language of the Esqui-maux, I learned a great deal from Maria. Before all else I learned that these playthings were not mere idle trifles invented by manufacturers and dealers for the purposes of gain. They were, on the contrary, a little or, rather, a big world, authoritative and beautiful, many sided, containing a multiplicity of things all of which had the one and only aim of serving love, refining the senses, giving life to the dead world around us, endowing it in a magical way with new instruments of love, from powder and scent to the dancing-show, from ring to cigarette-case, from waist-buckle to hand-bag. This bag was no bag, this purse no purse, flowers no flowers, the fan no fan. All were the plastic material of love, of magic and delight. Each was a messenger, a smuggler, a weapon, a battle-cry.

I often wondered who it was whom Maria really loved. I think she loved the young Pablo of the saxophone, with his melancholy black eyes and his long, white, distinguished, melancholy hands. I should have thought Pablo a somewhat sleepy lover, spoilt and passive, but Maria assured me that though it took a long time to wake him up he was then more strenuous and forward and virile than prize-fighter or riding master.

In this way I got to know many secrets about this person and that, jazz-musicians, actors and many of the women and girls and men of our circle. I saw beneath the surface of the various alliances and enmities and by degrees (though I had been such an entire stranger to this world) I was drawn in and treated with confidence. I learned a good deal about Hermine, too. It was of Herr Pablo, however, of whom Maria was fond, that I saw the most. At times she, too, availed herself of his secret drugs and was forever procuring these delights for me also; and Pablo was always most markedly on the alert to be of service to me. Once he said to me without more ado: "You are so very unhappy. That is bad. One shouldn't be like that. It makes me sorry. Try a mild pipe of opium." My opinion of this jolly, intelligent, childlike and, at the same time, unfathomable person gradually changed. We became friends, and I often took some of his specifics. He looked on at my affair with Maria with some amusement. Once he entertained us in his room on the top floor of an hotel in the suburbs. There was only one chair, so Maria and I had to sit on the bed. He gave us a drink from three little bottles, a mysterious and wonderful draught. And then when I had got into a very good humour, he proposed, with beaming eyes, to celebrate a love-orgy for three. I declined abruptly. Such a thing was inconceivable to me. Nevertheless I stole a glance at Maria to see how she took it, and though she at once backed up my refusal I saw the gleam in her eyes and observed that the renunciation cost her some regret. Pablo was disappointed by my refusal but not hurt. "Pity," he said. "Harry is too morally minded. Nothing to be done. All the same it would have been so beautiful, so very beautiful! But I've got another idea." He gave us each a little opium to smoke, and sitting motionless with open eyes we all three lived through the scenes that he suggested to us while Maria trembled with delight. As I felt a little unwell after this, Pablo laid me on the bed and gave me some drops, and while I lay with closed eyes I felt the fleeting breath of a kiss on each eyelid. I took the kiss as though I believed it came from Maria, but I knew very well it came from him.

And one evening he surprised me still more. Coming to me in my room he told me that he needed twenty francs and would I oblige him? In return he offered that I instead of him should have Maria for the night.

"Pablo," I said, very much shocked, "you don't know what you say. Barter for a woman is counted among us as the last degradation. I have not heard your proposal, Pablo."

He looked at me with pity. "You don't want to, Herr Harry. Very good. You're always making difficulties for yourself. Don't sleep tonight with Maria if you would rather not. But give me the money all the same. You shall have it back. I have urgent need of it."

"What for?"

"For Agostino, the little second violin, you know. He has been ill for a week and there's no one to look after him. He hasn't a son, nor have I at the moment."

From curiosity and also partly to punish myself, I went with him to Agostino. He took milk and medicine to him in his attic, and a wretched one it was. He made his bed and aired the room and made a most professional compress for the fevered head, all quickly and gently and efficiently like a good sick-nurse. The same evening I saw him playing till dawn in the City Bar.

I often talked at length and in detail about Maria with Hermine, about her hands and shoulders and hips and her way of laughing and kissing and dancing.

"Has she shown you this?" asked Hermine on one occasion, describing to me a peculiar play of the tongue in kissing. I asked her to show it me herself, but she was most earnest in her refusal. "That is for later. I am not your love yet."

I asked her how she was acquainted with Maria's ways of kissing and with many secrets as well that could be known only to her lovers.

"Oh," she cried, "we're friends, after all. Do you think we'd have secrets from one another? I must say you've got hold of a beautiful girl. There's no one like her."

"All the same, Hermine, I'm sure you have some secrets from each other, or have you told her everything you know about me?"

"No, that's another matter. Those are things she would not understand. Maria is wonderful. You are fortunate. But between you and me there are things she has not a notion of. Naturally I told her a lot about you, much more than you would have liked at the time. I had to win her for you, you see. But neither Maria nor anyone else will ever understand you as I understand you. I've learnt something about you from her besides, for she's told me all about you as far as she knows you at all. I know you nearly as well as if we had often slept together."

It was curious and mysterious to know, when I was with Maria again, that she had had Hermine in her arms just as she had me…. New, indirect and complicated relations rose before me, new possibilities in love and life; and I thought of the thousand souls of the Steppenwolf treatise.

* * * *

In the short interval between the time that I got to know Maria and the Fancy Dress Ball I was really happy; and yet I never had the feeling that this was my release and the attainment of felicity. I had the distinct impression, rather, that all this was a prelude and a preparation, that everything was pushing eagerly forward, that the gist of the matter was to come.

I was now so proficient in dancing that I felt quite equal to playing my part at the Ball of which everybody was talking. Hermine had a secret. She took the greatest care not to let out what her costume was to be. I would recognise her soon enough, she said, and should I fail to do so, she would help me; but beforehand I was to know nothing. She was not in the least inquisitive to know my plans for a fancy dress and I decided that I should not wear a costume at all. Maria, when I asked her to go with me as my partner, explained that she had a cavalier already and a ticket too, in fact; and I saw with some disappointment that I should have to attend the festivity alone. It was the principal Fancy Dress Ball of the town, organised yearly by the Society of Artists in the Globe Rooms.

During these days I saw little of Hermine, but the day before the Ball she paid me a brief visit. She came for her ticket, which I had got for her, and sat quietly with me for a while in my room. We fell into a conversation so remarkable that it made a deep impression on me.

"You're really doing splendidly," she said. "Dancing suits you. Any one who hadn't seen you for the last four weeks would scarcely know you."

"Yes," I agreed. "Things haven't gone so well with me for years. That's all your doing, Hermine."

"Oh, not the beautiful Maria's?"

"No. She is a present from you like all the rest. She is wonderful."

"She is just the girl you need, Steppenwolf—pretty, young, light hearted, an expert in love and not to be had every day. If you hadn't to share her with others, if she weren't always merely a fleeting guest, it would be another matter."

Yes, I had to concede this too.

"And so have you really got everything you want now?"

"No, Hermine. It is not like that. What I have got is very beautiful and delightful, a great pleasure, a great consolation. I'm really happy—"

"Well then, what more do you want?"

"I do want more. I am not content with being happy. I was not made for it. It is not my destiny. My destiny is the opposite."

"To be unhappy in fact? Well, you've had that and to spare, that time when you couldn't go home because of the razor."

"No, Hermine, it is something else. That time, I grant you, I was very unhappy. But it was a stupid unhappiness that led to nothing."

"Why?"

"Because I should not have had that fear of death when I wished for it all the same. The unhappiness that I need and long for is different. It is of the kind that will let me suffer with eagerness and lust after death. That is the unhappiness, or happiness, that I am waiting for."

"I understand that. There we are brother and sister. But what have you got against the happiness that you have found now with Maria? Why aren't you content?"

"I have nothing against it. Oh, no, I love it. I'm grateful for it. It is as lovely as a sunny day in a wet summer. But I suspect that it can't last. This happiness leads to nothing either. It gives content, but content is no food for me. It lulls the Steppenwolf to sleep and satiates him. But it is not a happiness to die for."

"So it's necessary to be dead, Steppenwolf?"

"I think so, yes. My happiness fills me with content and I can bear it for a long while yet. But sometimes when happiness leaves a moment's leisure to look about me and long for things, the longing I have is not to keep this happiness forever, but to suffer once again, only more beautifully and less meanly than before. I long for the sufferings that make me ready and willing to die."

Hermine looked tenderly in my eyes with that dark look that could so suddenly come into her face. Lovely, fearful eyes! Picking her words one by one and piecing them together, and speaking slowly and so low that it was an effort to hear her, she said:

"I want to tell you something today, something that I have known for a long while, and you know it too; but perhaps you have never said it to yourself. I am going to tell you now what it is that I know about you and me and our fate. You, Harry, have been an artist and a thinker, a man full of joy and faith, always on the track of what is great and eternal, never content with the trivial and petty. But the more life has awakened you and brought you back to yourself, the greater has your need been and the deeper the sufferings and dread and despair that have overtaken you, till you were up to the neck in them. And all that you once knew and loved and revered as beautiful and sacred, all the belief you once had in mankind and our high destiny, has been of no avail and has lost its worth and gone to pieces. Your faith found no more air to breathe. And suffocation is a hard death. Is that true, Harry? Is that your fate?"

I nodded again and again.

"You have a picture of life within you, a faith, a challenge, and you were ready for deeds and sufferings and sacrifices, and then you became aware by degrees that the world asked no deeds and no sacrifices of you whatever, and that life is no poem of heroism with heroic parts to play and so on, but a comfortable room where people are quite content with eating and drinking, coffee and knitting, cards and wireless. And whoever wants more and has got it in him—the heroic and the beautiful, and the reverence for the great poets or for the saints—is a fool and a Don Quixote. Good. And it has been just the same for me, my friend. I was a gifted girl. I was meant to live up to a high standard, to expect much of myself and do great things. I could have played a great part. I could have been the wife of a king, the beloved of a revolutionary, the sister of a genius, the mother of a martyr. And life has allowed me just this, to be a courtesan of fairly good taste, and even that has been hard enough. That is how things have gone with me. For a while I was inconsolable and for a long time I put the blame on myself. Life, thought I, must in the end be in the right, and if life scorned my beautiful dreams, so I argued, it was my dreams that were stupid and wrong-headed. But that did not help me at all. And as I had good eyes and ears and was a little inquisitive too, I took a good look at this so-called life and at my neighbours and acquaintances, fifty or so of them and their destinies, and then I saw you. And I knew that my dreams had been right a thousand times over, just as yours had been. It was life and reality that were wrong. It was as little right that a woman like me should have no other choice than to grow old in poverty and in a senseless way at a typewriter in the pay of a money-maker, or to marry such a man for his money's sake, or to become some kind of drudge, as for a man like you to be forced in his loneliness and despair to have recourse to a razor. Perhaps the trouble with me was more material and moral and with you more spiritual—but it was the same road. Do you think I can't understand your horror of the fox-trot, your dislike of bars and dancing floors, your loathing of jazz music and the rest of it? I understand it only too well, and your dislike of politics as well, your despondence over the chatter and irresponsible antics of the parties and the press, your despair over the war, the one that has been and the one that is to be, over all that people nowadays think, read and build, over the music they play, the celebrations they hold, the education they carry on. You are right, Steppenwolf, right a thousand times over, and yet you must go to the wall. You are much too exacting and hungry for this simple, easy-going and easily contented world of today. You have a dimension too many. Whoever wants to live and enjoy his life today must not be like you and me. Whoever wants music instead of noise, joy instead of pleasure, soul instead of gold, creative work instead of business, passion instead of foolery, finds no home in this trivial world of ours—"

She looked down and fell into meditation.

"Hermine," I cried tenderly, "sister, how clearly you see! And yet you taught me the fox-trot! But how do you mean that people like us with a dimension too many cannot live here? What brings it about? Is it only so in our days, or was it so always?"

"I don't know. For the honour of the world, I will suppose it to be in our time only—a disease, a momentary misfortune. Our leaders strain every nerve, and with success, to get the next war going, while the rest of us, meanwhile, dance the fox-trot, earn money and eat pralinées—in such a time the world must indeed cut a poor figure. Let us hope that other times were better, and will be better again, richer, broader and deeper. But that is no help to us now. And perhaps it has always been the same—"

"Always as it is today? Always a world only for politicians, profiteers, waiters and pleasure-seekers, and not a breath of air for men?"

"Well, I don't know. Nobody knows. Anyway, it is all the same. But I am thinking now of your favourite of whom you have talked to me sometimes, and read me, too, some of his letters, of Mozart. How was it with him in his day? Who controlled things in his times and ruled the roost and gave the tone and counted for something? Was it Mozart or the business people, Mozart or the average man? And in what fashion did he come to die and be buried? And perhaps, I mean, it has always been the same and always will be, and what is called history at school, and all we learn by heart there about heroes and geniuses and great deeds and fine emotions, is all nothing but a swindle invented by the schoolmasters for educational reasons to keep children occupied for a given number of years. It has always been so and always will be. Time and the world, money and power belong to the small people and the shallow people. To the rest, to the real men belongs nothing. Nothing but death."

"Nothing else?"

"Yes, eternity."

"You mean a name, and fame with posterity?"

"No, Steppenwolf, not fame. Has that any value? And do you think that all true and real men have been famous and known to posterity?"

"No, of course not."

"Then it isn't fame. Fame exists in that sense only for the schoolmasters. No, it isn't fame. It is what I call eternity. The pious call it the kingdom of God. I say to myself: all we who ask too much and have a dimension too many could not contrive to live at all if there were not another air to breathe outside the air of this world, if there were not eternity at the back of time; and this is the kingdom of truth. The music of Mozart belongs there and the poetry of your great poets. The saints, too, belong there, who have worked wonders and suffered martyrdom and given a great example to men. But the image of every true act, the strength of every true feeling, belongs to eternity just as much, even though no one knows of it or sees it or records it or hands it down to posterity. In eternity there is no posterity."

"You are right."

"The pious," she went on meditatively, "after all know most about this. That is why they set up the saints and what they call the communion of the saints. The saints, that is to say, the true men, the younger brothers of the Saviour. We are with them all our lives long in every good deed, in every brave thought, in every love. The communion of the saints, in earlier times it was set by painters in a golden heaven, shining, beautiful and full of peace, and it is nothing else but what I meant a moment ago when I called it eternity. It is the kingdom on the other side of time and appearances. It is there we belong. There is our home. It is that which our heart strives for. And for that reason, Steppenwolf, we long for death. There you will find your Goethe again and Novalis and Mozart, and I my saints, Christopher, Philip of Neri and all. There are many saints who at first were sinners. Even sin can be a way to saintliness, sin and vice. You will laugh at me, but I often think that even my friend Pablo might be a saint in hiding. Ah, Harry, we have to stumble through so much dirt and humbug before we reach home. And we have no one to guide us. Our only guide is our home-sickness."

With the last words her voice had sunk again and now there was a stillness of peace in the room. The sun was setting; it lit up the gilt lettering on the back of my books. I took Hermine's head in my hands and kissed her on the forehead and leant my cheek to hers as though she were my sister, and so we stayed for a moment. And so I should have liked best to stay and to have gone out no more that day. But Maria had promised me this night, the last before the great Ball.

But on my way to join Maria I thought, not of her, but of what Hermine had said. It seemed to me that it was not, perhaps, her own thoughts but mine. She had read them like a clairvoyant, breathed them in and given them back, so that they had a form of their own and came to me as something new. I was particularly thankful to her for having expressed the thought of eternity just at this time. I needed it, for without it I could not live and neither could I die. The sacred sense of beyond, of timelessness, of a world which had an eternal value and the substance of which was divine had been given back to me today by this friend of mine who taught me dancing.

I was forced to recall my dream of Goethe and that vision of the old wiseacre when he laughed so inhumanly and played his joke on me in the fashion of the immortals. For the first time I understood Goethe's laughter, the laughter of the immortals. It was a laughter without an object. It was simply light and lucidity. It was that which is left over when a true man has passed through all the sufferings, vices, mistakes, passions and misunderstandings of men and got through to eternity and the world of space. And eternity was nothing else than the redemption of time, its return to innocence, so to say, and its transformation again into space.

I went to meet Maria at the place where we usually dined. However, she had not arrived, and while I sat waiting at the table in the quiet and secluded restaurant, my thoughts still ran on the conversation I had had with Hermine. All these thoughts that had arisen between her and me seemed so intimate and well known, fashioned from a mythology and an imagery so entirely my own. The immortals, living their life in timeless space, enraptured, re-fashioned and immersed in a crystalline eternity like ether, and the cool starry brightness and radiant serenity of this world outside the earth—whence was all this so intimately known? As I reflected, passages of Mozart's *Cassations*, of Bach's *Well-tempered Clavier* came to my mind and it seemed to me that all through this music there was the radiance of this cool starry brightness and the quivering of this clearness of ether. Yes, it was there. In this music there was a feeling as of time frozen into space, and above it there quivered a never-ending and superhuman serenity, an eternal, divine laughter. Yes, and how well the aged Goethe of my dreams fitted in too! And suddenly I heard this fathomless laughter around me. I heard the immortals laughing. I sat entranced. Entranced, I felt for a pencil in my waistcoat pocket, and looking for paper saw the wine card lying on the table. I turned it over and wrote on the back. I wrote verses and forgot about them till one day I discovered them in my pocket. They ran:

THE IMMORTALS

Ever reeking from the vales of earth
Ascends to us life's fevered surge,
Wealth's excess, the rage of dearth,
Smoke of death-meals on the gallow's verge;
Greed without end, imprisoned air;
Murderers' hands, usurers' hands, hands of prayer;
Exhales in fœtid breath the human swarm
Whipped on by fear and lust, blood raw, blood warm,
Breathing blessedness and savage heats,
Eating itself and spewing what it eats,
Hatching war and lovely art,
Decking out with idiot craze
Bawdy houses while they blaze,
Through the childish fair-time mart
Weltering to its own decay
In the glare of pleasure's way,
Rising for each new-born and then
Sinking for each to dust again.
But we above you ever more residing
In the ether's star translumined ice
Know not day nor night nor time's dividing,
Wear nor age nor sex for our device.
All your sins and anguish self-affrighting,
Your murders and lascivious delighting
Are to us but as a show
Like the suns that circling go
Changing not our day for night;
On your frenzied life we spy,
And refresh ourselves thereafter
With the stars in order fleeing;
Our breath is winter; in our sight

Fawns the dragon of the sky;
Cool and unchanging is our eternal being,
Cool and star bright is our eternal laughter.

Then Maria came and after a cheerful meal I accompanied her to our little room. She was lovelier that evening, warmer and more intimate than she had ever been. The love she gave me was so tender that I felt it as the most complete abandon. "Maria," said I, "you are as prodigal today as a goddess. Don't kill us both quite. Tomorrow after all is the Ball. Whom have you got for a cavalier tomorrow? I'm very much afraid it is a fairy prince who will carry you off and I shall never see you any more. Your love tonight is almost like that of good lovers who bid each other farewell for the last time."

She put her lips close to my ear and whispered:

"Don't say that, Harry. Any time might be the last time. If Hermine takes you, you will come no more to me. Perhaps she will take you tomorrow."

Never did I experience the feeling peculiar to those days, that strange, bitter-sweet alternation of mood, more powerfully than on that night before the Ball. It was happiness that I experienced. There was the loveliness of Maria and her surrender. There was the sweet and subtle sensuous joy of inhaling and tasting a hundred pleasures of the senses that I had only begun to know as an elderly man. I was bathed in sweet joy like a rippling pool. And yet that was only the shell. Within all was significant and tense with fate, and while, love-lost and tender, I was busied with the little sweet appealing things of love and sank apparently without a care in the caress of happiness, I was conscious all the while in my heart how my fate raced on at breakneck speed, racing and chasing like a frightened horse, straight for the precipitous abyss, spurred on by dread and longing to the consummation of death. Just as a short while before I had started aside in fear from the easy thoughtless pleasure of merely sensual love and felt a dread of Maria's beauty that laughingly offered itself, so now I felt a dread of death, a dread, however, that was already conscious of its approaching change into surrender and release.

Even while we were lost in the silent and deep preoccupation of our love and belonged more closely than ever we had to one another, my soul bid adieu to Maria, and leave of all that she had meant to me. I had learnt from her, once more before the end, to confide myself like a child to life's surface play, to pursue a fleeting joy, and to be both child and beast in the innocence of sex—a state that (in earlier life) I had only known rarely and as an exception. The life of the senses and of sex had nearly always had for me the bitter accompaniment of guilt, the sweet but dread taste of forbidden fruit that puts a spiritual man on his guard. Now, Hermine and Maria had shown me this garden in its innocence, and I had been a guest there and thankfully. But it would soon be time to go on further. It was too agreeable and too warm in this garden. It was my destiny to make another bid for the crown of life in the expiation of its endless guilt. An easy life, an easy love, an easy death—these were not for me.

From what the girls told me I gathered that for the Ball next day, or in connection with it, quite unusual delights and extravagances were on foot. Perhaps it was the climax, and perhaps Maria's suspicion was correct. Perhaps this was our last night together and perhaps the morning would bring a new unwinding of fate. I was aflame with longing and breathless with dread; I clung wildly to Maria; and there flared within me a last burst of wild desire....

* * * *

I made up by day for the sleep I had lost at night. After a bath I went home dead tired. I darkened my bedroom and as I undressed I came on the verses in my pocket; but I forgot them again and lay down forthwith. I forgot Maria and Hermine and the Masked Ball and slept the clock round. It was not till I had got up in the evening and was shaving that I remembered that the Ball began in an hour and that I had to find a dress shirt. I got myself ready in very good humour and went out thereafter to have dinner.

It was the first Masked Ball I was to participate in. In earlier days, it is true, I had now and again attended such festivities and even sometimes found them very entertaining, but I had never danced. I had been a spectator merely. As for the enthusiasm with which others had talked and rejoiced over them in my hearing, it had always struck me as comic. And now the day had come for me too to find the occasion one of almost painful suspense. As I had no partner to take, I decided not to go till late. This, too, Hermine had counselled me.

I had seldom of late been to the Steel Helmet, my former refuge, where the disappointed men sat out their evenings, soaking in their wine and playing at bachelor life. It did not suit the life I had come to lead since. This evening, however, I was drawn to it before I was aware. In the mood between joy and fear that fate and parting imposed on me just now, all the stations and shrines of meditation in my life's pilgrimage caught once more that gleam of pain and beauty that comes from things past; and so too had the little tavern, thick with smoke, among whose patrons I had lately been numbered and whose primitive opiate of a bottle of land-wine had lately heartened me enough to spend one more night in my lonely bed and to endure life for one more day. I had tasted other specifics and stronger stimulus since then, and sipped a sweeter poison. With a smile I entered the ancient hostel. The landlady greeted me and so, with a nod, did the silent company of habitués. A roast chicken was commended and soon set before me. The limpid Elsasser sparkled in the thick peasant glass. The clean white wooden tables and the old yellow wainscoting had a friendly look. And while I ate and drank there came over me that feeling of change and decay and of farewell celebrations, that sweet and inwardly painful feeling of being a living part of all the scenes and all the things of an earlier life that has never yet been parted from, and from which the time to part has come. The modern man calls this sentimentality. He has lost the love of inanimate objects. He does not even love his most sacred object, his motorcar, but is ever hoping to exchange it as soon as he can for a later model. This modern man has energy and ability. He is healthy, cool and strenuous—a splendid type, and in the next war he will be a miracle of efficiency. But all that was no concern of mine. I was not a modern man, nor an old-fashioned one either. I had escaped time altogether, and went my way, with death at my elbow and death as my resolve. I had no objection to sentimentalities. I was glad and thankful to find a trace of anything like a feeling still remaining in my burnt-out heart. So I let my memories of the old tavern and my attachment to the solid wooden chairs and the smell of smoke and wine and the air of use and wont and warmth and homeliness that the place had carry me away. There is beauty in farewells and a gentleness in their very tone. The hard seat was dear to me, and so was the peasant glass and the cool racy taste of the Elsasser and my intimacy with all and everything in this room, and the faces of the bent and dreaming drinkers, those disillusioned ones, whose brother I had been for so long. All this was bourgeois sentimentality, lightly seasoned with a touch of the old-fashioned romance of inns, a romance coming from my boyhood when inns and wine and cigars were still forbidden things—strange and wonderful. But no Steppenwolf rose before me baring his teeth to tear my sentiment to pieces. I sat there in peace in the glow of the past whose setting still shed a faint after-glow.

A street seller came in and I bought a handful of roasted chestnuts. An old dame came in with flowers and I bought a bunch of violets and presented them to the landlady. It was not till I was about to pay my bill and felt in vain for the pocket of the coat I usually wore that I realised once more than I was in evening dress. The Masked Ball. And Hermine!

It was still early enough, however. I could not convince myself to go to the Globe Rooms straight away. I felt too—as I had in the case of all the pleasures that had lately come my way—a whole array of checks and resistances. I had no inclination to enter the large and crowded and noisy rooms. I had a schoolboy's shyness of the strange atmosphere and the world of pleasure and dancing.

As I sauntered along I passed by a cinema with its dazzling lights and huge coloured posters. I went on a few steps, then turned again and went in. There till eleven I could sit quietly and comfortably in the dark. Following the attendant with the pocket light I stumbled through the curtains into the darkened hall, found a seat and was suddenly in the middle of the Old Testament.

The film was one of those that are nominally not shown for money. Much expense and many refinements are lavished upon them in a more sacred and nobler cause, and at midday even school-children are brought to see them by their religious teachers. This one was the story of Moses and the Israelites in Egypt, with a huge crowd of men, horses, camels, palaces, splendours of the Pharaohs and tribulations of the Jews in the desert. I saw Moses, whose hair recalled portraits of Walt Whitman, a splendidly theatrical Moses, wandering through the desert at the head of the Jews, with a dark and fiery eye and a long staff and the stride of a Wotan. I saw him pray to God at the edge of the Red Sea, and I saw the Red Sea parted to give free passage, a deep road between piled-up mountains of water (the confirmation classes conducted by the clergy to see this religious film could argue without end as to how the film people managed this). I saw the prophet and his awestruck people pass through to the other side, and behind them I saw the war-chariots of Pharaoh come into sight and the Egyptians stop and start on the brink of the sea, and then, when they ventured courageously on, I saw the mountainous waters close over the heads of Pharaoh in all the splendour of his gold trappings and over all his chariots and all his men, recalling, as I saw it, Handel's wonderful duet for two basses in which this event is magnificently sung. I saw Moses, further, climbing Sinai, a gloomy hero in a gloomy wilderness of rocks, and I looked on as Jehovah in the midst of storm and thunder and lightning imparted the Ten Commandments to him, while his worthless people set up the golden calf at the foot of the mountain and gave themselves over to somewhat roisterous celebrations. I found it so strange and incredible to be looking on at all this, to be seeing the sacred writ, with its heroes and its wonders, the source in our childhood of the first dawning suspicion of another world than this, presented for money before a grateful public that sat quietly eating the provisions brought with it from home. A nice little picture, indeed, picked up by chance in the huge wholesale clearance of culture in these days! My God, rather than come to such a pass it would have been better for the Jews and every one else, let alone the Egyptians, to have perished in those days and forthwith of a violent and becoming death instead of this dismal pretence of dying by inches that we go in for today. Yes indeed!

My secret repressions and unconfessed fright in face of the Masked Ball were by no means lessened by the feelings provoked in me by the cinema. On the contrary, they had grown to uncomfortable proportions and I had to shake myself and think of Hermine before I could go to the Globe Rooms and dared to enter. It was late, and the Ball had been for a long time in full swing. At once before I had even taken off my things I was caught up, shy and sober as I was, in the swirl of the masked throng. I was accosted familiarly. Girls summoned me to the champagne rooms. Clowns slapped me on the back, and I was addressed on all sides as an old friend. I responded to none of it, but fought my way through the crowded rooms to the cloak-room, and when I got my cloak-room ticket I put it in my pocket with great care, reflecting that I might need it before very long when I had had enough of the uproar.

Every part of the great building was given over to the festivities. There was dancing in every room and in the basement as well. Corridors and stairs were filled to overflowing with masks and dancing and music and laughter and tumult. Oppressed in heart I stole through the throng, from the jazz orchestra to the peasant band, from the large and brilliantly lighted principal room into the passages and on to the stairs, to bars, buffets and champagne parlours. The walls were mostly hung with wild and cheerful paintings by the latest artists. All the world was there, artists, journalists, professors, business men, and of course every adherent of pleasure in the town. In one of the orchestras sat Pablo, blowing with enthusiasm in his curved mouth-piece. As soon as he saw me he sang out a greeting. Pushed hither and thither in the crowd I found myself in one room after another, upstairs here and downstairs there. A corridor in the basement had been staged as hell by the artists and there a band of devils played furiously. After a while, I began to look for Hermine or Maria and strove time after time to reach the principal room; but either I missed my way or had to meet the current. By midnight I had found no one, and though I had not danced I was hot and giddy. I threw myself into the nearest chair among utter strangers and ordered some wine, and came to the conclusion that joining in such rowdy festivals was no part for an old man like me. I drank my glass of wine while I stared at the naked arms and backs of the women, watched the crowd of grotesquely masked figures drifting by and silently declined the advances of a few girls who wished to sit on my knee or get me to dance. "Old Growler," one called after me; and she was right. I decided to raise my spirits with the wine, but even the wine went against me and I could scarcely swallow a second glass. And then the feeling crept over me that the Steppenwolf was standing behind me with his tongue out. Nothing pleased me. I was in the wrong place. To be sure, I had come with the best intentions, but this was no place for me to be merry in; and all this loud effervescence of pleasure, the laughter and the whole foolery of it on every side, seemed to me forced and stupid.

Thus it was that, at about one o'clock, in anger and disillusionment I steered a course for the cloak-room, to put on my coat again and go. It was surrender and backsliding into my wolfishness, and Hermine would scarcely forgive it me. But I could not do otherwise. All the way as I squeezed through the throng to the cloak-room, I still kept a careful look-out in case I might yet see one of my friends, but in vain. Now I stood at the counter. Already the attendant was politely extending his hand for my number. I felt in my waistcoat pocket—the number was no longer there! The devil was in it if even this failed me. Often enough during my forlorn wanderings through the rooms and while I sat over my tasteless wine I had felt in my pocket, fighting back the resolve to go away again, and I had always found the round flat check in its place. And now it was gone. Everything was against me.

"Lost your number?" came in a shrill voice from a small red and yellow devil at my elbow. "Here, comrade, you can take mine," and he held it out to me without more ado. While I mechanically took it and turned it over in my fingers the brisk little fellow rapidly disappeared.

When, however, I examined the pasteboard counter for a number, no number was to be seen. Instead there was a scribble in a tiny hand. I asked the attendant to wait and went to the nearest light to read it. There in little crazy letters that were scarcely legible was scrawled:

TONIGHT AT THE MAGIC THEATRE

FOR MADMEN ONLY

PRICE OF ADMITTANCE YOUR MIND.
NOT FOR EVERYBODY. HERMINE IS IN HELL.

As a marionette whose thread the operator has let go for a moment wakes to new life after a brief paralysis of death and coma and once more plays its lively part, so did I at this jerk of the magic thread throw myself with the elasticity and eagerness of youth into the tumult from which I had just retreated in the listlessness and weariness of elderly years. Never did sinner show more haste to get to hell. A moment before my patent-leather shoes had galled me, the heavily scented air disgusted me, and the heat undone me. Now on my winged feet I nimbly one-stepped through every room on the way to hell. The very air had a charm. The warmth embedded me and wafted me on, and so no less did the riotous music, the intoxication of colours, the perfume of women's shoulders, the clamour of the hundred tongues, the laughter, the rhythm of the dance, and the glances of all the kindled eyes.

A Spanish dancing girl flung herself into my arms: "Dance with me!"

"Can't," said I. "I'm bound for hell. But I'll gladly take a kiss with me."

The red mouth beneath the mask met mine and with the kiss I recognised Maria. I caught her tight in my arms and like a June rose bloomed her full lips. By this time we were dancing, our lips still joined. Past Pablo we danced, who hung like a lover over his softly wailing instrument. Those lovely animal eyes embraced us with their half-abstracted radiance. But before we had gone twenty steps the music broke off and regretfully I let go of Maria.

"I'd have loved to have danced with you again," I said, intoxicated with her warmth. "Come with me a step or two, Maria. I'm in love with your beautiful arm. Let me have it a moment longer! But, you see, Hermine has summoned me. She is in hell."

"I thought so. Farewell, Harry. I won't forget you." She left me—left me indeed. Yes, it was autumn, it was fate, that had given the summer rose so full and ripe a scent.

On I went through the long corridors, luxuriously thronged, and down the stairs to hell. There, on pitch-black walls shone wicked garish lights, and the orchestra of devils was playing feverishly. On a high stool at the bar there was seated a pretty young fellow without a mask and in evening dress who scrutinised me with a cursory and mocking glance. Pressed to the wall by the swirl of dancers—about twenty couples were dancing in this very confined space—I examined all the women with eager suspense. Most were still in masks and smiled at me, but none was Hermine. The handsome youth on the high stool glanced mockingly at me. At the next pause, thought I, she will come and summon me. The dance ended but no one came.

I went over to the bar which was squeezed into a corner of the small and low room, and taking a seat near the young man ordered a whisky. While I drank it I saw his profile. It had a familiar charm, like a picture from long ago, precious for the very dust that has settled on it from the past. Oh, then it flashed through me. It was Herman, the friend of my youth.

"Herman!" I stammered.

She smiled. "Harry? Have you found me?"

It was Hermine, barely disguised by the make-up of her hair and a little paint. The stylish collar gave an unfamiliar look to the pallor of her intelligent face, the wide black sleeves of her dress-coat and the white cuffs made her hands look curiously small, and the long black trousers gave a curious elegance to her feet in their black and white silk socks.

"Is this the costume, Hermine, in which you mean to make me fall in love with you?"

"So far," she said, "I have contented myself with turning the heads of the ladies. But now your turn has come. First, let's have a glass of champagne."

So we did, perched on our stools, while the dance went on around us to the lively and fevered strain of the strings. And without Hermine appearing to give herself the least trouble I was very soon in love with her. As she was dressed as a boy, I could not dance with her nor allow myself any tender advances, and while she seemed distant and neutral in her male mask, her looks and words and gestures encircled me with all her feminine charm. Without so much as having touched her I surrendered to her spell, and this spell itself kept within the part she played. It was the spell of a hermaphrodite. For she talked to me about Herman and about childhood, mine and her own, and about those years of childhood when the capacity for love, in its first youth, embraces not only both sexes, but all and everything, sensuous and spiritual, and endows all things with a spell of love and a fairy-like ease of transformation such as in later years comes again only to a chosen few and to poets, and to them rarely. Throughout she kept up the part of a young man, smoking cigarettes and talking with a spirited ease that often had a little mockery in it; and yet it was all iridescent with the rays of desire and transformed, as it reached my senses, into a charming seduction.

How well and thoroughly I thought I knew Hermine, and yet what a completely new revelation of herself she opened up to me that night! How gently and inconspicuously she cast the net I longed for around me, and how playfully and how like a pixie she gave the sweet poison to drink!

We sat and talked and drank champagne. We strolled through the rooms and looked about us. We went on voyages of exploration to discover couples whose love-making it amused us to spy upon. She pointed out women whom she recommended me to dance with, and gave me advice as to the methods of attack to be employed with each. We took the floor as rivals and paid court for a while to the same girl, danced with her by turns and both tried to win her heart. And yet it was all only a carnival, only a game between the two of us that caught us more closely together in our own passion. It was all a fairy tale. Everything had a new dimension, a deeper meaning. Everything was fanciful and symbolic. There was one girl of great beauty but looking tragic and unhappy. Herman danced with her and drew her out. They disappeared to drink champagne together, and she told me afterwards that she had made a conquest of her not as a man but as a woman, with the spell of Lesbos. For my part, the whole building, reverberating everywhere with the sound of dancing, and the whole intoxicated crowd of masks, became by degrees a wild dream of paradise. Flower upon flower wooed me with its scent. I toyed with fruit after fruit. Serpents looked at me from green and leafy shadows with mesmeric eyes. Lotus blossoms luxuriated over black bogs. Enchanted birds sang allurement from the trees. Yet all was a progress to one longed-for goal, the summons of a new yearning for one and one only. Once I was dancing with a girl I did not know. I had swept her with the ardour of a lover into the giddy swirl of dancers and while we hung in this unreal world, she suddenly remarked with a laugh: "One wouldn't know you. You were so dull and flat before." Then I recognised the girl who had called me "Old Growler" a few hours before. She thought she had got me now, but with the next dance it was another for whom my ardour glowed. I danced without ceasing for two hours or more—every dance and some, even, that I had never danced before. Every now and then Herman was near me, and gave me a nod and a smile as he disappeared in the throng.

An experience fell to my lot this night of the Ball that I had never known in all my fifty years, though it is known to every flapper and student—the intoxication of a general festivity, the mysterious merging of the personality in the mass, the mystic union of joy. I had often heard it spoken of. It was known, I knew, to every servant girl. I had often observed the sparkle in the eye of those who told me of it and I had always treated it with a half-superior, half-envious smile. A hundred times in my life I had seen examples of those whom rapture had intoxicated and released from the self, of that smile, that half-crazed absorption, of those whose heads have been turned by a common enthusiasm. I had seen it in drunken recruits and sailors, and also in great artists in the enthusiasm, perhaps, of a musical festival; and not less in young soldiers going to war. Even in recent days I had marvelled at and loved and mocked and envied this gleam and this smile in my friend, Pablo, when he hung over his saxophone in the blissful intoxication of playing in the orchestra, or when, enraptured and ecstatic, he looked over to the conductor, the drum, or the man with the banjo. It had sometimes occurred to me that such a smile, such a childlike radiance could be possible only to quite young persons or among those peoples whose customs permitted no marked differences between one individual and another. But today, on this blessed night, I myself, the Steppenwolf, was radiant with this smile. I myself swam in this deep and childlike happiness of a fairy-tale. I myself breathed the sweet intoxication of a common dream and of music and rhythm and wine and women—I, who had in other days so often listened with amusement, or dismal superiority, to its panegyric in the ball-room chatter of some student. I was myself no longer. My personality was dissolved in the intoxication of the festivity like salt in water. I danced with this woman or that, but it was not only the one I had in my arms and whose hair brushed my face that belonged to me. All the other women who were dancing in the same room and the same dance and to the same music, and whose radiant faces floated past me like fantastic flowers, belonged to me, and I to them. All of us had a part in one another. And the men too. I was with them also. They, too, were no strangers to me. Their smile was mine, and mine their wooing and theirs mine.

A new dance, a fox-trot, with the title *Yearning*, had swept the world that winter. Once we had heard it we could not have enough of it. We were all soaked in it and intoxicated with it and every one hummed the melody whenever it was played. I danced without stop and with anyone who came in my way, with quite young girls, with women in their earlier or their latter prime, and with those who had sadly passed them both; and with them all I was enraptured—laughing, happy, radiant. And when Pablo saw me so radiant, me whom he had always looked on as a very lamentable poor devil, his eyes beamed blissfully upon me and he was so inspired that he got up from his chair and blowing lustily in his horn climbed up on it. From this elevation he blew with all his might, while at the same time his whole body, and his instrument with it, swayed to the tune of *Yearning*. I and my partner kissed our hands to him and sang loudly in response. Ah, thought I, meanwhile, let come to me what may, for once at least, I, too, have been happy, radiant, released from myself, a brother of Pablo's, a child.

I had lost the sense of time, and I don't know how many hours or moments the intoxication of happiness lasted. I did not observe either that the brighter the festal fire burned the narrower were the limits within which it was confined. Most people had already left. The corridors were silent and many of the lights out. The stairs were deserted and in the rooms above one orchestra after another had stopped playing and gone away. It was only in the principal room and in Hell below that the orgy still raged in a crescendo. Since I could not dance with Hermine as a boy, we had only had fleeting encounters in the pauses between the dances, and at last I lost sight of her entirely—and not only sight but thought. There were no thoughts left. I was lost in the maze and whirl of the dance. Scents and tones and sighs and words stirred me. I was greeted and kindled by strange eyes, encircled by strange faces, borne hither and thither in time to the music as though by a wave.

And then of a sudden I saw, half coming to my senses for a moment, among the last who still kept it up in one of the smaller rooms, and filled it to overflowing—the only one in which the music still sounded—of a sudden I saw a black Pierrette with face painted white. She was fresh and charming, the only masked figure left and a bewitching apparition that I had never in the whole course of the night seen before. While in every one else the late hour showed itself in flushed and heated faces, crushed dresses, limp collars and crumpled ruffs, the black Pierrette stood there fresh and neat with her white face beneath her mask. Her costume had not a crease and not a hair was out of place. Her ruff and pointed cuffs were untouched. I rushed towards her, put my arms around her, and drew her into the dance. Her perfumed ruff tickled my chin. Her hair brushed my cheek. The young vigour of her body answered my movements as no one's else had done that night, yielding to them with an inward tenderness and compelling them to new contacts by the play of her allurements. I bent down to kiss her mouth as we danced. Its smile was triumphant and long familiar. Of a sudden I recognised the firm chin, the shoulders, arms and hands. It was Hermine, Herman no longer. Hermine in a change of dress, fresh, perfumed, powdered. Our lips met passionately. For a moment her whole body to her knees clung in longing and surrender to mine. Then she drew her mouth away and, holding back, fled from me as we danced. When the music broke off we were still clasped where we stood. All the excited couples round us clapped, stamped, cried out and urged the exhausted orchestra to play *Yearning* over again. And now a feeling that it was morning fell upon us all. We saw the ashen light behind the curtains. It warned us of pleasure's approaching end and gave us symptoms of the weariness to come. Blindly, with bursts of laughter, we flung ourselves desperately into the dance once more, into the music, and the light that began to flood the room. Our feet moved in time to the music as though we were possessed, every couple touching, and once more we felt the great wave of bliss break over us. Hermine abandoned her triumphant air, her mockery and coolness. She knew that there was no more to do to make me in love with her. I was hers, and her way of dancing, her looks and smiles and kisses all showed that she gave herself to me. All the women of this fevered night, all that I had danced with, all whom I had kindled or who had kindled me, all whom I had courted, all who had clung to me with longing, all whom I had followed with enraptured eyes were melted together and had become one, the one whom I held in my arms.

On and on went this nuptial dance. Time after time the music flagged. The wind let their instruments fall. The pianist got up from the piano. The first fiddle shook his head. And every time they were won over by the imploring persistence of the last intoxicated dancers and played once more. They played faster and more wildly. Then at last, as we stood, still entwined and breathless after the last eager dance, the piano was closed with a bang, and our arms fell wearily to our sides like those of the wind and strings and the flutist, blinking sleepily, put his flute away in its case. Doors opened, the cold air poured in, attendants appeared with cloaks and the bar-waiter turned off the light. The whole scene vanished eerily away and the dancers who a moment ago had been all on fire shivered as they put on coats and cloaks and turned up their collars. Hermine was pale but smiling. Slowly she raised her arm and pushed back her hair. As she did so one arm caught the light and a faint and indescribably tender shadow ran from her arm-pit to her hidden breast, and this little trembling line of shadow seemed to me to sum up all the charm and fascination of her body like a smile.

We stood looking at one another, the last in the hall, the last in the whole building. Somewhere below I heard a door bang, a glass break, a titter of laughter die away, mixed with the angry hurried noise of motorcars starting up. And somewhere, at an indeterminable distance and height, I heard a laugh ring out, an extraordinarily clear and merry peal of laughter. Yet it was eerie and strange. It was a laugh, made of crystal and ice, bright and radiant, but cold and inexorable. Where had I heard this laugh before? I could not tell.

We stood and looked at one another. For a moment I came to my sober self. I felt a fearful weariness descend upon me. I felt with repugnance how moist and limp my clothing hung around me. I saw my hands emerging red and with swollen veins from my crumpled and wilted cuffs. But all at once the mood passed, banished by a look from Hermine. At this look that seemed to come from my own soul all reality fell away, even the reality of my sensuous love of her. Bewitched we looked at one another, while my poor little soul looked at me.

"You're ready?" asked Hermine, and her smile fled away like the shadows on her breast. Far up in unknown space rang out that strange and eerie laughter.

I nodded. Oh, yes, I was ready.

At this moment Pablo appeared in the doorway and beamed on us out of his jolly eyes that really were animal's eyes except that animal's eyes are always serious, while his always laughed, and this laughter turned them into human eyes. He beckoned to us with his usual friendly cordiality. He had put on a gorgeous silk smoking-jacket. His limp collar and tired white face had a withered and pallid look above its red facings; but the impression was erased by his radiant black eyes. So was reality erased, for they too had the witchery.

We joined him when he beckoned and in the doorway he said to me in a low voice: "Brother Harry, I invite you to a little entertainment. For madmen only, and one price only—your mind. Are you ready?"

Again I nodded.

The dear fellow gave us each an arm with kind solicitude, Hermine his right, me his left, and conducted us upstairs to a small round room that was lit from the ceiling with a bluish light and nearly empty. There was nothing in it but a small round table and three easy chairs in which we sat ourselves.

Where were we? Was I asleep? Was I at home? Was I driving in a car? No, I was sitting in a blue light in a round room and a rare atmosphere, in a stratum of reality that had become rarefied in the extreme.

Why then was Hermine so white? Why was Pablo talking so much? Was it not perhaps I who made him talk, spoke, indeed, with his voice? Was it not, too, my own soul that contemplated me out of his black eyes like a lost and frightened bird, just as it had out of Hermine's grey ones?

Pablo looked at us good-naturedly as ever and with something ceremonious in his friendliness; and he talked much and long. He whom I had never heard say two consecutive sentences, whom no discussion nor thesis could interest, whom I had scarcely credited with a single thought, discoursed now in his good-natured warm voice fluently and without a fault.

"My friends, I have invited you to an entertainment that Harry has long wished for and of which he has long dreamed. The hour is a little late and no doubt we are all slightly fatigued. So, first, we will rest and refresh ourselves a little."

From a recess in the wall he took three glasses and a quaint little bottle, also a small oriental box inlaid with differently coloured woods. He filled the three glasses from the bottle and taking three long thin yellow cigarettes from the box and a box of matches from the pocket of his silk jacket he gave us a light. And now we all slowly smoked the cigarettes whose smoke was as thick as incense, leaning back in our chairs and slowly sipping the aromatic liquid whose strange taste was so utterly unfamiliar. Its effect was immeasurably enlivening and delightful—as though one were filled with gas and had no longer any gravity. Thus we sat peacefully exhaling small puffs and taking little sips at our glasses, while every moment we felt ourselves growing lighter and more serene.

From far away came Pablo's warm voice.

"It is a pleasure to me, my dear Harry, to have the privilege of being your host in a small way on this occasion. You have often been sorely weary of your life. You were striving, were you not, for escape? You have a longing to forsake this world and its reality and to penetrate to a reality more native to you, to a world beyond time. You know, of course, where this other world lies hidden. It is the world of your own soul that you seek. Only within yourself exists that other reality for which you long. I can give you nothing that has not already its being within yourself. I can throw open to you no picture-gallery but your own soul. All I can give you is the opportunity, the impulse, the key. I help you to make your own world visible. That is all."

Again he put his hand into the pocket of his gorgeous jacket and drew out a round looking-glass.

"Look, it is thus that you have so far seen yourself."

He held the little glass before my eyes (a childish verse came to my mind: "Little glass, little glass in the hand") and I saw, though indistinctly and cloudily, the reflection of an uneasy self-tormented, inwardly labouring and seething being—myself, Harry Haller. And within him again I saw the Steppenwolf, a shy, beautiful, dazed wolf with frightened eyes that smouldered now with anger, now with sadness. This shape of a wolf coursed through the other in ceaseless movement, as a tributary pours its cloudy turmoil into a river. In bitter strife, each tried to devour the other so that his shape might prevail. How unutterably sad was the look this fluid inchoate figure of the wolf threw from his beautiful shy eyes.

"There you see yourself," Pablo remarked and put the mirror away in his pocket. I was thankful to close my eyes and take a sip of the elixir.

"And now," said Pablo, "we have had our rest. We have had our refreshment and a little talk. If your fatigue has passed off I will conduct you to my peep-show and show you my little theatre. Will you come?"

We got up. With a smile Pablo led. He opened a door, and drew a curtain aside and we found ourselves in the horseshoe-shaped corridor of a theatre, and exactly in the middle. On either side, the curving passage led past a large number, indeed an incredible number, of narrow doors into the boxes.

"This," explained Pablo, "is our theatre, and a jolly one it is. I hope you'll find lots to laugh at." He laughed aloud as he spoke, a short laugh, but it went through me like a shot. It was the same bright and peculiar laugh that I had heard before from below.

"This little theatre of mine has as many doors into as many boxes as you please, ten or a hundred or a thousand, and behind each door exactly what you seek awaits you. It is a pretty cabinet of pictures, my dear friend; but it would be quite useless for you to go through it as you are. You would be checked and blinded at every turn by what you are pleased to call your personality. You have no doubt guessed long since that the conquest of time and the escape from reality, or however else it may be that you choose to describe your longing, means simply the wish to be relieved of your so-called personality. That is the prison where you lie. And if you were to enter the theatre as you are, you would see everything through the eyes of Harry and the old spectacles of the Steppenwolf. You are therefore requested to lay these spectacles aside and to be so kind as to leave your highly esteemed personality here in the cloak-room where you will find it again when you wish. The pleasant dance from which you have just come, the treatise on the Steppenwolf, and the little stimulant that we have only this moment partaken of may have sufficiently prepared you. You, Harry, after having left behind your valuable personality, will have the left side of the theatre at your disposal, Hermine the right. Once inside, you can meet each other as you please. Hermine will be so kind as to go for a moment behind the curtain. I should like to introduce Harry first."

Hermine disappeared to the right past a gigantic mirror that covered the rear wall from floor to vaulted ceiling.

"Now, Harry, come along be as jolly as you can. To make it so and to teach you to laugh is the whole aim in getting up this entertainment—I hope you will make it easy for me. You feel quite well, I trust? Not afraid? That's good, excellent. You will now, without fear and with unfeigned pleasure, enter our visionary world. You will introduce yourself to it by means of a trifling suicide, since this is the custom."

He took out the pocket-mirror again and held it in front of my face. Again I was confronted by the same indistinct and cloudy reflection, with the wolf's shape encircling it and coursing through it. I knew it too well and disliked it too sincerely for its destruction to cause me any sorrow.

"You will now extinguish this superfluous reflection, my dear friend. That is all that is necessary. To do so, it will suffice that you greet it, if your mood permits, with a hearty laugh. You are here in a school of humour. You are to learn to laugh. Now, true humour begins when a man ceases to take himself seriously."

I fixed my eyes on the little mirror, where the man Harry and the wolf were going through their convulsions. For a moment there was a convulsion deep within me too, a faint but painful one like remembrance, or like homesickness, or like remorse. Then the slight oppression gave way to a new feeling like that a man feels when a tooth has been extracted with cocaine, a sense of relief and of letting out a deep breath, and of wonder, at the same time, that it has not hurt in the least. And this feeling was accompanied by a buoyant exhilaration and a desire to laugh so irresistible that I was compelled to give way to it.

The mournful image in the glass gave a final convulsion and vanished. The glass itself turned grey and charred and opaque, as though it had been burnt. With a laugh Pablo threw the thing away and it went rolling down the endless corridor and disappeared.

"Well laughed, Harry," cried Pablo. "You will learn to laugh like the immortals yet. You have done with the Steppenwolf at last. It's no good with a razor. Take care that he stays dead. You'll be able to leave the farce of reality behind you directly. At our next meeting we'll drink brotherhood, dear fellow. I never liked you better than I do today. And if you still think it worth your while we can philosophise together and argue and talk about music and Mozart and Gluck and Plato and Goethe to your heart's content. You will understand now why it was so impossible before. I wish you good riddance of the Steppenwolf for today at any rate. For naturally, your suicide is not a final one. We are in a magic theatre; a world of pictures, not realities. See that you pick out beautiful and cheerful ones and show that you really are not in love with your highly questionable personality any longer. Should you still, however, have a hankering after it, you need only have another look in the mirror that I will now show you. But you know the old proverb: 'A mirror in the hand is worth two on the wall?' Ha ha!" (again that laugh, beautiful and frightful!) "And now there only remains one little ceremony and quite a jolly one. You have now to cast aside the spectacles of your personality. So come here and look in a proper looking-glass. It will give you some fun."

Laughingly with a few droll caresses he turned me about so that I faced the gigantic mirror on the wall. There I saw myself.

I saw myself for a brief instant as my usual self, except that I looked unusually good-humoured, bright and laughing. But I had scarcely had time to recognise myself before the reflection fell to pieces. A second, a third, a tenth, a twentieth figure sprang from it till the whole gigantic mirror was full of nothing but Harrys or bits of him, each of which I saw only for the instant of recognition. Some of these multitudinous Harrys were as old as I, some older, some very old. Others were young. There were youths, boys, schoolboys, scamps, children. Fifty-year-olds and twenty-year-olds played leap frog. Thirty-year-olds and five-year-olds, solemn and merry, worthy and comic, well dressed and unpresentable, and even quite naked, long haired, and hairless, all were I and all were seen for a flash, recognised and gone. They sprang from each other in all directions, left and right and into the recesses of the mirror and clean out of it. One, an elegant young fellow, leapt laughing into Pablo's arms and embraced him and they went off together.

And one who particularly pleased me, a good looking and charming boy of sixteen or seventeen years, sprang like lightning into the corridor and began reading the notices on the doors. I went after him and found him in front of a door on which was inscribed:

ALL GIRLS ARE YOURS
ONE QUARTER IN THE SLOT

The dear boy hurled himself forward, made a leap and, falling head first into the slot himself, disappeared behind the door.

Pablo too had vanished. So apparently had the mirror and with it all the countless figures. I realised that I was now left to myself and to the theatre, and I went with curiosity from door to door and read on each its alluring invitation.

The inscription:

JOLLY HUNTING
GREAT HUNT IN AUTOMOBILES

attracted me. I opened the narrow door and stepped in.

I was swept at once into a world of noise and excitement. Motor-cars, some of them armoured, were run through the streets chasing the pedestrians. They ran them down and either left them mangled on the ground or crushed them to death against the walls of the houses. I saw at once that it was the long-prepared, long-awaited and long-feared war between men and machines, now at last broken out. On all sides lay dead and decomposing bodies, and on all sides, too, smashed and distorted and half-burnt motorcars. Aeroplanes circled above the frightful confusion and were being fired upon from many roofs and windows with rifles and machine guns. On every wall were wild and magnificently stirring placards, whose giant letters flamed like torches, summoning the nation to side with the men against the machines, to make an end at last of the fat and well-dressed and perfumed plutocrats who used machines to squeeze the fat from other men's bodies, of them and their huge fiendishly purring automobiles. Set factories afire at last! Make a little room on the crippled earth! Depopulate it so that the grass may grow again, and woods, meadows, heather, stream and moor return to this world of dust and concrete. Other placards, on the other hand, in wonderful colours and magnificently phrased, warned all those who had a stake in the country and some share of prudence (in more moderate and less childish terms which testified to the remarkable cleverness and intellect of those who had composed them) against the rising tide of anarchy. They depicted in a truly impressive way the blessings of order and work and property and education and justice, and praised machinery as the last and most sublime invention of the human mind. With its aid, men would be equal to the gods. I studied these placards, both the red and the green, and reflected on them and marvelled at them. The flaming eloquence affected me as powerfully as the compelling logic. They were right, and I stood as deeply convinced in front of one as in front of the other, a good deal disturbed all the time by the rather juicy firing that went on all round me. Well, the principal thing was clear. There was a war on, a violent, genuine and highly sympathetic war where there was no concern for Kaiser or republic, for frontiers, flags or colours and other equally decorative and theatrical matters, all nonsense at bottom; but a war in which every one who lacked air to breathe and no longer found life exactly pleasing gave emphatic expression to his displeasure and strove to prepare the way for a general destruction of this iron-cast civilisation of ours. In every eye I saw the unconcealed spark of destruction and murder, and in mine too these wild red roses bloomed as rank and high, and sparkled as brightly. I joined the battle joyfully.

The best of all, however, was that my school-friend, Gustav, turned up close beside me. I had lost sight of him for dozens of years, the wildest, strongest, most eager and venturesome of the friends of my childhood. I laughed in my heart as I saw him beckon me with his bright blue eyes. He beckoned and at once I followed him joyfully.

"Good Lord, Gustav," I cried happily, "fancy seeing you again. Whatever has become of you?"

"Keep quiet with your questions and chatter! I'm a professor of theology if you want to know. But, the Lord be praised, there's no occasion for theology now, my boy. It's war. Come on!"

He shot the driver of a small car that came snorting towards us and leaping into it as nimbly as a monkey, brought it to a standstill for me to get in. Then we drove like the devil between bullets and crashed cars out of town and suburbs.

"Are you on the side of the manufacturers?" I asked my friend.

"Oh, Lord, that's a matter of taste, so we can leave it out of account—though now you mention it, I rather think we might take the other side, since at bottom it's all the same, of course. I'm a theologian and my predecessor, Luther, took the side of the princes and plutocrats against the peasants. So now we'll establish the balance a little. This rotten car, I hope she'll hold out another mile or two."

Swift as the wind, that child of heaven, we rattled on, and reached a green and peaceful countryside many miles distant. We traversed a wide plain and then slowly climbed into the mountains. Here we made a halt on a smooth and glistening road that led in bold curves between the steep wall of rock and the low retaining wall. Far below shone the blue surface of a lake.

"Lovely view," said I.

"Very pretty. We'll call it the Axle Way. A good many axles of one sort or another are going to crash here, Harry, my boy. So watch out!"

A tall pine grew by the roadside, and among the tall branches we saw something like a little hut made of boards to serve as an outlook and point of vantage. Gustav smiled with a knowing twinkle in his blue eyes. We hurried out of the car, climbed up the trunk and, breathing hard, concealed ourselves in the outlook post, which pleased us much. We found rifles and revolvers there and boxes of ammunition. We had scarcely cooled down when we heard the hoarse imperious hoot of a large touring-car from the next bend of the road. It came purring at top speed up the smooth road. Our rifles were ready in our hands. The excitement was intense.

"Aim at the chauffeur," commanded Gustav quickly just as the heavy car went by beneath us. I aimed, and fired at the chauffeur in his blue cap. The man fell in a heap. The car careened on, charged the cliff face, rebounded, attacked the lower wall furiously with all its unwieldy weight like a great bumble bee and, tumbling over, crashed with a brief and distant report into the depths below.

"Got him!" Gustav laughed. "My turn next."

Another came as he spoke. There were three or four occupants packed in the back seat. From the head of a woman a bright blue veil streamed out behind. It filled me with genuine remorse. Who could say how pretty a face it might adorn? Good God, though we did play the brigand we might at least emulate the illustrious and spare pretty women. Gustav, however, had already fired. The driver shuddered and collapsed. The car leapt against the perpendicular cliff, fell back and overturned, wheels uppermost. Its engine was still running and the wheels turned absurdly in the air; but suddenly with a frightful explosion it burst into flames.

"A Ford," said Gustav. "We must get down and clear the road."

We climbed down and watched the burning heap. It soon burnt out. Meanwhile we made levers of green wood and hoisted it to the side of the road and over the wall into the abyss, where for a long time it went crashing through the undergrowth. Two of the dead bodies had fallen out as we turned the car over and lay on the road with their clothing partly burnt. One wore a pretty good coat. I searched the pockets to see who he was. A leather case came to hand with some cards in it. I took one and read: Tat Twam Asi.

"Very witty," said Gustav. "Though, as a matter of fact, it is all one what our victims are called. They're poor devils just as we are. Their names don't matter. This world is done for and so are we. The least painful solution would be to hold it under water for ten minutes. Now to work—"

We threw the bodies after the car. Already another one was tooting. We shot it down with a volley where we stood. It made a drunken swerve and reeled on for a stretch, then turned over and lay gasping. One passenger was still sitting inside, but a pretty young girl got out uninjured, though she was white and trembling violently. We greeted her politely and offered our assistance. She was too much shaken to speak and stared at us for a while quite dazed.

"Well, first let us look after the old boy," said Gustav and turned to the occupant of the car who still clung to his seat behind the chauffeur. He was a gentleman with short grey hair. His intelligent, clear grey eyes were open, but he seemed to be seriously hurt; at least, blood flowed from his mouth and he held his neck askew and rigid.

"Allow me to introduce myself. My name is Gustav. We have taken the liberty of shooting your chauffeur. May we inquire whom we have the honour to address?"

The old man looked at us coolly and sadly out of his small grey eyes.

"I am the Attorney-General Loering," he said slowly. "You have not only killed my poor chauffeur, but me too, I fancy. Why did you shoot on us?"

"For exceeding the speed limit."

"We were not travelling at more than normal speed."

"What was normal yesterday is no longer normal today, Mr. Attorney-General. We are of the opinion that whatever speed a motorcar travels is too great. We are destroying all motorcars and all other machines also."

"Your rifles too?"

"Their turn will come, granted we have the time. Presumably by tomorrow or the day after we shall all be done for. You know, of course, that this part of the world was shockingly overpopulated. Well, now we are going to let in a little air."

"Are you shooting every one, without distinction?"

"Certainly. In many cases it may no doubt be a pity. I'm sorry, for example, about this charming young lady. Your daughter, I presume."

"No. She is my stenographer."

"So much the better. And now will you please get out, or let us carry you out, as the car is to be destroyed."

"I prefer to be destroyed with it."

"As you wish. But allow me to ask you one more question. You are a public prosecutor. I never could understand how a man could be a public prosecutor. You make your living by bringing other men, poor devils mostly, to trial and passing sentence on them. Isn't that so?"

"It is. I do my duty. It was my office. Exactly as it is the office of the hangman to hang those whom I condemn to death. You too have assumed a like office. You kill people also."

"Quite true. Only we do not kill from duty, but pleasure, or much more, rather, from displeasure and despair of the world. For this reason we find a certain amusement in killing people. Has it never amused you?"

"You bore me. Be so kind as to do your work. Since the conception of duty is unknown to you—"

He was silent and made a movement of his lips as though to spit. Only a little blood came, however, and clung to his chin.

"One moment!" said Gustav politely. "The conception of duty is certainly unknown to me—now. Formerly I had a great deal of official concern with it. I was a professor of theology. Besides that, I was a soldier and went through the war. What seemed to me to be duty and what the authorities and my superior officers from time to time enjoined upon me was not by any means good. I would rather have done the opposite. But granting that the conception of duty is no longer known to me, I still know the conception of guilt—perhaps they are the same thing. In so far as a mother bore me, I am guilty. I am condemned to live. I am obliged to belong to a State, to serve as a soldier, to kill and to pay taxes for armaments. And now at this moment the guilt of life has brought me once more to the necessity of killing people as it did in the war. And this time I have no repugnance. I am resigned to the guilt. I have no objection to this stupid congested world going to bits. I am glad to help and glad to perish with it."

The public prosecutor made an effort to smile a little with his lips on which the blood had coagulated. He did not succeed very well, though the good intention was manifest.

"Good," said he. "So we are colleagues. Well, as such, please do your duty."

The pretty girl had meanwhile sat down by the side of the road and fainted.

At this moment there was again the tooting of a car coming down the road at full speed. We drew the girl a little to one side and, standing close against the cliff, let the approaching car run into the ruins of the other. The brakes were applied violently and the car reared up in the air. It came to a standstill undamaged. We seized our rifles and quickly had the newcomers covered.

"Get out!" commanded Gustav. "Hands up!"

Three men got out of the car and obediently held up their hands.

"Is anyone of you a doctor?" Gustav asked.

They shook their heads.

"Then be so good as to remove this gentleman. He is seriously hurt. Take him in your car to the nearest town. Forward, and get on with it."

The old gentleman was soon lying in the other car. Gustav gave the word and off they went.

The stenographer meanwhile had come to herself and had been watching these proceedings. I was glad we had made so fair a prize.

"Madam," said Gustav, "you have lost your employer. I hope you were not bound to the old gentleman by other ties. You are now in my service. So be our good comrade. So much for that; and now time presses. It will be uncomfortable here before long. Can you climb, Madam? Yes? Then go ahead and we'll help you up between us."

We all climbed up to our hut in the tree as fast as we could. The lady did not feel very well up there, but we gave her some brandy, and she was soon so much recovered that she was able to admire the wonderful view over lake and mountains and to tell us also that her name was Dora.

Immediately after this, there was another car below us. It steered carefully past the overturned one without stopping and then gathered speed.

"Poltroon!" laughed Gustav and shot the driver. The car zig-zagged and dashing into the wall stove it in and hung suspended over the abyss.

"Dora," I said, "can you use firearms?"

She could not, but we taught her how to load. She was clumsy at first and hurt her finger and cried and wanted court-plaster. But Gustav told her it was war and that she must show her courage. Then it went better.

"But what's going to become of us?" she asked.

"Don't know," said Gustav. "My friend Harry is fond of pretty girls. He'll look after you."

"But the police and the soldiers will come and kill us."

"There aren't any police and such like any more. We can choose, Dora. Either we stay quietly up here and shoot down every car that tries to pass, or else we can take a car and drive off in it and let others shoot at us. It's all the same which side we take. I'm for staying here."

And now there was the loud tooting of another car beneath us. It was soon accounted for and lay there wheels uppermost.

Gustav smiled. "Yes, there are indeed too many men in the world. In earlier days it wasn't so noticeable. But now that every one wants air to breathe, and a car to drive as well, one does notice it. Of course, what we are doing isn't rational. It's childishness, just as war is childishness on a gigantic scale. In time, mankind will learn to keep its numbers in check by rational means. Meanwhile, we are meeting an intolerable situation in a rather irrational way. However, the principle's correct—we eliminate."

"Yes," said I, "what we are doing is probably mad, and probably it is good and necessary all the same. It is not a good thing when man overstrains his reason and tries to reduce to rational order matters that are not susceptible of rational treatment. Then there arise ideals such as those of the Americans or of the Bolsheviks. Both are extraordinarily rational, and both lead to a frightful oppression and impoverishment of life, because they simplify it so crudely. The likeness of man, once a high ideal, is in process of becoming a machine-made article. It is for madmen like us, perhaps, to ennoble it again."

With a laugh Gustav replied: "You talk like a book, my boy. It is a pleasure and a privilege to drink at such a fount of wisdom. And perhaps there is even something in what you say. But now kindly re-load your piece. You are rather too dreamy for my taste. Any moment may bring a few buck, and we cannot kill them with philosophy. We must have ball in our barrels."

A car came and was dropped at once. The road was blocked. A survivor, a stout red-faced man, gesticulated wildly over the ruins. Then he stared up and down and, discovering our hiding place, came for us bellowing and shooting up at us with a revolver.

"Get off with you or I'll shoot," Gustav shouted down. The man took aim at him and fired again. Then we shot him.

After this two more came and were bagged. Then the road was silent and deserted. Apparently the news had got about that it was dangerous. We had time to enjoy the beauty of the view. On the far side of the lake a small town lay in the valley. Smoke rose from it and soon we saw fire leaping from roof to roof. Shooting could be heard. Dora cried a little and I stroked her wet cheeks.

"Have we all got to die then?" she asked. There was no reply. Meanwhile a man on foot went past below. He saw the smashed-up motorcars and began nosing round them. Leaning over into one of them he pulled out a gay parasol, a ladies' hand-bag and a bottle of wine. Then he sat down contentedly on the wall, took a drink from the bottle and ate something wrapped in tinfoil out of the hand-bag. After emptying the bottle he went on, well pleased, with the parasol clasped under his arm; and I said to Gustav: "Could you find it in you to shoot at this good fellow and make a hole in his head? God knows, I couldn't."

"You're not asked to," my friend growled. But he did not feel very comfortable either. We had no sooner caught sight of a man whose behaviour was harmless and peaceable and childlike and who was still in a state of innocence than all our praiseworthy and most necessary activities became stupid and repulsive. Pah—all that blood! We were ashamed of ourselves. But in the war there must have been Generals even who felt the same.

"Don't let us stay here any longer," Dora implored. "Let's go down. We are sure to find something to eat in the cars. Aren't you hungry, you Bolsheviks?"

Down in the burning town the bells began to peal with a wild terror. We set ourselves to climb down. As I helped Dora to climb over the breast work, I kissed her knee. She laughed aloud, and then the planks gave way and we both fell into vacancy—

* * * *

Once more I stood in the round corridor, still excited by the hunting adventure. And everywhere on all the countless doors were the alluring inscriptions:

MUTABOR
TRANSFORMATION INTO ANY ANIMAL
OR PLANT YOU PLEASE

KAMASUTRAM
INSTRUCTION IN THE INDIAN ARTS OF LOVE
COURSE FOR BEGINNERS; FORTY-TWO DIFFERENT
METHODS AND PRACTICES

DELIGHTFUL SUICIDE
YOU LAUGH YOURSELF TO BITS

DO YOU WANT TO BE ALL SPIRIT?
THE WISDOM OF THE EAST.

DOWNFALL OF THE WEST
MODERATE PRICES. NEVER SURPASSED.

COMPENDIUM OF ART
TRANSFORMATION FROM TIME INTO SPACE
BY MEANS OF MUSIC

LAUGHING TEARS
CABINET OF HUMOUR

SOLITUDE MADE EASY
COMPLETE SUBSTITUTE FOR
ALL FORMS OF SOCIABILITY.

The series of inscriptions was endless. One was:

GUIDANCE IN THE BUILDING UP OF
THE PERSONALITY. SUCCESS GUARANTEED

This seemed to me to be worth looking into and I went in at this door.

I found myself in a quiet twilit room where a man with something like a large chess-board in front of him sat in Eastern fashion on the floor. At the first glance I thought it was friend Pablo. He wore at any rate a similar gorgeous silk jacket and had the same dark and shining eyes.

"Are you Pablo?" I asked.

"I am not anybody," he replied amiably. "We have no names here and we are not anybody. I am a chess-player. Do you wish for instruction in the building up of the personality?"

"Yes, please."

"Then be so kind as to place a few dozen of your pieces at my disposal."

"My pieces—?"

"Of the pieces into which you saw your so-called personality broken up. I can't play without pieces."

He held a glass up to me and again I saw the unity of my personality broken up into many selves whose number seemed even to have increased. The pieces were now, however, very small, about the size of chessmen. The player took a dozen or so of them in his sure and quiet fingers and placed them on the ground near the board. As he did so he began to speak in the monotonous way of one who goes through a recitation or reading that he has often gone through before.

"The mistaken and unhappy notion that a man is an enduring unity is known to you. It is also known to you that man consists of a multitude of souls, of numerous selves. The separation of the unity of the personality into these numerous pieces passes for madness. Science has invented the name Schizomania for it. Science is in this so far right as no multiplicity may be dealt with unless there be a series, a certain order and grouping. It is wrong in so far as it holds that one only and binding and lifelong order is possible for the multiplicity of subordinate selves. This error of science has many unpleasant consequences, and the single advantage of simplifying the work of the state-appointed pastors and masters and saving them the labours of original thought. In consequence of this error many persons pass for normal, and indeed for highly valuable members of society, who are incurably mad; and many, on the other hand, are looked upon as mad who are geniuses. Hence it is that we supplement the imperfect psychology of science by the conception that we call the art of building up the soul. We demonstrate to anyone whose soul has fallen to pieces that he can rearrange these pieces of a previous self in what order he pleases, and so attain to an endless multiplicity of moves in the game of life. As the playwright shapes a drama from a handful of characters, so do we from the pieces of the disintegrated self build up ever new groups, with ever new interplay and suspense, and new situations that are eternally inexhaustible. Look!"

With the sure and silent touch of his clever fingers he took hold of my pieces, all the old men and young men and children and women, cheerful and sad, strong and weak, nimble and clumsy, and swiftly arranged them on his board for a game. At once they formed themselves into groups and families, games and battles, friendships and enmities, making a small world. For a while he let this lively and yet orderly world go through its evolutions before my enraptured eyes in play and strife, making treaties and fighting battles, wooing, marrying and multiplying. It was indeed a crowded stage, a moving breathless drama.

Then he passed his hand swiftly over the board and gently swept all the pieces into a heap; and, meditatively with an artist's skill, made up a new game of the same pieces with quite other groupings, relationships and entanglements. The second game had an affinity with the first, it was the same world built of the same material, but the key was different, the time changed, the motif was differently given out and the situations differently presented.

And in this fashion the clever architect built up one game after another out of the figures, each of which was a bit of myself, and every game had a distant resemblance to every other. Each belonged recognisably to the same world and acknowledged a common origin. Yet each was entirely new.

"This is the art of life," he said dreamily. "You may yourself as an artist develop the game of your life and lend it animation. You may complicate and enrich it as you please. It lies in your hands. Just as madness, in a higher sense, is the beginning of all wisdom, so is schizomania the beginning of all art and all fantasy. Even learned men have come to a partial recognition of this, as may be gathered, for example, from *Prince Wunderhorn*, that enchanting book, in which the industry and pains of a man of learning, with the assistance of the genius of a number of madmen and artists shut up as such, are immortalised. Here, take your little pieces away with you. The game will often give you pleasure. The piece that today grew to the proportions of an intolerable bugbear, you will degrade tomorrow to a mere lay figure. The luckless Cinderella will in the next game be the princess. I wish you much pleasure, my dear sir."

I bowed low in gratitude to the gifted chess-player, put the little pieces in my pocket and withdrew through the narrow door.

My real intention was to seat myself at once on the floor in the corridor and play the game for hours, for whole eternities; but I was no sooner in the bright light of the circular theatre passage than a new and irresistible current carried me along. A dazzling poster flashed before my eyes:

MARVELLOUS TAMING OF
THE STEPPENWOLF

Many different emotions surged up in me at the sight of this announcement. My heart was painfully contracted by all kinds of fears and repressions from my former life and the reality I had left behind. With trembling hand I opened the door and found myself in the booth of a Fair with an iron rail separating me from a wretched stage. On the stage I saw an animal-tamer—a cheap-jack gentleman with a pompous air—who in spite of a large moustache, exuberantly muscular biceps and his absurd circus get-up had a malicious and decidedly unpleasant resemblance to myself. The strong man led on a leash like a dog—lamentable sight—a large, beautiful but terribly emaciated wolf, whose eyes were cowed and furtive; and it was as disgusting as it was intriguing, as horrible as it was all the same secretly entertaining, to see this brutal tamer of animals put the noble and yet so ignominiously obedient beast of prey through a series of tricks and sensational turns.

At any rate, the man, my diabolically distorted double, had his wolf marvellously broken. The wolf was obediently attentive to every command and responded like a dog to every call and every crack of the whip. He went down on his knees, lay for dead, and, aping the lord of creation, carried a loaf, an egg, a piece of meat, a basket in his mouth with cheerful obedience; and he even had to pick up the whip that the tamer had let fall and carry it after him in his teeth while he wagged his tail with an unbearable submissiveness. A rabbit was put in front of him and then a white lamb. He bared his teeth, it is true, and the saliva dropped from his mouth while he trembled with desire, but he did not touch either of the animals; and at the word of command he jumped over them with a graceful leap, as they cowered trembling on the floor. More—he laid himself down between the rabbit and the lamb and embraced them with his foremost paws to form a touching family group, at the same time eating a stick of chocolate from the man's hand. It was an agony to witness the fantastic extent to which the wolf had learnt to belie his nature; and I stood there with my hair on end.

There was some compensation, however, both for the horrified spectator and for the wolf himself, in the second part of the programme. For after this refined exhibition of animal-taming and when the man with a winning smile had made his triumphant bow over the group of the wolf and the lamb, the rôles were reversed. My engaging double suddenly with a low reverence laid his whip at the wolf's feet and became as agitated, as shrunken and wretched, as the wolf had been before. The wolf, however, licked his chops with a grin, his constraint and dissimulation erased. His eyes kindled. His whole body was taut and showed the joy he felt at recovering his wild nature.

And now the wolf commanded and the man obeyed. At the word of command the man sank on his knees, let his tongue loll out and tore his clothes off with his filed teeth. He went on two feet or all-fours just as the wolf ordered him, played the human being, lay for dead, let the wolf ride on his back and carried the whip after him. With the aptness of a dog he submitted gladly to every humiliation and perversion of his nature. A lovely girl came on to the stage and went up to the tamed man. She stroked his chin and rubbed her cheek against his; but he remained on all-fours, remained a beast. He shook his head and began to show his teeth at the charming creature—so menacingly and wolfishly at last, that she ran away. Chocolate was put before him, but with a contemptuous sniff he thrust it from him with his snout. Finally the white lamb and the fat piebald rabbit were brought on again and the docile man gave his last turn and played the wolf most amusingly. He seized the shrieking creatures in his fingers and teeth, tore them limb from limb, grinningly chewed the living flesh and rapturously drank their warm blood while his eyes closed in a dreamy delight.

I made for the door in horror and dashed out. This Magic Theatre was clearly no paradise. All hell lay beneath its charming surface. O God, was there even here no release?

In fear I hurried this way and that. I had the taste of blood and chocolate in my mouth, the one as hateful as the other. I desired nothing but to be beyond this wave of disgust. I wrestled with myself for more bearable, friendlier pictures. "O Friend, not these notes!" sang in my head, and with horror I remembered those terrible photographs from the Front that one saw occasionally during the war—those heaps of bodies entangled with each other, whose faces were changed to grinning ghouls by their gas-masks. How silly and childish of me, a humanely minded opponent of war though I was, to have been horrified by those pictures. Today I knew that no tamer of beasts, no General, no insane person could hatch a thought or a picture in his brain that I could not match myself with one every bit as frightful, every bit as savage and wicked, as crude and stupid.

With an immense relief I remembered the notice I had seen on first entering the theatre, the one that the nice boy had stormed so furiously—

ALL GIRLS ARE YOURS

and it seemed to me, all in all, that there was really nothing else so desirable as this. I was greatly cheered at finding that I could escape from that cursed wolf-world, and went in.

The fragrance of spring-time met me. The very atmosphere of boyhood and youth, so deeply familiar and yet so legendary, was around me and in my veins flowed the blood of those days. All that I had done and thought and been since, fell away from me and I was young again. An hour, a few minutes before, I had prided myself on knowing what love was and desire and longing, but it had been the love and the longing of an old man. Now I was young again and this glowing current of fire that I felt in me, this mighty impulse, this unloosening passion like that wind in March that brings the thaw, was young and new and genuine. How the flame that I had forgotten leaped up again, how darkly stole on my ears the tones of long ago! My blood was on fire, and blossomed forth as my soul cried aloud and sang. I was a boy of fifteen or sixteen with my head full of Latin and Greek and poetry. I was all ardour and ambition and my fancy was laden with the artist's dreams. But far deeper and stronger and more awful than all there burned and leapt in me the flame of love, the hunger of sex, the fever and the foreboding of desire.

I was standing on a spur of the hills above the little town where I lived. The wind wafted the smell of spring and violets through my long hair. Below in the town I saw the gleam of the river and the windows of my home, and all that I saw and heard and smelt overwhelmed me, as fresh and reeling from creation, as radiant in depth of colour, swayed by the wind of spring in as magical a transfiguration, as when once I looked on the world with the eyes of youth—first youth and poetry. With wandering hand I pulled a half-opened leaf-bud from a bush that was newly green. I looked at it and smelt it (with the smell everything of those days came back in a glow) and then I put it between my lips, lips that no girl had ever kissed, and began playfully to bite it. At the sour and aromatically bitter taste I knew at once and exactly what it was that I was living over again. It all came back. I was living again an hour of the last years of my boyhood, a Sunday afternoon in early spring, the day that on a lonely walk I met Rosa Kreisler and greeted her so shyly and fell in love with her so madly.

She came, that day, alone and dreamingly up the hill towards me. She had not seen me and the sight of her approaching filled me with apprehension and suspense. I saw her hair, tied in two thick plaits, with loose strands on either side, her cheeks blown by the wind. I saw for the first time in my life how beautiful she was, and how beautiful and dreamlike the play of the wind in her delicate hair, how beautiful and provocative the fall of her thin blue dress over her young limbs; and just as the bitter spice of the chewed bud coursed through me with the whole dread pleasure and pain of spring, so the sight of the girl filled me with the whole deadly foreboding of love, the foreboding of woman. In that moment was contained the shock and the fore-warning of enormous possibilities and promises, nameless delight, unthinkable bewilderments, anguish, suffering, release to the innermost and deepest guilt. Oh, how sharp was the bitter taste of spring on my tongue! And how the wind streamed playfully through the loose hair beside her rosy cheeks! She was close now. She looked up and recognised me. For a moment she blushed a little and looked aside; but when I took off my school-cap, she was self-possessed at once and, raising her head, returned my greeting with a smile that was quite grownup. Then, entirely mistress of the situation, she went slowly on, in a halo of the thousand wishes, hopes and adorations that I sent after her.

So it had once been on a Sunday thirty-five years before and all that had been then came back to me in this moment. Hill and town, March wind and buddy taste, Rosa and her brown hair, the welling-up of desire and the sweet suffocation of anguish. All was as it was then, and it seemed to me that I had never in my life loved as I loved Rosa that day. But this time it was given me to greet her otherwise than on that occasion. I saw her blush when she recognised me, and the pains she took to conceal it, and I knew at once that she had a liking for me and that this encounter meant the same for her as for me. And this time instead of standing ceremoniously cap in hand till she had gone by, I did, in spite of anguish bordering on obsession, what my blood bade me do. I cried: "Rosa! Thank God, you've come, you beautiful, beautiful girl. I love you so dearly." It was not perhaps the most brilliant of all the things that might have been said at this moment, but there was no need for brilliance, and it was enough and more. Rosa did not put on her grownup air, and she did not go on. She stopped and looked at me and, growing even redder than before, she said: "Heaven be praised, Harry—do you really like me?" Her brown eyes lit up her strong face, and they showed me that my past life and loves had all been false and perplexed and full of stupid unhappiness from that very moment on a Sunday afternoon when I had let Rosa pass me by. Now, however, the blunder was put right. Everything went differently and everything was good.

We clasped hands, and hand in hand walked slowly on as happy as we were embarrassed. We did not know what to do or to say, so we began to walk faster from embarrassment and then broke into a run, and ran till we lost our breath and had to stand still. But we did not let go our hands. We were both still children and did not know quite what to do with each other. That Sunday we did not even kiss, but we were immeasurably happy. We stood to get our breath. We sat on the grass and I stroked her hand while she passed the other one shyly over my hair. And then we got up again and tried to measure which of us was the taller. In reality, I was the taller by a finger's breath, but I would not have it so. I maintained that we were of exactly the same height and that God had designed us for each other and that later on we would marry. Then Rosa said that she smelt violets and we knelt in the short spring grass and looked for them and found a few with short stalks and I gave her mine and she gave me hers, and as it was getting chill and the sun slanted low over the cliffs, Rosa said she must go home. At this we both became very sad, for I dared not accompany her. But now we shared a secret and it was our dearest possession. I stayed behind on the cliffs and lying down with my face over the edge of the sheer descent, I looked down over the town and watched for her sweet little figure to appear far below and saw it pass the spring and over the bridge. And now I knew that she had reached her home and was going from room to room, and I lay up there far away from her; but there was a bond between her and me. The same current ran in both of us and a secret passed to and fro.

We saw each other again here and there all through this spring, sometimes on the cliffs, sometimes over the garden hedge; and when the elder began to bloom we gave each other the first shy kiss. It was little that children like us had to give each other and our kiss lacked warmth and fullness. I scarcely ventured to touch the strands of her hair about her ears. But all the love and all the joy that was in us were ours. It was a shy emotion and the troth we plighted was still unripe, but this timid waiting on each other taught us a new happiness. We climbed one little step up on the ladder of love. And thus, beginning from Rosa and the violets, I lived again through all the loves of my life—but under happier stars. Rosa I lost, and Irmgard appeared; and the sun was warmer and the stars less steady, but Irmgard no more than Rosa was mine. Step by step I had to climb. There was much to live through and much to learn; and I had to lose Irmgard and Anna too. Every girl that I had once loved in youth, I loved again, but now I was able to inspire each with love. There was something I could give to each, something each could give to me. Wishes, dreams and possibilities that had once had no other life than my own imagination were lived now in reality. They passed before me like beautiful flowers, Ida and Laura and all whom I had loved for a summer, a month, or a day.

I was now, as I perceived, that good looking and ardent boy whom I had seen making so eagerly for love's door. I was living a bit of myself only—a bit that in my actual life and being had not been expressed to a tenth or a thousandth part, and I was living it to the full. I was watching it grow unmolested by any other part of me. It was not perturbed by the thinker, nor tortured by the Steppenwolf, nor dwarfed by the poet, the visionary or the moralist. No—I was nothing now but the lover and I breathed no other happiness and no other suffering than love. Irmgard had already taught me to dance and Ida to kiss, and it was Emma first, the most beautiful of them all, who on an autumn evening beneath a swaying elm gave me her brown breasts to kiss and the cup of passion to drink.

I lived through much in Pablo's little theatre and not a thousandth part can be told in words. All the girls I had ever loved were mine. Each gave me what she alone had to give and to each I gave what she alone knew how to take. Much love, much happiness, much indulgence, and much bewilderment, too, and suffering fell to my share. All the love that I had missed in my life bloomed magically in my garden during this hour of dreams. There were chaste and tender blooms, garish ones that blazed, dark ones swiftly fading. There were flaring lust, inward reverie, glowing melancholy, anguished dying, radiant birth. I found women who were only to be taken by storm and those whom it was a joy to woo and win by degrees. Every twilit corner of my life where, if but for a moment the voice of sex had called me, a woman's glance kindled me or the gleam of a girl's white skin allured me, emerged again and all that had been missed was made good. All were mine, each in her own way. The woman with the remarkable dark brown eyes beneath flaxen hair was there. I had stood beside her for a quarter of an hour in the corridor of an express and afterwards she often appeared in my dreams. She did not speak a word, but what she taught me of the art of love was unimaginable, frightful, deathly. And the sleek, still Chinese, from the harbour of Marseilles, with her glassy smile, her smooth dead-black hair and swimming eyes—she too knew undreamed-of things. Each had her secret and the bouquet of her soil. Each kissed and laughed in a fashion of her own, and in her own peculiar way was shameful and in her own peculiar way shameless. They came and went. The stream carried them towards me and washed me up to them and away. I was a child in the stream of sex at play in the midst of all its charm, its danger and surprise. And it astonished me to find how rich my life—the seemingly so poor and loveless life of the Steppenwolf—had been in the opportunities and allurements of love. I had missed them. I had fled before them. I had stumbled on over them. I had made haste to forget them. But here they all were stored up in their hundreds, and not one missing. And now that I saw them I gave myself up to them without defence and sank down into the rosy twilight of their underworld. Even that seduction to which Pablo had once invited me came again, and other earlier ones, none of which at the time I had even fully grasped, fantastic games for three or four, caught me into their gambols with a laugh. Many things happened and many games were played not to be said in words.

When I rose once more to the surface of the unending stream of allurement and vice and entanglement, I was calm and silent. I was equipped, far gone in knowledge, wise, expert—ripe for Hermine. She rose as the last figure in my populous mythology, the last name of an endless series; and at once I came to myself and made an end of this fairy-tale of love; for I did not wish to meet her in this twilight of a magic mirror. I belonged to her not just as this one piece in my game of chess—I belonged to her wholly. Oh, I would now so lay out the pieces in my game that all was centred in her and led to fulfilment.

The stream had washed me ashore. Once again I stood in the silent theatre passage. What now? I felt for the little figures in my pocket—but already this impulse died away. Around me was the inexhaustible world of doors, notices and magic mirrors. Listlessly I read the first words that caught my eye, and shuddered.

HOW ONE KILLS FOR LOVE

was what it said.

Swiftly a picture was flashed upon my memory with a jerk and remained there one instant. Hermine at the table of a restaurant, turning all at once from the wine and food, lost in an abyss of speech, with a terrifying earnestness in her face as she said that she would have one aim only in making me her lover, and it was that she should die by my hand. A heavy wave of anguish and darkness flooded my heart. Suddenly everything confronted me once more. Suddenly once more the sense of the last call of fate gripped my heart. Desperately I felt in my pocket for the little figures so that I might practise a little magic and rearrange the lay-out of the board. The figures were no longer there. Instead of them I pulled out a knife. In mortal dread I ran along the corridor, past every door. I stood opposite the gigantic mirror. I looked into it. In the mirror there stood a beautiful wolf as tall as myself. He stood still, glancing shyly from unquiet eyes. As he leered at me, his eyes blazed and he grinned a little so that his chops parted and showed his red tongue.

Where was Pablo? Where was Hermine? Where was that clever fellow who had discoursed so pleasantly about the building up of the personality?

Again I looked into the mirror. I had been mad. I must have been mad. There was no wolf in the mirror, lolling his tongue in his maw. It was I, Harry. My face was grey, forsaken of all fancies, fordone with all vice, horribly pale. Still it was a human being, someone one could speak to.

"Harry," I said, "what are you doing there?"

"Nothing," said he in the mirror, "I am only waiting. I am waiting for death."

"Where is death then?"

"Coming," said the other. And I heard from the empty spaces within the theatre the sound of music, a beautiful and awful music, that music from *Don Giovanni* that heralds the approach of the guest of stone. With an awful and an iron clang it rang through the ghostly house, coming from the other world, from the immortals.

"Mozart," I thought, and with the word conjured up the most beloved and the most exalted picture that my inner life contained.

At that, there rang out behind me a peal of laughter, a clear and ice-cold laughter out of a world beyond unknown to men, a world born of sufferings, purged and divine humour. I turned about, frozen through with the blessing of this laughter, and there came Mozart. He passed by me laughing as he went and, strolling quietly on, he opened the door of one of the boxes and went in. Eagerly I followed the god of my youth, the object, all my life long, of love and veneration. The music rang on. Mozart was leaning over the front of the box. Of the theatre nothing was to be seen. Darkness filled the boundless space.

"You see," said Mozart, "it goes all right without the saxophone—though to be sure, I shouldn't wish to tread on the toes of that famous instrument."

"Where are we?" I asked.

"We are in the last act of *Don Giovanni*. Leporello is on his knees. A superb scene, and the music is fine too. There is a lot in it, certainly, that's very human, but you can hear the other world in it—the laughter, eh?"

"It is the last great music ever written," said I with the pomposity of a schoolmaster. "Certainly, there was Schubert to come. Hugo Wolf also, and I must not forget the poor, lovely Chopin either. You frown, Maestro? Oh, yes, Beethoven—he is wonderful too. But all that—beautiful as it may be—has something rhapsodical about it, something of disintegration. A work of such plentitude and power as *Don Giovanni* has never since arisen among men."

"Don't overstrain yourself," laughed Mozart, in frightful mockery. "You're a musician yourself, I perceive. Well, I have given up the trade and retired to take my ease. It is only for amusement that I look on at the business now and then."

He raised his hands as though he were conducting, and a moon, or some pale constellation, rose somewhere. I looked over the edge of the box into immeasurable depths of space. Mist and clouds floated there. Mountains and sea-shores glimmered, and beneath us extended world-wide a desert plain. On this plain we saw an old gentleman of a worthy aspect, with a long beard, who drearily led a large following of some ten thousand men in black. He had a melancholy and hopeless air; and Mozart said:

"Look, there's Brahms. He is striving for redemption, but it will take him all his time."

I realised that the thousands of men in black were the players of all those notes and parts in his scores which according to divine judgment were superfluous.

"Too thickly orchestrated, too much material wasted," Mozart said with a nod.

And thereupon we saw Richard Wagner marching at the head of a host just as vast, and felt the pressure of those thousands as they clung and closed upon him. Him, too, we watched as he dragged himself along with slow and sad step.

"In my young days," I remarked sadly, "these two musicians passed as the most extreme contrasts conceivable."

Mozart laughed.

"Yes, that is always the way. Such contrasts, seen from a little distance, always tend to show their increasing similarity. Thick orchestration was in any case neither Wagner's nor Brahms' personal failing. It was a fault of their time."

"What? And have they got to pay for it so dearly?" I cried in protest.

"Naturally. The law must take its course. Until they have paid the debt of their time it cannot be known whether anything personal to themselves is left over to stand to their credit."

"But they can't either of them help it!"

"Of course not. They cannot help it either that Adam ate the apple. But they have to pay for it all the same."

"But that is frightful."

"Certainly. Life is always frightful. We cannot help it and we are responsible all the same. One's born and at once one is guilty. You must have had a remarkable sort of religious education if you did not know that."

I was now thoroughly miserable. I saw myself as a dead-weary pilgrim, dragging myself across the desert of the other world, laden with the many superfluous books I had written, and all the articles and feuilletons; followed by the army of compositors who had had the type to set up, by the army of readers who had had it all to swallow. My God—and over and above it all there was Adam and the apple, and the whole of original sin. All this, then, was to be paid for in endless purgatory. And only then could the question arise whether, behind all that, there was anything personal, anything of my own, left over; or whether all that I had done and all its consequences were merely the empty foam of the sea and a meaningless ripple in the flow of what was over and done.

Mozart laughed aloud when he saw my long face. He turned a somersault in the air for laughter's sake and played trills with his heels. At the same time he shouted at me: "Hey, my young man, you are biting your tongue, man, with a gripe in your lung, man? You think of your readers, those carrion-feeders, and all your type-setters, those wretched abettors, and sabre-whetters. You dragon, you make me laugh till I shake me and burst the stitches of my breeches. O heart of a gull, with printer's ink dull, and soul sorrow-full. A candle I'll leave you, if that'll relieve you. Betittled, betattled, spectackled and shackled, and pitifully snagged and by the tail wagged, with shilly and shally no more shall you dally. For the devil, I pray, will bear you away and slice you and splice you till that shall suffice you for your writings and rotten plagiarisings ill-gotten."

This, however, was too much for me. Anger left me no time for melancholy. I caught hold of Mozart by the pig-tail and off he flew. The pig-tail grew longer and longer like the tail of a comet and I was whirled along at the end of it. The devil—but it was cold in this world we traversed! These immortals put up with a rarefied and glacial atmosphere. But it was delightful all the same—this icy air. I could tell that, even in the brief moment that elapsed before I lost my senses. A bitter-sharp and steel-bright icy gaiety coursed through me and a desire to laugh as shrilly and wildly and unearthily as Mozart had done. But then breath and consciousness failed me.

* * * *

When I came to myself I was bewildered and done-up. The white light of the corridor shone in the polished floor. I was not among the immortals, not yet. I was still, as ever, on this side of the riddle of suffering, of wolf-men and torturing complexities. I had found no happy spot, no endurable resting place. There must be an end of it.

In the great mirror, Harry stood opposite me. He did not appear to be very flourishing. His appearance was much the same as on that night when he visited the professor and sat through the dance at the Black Eagle. But that was far behind, years, centuries behind. He had grown older. He had learnt to dance. He had visited the magic theatre. He had heard Mozart laugh. Dancing and women and knives had no more terrors for him. Even those who have average gifts, given a few hundred years, come to maturity. I looked for a long time at Harry in the looking-glass. I still knew him well enough, and he still bore a faint resemblance to the boy of fifteen who one Sunday in March had met Rosa on the cliffs and taken off his school-cap to her. And yet he had grown a few centuries older since then. He had pursued philosophy and music and had his fill of war and his Elsasser at the Steel Helmet and discussed Krishna with men of honest learning. He had loved Erica and Maria, and had been Hermine's friend, and shot down motorcars, and slept with the sleek Chinese, and encountered Mozart and Goethe, and made sundry holes in the web of time and rents in reality's disguise, though it held him a prisoner still. And suppose he had lost his pretty chessmen again, still he had a fine blade in his pocket. On then, old Harry, old weary loon.

Bah, the devil—how bitter the taste of life! I spat at Harry in the looking-glass. I gave him a kick and kicked him to splinters. I walked slowly along the echoing corridor, carefully scanning the doors that had held out so many glowing promises. Not one now showed a single announcement. Slowly I passed by all the hundred doors of the Magic Theatre. Was not this the day I had been to a Masked Ball? Hundreds of years had passed since then. Soon years would cease altogether. Something, though, was still to be done. Hermine awaited me. A strange marriage it was to be, and a sorrowful wave it was that bore me on, drearily bore me on, a slave, a wolf-man. Bah, the devil!

I stopped at the last door. So far had the sorrowful wave borne me. O Rosa! O departed youth! O Goethe! O Mozart!

I opened it. What I saw was a simple and beautiful picture. On a rug on the floor lay two naked figures, the beautiful Hermine and the beautiful Pablo side by side in a sleep of deep exhaustion after love's play. Beautiful, beautiful figures, lovely pictures, wonderful bodies. Beneath Hermine's left breast was a fresh round mark, darkly bruised—a love bite of Pablo's beautiful, gleaming teeth. There, where the mark was, I plunged in my knife to the hilt. The blood welled out over her white and delicate skin. I would have kissed away the blood if everything had happened a little differently. As it was, I did not. I only watched how the blood flowed and watched her eyes open for a little moment in pain and deep wonder. What makes her wonder? I thought? Then it occurred to me that I had to shut her eyes. But they shut again of themselves. So all was done. She only turned a little to one side, and from her arm-pit to her breast I saw the play of a delicate shadow. It seemed that it wished to recall something, but what I could not remember. Then she lay still.

For long I looked at her and at last I waked with a shudder and turned to go. Then I saw Pablo stretch himself. I saw him open his eyes and stretch his limbs and then bend over the dead girl and smile. Never, I thought, will this fellow take anything seriously. Everything makes him smile. Pablo, meanwhile, carefully turned over a corner of the rug and covered Hermine up as far as her breast so that the wound was hidden, and then he went silently out of the box. Where was he going? Was everybody leaving me alone? I stayed there, alone with the half-shrouded body of her whom I loved—and envied. The boyish hair hung low over the white forehead. Her lips shone red against the dead pallor of her blanched face and they were a little parted. Her hair diffused its delicate perfume and through it glimmered the little shell-like ear.

Her wish was fulfilled. Before she had ever been mine, I had killed my love. I had done the unthinkable, and now I kneeled and stared and did not know at all what this deed meant, whether it was good and right or the opposite. What would the clever chess-player, what would Pablo have to say to it? I knew nothing and I could not think. The painted mouth glowed more red on the growing pallor of the face. So had my whole life been. My little happiness and love were like this staring mouth, a little red upon a mask of death.

And from the dead face, from the dead white shoulders and the dead white arms, there exhaled and slowly crept a shudder, a desert wintriness and desolation, a slowly, slowly increasing chill in which my hands and lips grew numb. Had I quenched the sun? Had I stopped the heart of all life? Was it the coldness of death and space breaking in?

With a shudder I stared at the stony brow and the stark hair and the cool pale shimmer of the ear. The cold that streamed from them was deathly and yet it was beautiful, it rang, it vibrated. It was music!

Hadn't I once felt this shudder before and found it at the same time a joy? Hadn't I once caught this music before? Yes, with Mozart and the immortals.

Verses came into my head that I had once come upon somewhere:

> We above you ever more residing
> In the ether's star translumined ice
> Know nor day nor night nor time's dividing,
> Wear nor age nor sex as our device.
> Cool and unchanging is our eternal being,
> Cool and star bright is our eternal laughter.

Then the door of the box opened and in came Mozart. I did not recognise him at the first glance, for he was without pigtail, knee-breeches and buckled shoes, in modern dress. He took a seat close beside me, and I was on the point of holding him back because of the blood that had flowed over the floor from Hermine's breast. He sat there and began busying himself with an apparatus and some instruments that stood beside him. He took it very seriously, tightening this and screwing that, and I looked with wonder at his adroit and nimble fingers and wished that I might see them playing a piano for once. I watched him thoughtfully, or in a reverie rather, lost in admiration of his beautiful and skilful hands, warmed too, by the sense of his presence and a little apprehensive as well. Of what he was actually doing and of what it was that he screwed and manipulated, I took no heed whatever.

I soon found, however, that he had fixed up a wireless set and put it in going order, and now he inserted the loud-speaker and said: "Munich calling. Concerto Grosso in F major of Handel."

At once, to my indescribable astonishment and horror, the devilish metal funnel spat out, without more ado, its mixture of bronchial slime and chewed rubber; that noise that possessors of gramophones and wireless sets are prevailed upon to call music. And behind the slime and the croaking there was, sure enough, like an old master beneath a layer of dirt, the noble outline of that divine music. I could distinguish the majestic structure and the deep wide breath and the full broad bowing of the strings.

"My God," I cried in horror, "what are you doing, Mozart? Do you really mean to inflict this mess on me and yourself, this triumph of our day, the last victorious weapon in the war of extermination against art? Must this be, Mozart?"

How the uncomfortable man laughed! And what a cold and eerie laugh! It was noiseless and yet everything went to smithereens in it. He marked my torment with deep satisfaction while he bent over the cursed screws and attended to the metal trumpet. Laughing still, he let the distorted, the murdered and murderous music ooze out and on; and laughing still, he replied:

"Please, no pathos, my friend! Anyway, did you observe the ritardando? An inspiration, eh? Yes, and now you tolerant man, let the sense of this ritardando touch you. Do you hear the basses? They stride like gods. And let this inspiration of old Handel penetrate your restless heart and give it peace. Just listen, you poor creature, listen without either pathos or mockery, while far away behind the veil of this hopelessly idiotic and ridiculous apparatus the form of this divine music passes by. Pay attention and you will learn something. Observe what this crazy speaking-trumpet, apparently the most stupid, the most useless and the most damnable thing that the world contains, contrives to do. It takes hold of some music played where you please, without distinction or discretion, lamentably distorted, to boot, and chucks it into space to land where it has no business to be; and yet after all this it cannot destroy the original spirit of the music; it can only, however it may meddle and mar, lay its senseless mechanism at its feet. Listen, then, you poor thing. Listen well. You have need of it. And now you hear not only a Handel who, disfigured by wireless, is, all the same, in this most ghastly of disguises still divine; you hear as well and you observe, most worthy sir, a most admirable symbol of all life. When you listen to wireless, you are a witness of the everlasting war between idea and appearance, between time and eternity, between the human and the divine. Exactly, my dear sir, as the wireless for ten minutes together projects the most lovely music without regard into the most impossible places, into snug drawing-rooms and attics and into the midst of chattering, guzzling, yawning and sleeping listeners, and exactly as it strips this music of its sensuous beauty, spoils and scratches and beslimes it and yet cannot altogether destroy its spirit, just so does life, the so-called reality, deal with the sublime picture-play of the world and make a hurley-burley of it. It makes its unappetising tone—slime of the most magic orchestral music. Everywhere it obtrudes its mechanism, its activity, its dreary exigencies and vanity between the ideal and the real, between orchestra and ear. All life is so, my child, and we must let it be so; and, if we are not asses, laugh at it. It little becomes people like you to be critics of wireless or of life either. Better learn to listen first! Learn what is to be taken seriously and laugh at the rest. Or is it that you have done better yourself, more nobly and fitly and with better taste? Oh, no, Mr. Harry, you have not. You have made a frightful history of disease out of your life, and a misfortune of your gifts. And you have, as I see, found no better use for so pretty, so enchanting a young lady than to stick a knife into her body and destroy her. Was that right, do you think?"

"Right?" I cried in despair. "No! My God, everything is so false, so hellishly stupid and wrong! I am a beast, Mozart, a stupid, angry beast, sick and rotten. There you're right a thousand times. But as for this girl—it was her own desire. I have only fulfilled her own wish."

Mozart laughed his noiseless laughter. But he had the great kindness to turn off the wireless.

My self-extenuation sounded unexpectedly and thoroughly foolish even to me who had believed in it with all my heart. When Hermine had once, so it suddenly occurred to me, spoken about time and eternity, I had been ready forthwith to take her thoughts as a reflection of my own. That the thought, however, of dying by my hand had been her own inspiration and wish and not in the least influenced by me I had taken as a matter of course. But why on that occasion had I not only accepted that horrible and unnatural thought, but even guessed it in advance. Perhaps because it had been my own. And why had I murdered Hermine just at the very moment when I saw her lying naked in another's arms? All-knowing and all-mocking rang Mozart's soundless laughter.

"Harry," said he, "you're a great joker. Had this beautiful girl really nothing to desire of you but the stab of a knife? Keep that for someone else! Well, at least you have stabbed her properly. The poor child is as dead as a mouse. And now perhaps would be an opportune moment to realise the consequences of your gallantry towards this lady. Or do you think of evading the consequences?"

"No," I cried. "Don't you understand at all? I evade the consequences? I have no other desire than to pay and pay and pay for them, to lay my head beneath the axe and pay the penalty of annihilation."

Mozart looked at me with intolerable mockery.

"How pathetic you always are. But you will learn humour yet, Harry. Humour is always gallows-humour, and it is on the gallows you are now constrained to learn it. You are ready? Good. Then off with you to the public prosecutor and let the law take its course with you till your head is coolly hacked off at break of dawn in the prison-yard. You are ready for it?"

Instantly a notice flashed before my eyes:

HARRY'S EXECUTION

and I consented with a nod. I stood in a bare yard enclosed by four walls with barred windows and shivered in the air of a grey dawn. There were a dozen gentlemen there in morning coats and gowns, and a newly erected guillotine. My heart was contracted with misery and dread, but I was ready and acquiescent. At the word of command, I stepped forward and at the word of command I knelt down. The public prosecutor removed his cap and cleared his throat, and all the other gentlemen cleared their throats. He unfolded an official document and held it before him and read out:

"Gentlemen, there stands before you Harry Haller, accused and found guilty of the wilful misuse of our magic theatre. Haller has not alone insulted the majesty of art in that he confounded our beautiful picture gallery with so-called reality and stabbed to death the reflection of a girl with the reflection of a knife; he has in addition displayed the intention of using our theatre as a mechanism of suicide and shown himself devoid of humour. Wherefore we condemn Haller to eternal life, and we suspend for twelve hours his permit to enter our theatre. The penalty also of being laughed out of court may not be remitted. Gentlemen, all together, one-two-three!"

On the word "three" all who were present broke into one simultaneous peal of laughter, a laughter in full chorus, a frightful laughter of the other world that is scarcely to be borne by the ears of men.

When I came to myself again, Mozart was sitting beside me as before. He clapped me on the shoulder and said: "You have heard your sentence. So, you see, you will have to learn to listen to more of the wireless music of life. It'll do you good. You are uncommonly poor in gifts, a poor blockhead, but by degrees you will come to grasp what is required of you. You have got to learn to laugh. That will be required of you. You must apprehend the humour of life, its gallows-humour. But of course you are ready for everything in the world except what will be required of you. You are ready to stab girls to death. You are ready to be executed with all solemnity. You would be ready, no doubt, to mortify and scourge yourself for centuries together. Wouldn't you?"

"Oh, yes, ready with all my heart," I cried in my misery.

"Of course! When it's a question of anything stupid and pathetic and devoid of humour or wit, you're the man, you tragedian. Well, I am not. I don't care a fig for all your romantics of atonement. You wanted to be executed and to have your head chopped off, you Berserker! For this imbecile ideal you would suffer death ten times over. You are willing to die, you coward, but not to live. The devil, but you shall live! It would serve you right if you were condemned to the severest of penalties."

"Oh, and what would that be?"

"We might, for example, restore this girl to life again and marry you to her."

"No, I should not be ready for that. It would bring unhappiness."

"As if there were not enough unhappiness in all you have designed already! However, enough of pathos and death-dealing. It is time to come to your senses. You are to live and to learn to laugh. You are to listen to life's wireless music and to reverence the spirit behind it and to laugh at the bimbim in it. So there you are. More will not be asked of you."

Gently from behind clenched teeth I asked: "And if I do not submit? And if I deny your right, Mozart, to interfere with the Steppenwolf, and to meddle in his destiny?"

"Then," said Mozart calmly, "I should invite you to smoke another of my charming cigarettes." And as he spoke and conjured up a cigarette from his waistcoat pocket and offered it me, he was suddenly Mozart no longer. It was my friend Pablo looking warmly at me out of his dark exotic eyes and as like the man who had taught me to play chess with the little figures as a twin.

"Pablo!" I cried with a convulsive start. "Pablo, where are we?"

"We are in my Magic Theatre," he said with a smile, "and if you wish at any time to learn the Tango or to be a General or to have a talk with Alexander the Great, it is always at your service. But I'm bound to say, Harry, you have disappointed me a little. You forgot yourself badly. You broke through the humour of my little theatre and tried to make a mess of it, stabbing with knives and spattering our pretty picture-world with the mud of reality. That was not pretty of you. I hope, at least, you did it from jealousy when you saw Hermine and me lying there. Unfortunately, you did not know what to do with this figure. I thought you had learnt the game better. Well, you will do better next time."

He took Hermine who at once shrank in his fingers to the dimensions of a toy-figure and put her in the very same waistcoat-pocket from which he had taken the cigarette.

Its sweet and heavy smoke diffused a pleasant aroma. I was utterly done-up and ready to sleep for a year.

I understood it all. I understood Pablo. I understood Mozart, and somewhere behind me I heard his ghastly laughter. I knew that all the hundred thousand pieces of life's game were in my pocket. A glimpse of its meaning had stirred my reason, and I was determined to begin the game afresh. I would sample its tortures once more and shudder again at its senselessness. I would traverse not once more, but often, the hell of my inner being.

One day I would be a better hand at the game. One day I would learn how to laugh. Pablo was waiting for me, and Mozart too.